A CRUCIBLE OF FIRE AND STEEL

BOOK TWO OF HEIRS OF WAR

JAMIE EDMUNDSON

Rarn Publishing

BY JAMIE EDMUNDSON

A CRUCIBLE OF FIRE AND STEEL

Book Two of Heirs of War

Author website jamieedmundson.com

Cover: Bastien Jez

Visit the Heirs of War page which includes downloadable colour maps of key locations:

For Kath and Dave

DRAMATIS PERSONAE

DALRIYA

Guivergne
    Esterel, King of Guivergne
    Peyre, Esterel's brother, Duke of Morbaine
    Sanc, Esterel's younger brother
    Rab, Sanc's dog
    Loysse, Esterel's sister
    Cebelia, Loysse's lady maid
    Brayda, a maid
    Brancat, castellan of the Bastion
    Lord Russell, steward of Morbaine
    Umbert, son of Russell, Peyre's friend
    Domard, Duke of Martras
    Ragonde, Domard's man
    Auberi, Duke of Famiens
    Gosse, a border lord
    Sul, Gosse's man
    Caisin, Lord Chancellor of Guivergne
    Sacha, Lord Courion, Royal Steward

Coleta, Sacha's sister
Miles, Lord of Corbenay, Marshall of Guivergne
Florent, Esterel's friend
Raymon, Lord of Auriac
Robert, Raymon's son
Arnoul, Lord of Saliers
Benoit, Arnoul's son
Jehan, guardsman in The Bastion
Inhan, a warrior in the Barissian Guard

Empire of Brasingia

Kelland & Luderia
Leopold, Duke of Kelland & Luderia
Hannelore, Leopold's mother
Liesel, his sister
Inge, adviser to Leopold
Gervase Salvinus, adviser to Leopold
Lord Kass, a nobleman
Olbrecht & Heinke, young noblemen
Teuchenberg & Wechlitz, older noblemen

Barissia
Walter, Duke of Barissia
Farred, Walter's partner
Elger, captain of the Barissian Guard
Syele, warrior
Mixo, a nobleman

Atrabia
Emlyn, Prince of Atrabia
Ilar & Macsen, Emlyn's sons
Bron, Emlyn's sister in law
Tegyn, Emlyn's niece
Idris, Emlyn's nephew

Elsewhere in Brasingia

Jeremias, Duke of Rotelegen
Katrina, Duchess of Rotelegen, sister of Leopold & Liesel
Friedrich, Duke of Thesse
Otto, Friedrich's chamberlain
Emmett, Archbishop of Gotbeck

Magnia

King Ida
Elfled, his mother
Brictwin, Ida's bodyguard
Morlin, Elfled's bodyguard
Herin, a warrior
Belwynn Godslayer

The Midder Steppe

Cuenin, a chieftain
Jorath, a chieftain
Frayne, a chieftain
Brock, a chieftain

The Confederacy

Gethin, King of Ritherys
Rhain, King of Corieltes

Others in Dalriya

Ezenachi, Lord of the Avakaba
Jesper, a Halvian
Maragin, a Krykker chieftain
Stenk, a Krykker chieftain
Lorant, King of the Blood Caladri
Theron, King of Kalinth
Leontios, Grand Master of the Knights of Kalinth
Zared, King of Persala
Gansukh, Khan of the Jalakh Empire

Bolormaa, Gansukh's mother
Oisin, King of the Orias (Giants)
Gunnhild, a Vismarian warrior

SILB

Scorgians
Lenzo, Prince of Scorgia
Gaida, Lenzo's lieutenant
Cleph, a fisherman
Wacho, Master of the Breath Forts
Amelia the Widow, merchant of Arvena
Dag, Amelia's agent
Transamund, trader of Arvena
Nolf Money Bags, merchant of Arvena
Tassia, a prostitute

Kassites
Grindan Won't Stop Eating, chieftain
Holt Slender Legged, chieftain
List the Castrator, chieftain
Rinc the Black, chieftain
Tredan Late to Battle, chieftain
Mildrith, Kassite champion
Sweterun, Mildrith's friend

Nerisians and Gadenzians
Lothar, King of Nerisia
Temyl, Nerisian champion
Guntram, Gadenzian champion
Erstein, Count of Obernai

Rasidi, Telds and Egers
Ordono, King of the Rasidi
Mergildo, Rasidi champion

Domeka, Teld servant in Aguilas
Kepa, Teld champion
Haritz, King of the Telds
The Eger Khan, ruler of the Egers
Hamzat, brother of the Eger Khan
Tagir, father of the Eger Khan

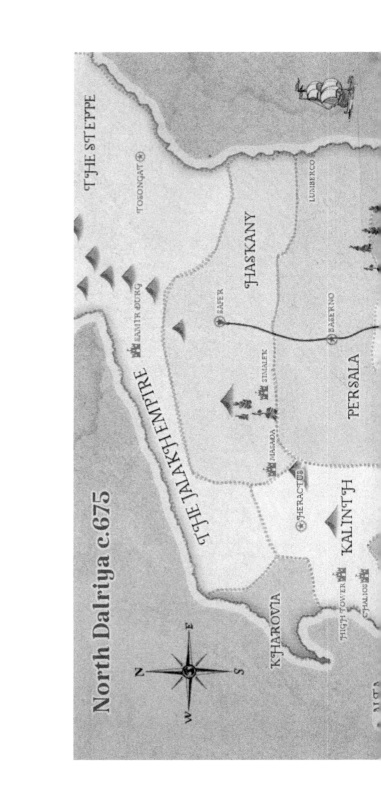

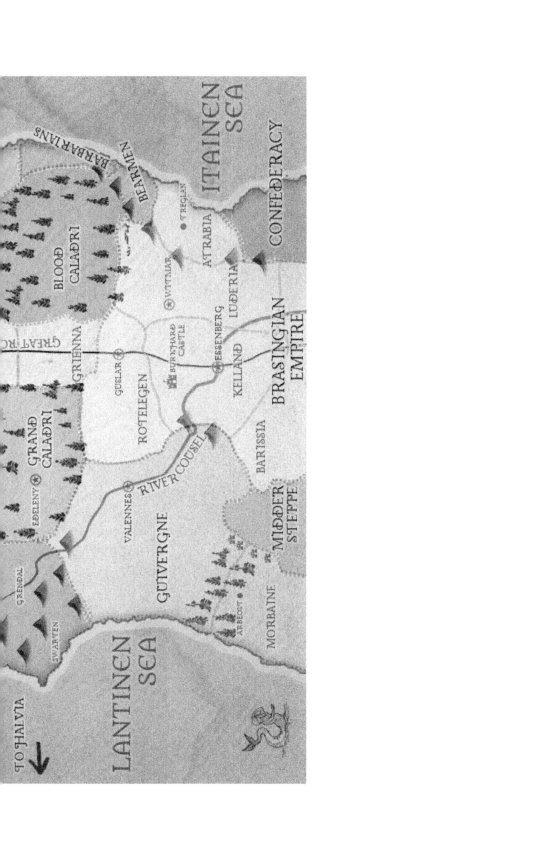

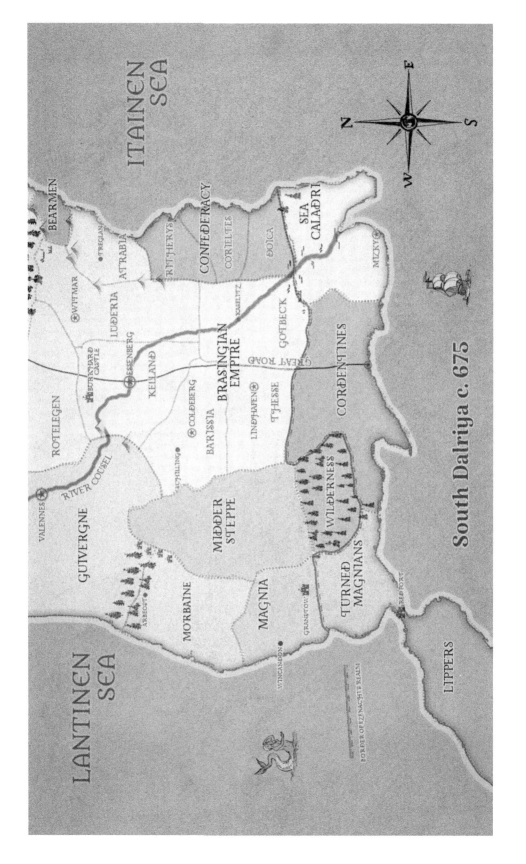

South Dalriya c. 675

PART I
THE LURE OF EMPIRE

SANC * PEYRE * LIESEL

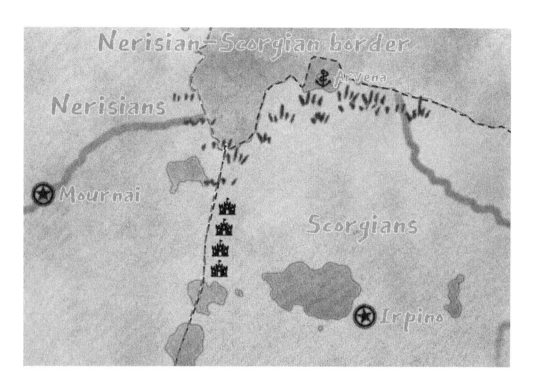

SANC

UNKNOWN LANDS, 675

S anc was woken by a dog licking his face.

'Get off, Rab,' he croaked, pushing him away.

He sat up, feeling groggy. The sun was high in the sky, suggesting it was the middle of the day. He and Rab were alone, on a grassy slope that looked like pasture land. He had no idea how long they'd been there. The effect of the teleportation combined with the amount of magic used to power it must have left him out cold.

'Where's Herin?' he mumbled. He recalled Rab jumping at him, just as Rimmon's spell had begun to teleport him away. He'd grabbed the dog, letting go of Herin as he did so. Did that mean Herin hadn't been transported?

He got to his feet. Standing made him dizzy. He tried walking it off but almost fainted and sat back down. If, as Rimmon had planned, he had indeed travelled to another world, it was no surprise his body suffered for it.

Rab seemed alright, if a little confused. But he was a good boy and lay next to his master, assuming that Sanc was going to sleep again.

'I'm sorry, boy,' Sanc said, patting him.

The area seemed uninhabited which made him feel safe for now.

He tried to think. Was it possible that Herin had come with him and decided to explore alone while Sanc slept? Surely, he would have tried to wake Sanc? Sanc looked about. There was no other depression in the grass or signs of footsteps. No object had been left to let Sanc know Herin was here.

'Looks like we're on our own, Rab,' he said. 'In a strange world. I wish you hadn't done that. I could have done with Herin's help.'

But he couldn't be angry. After allowing himself some more rest, he tried walking again. It was better the second time. Taking it easy, he walked up the slope, thinking he might get to a view of the surrounding area.

The enormity of the task he faced threatened to overwhelm him. Alone in an unknown land, he had to find someone to help him defeat Ezenachi. The more he considered it, the more it sounded like madness.

He reached the top. It afforded him a good view of the area. In the direction he had walked, he could see hilly land, probably given over to pasture like the one he stood on. Back in the direction he had come from, the land was flatter.

He could see a vast lake, its far end somewhere beyond the horizon. There were settlements along its shore. He looked back and forth, weighing up the options. He might hide safely in the empty, undulating lands. But he was here to find help, so what was the point of that? The settled area by the lake might have people who could help him. He carried provisions in his pack, but they wouldn't last forever. On the other hand, a stranger from another land, who didn't speak their language, would likely be met with hostility.

Think, Sanc, he urged himself.

The language. That was the first barrier. He remembered how he had entered the mind of the Lipper prisoner in Magnia. That connection had allowed him to understand the Lipper's thoughts. Once he had, he'd discovered the Lipper didn't want to be rescued, like Herin had. He'd been loyal to Ezenachi.

Still, it was the principle that mattered. He must try to do the same with the people who lived here. Once he could communicate with them, his quest would become easier.

'I will wait until night,' he said.

Rab tilted his head at the words, as if trying to understand Sanc's plan.

'I can see the light of every mind as it sleeps. That will allow me to approach someone without the risk of alarming them.'

Content that he had a plan of sorts, Sanc made his way back down the slope towards the lake. He moved into a wooded area. It allowed him to approach the outskirts of one of the lake settlements without being seen. The wooden houses were attractive and spaced out, suggesting this was a well-off little community.

He decided to retreat a safer distance into the woods, settling down by a fallen white oak. He knew he should ration the food Queen Elfled had provided in his pack. But eating a little of it relieved the boredom. He had to give some to Rab, anyway. He worried if he wasn't fed, Rab might go off to hunt and get himself in trouble.

At last, the sun began to set. Sanc looked at the sky. It was no different from the sky over Dalriya. Was he really in another world? Or had he simply travelled a huge distance, somewhere beyond the sea? He didn't know how to find the answer. Occasionally, voices drifted to him from the nearby settlement, but not loud enough to hear what was being said. He waited until twilight. Only then did he close his eyes and search for the sources of light. There were a few, all of them located towards the lake area. But it was still too early. Most people must still be awake.

As dusk came, he was surprised to hear voices again, but this time coming from behind him. He peered through the darkness, listening. What he heard put him on edge. The heavy footsteps and male voices put him in mind of soldiers. He couldn't tell how close they were, but he was sure they were getting nearer.

It would be foolish to take risks, he told himself. Gathering Rab to him, he began to cast his magic. As the soldiers neared, they were persuaded Sanc wasn't there, crouching by the oak, hand on the hilt of his sword. The magic told them they couldn't hear Rab's nervous growling as they passed by, on their way to the lake; perhaps forty of them in all. They were warriors, alright. They seemed well armed, but looked dirty, bedraggled and unshaven. Sanc knew that look. Men who were at war—who had been away from the comforts of home for some time.

Sanc heard them talking to one another. At least one question was resolved. He couldn't understand a thing they were saying. They were whispering, and it sounded like some of them were giving orders to the others. He let out a sigh of relief as they passed by without seeing him.

Paranoia hit him then. Could it be coincidence they had arrived at his precise location? Surely it had to be? Yet sorcerers were capable of detecting one another, especially when they used magic. There was no doubt he and Rimmon had expended a serious amount of magic to get Sanc here. Might a native magic user have detected the source and sent the warriors out to find him? The idea that a sorcerer might be out there in the darkness put him even more on edge.

Then the screaming started.

Sanc hadn't considered that the troop of warriors might attack the settlement on the lake. It struck home, even further, how completely ignorant he was of the land he had travelled to. He didn't know who the lake dwellers were or who their enemies were. Didn't know who was in the wrong and who in the right. But the screams of women and children unsettled him. He doubted they had done anything to deserve punishment. He got to his feet and stood irresolute. The sensible thing was to stay out of it, surely.

No. I can't.

'Wait,' he instructed Rab.

He drew his sword and walked after the warriors. Turning, he saw Rab was following him. *He's not going to wait while I walk into danger,* Sanc realised.

'I can't treat you like a baby,' he told the dog. 'If you're coming, you must look after yourself.'

Sanc continued towards the sound of fighting and screaming. Firelight cast flickering shadows on the scene before him. Some houses had been set alight. It was still impossible to tell what the objective of the attackers was. As he reached the first houses, two warriors came to meet him.

Their leather mail looked bulky, suggesting they had a second layer of protection underneath. Both carried spear and shield and had short swords at their belts. It made Sanc wish he had a shield with him. He patted the knife at his belt: the bone-handled weapon had been a gift from his father. Then he thought better of it. A spare hand was more useful to him than a shield or knife.

One of the men peered at him, as if trying to work out who he was. He shouted something that sounded like a challenge. Rab growled back.

Sanc kept on walking. He was committed now. He needed to find out what was happening. If it was a massacre, he had to stop it.

The warrior gave up on talking. Sanc saw him balance his weight and draw his arm backwards; he knew what was coming. The spear shot towards him.

Anger, frustration, and fear spurred Sanc on. He raised a hand, catching the spear in his magic. He turned it around in mid-air, sending it back to his enemy with interest.

The man's eyes shot wide open, but his training kicked in. He raised his shield to block the returning spear. At the last moment, Sanc tugged the man's arm to the side. The spear slammed into his chest. The blade sliced through his armour, and he was sent flying backwards by the impact.

His comrade turned and ran.

Sanc reacted quickly, desperate to stop the man from giving a warning. Sanc held him in place as he ran for the warrior. The man fought Sanc's restraints, pushing to free himself and it took concentration for Sanc to hold him and move at the same time. As Sanc neared, the man gave up and turned to face him. The warrior led with his shield, trying to clatter into Sanc.

Holding his hand up, Sanc stopped his enemy's shield-arm. The warrior thrust with his spear. Sanc moved to one side. Just as he had been taught to do by Brancat, he raked his sword blade along the length of the pole. He caught the man's gloved hand, disarming him. His opponent tried to move, but Sanc still held his shield-arm immobile. Sanc launched an overhead swing. Seeing it, the warrior raised his free arm up to catch the blow. Changing course, Sanc shifted to the side. As he did so, he swung his sword around at shoulder height. It bit into the back of the warrior's neck, nearly severing it off. His body sank to the ground.

Sanc looked at his kills. It wasn't how he had been taught to fight, and if Brancat or anyone from Arbeost had been watching, they'd have called it dishonourable. He felt the same. But he hadn't come to this place to seek honour. He'd come to save all those people back home.

Wasting no more time, he made his way through the settlement. There was a central green that faced the lake, where a dock was full of boats. It occurred to Sanc that these vessels might be a prize worth taking in time of war. There seemed little else of value.

Twenty or so warriors gathered in this area. Kneeling or sitting on the ground, weapons pointed their way, was a large group of residents. *So, it seems they're not killing everyone. Not yet, at least.* He witnessed this group of captives added to, as four warriors arrived with a woman and her two children. Once their catch was deposited, they left again. Presumably to find more.

Sanc and Rab padded away, leaving this scene for now. Better to find smaller numbers of the enemy first. He heard a struggle coming from one house. Wasting no time, he entered through the open door. Inside the open plan home, a woman and children cowered in one corner, while three warriors beat at a bloodied man.

The warriors didn't know what hit them. Sanc took one from behind while holding another still. Rab bit into the ankle of the other. He screamed in fright, before raising his weapon to strike at the dog. Sanc thrust again, into the man's armpit. His blade sunk deep as the man cried in agony. He twisted away, crashing to the floor, taking Sanc's sword with him. Sanc let Rab deal with him for the moment. He took his knife and slit the throat of the man he was holding.

The man on the floor shouted at him as he approached, probably pleading for his life. But that wasn't possible. Sanc stamped down when he tried to move and then knelt on him. They struggled for a few moments before Sanc's knife opened another neck. He stood carefully. The floor of the house was slippery now. He was covered in blood and worse; stunk of it. But it couldn't be helped. The man of the house had positioned himself in front of his family, perhaps trying to protect them from Sanc. Sanc pointed outside. It would be best if they left and hid in the woods until it was all over.

He'd killed five now. But that wasn't enough. Sanc wasn't ready to approach the main force on the green yet. Instead, he walked between the houses of the settlement, using the darkness as cover. He used his magic, too. He was sure the illusion of invisibility was broken if he was spotted moving about. But in these conditions, he thought it might give him an extra layer of protection.

Rab was his shadow. He understood they were hunting, and stayed silent as they tracked their prey.

Five became eight; became twelve; became fifteen. By that point, the warriors knew something was up—had probably discovered some of their fallen. Sanc studied them from behind a garden wall. There were still a score of them. He didn't think he was rating his magic too highly to think he could probably defeat all twenty.

But something could easily go wrong—it would only take one unseen archer, hiding somewhere, to kill him. He also had to consider the consequences. A massive display of magic like that could get him into trouble. The people who witnessed it would talk. It would be better to keep his abilities secret.

Meanwhile, the enemy seemed unsure what to do. There were plenty of raised voices, but Sanc couldn't work out what was going on. *Maybe I should do it?* he asked himself. *After all, they could have reinforcements coming for all I know. Now might be the best time.*

Then another thought hit him as if from nowhere. There was another thing he could hide if he so chose. His eyes. They had done nothing but cause him harm, his entire life. They could be the death of him here. He cast yet another illusion. This time, anyone who looked at him would convince themselves he had brown eyes. He had no way to test it. *If it doesn't work so be it. I have nothing to lose.* He readied himself to leave his hiding place and face the enemy.

Just as he was convincing himself to move, the warriors acted. Whoever was in charge divided them into three groups. Two groups left the green, walking in different directions through the settlement. *Looking for me.* The third stayed with their prisoners. Only eight of them guarding around four times that number.

Sanc put a hand on Rab as one of the search groups passed nearby. Again, he used his magic to suppress sight and sound. When they were gone, he knew it was time to act. He wouldn't get a better chance.

He walked towards the group guarding the prisoners with purpose, sword in hand, limiting their time to think. They shouted at him. One put a blade at a girl's throat. Sanc ignored it all.

One of their number stepped towards him. He was large, muscular; metal rings circled his huge arms and decorated his beard, while his face was red with anger. He held a war axe two-handed. It was a fearsome looking weapon, no doubt capable of splitting Sanc in two. When his comrades came with him, he gave a curt command. He would take Sanc alone.

Sanc supposed he understood the man's confidence. Sanc wasn't much to look at compared to this warrior—a one-handed sword the only perceivable threat. He could only guess what else prompted the single challenge—perhaps if he was the leader, honour demanded he take Sanc out himself. But it played straight into Sanc's hands. If he could defeat these warriors without alerting anyone to his powers, he would feel a lot better.

'Wait,' Sanc commanded Rab.

Rab growled at the man but did as he was told.

Not giving the leader a chance to change his mind, Sanc dashed towards him. With a grin that showed his yellowed teeth, the warrior bounded towards him. He barely drew back his axe before swinging it towards Sanc. But that was as far as he got. Taking no risks, Sanc held him in place. He didn't slow his own movement and, with time to be accurate, sank his sword blade point first through his opponent's neck. Releasing his magical hold, he gripped the hilt tight with both hands. His sword came free as the man sank to the ground.

The killing may have looked odd, but Sanc was satisfied that there had been nothing obvious to mark him out as a sorcerer. As the leader's men now came to avenge him, Sanc rushed towards them. Years of training, combined with his growing powers, kicked in. As the nearest, spear-wielding warrior came within range, an invisible blast of magic sent the man immediately behind him tumbling to the ground. Rab, unable to hold back any longer, was onto him, locking his jaw onto a hand.

Sanc held the first warrior in the middle of his spear thrust and used all his strength to slash his sword into the man's face. As he released his hold on the warrior, two thrown axes came for him. Sanc sent them wide and ran, making for the axe throwers, as they desperately drew their swords. Behind them, he saw another throwing axe hurtling towards him. He made sure it hit the back of the head of one axe thrower, while he ran through the other.

He'd killed four warriors in a matter of moments. As he drew breath, the fight resolved itself. A sixth warrior was bundled to the ground by a group of captives, while the remaining two turned and ran.

The people of the settlement—a few men among women and children—gaped at him. Sanc understood they didn't know what to make of him. 'Pick up the weapons,' he said, pointing at the swords and axes of the men he had killed.

They didn't understand his words, but the gesture was clear enough, and once one woman grabbed a sword, others wasted no time in arming themselves. One man, who had claimed the two-handed axe, tried speaking to Sanc. Sanc could only shrug. The man gestured at his town. Some buildings were still aflame, but with access to so much water, Sanc didn't think they would have a problem putting them out.

He gestured in the same direction. 'I will come with you to fight the other warriors,' he said, assuming that would be the man's main concern. He walked towards the buildings, and everyone came with him.

With growing confidence that Sanc was an ally, they led him through the settlement, scouring for the enemy. They found none living. The family Sanc had rescued appeared, the father's face still bloody from his beating. He pointed towards the woodland Sanc had hidden in, talking fast. The man who had claimed the axe looked that way too, talking quietly. Sanc guessed the warriors had retreated into the trees.

The axeman organised things. He gestured at Sanc to follow him. Half a dozen of them walked towards the wooded area, then stopped, peering into the trees. Gradually, the plan became clear to Sanc. They stood guard while the rest of the people put out the fires. Sanc had to tell Rab to stay put, since the dog seemed keen to enter the woods. After a while, when the fires were out and there had been no more sign of the attackers, the man led them back into the settlement. The bodies of the dead had been collected. The people stood around for a while. The shock of the attack turned to grief as children cried and women wailed.

The axeman spoke to Sanc. He looked as frustrated as Sanc felt at their inability to communicate. Sanc put the palm of his hand to his own chest then pointed to the man, who seemed to be a leader here, before gesturing towards a house. Seeming to understand, the man gave out some orders to those around him before leading Sanc to the house.

They entered. It was an open plan design like the others Sanc had been in. Sanc sat down by the fire, placing his sword on the ground. The man did the same, depositing his axe while he muttered some words.

Holding his hands up, Sanc leaned forward, then slowly moved his arms. The man looked at him questioningly, his round eyes hesitant about whether to trust this strange newcomer.

'It's alright,' Sanc said, knowing the man didn't understand the words, but might be reassured by the tone. 'I just need to learn your damned language.'

The man allowed Sanc to place his hands on each side of his head. Sanc closed his eyes and searched for the connection to the man's mind. It was there, glowing with a faint light. Just as it happened in Magnia, the process of trying to speak to him telepathically led Sanc to the part of his mind that controlled language. Once he identified it, he found he could draw the information he needed.

Sanc gasped as he withdrew his hands. He felt woozy now. He'd drawn on the last of his reserves. He'd hardly been careful with the amount of magic he had used today. Rimmon had warned him countless times. *I must learn to be more disciplined,* he told himself. *Work within my limits. I could have tried this task tomorrow, after a night's sleep. What if more warriors come?*

He opened his eyes, focusing on the man before him. He frowned as he concentrated on what to say. Understanding a language did not mean it was easy to speak it. 'Can you understand my words now?' he asked.

The man's eyes shot open in surprise. He spoke quickly, excitedly, and Sanc couldn't follow what he said.

'Slower.'

Now it was the other man's turn to frown in concentration as he chose what to say. 'Thank you for saving us.'

'You are welcome.'

'Did the king send you to help us?'

So, there is a king somewhere. Sanc had so many questions, but he had to be wary of revealing too much. If these people realised how little he knew—that he had come here from some other world—they might become scared of him. At the same time, lying might cause problems later.

'No. I sent myself.'

The man frowned. Sanc didn't think he'd said that last bit very well. But being vague about who he was wasn't such a bad idea.

'My name is Sanc,' he offered.

That was a better place to start. The man put a hand to his chest. 'Cleph. You will stay in this house tonight.'

'Thank you' Sanc said.

Cleph smiled. Then his face became serious again. 'First. Will you help us bury our dead?'

SANC

UNKNOWN LANDS, 675

Sanc barely slept the rest of the night. Perhaps the only reason he did at all was because his expenditure of magic had left him exhausted. As for the inhabitants of the settlement, he doubted they got any. When he woke, Rab was curled next to him.

'You had a busy night too, boy,' Sanc murmured.

He found the people gathered on the green, amongst an early morning mist. Daylight made the settlement seem smaller. Even the moored boats were tinier than he had thought last night.

Cleph approached him. 'We are debating whether it is safe to go fishing, or if we should leave our village.'

Sanc imagined it was a tough decision. The daily catch must be their livelihood; but he didn't see how they could leave the women and children here alone. He shrugged, no idea who their enemies were, never mind the odds of them returning.

Cleph frowned. He seemed irritated, as if Sanc should have advised him. The gratitude of last night was disappearing. 'Where are you from?' he asked.

'A long way from here,' Sanc answered, hoping that more vague answers would suffice. 'Where are your leaders?' he said, preferring to ask the questions. He needed to learn about this world as soon as possible, and he doubted these villagers could put him in touch with a god who could defeat Ezenachi.

Cleph pointed across the lake. 'They were in Irpino. But the Nerisians are there.'

Sanc looked at the position of the sun compared to Cleph's gesture. If things worked the same here as in Dalriya, this place called Irpino was somewhere to the south. The Nerisians must be the people he had fought last night. Already, those small items of information gave him a firmer grip on what was going on than he had until now. He remembered last night Cleph had asked him if their king had sent him.

'Your king is at Irpino? Have the Nerisians taken it?'

'I don't know,' Cleph said. Again, there was the faint hint of irritation, or suspicion, at Sanc's ignorance. 'But their warriors are here.'

Sanc took this to mean the Nerisians had invaded from the south. Their presence here implied that Irpino, probably the capital, had fallen. Unknowingly, he had helped a people facing an invasion from a foreign army. The thought crossed his mind that he might have been better allying with the successful invaders.

Shouts of alarm interrupted his thinking. A dozen armed men had arrived on the scene. At first, Sanc assumed, along with many others, that these were the warriors from last night. Cleph soon disabused him.

'Quiet!' he shouted. 'These are Scorgians!'

'Not just any Scorgians!' one warrior shouted, a large man with a sizeable gut. 'Kneel for your prince!'

Sanc joined the villagers in kneeling. He studied the man who approached and signalled for them to rise. He looked young, probably a few years older than Esterel. Tall, with green eyes in a handsome face. His hair was golden brown, and he had a long beard, like nearly all his warriors. They wore chain mail and carried expensive weapons, as would befit the entourage of a prince of the realm.

'What happened here?' he asked, glancing from the fire damaged buildings to the pit where they had buried the enemy.

Despite Cleph's loud voice, many spoke at once. The prince didn't stop them. Soon, he was turning his attention to Sanc.

'Sounds like you saved these people. Your name?'

'I am Sanc. From far from here. I am a great warrior.'

The prince raised an eyebrow at this. 'So it would seem. I am Prince Lenzo. From here. And I am sorely in need of great warriors. You will come with me?'

'Yes,' Sanc said. He dared to think he had struck lucky. A prince, even one facing an invasion, was the kind of person he needed to befriend. 'Where are we going?' he added as an afterthought.

Lenzo smiled at that. 'Irpino has fallen,' he said, his voice rising so all could hear clearly. 'King Domizio is captured. These are dark days for our people. I must head west with all speed to our border garrisons and collect our forces there before they are lost to the enemy. I will need your boats to make this journey.'

A deflated silence followed this statement.

'What should we do?' Cleph asked.

'Take your families to Arvena. That is where I will go.'

'Arvena? But that is a long way. We are fishermen—'

'There are plenty of fish in the sea.'

'But we won't have our boats, or—'

'Arvena will be a place of safety,' Lenzo interrupted again. 'There is nowhere else. You can take your chances here and be ruled by Lothar of Nerisia.' He looked back at the pit. 'It's not like the Nerisians are going to kill *everyone*. Come, Sanc.'

Lenzo and his men headed for the dock. Sanc whistled for Rab to come and they followed behind. Fearful, disbelieving faces stared at them as they left. The warriors wasted no time in clambering aboard the larger boats.

'What is this creature?' the prince asked, some alarm in his voice, as Rab came bounding over.

'A dog.'

'Is it safe?'

'He's called Rab. He's a good boy.'

'Very well. I shall trust Rab.'

19

'Never mind the creature. Are you sure about *him?*' the warrior with the gut asked his prince, with a nod at Sanc, as they waited to board.

'How can I not bring him? By all accounts, he killed over twenty Nerisian warriors.'

'Yes. But he talks like a baby.'

'Gaida. You appear to be under the impression that I have the luxury of choosing only the perfect companions. When the truth is, I must take anyone I can get.' The prince clambered onto the largest of the boats. 'Sanc, travel with me,' he said. 'Bring your beast. It will be a tiresome voyage, and at the very least, you offer a new brand of tedium.'

Sanc took his place as one of five men on the boat. As soon as he was settled onto a bench, he was handed an oar. One of the warriors unfurled the sail. Leaning over, Sanc took in the mooring line and then pushed their craft away from the dock. He avoided the faces of the children he was leaving behind.

'Better to leave a hero,' Prince Lenzo said next to him, 'than stay and be revealed a fool.'

THE LAKE WAS LARGER than Sanc had imagined. They sailed westward all morning, rowing when they had to. Still, Sanc couldn't see the opposite shore. They kept the north shore in view the entire time. Sanc was glad about that. He took surreptitious glances beneath the surface. He couldn't stop himself from imagining the size of creatures that could live in its depths. But no one else seemed worried. They passed many small settlements just like the one they had left. Their fishing boats were out, working their own patch of water.

'They have no idea what's coming,' Lenzo commented when he saw Sanc watching them.

'Should we warn them?'

The prince shrugged. 'There's little point. Most Scorgians are not in great danger. They'll go on catching fish when this is over. They'll just be selling their surplus to Nerisian lords. No doubt some won't even notice the difference. I'm the true loser in all of this.'

'The war is over?' Sanc asked, confused. 'I thought we were going to get reinforcements.'

'Not to fight the Nerisians. To take with us north, to Arvena. It's an island city. With a few thousand warriors, we can hold it quite comfortably.'

Sanc thought about this. 'Then why did the Nerisians attack that settlement?'

'I'm not sure,' Lenzo admitted. 'Either they were looking for me,' he said, turning his green eyes to study Sanc, 'or you. What exactly are you doing here, friend? You don't speak like any of the seven peoples of Silb.'

'I've come to find help,' Sanc said, relieved to share his mission with the prince. 'My people face a great enemy.'

Lenzo gave him a sardonic smile. 'Are they in worse straits than we are?'

Sanc had to admit it was a fair point. 'This threat is to all the people of my lands. Rich or poor; whatever kingdom they live in.'

'And who in Silb did you expect might come to your rescue?'

'I don't know. I was hoping you'd be able to tell me.'

Lenzo laughed, the sound echoing across the water. 'Are you hearing this, Gaida?' he asked the big warrior who sat on the opposite side of the prince.

'Aye. I say chuck him overboard, Your Highness.'

'I'm not convinced that would kill him. Would it, Sanc?' he asked, a meaningful look in his eyes.

Does he suspect me a sorcerer? Sanc wondered. He supposed that a clever man, such as this prince, would naturally question the idea that Sanc single-handedly killed twenty Nerisian warriors. But what would he do if Sanc admitted to such powers? 'I can swim,' he said in reply.

Lenzo laughed again. 'See, Gaida? Sanc is a great warrior who can swim. Perhaps he is immortal.'

Gaida grunted. 'Wouldn't that be wonderful.'

. . .

THEY CONTINUED INTO THE AFTERNOON, Prince Lenzo pushing them to go as fast as they could. There were no stops and Sanc was grateful for the food Queen Elfled had packed for him. He thought of those he had left behind. Edgar and Elfled, struggling to contain an existential threat to their kingdom. Rimmon, who had sent him here out of desperation. Jesper, who had always been there to protect him, until he had left Magnia to ask for help from Guivergne. He wondered how his family had reacted. Peyre in Morbaine; Esterel in Valennes; Loysse, now the duchess of Famiens. Would his siblings help the Magnians? And what would be the consequences for them if they did?

At last, the end of the great lake came into view and the three boats turned towards the shore. A large town sprawled along the lakeside. Lenzo named it Carraia. By its size, Sanc determined it must be more than just another fishing village.

'What's the plan, Your Highness?' Gaida asked.

'Find out what they know. Which will probably be nothing. Then we need horses. I'm determined to reach the Breath Forts today. We've got ourselves ahead of them, but the Nerisians are still not far behind.'

'Do we buy horses or commandeer them?'

'Can we afford to buy thirteen horses?'

'No.'

'Then commandeer them, Gaida. Tell them we have three boats as a down payment and I'll settle the outstanding balance as soon as I can.'

They wasted no time in Carraia. As Lenzo predicted, the towns-folk they spoke with knew nothing of a Nerisian invasion. The prince took it as a good sign. It suggested the forts on the Scorgians' western border were intact.

'Can you ride a horse?' Lenzo asked Sanc as he climbed into his saddle.

'Yes.' He recalled riding out with Peyre and Umbert in Arbeost.

Such carefree days: he wished he had appreciated them a little more at the time.

'Then this other land you are from sounds little different to Silb.'

'It seems so,' Sanc said.

They made their way through the outskirts of the town and took a well-worn track heading north-west, through fields of grain. Rab tracked them, staying far enough from the horses to avoid worrying them.

'Why do you call them the Breath Forts?' he asked the prince.

'The Nerisians have been a threat for decades. A few generations ago, we built the chain of forts to protect our border. If we hadn't, we'd have been defeated long before now. They became known as the Breath Forts because they eased the pressure on us—allowed us to breathe. Only, the damned Nerisians came at us through a back door —into the south-west of the country. The forts are doomed now. But they can provide us with enough armed warriors to survive. At least a little longer.'

'You shouldn't tell this outlander so much when he tells you nothing,' Gaida complained to his prince.

'Well, he has us at a disadvantage, doesn't he? He's here. If I asked him about his lands, he could lie to me, and I'd never know.'

'I wouldn't do that,' Sanc said.

'Alright, then,' Lenzo said. 'Tell us about this threat that made you leave your lands behind.'

'He is a god named Ezenachi,' Sanc told them. 'He inhabits a human's form and walks the land.'

'Why would a god do this?' Lenzo asked. 'It makes him vulnerable. He must be a desperate god to behave this way.'

'There are no other gods in Dalriya to stop him. He is invincible, scared of no one.'

'No other gods?' Lenzo repeated, exchanging a look with Gaida. 'Where is your god?'

'Dead. Madria was killed. Seventeen years ago.' *The year I was born.* 'So, you see why we need help from someone else.' He paused, trying to read the reactions of Lenzo and Gaida. 'You have gods in Silb?'

'Of course,' Lenzo answered. 'The Scorgians are blessed to have Salacus watching over us. Each of the seven peoples has a god. And none would be so foolish as to take a human form and risk extermination.'

'Then how do they influence the world?'

'They make a champion among us.'

A champion? Like Madria had Pentas? 'Who is your champion?'

'Who *was*, you mean. Vultas. He led our armies in battle. The Nerisians killed him three weeks ago.'

'Can Salacus not make another one?'

'He has. Somewhere in Scorgia, there was a babe born three weeks ago.'

A new champion born? Like me? Rimmon had told him that the death of Pentas had led Madria to create a new sorcerer.

Lenzo looked at him with irritation. 'How can you not know this, outlander?'

'I know some of it,' Sanc said. 'But if your champion is dead and your people in trouble, wouldn't Salacus come to your aid?'

'Salacus aids us,' Lenzo replied, as if speaking to a child. 'But it is *we* who have failed. It is the Scorgians who have let *him* down. Why should he set foot among us and risk death? What would happen to us then? We would be as defenceless as your people.'

Sanc nodded, grateful for the prince's explanation. It helped him to understand, even if it was just a little more than he had before, about the world of gods. *But it doesn't get me any closer to a solution to the problem of Ezenachi.*

They rode hard to reach the chain of forts that marked the Scorgians' western border. Stone-built forts, with a stone wall linking one to the next, they were a testament to the threat the Nerisians had posed this kingdom.

There was no fighting here; no Nerisian army come to besiege the defences. But in the growing darkness, it was easy to believe they were close—merely biding time until they could attack from both directions. It reminded Sanc so much of the Magnian forts that had defended against the Avakabi that a chill ran down his spine. Vivid memories of the defence of the Red Fort came to him: Ezenachi's warriors, his mindless slaves, attacking with no thought of their own safety. Sanc didn't believe himself a coward. But he shrank from the idea of reliving that desperate siege.

Prince Lenzo led them to one of the largest forts, situated near the centre of the chain. It was late, and once they were admitted, their horses were stabled and Sanc and the rest of the prince's men were given beds in the barracks.

Only Lenzo and Gaida went to speak with the Master of the Breath Forts. The prince would demand the soldiers give up their posts and retreat, leaving the forts for the enemy. Even though he was a prince; his father defeated; their capital taken; their champion killed; Sanc thought Lenzo might have a difficult task persuading the master to do as he wished.

In the barracks, Sanc took off his outer garments and tested his straw mattress. It was uncomfortable and the woollen blanket atop it smelt bad; he tried not to wonder what bugs might infest his bed. But it was late, and he had slept little the night before. He used his own blanket and gave the other to Rab, who seemed not to mind the smell, and settled down on it by the side of the bed. Sanc closed his eyes and stopped the magic that had kept his eyes coloured brown all this time. Still, the mutterings of the warriors around him and his own agitated mind kept him from sleep for a long time.

* * *

THE FORT ROSE EARLY in the morning. It quickly became apparent that whatever conversation had taken place the night before, Prince Lenzo had got his way. Orders were shouted and soldiers were soon stripping the place of anything they could carry.

Gaida came for Lenzo's entourage and led them, Sanc included, to the mess hall. A feast of army rations lay before them: hard bread, wheels of cheese, salted pork and fish, and as much wine as they could drink. The Scorgians would take whatever food they could transport, but the rest they would ruin, rather than leave it to sustain the enemy.

Sanc joined the others in eating heartily, and refilled his pack with leftovers. Some soldiers laughed at the amount Rab put away until Sanc decided he'd had enough.

Afterwards, they went to the stables for their horses and joined up with Lenzo and a dozen riders outside the fort. They began their journey, heading northeast for the city of Arvena. Behind them, the rest of the soldiers were leaving too. The vast majority were on foot. There were a few oxen-pulled carts, but these were loaded high with supplies. More oxen were roped together, loaded with bags, and driven along with the soldiers.

'The same scene will be repeated up and down the Breath Forts,' Lenzo said to him, noticing how Sanc looked behind them.

'How many warriors altogether?' Sanc asked him.

'Well over two thousand,' Lenzo said. 'Though Master Wacho and I agree, we may not get them all to Arvena.'

Sanc nodded. He'd had enough experience of war in the last two years to know that in this situation, desertion would be rife.

'Master Wacho,' Lenzo said, raising his voice. 'This is the outlander I spoke of.'

The man riding at the front turned to look Sanc up and down. He had ten years on Lenzo and was tall and powerfully built. His hair was shaved to his scalp, with blue eyes under a prominent brow ridge, and he had the long beard of the Scorgian warrior class. He grunted at Sanc, a response that was calculatedly rude, putting him in his place. *At least*, Sanc told himself, *I have my red eyes hidden. I wouldn't have been accepted at all.* The thought didn't stop him from imagining a gust of wind suddenly knocking the man from his horse, however. But no, he couldn't do that.

'Don't mind our Master of the Breath Forts, Sanc,' Lenzo said lightly. 'Leaving one's kingdom to the mercy of the enemy is liable to put one in a bad mood.'

'Of course it does,' Wacho shot back with gritted teeth. 'How you can make fun of the situation is beyond me.'

There was no *'Your Highness'*, Sanc noted. Perhaps the conversation of last night had not been as congenial as events had led Sanc to believe.

'Because,' Lenzo retorted, 'whether one glowers and rages or laughs in the face of fate, it doesn't matter. Our plight remains exactly the same.'

An uneasy silence fell over the riders after that exchange. Lenzo and Wacho's warriors looked at one another with suspicion. *This is truly a realm that is falling apart*, Sanc realised. Not for the first time, he wondered if he wasn't better off riding back the way he had come and introducing himself to the King of the Nerisians. That was a man more likely to give him what he had come for. On the other hand, largely by chance, he had become a part of Prince Lenzo's retinue. He was learning much about the lands of Silb every day. If he needed to switch sides at some later point, there was nothing to prevent him.

Despite a full day's ride, the city of Arvena was apparently too far away to be reached in one day. Lenzo and Wacho found enough unity to agree on a location to stop. Neither wished to announce their presence in the region and so they made a rough camp for the night. There were two fires, however: one for Wacho and his men, one for Lenzo's.

'Last sleep without the stink of swamp or sea,' Lenzo commented as he settled down under a blanket.

'You can take your turn keeping watch,' Gaida said to Sanc, in a way that sounded part question and part order.

'Of course,' Sanc agreed.

Gaida nodded, looking relieved. No one could quite work out Sanc's status and he supposed that made Gaida's life a little difficult. The man seemed used to obeying his prince and telling everyone else what to do. 'First watch,' he said gruffly.

Sanc turned away from the fire and looked out in the direction they had come. Groups of Scorgian warriors would be out there doing the same as them. *How far behind them*, he wondered, *are the Nerisians?*

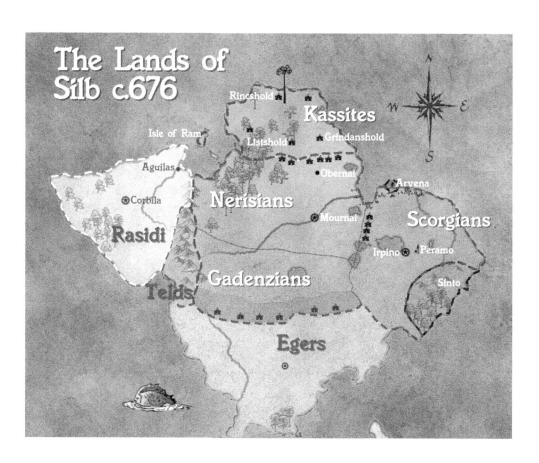

SANC

KINGDOM OF SCORGIA, 675

I don't like marshland, Sanc decided. He had entered the northern region of Scorgia with no preconceptions; it was experience only that led him to this conclusion. The going was slow, even once Lenzo had persuaded a couple of locals to act as guides through the fens. On his own, Sanc would have got hopelessly lost. Landmarks were few and far between. Everywhere looked the same: water, mud, and grass. Even when they stuck to the highest ground, the horses' legs were soon splattered in dark sludge. Then, their guides advised them to walk their horses.

At first, Sanc took care where to tread. But even the driest looking bits of land would give way to his weight, his feet sinking down. Soon, his shoes were soaking, and there was little point in taking care after that. Rab didn't escape the mud either, but he splattered in the pools of water to get the worst of it off, then shook himself dry.

Sanc wondered how the Scorgians' carts would get through this terrain. The answer was simple. They wouldn't. He didn't think he'd ever heard so much cursing at once. It was clear that neither Lenzo's nor Wacho's warriors were used to these conditions. They claimed they'd rather have fought and died against the Nerisians than this.

Wacho, losing his temper, told them to quit their moaning. Lenzo had a different approach.

'Once our warriors get here, they'll be safe,' he said. 'The Nerisians won't follow us into the marshes.'

'Why would they?' one of Wacho's soldiers dared to ask. He quietened with a glare from his leader.

Everyone knew the man had a point, however. Lenzo was ceding every city and town to the enemy. There was nothing of value here.

They passed a few mud huts as they continued north, the inhabitants presumably getting by on the catch they could take from the water. More sizeable settlements came into view as they approached the coast. A foul smell came too, however, doing nothing to raise spirits.

Gaida led them to one of these settlements, a collection of about two dozen dwellings gathered about a wooden dock that ran into the sea. Most of the houses were raised on wooden stilts. Gaida and their guides spoke with the locals, organising transport. Tired and irritable, the warriors sat or stood about, waiting for progress to be made.

There was a clear view to the coastline of the island. On it stood the city of Arvena, their destination; tantalisingly close.

At last, Gaida had things organised. He would stay here, with a few of Lenzo and Wacho's soldiers—none of them volunteers—to help organise things. The horses had to stay for the time being and more of Wacho's soldiers would arrive. Sanc was relieved to learn he and Rab would cross immediately. He sunk into the fishing boat and let out a sigh of relief when they cast off. There was a brisk sea breeze, soon seeing off the fetid smell that lingered on the coast. It carried them to the port of Arvena.

It was a short distance—swimmable, Sanc supposed—but as they approached the grand-looking docks, it was as if he had travelled to yet another world. Ships of varying shapes waited in harbour. High-sided warships with rows of oars, castles fore and aft and eyes painted on the bow sides; smaller fishing vessels; cargo ships of all sizes. The largest looked capable of holding the horses that Lenzo wanted transporting.

Then there was the rest of the city, rising slightly towards the centre, though it was otherwise a flat place. Yes, the immediate vicinity of the dock was all warehouses and shady looking taverns, as one might expect. But Sanc could also see church spires, whitewashed stone walls, marble facades, parkland, and a canal that wound its way from the docks into the centre of Arvena. The walled defences looked solid, and a stone keep occupied the highest ground. Immediately, he understood why Lenzo had set his stall on coming here. It was a city fit for a prince and its location made it highly defensible.

As soon as they disembarked, Lenzo was busy rounding up the city officials who could implement what he wanted. It was all carried out in the open near the docks. Sanc and the others had to wait patiently, their wet and dirty clothes slowly drying in the breeze.

First, the Prince had to explain the disaster that had befallen their kingdom. The Arvenans, shocked at the news, wanted all the details; Lenzo and Wacho, grim-faced, wanted action taken.

As the situation became clear, some of these burghers clearly balked at Lenzo's plan: their self-ruled trading city was to become the new capital of a diminished and defeated kingdom; their independence inevitably shackled by a resident ruler. But as Sanc watched them busily thinking through this unwelcome scenario, he wondered what other options they could offer. Rejecting Lenzo and submitting to the Nerisians had its own dangers as a strategy; and as the Prince and the Master of the Breath Forts repeatedly pressed home, there was an army two thousand strong heading their way.

It was only now that Sanc fully appreciated what Lenzo had achieved: those soldiers were his key to unlocking Arvena. Without them, he may have found himself taken into custody and sent back to Irpino as a gesture of the city's goodwill towards its new ruler. With them, he offered security—the burghers could continue making money, untroubled by the political turmoil on the mainland.

With obvious reluctance on the part of some, the officials gave the orders for the largest cogs to cross the channel and begin the operation to transport the troops over to the island.

Lenzo, meanwhile, began his conquest of the city. He and Wacho walked towards the centre of Arvena, half a dozen city leaders in tow, while Sanc and the other warriors followed closely behind.

'We can take rooms at The Dolphin for now,' the Prince told them, 'but I will need the finest house in the city as my residence. I will leave it to you to organise how its owner will be suitably compensated with other property.' The burghers attending him did their best to hide how appalled they were. 'Master Wacho will also require accommodation.'

'Some rooms in the keep will be adequate for me,' Wacho rumbled.

'Perfect!' Lenzo said. 'I need a hot bath. And then a woman or two. I've spent far too long in the company of stinking men in the last few days. Honestly, Master Wacho—I don't know how you do it.'

* * *

BY THE END of the next day, Lenzo was ensconced in his new house. It was beautiful both inside and out—a white marble front set the tone, with mosaic flooring and frescoed walls inside. It had its own private garden, a rare luxury in a city where space was at a premium. There was a separate building with sleeping quarters for staff and animals. Apart from Sanc, his warriors, and Rab, Lenzo had none; the previous owner, understandably, taking his with him.

Over the next few days, Lenzo politicked hard. He had endless meetings with merchants and officials, forming alliances and friendships. Some of these involved gifts and gradually the house became populated with the servants needed for it to run properly.

Sanc understood Lenzo needed to establish himself as the leader of the city. He had his rivals: merchant lords already in positions of power in the city council; and then there was Wacho. Operating from the keep, the Master of the Breath Forts was playing the same game. Meanwhile, Gaida was still in charge of transporting warriors across the channel from the mainland. They came in drips and drabs, but it wasn't long before hundreds of soldiers were in Arvena. The more that came, the more the balance of power swung towards Lenzo and Wacho.

All of which meant that everyone was busy except Sanc. He used the time to explore the city. He strolled alone around the wealthy neighbourhood where he now lived; the middling neighbourhood of shopkeepers and small traders; and back to the market area around the docks. He wore expensive armour and had a sword at his belt. No one quite knew who he was, and in the current turmoil, it worked in his favour. No one dared challenge him.

All the while, he was learning. He learned how the city worked and who was in charge of what. He learned who sent ships across the Tyrian Gulf to trade with the Nerisians; who had interests further west, among the Kassites or Rasidi; and who used the opposite route to trade in Scorgia and even as far as the Egers. In doing so, the lands of Silb were revealed to his mind's eye for the first time. And he learned that of all the places in Silb, he had found his way to the one that could get him wherever he wanted to go. For it became clear that while foreign vessels might come to Arvena to trade, no other kingdom had as large a fleet as the one based here.

Sanc even spent a day with Rab beyond the city's walls in the north of the island. Here there were a few smaller settlements where people farmed and fished. Not nearly big enough to feed the expanding population of the city, however. For that, trade abroad was vital.

Perhaps the most important thing Sanc learned was the language. His magic had given him understanding, but he spoke it like a foreigner. Now he could practise accent and dialect and learn the subtle differences in speech that could tell him the status of an individual; or when someone was using sarcasm or humour. He had made his choices and rode his luck to end up in this city. Now he had to work with the Arvenans to get what he wanted.

He still felt his best bet was Prince Lenzo. The man was clever and capable, and seemed to enjoy Sanc's company. Ultimately, of course, he saw Sanc as someone who might be useful to him. That didn't mean their relationship couldn't be mutually beneficial.

Sanc spent time with him in the evenings. They were rarely alone: Lenzo entertained important guests at dinner. After it, expensive wine and even more expensive whores occupied him long into the night. But Sanc found his moments.

'You have been out on an expedition again?' the Prince asked him as they drank wine from silver goblets—another present from a dinner guest.

'Arvena has the greatest fleet in Silb,' Sanc said.

'Correct.'

'So that can be the way to restore your kingdom?'

'No,' Lenzo said. 'Ships cannot do that alone. We also have the smallest army in Silb.' His face grew serious. 'You should have seen the numbers Lothar brought to Irpino. His resources in men and weaponry dwarfed ours, even before the invasion. The fields around the city glittered with iron—even the lowliest soldier wore metal armour. This is what grates on me more than anything else,' he said, gulping down the last of his drink before quickly refilling it. 'Lothar will be lauded as a great conqueror, while I will go down in history as a coward who ran with his tail between his legs. But if things had been the other way around—if I had inherited what he did—what greatness I could have achieved. Fate deals us each the hand that must be played. Mine was to be the heir to a crown that I had no chance of wearing.'

'So, what?' Sanc asked, genuinely confused. 'You will not even try to retake Scorgia?'

'How could I do that, Sanc? If you have an answer for me, I will gladly hear it. My only hope in that regard is for Lothar to be struck dead by some illness or accident. In that situation, maybe the Nerisians could be forced out.'

Sanc thought about it while he drank his wine. He was acquiring a taste for it. 'An assassination?'

'How powerful are you, killer of twenty warriors?' Lenzo asked him, green eyes suddenly fixed on Sanc like a predator. 'Because as well as his army, Lothar has two champions serving him.'

'Two?'

'Lothar is king of the Nerisians and the Gadenzians. Two gods look out for him, and two champions who wield magic.'

'I don't know how I compare,' Sanc admitted. 'What of the other kingdoms? Surely they have no interest in Lothar becoming so dominant? Diplomacy might work.'

'Diplomacy was, naturally, my father's principal tool. But the Nerisians have been on the rise for years, Sanc. Lothar's father stopped a Rasidi invasion in its tracks. Lothar himself fought off the Egers, killing their ruler, the Eger Khan. It's said there was such slaughter that it will take the Egers generations to recover. He created three great margravates which control his southern border.

'Then, in the last few years, Lothar warred with the Kassites. He subdued all but the most northern tribes, taking territory and oaths of allegiance. It's said that Kassite warriors even serve him now, in Scorgia. He did his groundwork; I'll give him that. He knew when he invaded Scorgia that his other borders were secure.' He gave Sanc a hard look. 'I am not stupid, you know.'

'Apologies,' Sanc said quickly. 'I am still ignorant of much. I just meant to help.'

'I understand,' Lenzo said, relenting. 'If my fate is to see out my days here, then I might as well enjoy it.'

He clicked his fingers and one of his whores came over to sit next to him. She was a raven-haired beauty, tall and slim, her looks not resembling either the Scorgian warrior class or its people. Lenzo placed a hand on her leg, drawing her silk dress up a little to reveal a shapely thigh.

'You know, you are a handsome boy, Sanc. You could join us tonight.'

The girl gave Sanc a steamy, inviting look.

Sanc gulped, intimidated. 'No thank you.'

Lenzo smiled. 'How old are you, Sanc?'

'Seventeen.'

The prince frowned. 'That is still young. You are right to decline my invitation. But you will have other opportunities in Arvena.' He studied Sanc in silence for a while. 'Now that you have educated yourself about this city, it is time for you to serve me.'

'Of course.'

'There are enough warriors here that I no longer worry about the city council turning against me. Most have shown themselves willing to accept my rule. It is Wacho who concerns me. I still hold out hope that he will be willing to play the role of loyal general. But he needs to be watched. What do you think about spying, Sanc? Is that something you could do?'

I can go invisible, Sanc said to himself. *Surely, that qualifies me for the role of spy.* 'I can do that,' he answered.

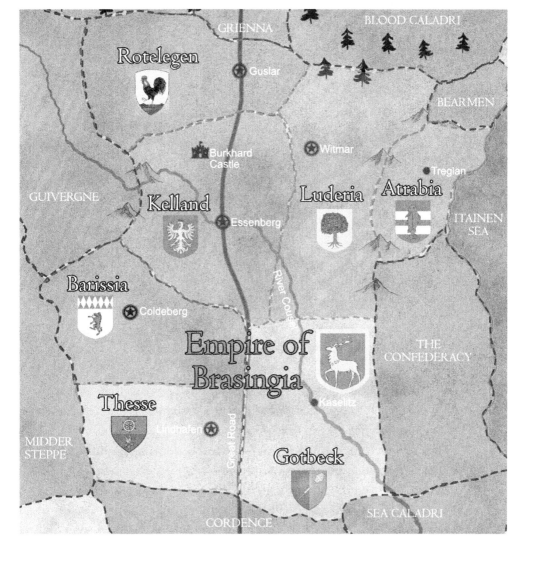

LIESEL

ESSENBERG, DUCHY OF KELLAND, 675

'At least I have you with me,' Liesel said to Tegyn, as they waited on their horses in the yard of Essenberg Castle.

'What difference do you think I can make?' her friend asked.

'Just to have you by my side makes me feel better,' Liesel told her.

'Oh,' Tegyn said, sounding unimpressed.

It was further proof that Liesel was trusted by Inge and Leopold. Not only that, but Idris had finally been moved from his cell to a room in the castle. He was still a prisoner and hadn't been seen by anyone Liesel trusted. She hoped he was in enough comfort to recover from his ordeal. Tegyn had dared to ask to see him. Inge had told her maybe later; but she hadn't said no. That was something to cling to.

Idris was useful to them—a threat to Emlyn, his uncle, that he could be replaced. A threat to Liesel if she were to step out of line again. Liesel thought there was more to it, as well. Leopold had developed a curious fondness for him; or at least, found him amusing. Even Inge smiled when his name was mentioned.

Prince Gavan had asked them to show steel and Idris had done it. He'd endured the torture meted out to him and the horrible living conditions; absorbed the news that they had killed his father. Somehow, his dry wit remained; or maybe it had helped him to survive.

Shouting told them it was time to leave, even if Liesel couldn't make out the words. Slowly, riders filtered out of the yard into the street that took them to the Great Road.

Inge and Leopold had assembled the entire cast for the journey to Guslar. As well as Liesel herself, her mother had come from Witmar—along with Salvinus, of course. She rode in a carriage near the front of the procession. The rulers of Grienna and Trevenza, who now styled themselves dukes, had also been invited along. Former provinces of Persala, Emperor Coen had allowed them to form a loose relationship with the empire. Not so close as to annoy King Zared of Persala, who had not given up his claims to them.

Then there was a ducal guard of warriors to accompany Leopold. More than Liesel thought was necessary to get her brother to Guslar and back. What, precisely, all these people added to Leopold's election prospects, Liesel had no idea.

It was a two-day journey to Guslar. A cool breeze from the north made it more pleasant than Liesel's last trip. The worst of the summer heat was over, and autumn was round the corner. When Liesel and Tegyn were allowed to ride together, with no one to bother them, it was actually quite enjoyable.

'I wonder if I will get a chance to get Friedrich alone,' Tegyn said.

'You remember,' Liesel said, 'that I pretended I wished to marry him?'

'Yes. But just to suck up to the witch, right?'

'Shh!' Tegyn was no good at the secretive game Liesel had been forced to play. 'I don't want to. But I will have to act like I do.'

Tegyn frowned. 'I see. That's going to make things tricky.'

'Maybe you could put off your seductions for another time?' Liesel suggested.

Tegyn sighed. 'I suppose. But you know, Liesel—'

'We aren't getting any younger,' Liesel got in before her friend finished the sentence. 'Yes, you have mentioned it.'

Tegyn made an effort to be quiet. 'What do you suppose will happen in Guslar?'

Liesel looked about them, checking for eavesdroppers, before she answered. 'I hope and pray that Leopold will lose. Though if he does, I fear what will happen next.'

'And Idris?' Tegyn asked.

'A new emperor may ask for his release.'

'But you don't think Leopold would agree to it?'

Liesel thought about it. 'Not for free,' she decided. 'Not unless he got something from it.'

'Hmm. How the Kellish love to use people to get what they want. No offence to you, honey.'

Liesel nodded. She was under no illusion that she was anything more than a possession, to be traded in for the best price. She looked at her friend. Had she been selfish in bringing Tegyn into the lion's den? She would have been safer back in Atrabia, there was no denying that. 'I'm Kellish too,' she said to her friend. 'I don't pretend otherwise anymore.'

WITH THE DATE and place agreed well in advance, the Rotelegen had been given plenty of time to make the arrangements for the election. Each ducal party had separate lodgings in the city and by the evening before election day they were all settled in to their respective quarters. As was traditional, now was the time for last-minute negotiations. It was an open secret that the outcome often fell on deals cut; bribes offered and accepted. The Kellish were no exception, Leopold and Inge sending their followers out with messages for one duke, then another.

Liesel knew this election was different, however. It mattered greatly who became the next emperor. Either you were prepared to accept Leopold—and that meant giving power to Inge—or you weren't. A chest full of thalers was unlikely to sway an Elector, as it may have done in the past.

The vote was scheduled for early the next morning. It was held in Guslar Cathedral, considered neutral ground. The leaders of the empire entered the church with their entourages. Six groups of seats circled a platform where a nervous Bishop of Guslar avoided eye contact with everyone.

Liesel took her seat with the other Kellish notables: her brother, mother, Inge and Salvinus. In the rows behind were other hangers-on whom Leopold had insisted on inviting. Flags with the Eagle of Kelland and the Green Tree of Luderia stood behind them. She studied the faces of those she sat with and those of the other duchies. She didn't see one that wasn't tight with tension.

Her sister sat with her husband, Jeremias; behind them the Red Rooster of Rotelegen. Her friend Tegyn took her seat with her uncle Emlyn and the Leaping Fish of Atrabia. Liesel's uncle, Walter of Barissia, Friedrich of Thesse, and Emmett of Gotbeck took the remaining places.

'Will the Electors please stand,' the bishop asked.

Six stood, as six had stood in the days before Atrabia was added to the Empire.

'With the gods and the peoples of Brasingia as witness, do you swear to abide by the judgement of your peers?'

'I swear,' the voices rang out.

Beside her, Liesel heard Leopold mutter something that she couldn't make out.

'Which of you offers to serve Brasingia as its sixth emperor?'

Liesel held her breath.

'I do,' Leopold said, looking across those assembled in the cathedral with confidence.

Liesel waited. *Surely, someone will stand against him?*

'I do.'

Jeremias. So, her brother-in-law had been persuaded by Walter's plan. Hannelore gasped, while Inge looked at the Duke of Rotelegen with a cold fury. Liesel looked across at Katrina. Her sister stared ahead, a fixed expression on her face. Liesel felt a sympathy then, that she hadn't felt when they had spoken a few weeks earlier. *You may become empress in the next few moments, sister. Either way, your husband has made you some dangerous enemies.*

The bishop waited until it was clear no one else wanted to stand.

'By virtue of their duchies, Leopold leads the voting two to one. We will now proceed in order of seniority. Walter of Barissia?'

'I vote for Rotelegen,' Walter replied, his voice steady and free of emotion.

The anger of those Liesel sat with was palpable. Their family had split down the middle for the whole of Brasingia to see.

'Emmett of Gotbeck?' the bishop called out.

'Rotelegen.'

Three votes to two. One more and Jeremias wins.

'Friedrich of Thesse?'

'Rotelegen.'

That was it. They'd done it. Relief flooded Liesel. Muttering filled the cathedral.

'Silence!' demanded the bishop. 'Respect our protocols. Emlyn of Atrabia?'

The new Prince of Atrabia gave a nervous look across at the Kellish. 'Kelland,' he said.

It didn't matter. The voting ended four to three.

'Then I declare—'

'Wait!' Leopold demanded. 'The dukes of Trevenza and Grienna are yet to vote.'

Liesel's mouth dropped as the two men got to their feet. What cheap trick was this?

'These men are not Electors!' Walter bellowed. 'For the sake of the empire, Leopold, stop this nonsense!'

Leopold gave his uncle a sneer as the two men gave their votes.

'Kelland.'

'Kelland.'

Leopold grinned. 'Five to four for me.'

'No,' said the bishop, as everyone present looked from one face to the other. 'I declare Jeremias to be the new emperor.'

'You would, wouldn't you?' Leopold shouted. 'You're in his pocket! It's five to four and I declare myself emperor!'

'That's treason, Leopold.' Jeremias looked at him, sternly. 'You swear allegiance now or I will have you arrested and tried.'

Oh, gods, Liesel said to herself. She'd had her fears, but this was even worse than those.

'How dare you?' Leopold said, sounding hysterical. He drew his sword and in an instant Salvinus was next to him, drawing his own blade.

The scrape of weapons sounded as men from all duchies drew weapons.

'Enough!' Inge's voice boomed as she got to her feet. She raised a hand, and that was more terrifying than any weapon. 'The last emperor was slain just weeks ago. You'll now slay the next? These are not normal times. Ezenachi wishes Leopold to be emperor. Make it so, and I will assure him we are loyal and trustworthy servants. Start a civil war over this and it will lead to the destruction of Brasingia.'

Inge stood only a couple of feet from Liesel. *I could grab her, drag her to the floor,* she told herself. *End this for good. No,* her sensible side kicked in. *She would kill you in an instant.*

'I hope you are not threatening me in my own city,' Jeremias said to Inge.

Liesel was impressed with how he carried himself. He must have known it wouldn't be as simple as collecting the votes.

'I have soldiers all around us,' he warned the witch. 'Either hand Leopold over or make him swear allegiance.'

'Neither will be happening,' Inge said. 'We are leaving now. If we are threatened by a single soldier, I will unleash. Maybe I can be stopped, eventually. But most of you will die in the attempt.'

'Let them go,' Walter warned.

He knows what she can do, Liesel said to herself. *Jeremias, too. They daren't act against her.*

The Kellish delegation backed away towards the exit to the cathedral. Salvinus gripped Hannelore by the arm and pulled her along. She was gasping for breath.

Liesel wished she could summon sympathy for her mother. She went with them. She locked eyes with her uncle as they retreated to the door. He gave her a barely perceptible nod. Now wasn't the time for her to add to the drama and escape. She was more useful in Essenberg than outside it. And at the back of her mind, there was always Idris. Liesel knew, with their plans in tatters, they wouldn't hesitate to take their wrath out on a prisoner.

Outside the cathedral, the Kellish retreated towards their lodgings. Rotelegen soldiers patrolled the square. Blue flames erupted in Inge's palm as she stalked away, her anger plain on her face. It was a threat to anyone that saw it, and Liesel decided no one would be foolhardy enough to take her on.

A group exited the cathedral, watching them go. Walter stood with Jeremias, talking to him.

Liesel looked at Inge's hand nervously. Was the witch tempted to hurl her magic and destroy the pair? Surely that would solve her problems. For whatever reason, she didn't, walking at such a pace that some in their party had to jog along to keep up.

Leopold spat on the ground in disgust. 'Only the Atrabians were loyal,' he muttered, incredulous.

Liesel studied her brother. *He now thinks himself emperor*, she realised. Despite witnessing the vote go against him. As if the votes of Trevenza and Grienna meant anything. *That is the world of fantasy he lives in. So powerful that it could become reality.*

She looked from Leopold back to Jeremias. *We have two emperors now. And a demon waiting on our border. How I could weep for Brasingia.*

A FEVERISH INTENSITY took hold of Essenberg Castle. Messengers came and went at all hours; spies and informants spoke with Inge. Leopold sent out orders to his lords and raised the Kellish army. In Witmar, Salvinus called up the warriors of Luderia. Their allies in Trevenza and Grienna were ready to march south on Rotelegen at his word. Jeremias was surrounded, and Liesel feared for him.

His allies, however, were quick to act. The Thessians and Gotbeckers brought their armies to Barissia. Walter led the armies of three duchies close to the Kellish border. That was a force impossible to ignore. Leopold's bold talk of invading the duchy of his brother-in-law and of the punishments he would mete out were allowed to slide. The Kellish looked to their southern border, fearful that Walter intended to take Essenberg.

The empire stood on the brink. Liesel knew the convulsions of a civil war would destroy Brasingia. Any spark might ignite the powder keg. Somehow, as the weeks went by, the leaders of each side restrained themselves. Autumn turned colder, making war less attractive. The costs of keeping so many men in the field mounted. At last, Walter's army departed, the warriors returning home. With reluctance, Leopold followed suit. War had been averted, but there was no sign of a resolution. Liesel looked to the future with dread. Next year, they would have the full campaign season to kill one another, while their real enemy was ignored.

It was into this bleak setting that the ship arrived in Essenberg. It was a fine vessel, newly built, with a stern deck that flew the Owl of Guivergne. The lords who came wore the finest of clothes—beneath their fur-lined cloaks were intricately worked scabbards at their belts. They led beautiful horses, each beast worth a small fortune. The horses were laden with gifts. When they reached the castle, these gifts were carried into the hall, where Leopold waited to greet them, seated on his throne. Liesel, Tegyn, and Inge stood amongst the lords and ladies of the court. The Imperial Guard—for that was what the castle soldiers now had to be called—stood to attention around the hall.

The leader of the Guivergnais went on one knee before Leopold.

Tegyn purred beside Liesel at the magnificence. Liesel barely registered. She was fixed on the leader of the Guivergnais.

Leopold gestured for him to stand.

'Your Imperial Majesty Leopold,' Peyre began. 'Please accept these gifts, humbly offered by my brother, King Esterel.'

Imperial Majesty Leopold, Liesel repeated to herself with derision. *If Peyre wants to get on the good side of Leopold, that is sufficient. No need for gifts. What game is he playing?*

Peyre snapped his fingers, and the gifts were placed before Leopold—the chests opened for him to see the treasure inside. There were gilt goblets and crockery; lavishly bound books, set with enamel and jewels; bolts of fabric and furs; equine equipment; musical instruments; jewellery; tapestries. Those gathered murmured in appreciation.

'The best of all, in my opinion, is not here,' Peyre said, 'but awaiting you in your stables. I have never seen a better stallion.'

'Duke Peyre,' Leopold said, 'your brother does me great honour. I cannot wait to accompany you to my stables, where we can examine this beast and talk together. It has been too long since we last spent time together.'

When you gave him that scar, Liesel told herself. *What is going on here?* she wondered. She glanced at Inge, who wore a smug look on her face. That was never a good sign.

'Indeed it has,' Peyre concurred.

'I feel a boor,' Leopold said, 'that I do not have a gift to give King Esterel in return.' It was said with a theatricality, for the benefit of the court.

'On the contrary,' Peyre said. 'King Esterel has sent me to request a gift from you far superior to these trifles that I have delivered.'

'What would that be, Your Grace?' Leopold asked, unconvincingly pretending he didn't already know.

If my brother joined a mummer's group, they would be careful to give him no lines, Liesel decided.

Peyre turned to Liesel then. He had a smile on his face, but it was affected for his audience, not her. 'Your Imperial Majesty. King Esterel formally requests the hand of your beautiful sister, Liesel, in marriage.'

Liesel's mouth dropped open in shock.

Leopold leered at her, triumphant.

* * *

'IT'S PERFECT,' Leopold crowed. 'Peyre is sure Esterel will intervene in the empire on our side. This could give us the swift victory we need.'

The three of them were in Leopold's private apartments. It was late, and Liesel's head was spinning with the Guivergnais marriage request.

'Of course, he will promise you everything to get the marriage,' Inge chided him. It was not said with venom, but Leopold still looked at the witch with cold eyes. 'Though I cannot pretend it's not very beneficial for us. At the very least, it will help keep Guivergne out of our affairs. Keep Esterel from marrying anyone else, too.'

'It will do rather more than that,' Leopold countered. 'I tell you, Peyre and I agree on many things. Two powerful realms in Dalriya, under myself and Esterel. He has grown up a bit since he was last here. Duke of Morbaine, now. I told you about his intervention in Magnia?'

'Yes,' said Inge. At times, she treated him like a little boy; indulging him, especially when he stubbornly refused to accept what she said.

Some emperor, Liesel thought. As for Peyre, he did seem to have changed. Not that she had yet been allowed to talk with him. According to Leopold, he had taken an army into Magnia mere days after his brother had made him Duke of Morbaine. There he had fought off the army of Ezenachi; until witnessing the demon's powers as she had done in Thesse. She longed to speak to him on all manner of subjects. But she knew she must play this game for all it was worth now. She must be hard as steel.

Inge studied her. 'I did once think a match with Esterel would be perfect for you, Liesel. I thought that ship had sailed. How strange that it comes back into port right when we need it.' She cocked her head at Liesel. 'You don't like the idea?'

Marrying Esterel of Guivergne would get her out of Brasingia for good. No more looking over her shoulder. She remembered Walter nodding to her in Guslar; her sister suggesting he had a plan for her. She was sure he was involved in this. But she mustn't seem eager to Inge or Leopold. Mustn't raise their suspicions in any way. She knew them both; had learned how to pull their strings. The more she disliked an idea, the more they would like it.

'I can't like the idea when I have never met him, can I?'

'Hardly a great obstacle,' Inge said. 'Esterel is said to be extraordinarily handsome and an accomplished warrior. He is young. You would be queen for many years.'

'It's just that I had expected to marry Friedrich. This has all come as a surprise. And neither of you warned me!'

'Friedrich?' Leopold said, outraged. 'You can forget that idea! I won't be satisfied until all four rebel dukes are in my dungeon, begging for mercy. I will smile contemptuously and give them none. I will make my sister a widow and laugh in her face.'

'Liesel, really,' said Inge, ignoring Leopold. 'Grow up a little. There have been careful talks with Valennes before Peyre came here. We couldn't risk the plan getting out.'

Liesel gave a shrug, as if mollified. 'Well, queen is higher ranking than duchess, I suppose. Even if it is in a foreign land. I would have servants and beautiful clothes and such. And a husband who chose me.'

'Ha!' Leopold snapped. 'Chose you because of *me!* Esterel will have you flat on your back as soon as you get there. He'll get you with child and then return to his mistress's bed, no doubt. You'll be popping out babies. And even if you survive childbirth, you'll have lost your looks in a few years.'

Liesel didn't have to fake the look of fear Leopold's words provoked. She worried about all those things. Marrying a stranger was a frightening prospect. Even if she knew that was always a likely prospect for someone of her status.

But it was still better than staying here with her brother. There was an undeniable pang of guilt and regret, as well. She would be leaving Idris behind. She wondered what he thought of her now— she'd done nothing to help him or improve his comfort. What would he think when she deserted him for good and married someone else?

Liesel noticed Inge studying her again. She hoped she'd given nothing away.

'Maybe we could arrange for me to meet with Esterel before I say yes?'

Leopold snorted. 'There's no time for that. I need this alliance firmly in place by spring. Besides, I'm the one who says yes, not you.'

Liesel glared at him. 'Then at least let me speak with his brother. The duke might assure me of Esterel's character.'

Inge waved a hand. 'You can speak with him tomorrow. He says he has messages of love for you straight from Esterel's mouth.' The witch smiled at this—a rare real one, Liesel thought. She obviously found the words amusing.

Liesel blushed.

Leopold laughed. 'Messages of love?' He looked incredulous. 'The Guivergnais are too much. You must come to see me straight afterwards, Liesel. Tell me word for word what he says.'

PEYRE

ESSENBERG, DUCHY OF KELLAND, 675

Y ou saw Ezenachi?' Inge asked him as they walked along the corridor of Essenberg Castle.

'Aye,' Peyre said. He was uneasy in her presence. Memories of the last time he was in the empire returned. She had been terrifying. In Witmar, she'd blasted him with her magic, knocking him unconscious. Now, she was polite; respectful. Of course, he was masking his own feelings as well. He would do whatever it took to get Liesel out of her control for good.

She stopped, making him stop as well. 'It is a sobering thing to witness such power. Makes you see the world differently. Both you and Liesel have now seen what he can do.'

'Liesel was in Thesse?'

'Yes, Your Grace. She understands the need for strong allies. Brasingia and Guivergne could become the strongest of all. Liesel could be the glue that binds them together. I hope your brother has the same reasons for the match. I know news of the contested election will have reached him.'

Peyre nodded. He was on dangerous ground, he knew. Inge wanted convincing that Guivergne's intentions were honourable. 'The

52

king was advised that Leopold would become the undisputed emperor in the end.'

Inge raised an eyebrow. 'I see. May I ask who advised the king this way?'

'I did, for one.' He looked at Inge. The girlish features that hid so much. 'I have witnessed some of your power, Inge. Your enemies have no sorcerers. The outcome seems inevitable. The only question is how you will do it.'

Inge looked surprised at his answer. But not displeased. 'When Ezenachi came against you in Magnia. I imagine he punished you. Like he punished Brasingia.'

Peyre saw no reason to lie. She would find out soon enough. 'He killed King Edgar, just like he killed Emperor Coen. Also, Rimmon the sorcerer.'

'Ah,' Inge whispered, a noise full of some emotion he couldn't decipher. 'And your other brother? It's alright. I know he is also a mage.'

Peyre stiffened at the mention of Sanc. But he saw little use in trying to fool her. 'Gone, before Ezenachi got there. Before I got there.'

'Gone?' Inge repeated.

Peyre shrugged. 'Sent away. I don't know the details of it. He and Rimmon did it before I got to Magnia.'

Inge considered this, chewing on her lower lip, staring into some distant place. It went on so long Peyre thought she had entered a trance, but then her eyes flicked back to his. 'I think that is the best for your brother. Maybe for all of us. Now I begin to fully understand Guivergne's motives for the marriage. Your country needs my protection as much as Brasingia.'

It wasn't a motive at all. It wasn't even a ruse Peyre had come up with. It was strange, though. When the witch said it, it sounded true. Except, it was the last thing Peyre wanted. He wanted Liesel in Valennes. Not Inge.

'I feel the alliance would benefit both sides,' he said.

'Of course, Peyre. Of course. I hope our personal disagreements are a thing of the past. I have made up with Liesel.' She pouted, like a girl who had asked for an expensive gift.

'Of course. That was a long time ago.'

Inge smiled. 'Look at you, all grown up.' She put a hand on his arm, and he fought off a shudder. 'Surely it will be your turn to marry next? You are quite the catch for some lucky girl, Your Grace.'

Peyre made himself give her a sickly smile. 'Maybe my turn will come soon.'

'I'm sure it will. Come, Liesel will be waiting for you.'

Inge led him to the castle gardens. Peyre saw Liesel waiting for him on a bench. Another lady sat next to her. As they approached, the two ladies stood.

There was an awkward silence. Inge sported one of her insincere smiles, and Peyre was sure she was leading up to some embarrassing comment. He was surprised when she turned and left, having said nothing at all.

'Lady Liesel,' Peyre said, giving her a nod. He had fallen in love with her three years ago. Sometimes he wondered if it had been a stupid, childish thing. But by the gods, if she didn't look even more beautiful now. His doubts were blown away. And here he was, come to persuade her to marry someone else.

'Your Grace,' Liesel said.

Her smile was small—hesitant, even. Yet it still said so much, acknowledging their friendship of three years ago. Peyre wished all they would talk about was one another; what had happened in the years since they had met. But that would only get in the way.

'I am pleased to get the chance to speak to you openly,' she said, her eyes widening with the last word. 'You will find me a much more obedient soul than when we met three years ago.'

The lady next to her raised a finger to her lips, as if Peyre were too stupid to get Liesel's hint. It marked her out as a friend of Liesel's. Presumably she was just here for the sake of decorum. She was petite but strong looking, her skin fair but her hair darker than most Brasingians.

'This is Tegyn,' Liesel said, pulling the girl's hand away from her mouth. 'Daughter of Prince Gavan and my good friend.'

Gavan? Peyre had heard the news. He'd died in Essenberg, the title passing to his brother. 'I'm sorry about the loss of your father, Lady Tegyn.'

'Thank you,' she said. 'They still have my brother here, you know. They've let me see him twice. He's doing alright. But maybe you could have a word with Leopold. Get him released?'

Peyre was taken aback. 'I could try,' he ventured. 'Though I am here to get agreement for the marriage and will do nothing to undermine that.'

Tegyn pursed her lips. 'I suppose that's fair. Anyway, I should let you two speak.'

Surely, you should, Peyre said to himself. 'I am here on behalf of King Esterel,' he said to Liesel.

The smile had gone, and she sat still, concentrating on what he had to say.

'His qualities and achievements are many and as his spokesperson, I will tell you all of those. But first, as his brother. I can tell you he is a good, kind man; and that is the most important thing of all.'

Liesel gave a little nod.

She will do it, he realised. *She will marry Esterel.* A sadness settled on his chest. It felt like grief.

'I THINK the marriage should go ahead as soon as possible,' Leopold told him.

Peyre nodded in agreement. *That is the easiest way to deal with the Duke of Kelland. Or Emperor of Brasingia,* he corrected himself. *Nod along.*

They were in Leopold's private rooms and were close to finishing a barrel of wine. Two of Leopold's thug friends were with them. Peyre knew one of them was the same man who had held him down the night Leopold had given him his scar. Peyre ached to wipe the smirk from his face. More than once he had come close to demanding that Leopold eject the bastard from his rooms. But he couldn't predict how Liesel's brother would react to that. He just daren't risk undoing things here when he was so close.

'It doesn't matter if I am not there,' Leopold continued earnestly. 'What matters is that Esterel can send his troops east in the spring.'

Leopold was convinced that Esterel would come charging into Rotelegen as soon as he was asked to. Peyre had done little of the convincing; the fool had convinced himself. This was the part of the equation Peyre didn't fully understand. Inge seemed hell bent on making Leopold the undisputed ruler of Brasingia when he was clearly ill-suited to it. As far as Peyre could see, that was the single most important cause of the empire's divisions—at a time when it needed strength and unity like never before.

'I understand,' he said.

Leopold looked pleased. 'Then I shall tell Liesel my decision,' he declared, as if it was anyone's but Inge's to make.

'My crew is ready to leave on my word,' Peyre informed him.

'I had hoped we would find time for a trip to the Shambles,' Leopold said. 'But maybe next time. You could bring Esterel for a visit?'

Peyre did his best to force a smile onto his face. 'All this talk of marriage, I wonder how you are yet to find a wife, Your Majesty.'

'Who is there in Dalriya who would be a worthy match for me?' Leopold asked him, straight-faced. 'Arguably your sister would have been, but she was married off to a mere duke of Guivergne? No offence, Peyre.'

Leopold's friend smirked.

Peyre resisted forming a fist. 'That was our father's doing. We weren't happy with it.'

'I'm sure. Well, get rid of her husband and maybe Esterel and I can talk about it. But her value has plummeted now.'

Over my dead body, Peyre said to himself. It was all he could do to keep the sentiment to himself. He had to get out of Essenberg. It made him wonder how Liesel had endured it for so long. 'What is the value of a prince?' he asked.

Leopold looked at him quizzically.

'I was told you had a prince locked up somewhere here.'

'Ah! Idris. Son of a prince, not a prince himself. I would say a prince usually ranks with a duke. Unless they're a prince of Atrabia. That's like being prince of a midden.' Leopold seemed to think about it. 'Except the Prince of Atrabia was the one Elector who stayed true to me.'

'Maybe you need to rethink your hierarchy?' Peyre suggested.

'I think you're right. The easiest thing to do would be strip the titles of duke and elector from those Brasingians who betrayed me. Give them to the rulers of Grienna and Trevenza. I would need to save some special punishment for the Rotelegen,' he said, his face twisting into a scowl. 'I will simply annex the duchy and add it to Kelland. The name Rotelegen will be forgotten; anyone who even speaks it will be punished.'

He is quite mad, Peyre reminded himself. 'And what of this son of a prince?' he asked Leopold. Peyre knew he shouldn't press the issue any further. But he found he couldn't stop thinking about Tegyn, Liesel's friend. *If I was imprisoned, I know Loysse would fight for my release with just as much persistence.*

'Idris? He is quite the character.' A gleam came to Leopold's eye. 'Come! Let us visit him,' he said, standing up on unsteady feet.

'Aye!' one of his friends enthused. 'The mad Atrabian!'

Peyre let them lead him through the castle. It was late and most people were abed, but no one was about to complain to the newly crowned Emperor of Brasingia. *The last time I drank and revelled with these bastards, they cut me up*, Peyre reminded himself. *I still haven't paid Leopold back for that. And here I am encouraging some fresh madness.* The sense of danger cut through the wine. But it was too late to turn them back now.

Two guards stood outside the Atrabian's room. They unlocked the door on Leopold's order and the four of them barged in.

A moan of complaint came from the darkness.

'Get some candles lit!' Leopold complained to his guards, and they were quick to oblige.

The flickering candlelight illuminated a pale figure sat up in the bed that took up most of the small room. Peyre could see the similarity to Tegyn. Idris had the same black hair. But his hair hung lank about his face and he was thin and gangly.

'Your Majesty,' the man said to Leopold, large eyes blinking owlishly.

'Thought I'd surprise you, Idris,' Leopold said.

'Oh, that's a shame,' the Atrabian said. 'Because I was expecting you to bring an unknown guest to my room in the middle of the night.'

'Ha!' Leopold grinned, finding the response amusing.

'Mad bastard!' said Leopold's friend.

'Shut up, Olbrecht!' Leopold told him. 'This is Peyre, Duke of Morbaine, Idris. Come to take Liesel away to marry his brother, the King of Guivergne.'

'Oh?' Idris said. He looked at Peyre questioningly.

Peyre recognised some sort of emotion there. If Liesel had become a close friend of Tegyn in Atrabia, then it was likely she was close to Idris, too. It seemed it, by the way Idris looked at him.

Some instinct told Peyre the man needed reassurance. 'I am afraid your sister has asked to come with us as well,' Peyre told him. 'So you won't see her again—or not until Leopold releases you at any rate.' He looked Idris in the eye and held his gaze for a moment. 'Don't worry. She'll be safe in Guivergne.'

Idris nodded, a look of gratitude briefly showing.

'Never mind all that,' Leopold said, sounding annoyed. 'We've come to show you just how mad this Atrabian bastard is, Peyre. Come on, Idris. Take that shirt off.'

'Oh goody,' the Atrabian said, removing his shirt.

Peyre gasped. Scars from knife wounds ran along his chest and sides.

'I know,' said Leopold. A leery grin came to his face, made worse by the flickering candlelight. 'I gave Peyre that, you know,' he said to Idris, pointing at Peyre's face. 'You screamed far more from that little cut than Idris has from any of these! Come on, let's add some fresh ones.'

Leopold and his two friends drew their knives from their belts.

'Where this time?' Leopold asked. 'There's not much room left anywhere,' he said, eyeing the Atrabian.

'How about my back?' Idris said, turning around. White and pink scars criss-crossed his skin.

'Mad bastard,' muttered Leopold's friend.

The three of them wasted no more time, each of them slicing long cuts into Idris's flesh that immediately welled with blood.

Peyre thought he would be sick. He glanced at the two guards, but they were stony faced. How regularly did they do this to the Atrabian? *It can't be that often,* he told himself, *since he has no fresh wounds. This is only happening because of me.* He went hot with shame and anger.

'Come on, Peyre,' Leopold said, handing him the hilt of his own knife. 'It's your turn.'

'I can't,' Peyre said. He was done pretending now. There were some things he couldn't do.

'We all have to do it,' Leopold insisted, sounding angry.

'It's alright, Your Grace,' Idris said. All Peyre could see was the back of his head. 'I've got a taste for it, you see. And there is very little to do in this tiny room, anyway. It soon heals.'

Peyre's hand closed over the hilt.

Leopold looked satisfied.

Now's the time to get my revenge on the bastard, Peyre realised. He saw Leopold's knife puncturing its owner's neck. He heard the gasp of surprise; the glugging noise as his throat filled with blood. He'd do in his two friends as well before the guards could react.

But what would happen to Liesel? What of Idris? Peyre's hand shook.

'Get on with it,' Leopold said, exasperated.

Peyre scored a line along the Atrabian's back and returned the knife to Leopold.

'Thank you,' Idris said.

* * *

THEY LEFT Essenberg the next day. Peyre's boat made steady enough progress—they used the horses of the river traders to help them travel upriver. They pulled on ropes attached to the craft from the river bank, switching the beasts at regular intervals. Autumn was only just holding off the onslaught of winter, when such a journey would have been unpleasant.

He eyed Liesel, sat up on the stern with Tegyn, furs clutched tight around her. If anything, she looked even more beautiful away from the city. Peyre wished to speak with her, but the vessel was too crowded to offer any privacy. He would have to wait.

The tension of the last few days eased when they passed from Brasingia into Guivergne. Peyre had not rested between the campaign in Magnia and his mission to Essenberg. An exhaustion of the body and mind came upon him, and he was grateful when they left the karst landscape of the border region and stopped at a settlement on the river capable of putting them up. His sailors would find sleeping spots on the floors of the various inns at the least. Peyre, meanwhile, found the best room in the best inn for Liesel and Tegyn to share.

'I will organise food to be brought up,' he told them. 'It won't be the finest Guivergne has to offer.'

'I'm not a snob, Peyre,' Liesel told him. 'I got by on Atrabian food for two years.'

Tegyn gave a little cry of complaint and slapped her on the arm.

'Sorry,' Peyre said. 'It's just with you being my future queen and all...'

Liesel gave him a fearful look. 'Don't. I'm overwhelmed enough as it is. Won't you join us? I have so many questions I need to ask you.'

'Of course. It would be my pleasure.'

When Peyre returned with their fish supper, the three of them perched on the beds and spoke. Liesel had not been exaggerating about the questions. She wanted to know everything about Guivergne —how its customs, people and way of life differed from Brasingia. When he was too vague with his answers, she told him off, telling him that since he had lived in both countries, he should know all the differences. She asked him to tell her about every individual he knew in Valennes; about the war of succession that had been fought on the death of Nicolas; about his intervention in Magnia. She wanted to be as prepared as possible.

Peyre found himself looking at Liesel beyond his own affection or desires. He saw someone determined to be a good queen. It did something to ease his pain that she would never be his. She would be his queen, and that was a consolation.

Finally, the subject they had been skirting around. Esterel.

'What does he want from his reign?' Liesel asked him.

That was a question that caught him off guard. Then he thought back to his brother's coronation speech. 'Honour and glory,' he said with a smile.

'Oh,' Liesel said. She did not sound thrilled with the idea. 'I suppose he has every chance of becoming a hero with a demon threatening Dalriya. What does he say about Ezenachi?'

'Well, this is something you should know. Guivergne is unlike most other parts of Dalriya. Except for Famiens, we weren't involved in the Isharite Wars. We have a tendency not to concern ourselves with events outside our borders unless they concern us directly. But after I told Esterel of my experience in Magnia, he understands the nature of the threat.'

'What did he say he will do?' Liesel asked him.

Peyre frowned. 'Well. Not long after I told him about it, I left Valennes for Essenberg. But I am sure he is doing much to warn our people of the threat.'

Liesel nodded.

Peyre got the feeling she had expected more, but what that might be, he didn't know.

'And this marriage plan? My uncle had a part in it?'

'I spoke with Walter at my sister's wedding.' *Be careful, Peyre,* he warned himself. He didn't want it to sound like Esterel was resistant to the idea of marrying Liesel. Or suggest that the marriage was merely an act of chivalry devised to rescue her. He could tell she was worried enough about the match without adding to her insecurities. 'We began careful negotiations after that.'

'No one said a word to me before you arrived,' she told him.

'I'm sorry,' Peyre said. 'You know, Esterel would never force you to marry him. If you don't want to, you just have to say. Tell me if you like.'

Liesel smiled and looked a lot happier.

I should have said that before, Peyre reprimanded himself.

'And what about the women in Esterel's life?' Liesel asked him. 'If he is as handsome and charismatic as everyone says, I'm sure he has turned a few heads.'

'Who has he bedded?' Tegyn demanded.

'Tegyn!' Liesel said, shocked.

The Atrabian girl rolled her eyes.

'That's not what I meant at all,' Liesel said. 'But if he has affections for another, I need to know. Or else I could put my foot in it.'

Peyre hesitated. Of course, there was Coleta. Esterel had talked of marrying Sacha's sister only a few weeks before. But he felt it would be doing both her and Esterel a wrong if he named her now.

'I'm sorry, Peyre,' Liesel said. 'That was an unfair question to ask. You have been so kind to me, as always, that I just asked it without thinking.'

'It's alright. What you say is true. Of course, it would be strange if Esterel hadn't had dalliances. But there is no one who would steal any of his attention once he meets you.'

Liesel blushed.

Have I overstepped the mark with that compliment, Peyre worried.

'Thank you, Peyre. I never thanked you properly the first time you helped me. For you to have come back to Essenberg after what Leopold did... I am just so grateful for what you have done. I am lucky and honoured to have you as a friend.'

She reached out to him a little; awkwardly. Peyre had no choice but to take her hands in his. He fought to pretend nothing in him stirred at that touch.

'Of course,' he said. 'We will always be friends.' He released her and they shared a smile. *Gods,* Peyre thought. *Now I wonder if I can bear this for the rest of my life. I am making some awful torture for myself.*

'Did you speak with Leopold about my brother?' Tegyn asked him.

Peyre was relieved for the change of subject. Though it was hardly an easy one. 'I met your brother last night,' he told her. *There is no way I am telling them what I did.* The memory of Idris in his room struck him and he could feel the shame of the encounter burning his cheeks.

'He is well?' Liesel asked, desperation in her voice.

Peyre wondered then. Two years, Liesel had lived in Atrabia with Prince Gavan's family. She was clearly close with Tegyn. It would be no great surprise if she were just as close to Idris. But as a brother, or something more?

'He is as well as can be expected,' Peyre answered. The Atrabian's scarred torso came to his mind's eye and Peyre forced it away. 'I am afraid I see no immediate prospect of him being released. I tried; as much as I could.'

'Thank you,' Tegyn said simply.

'My departure will help, I am sure,' Liesel said. 'Leopold and Inge saw him as a way to control me. Now that angle has gone, they may question the value in keeping him imprisoned forever.'

Peyre nodded in agreement, though it sounded unlikely. Surely, Liesel knew her own brother better than Peyre did. There was no sympathy in his character; not a shred of compassion for others.

LIESEL

VALENNES, KINGDOM OF GUIVERGNE, 675

'There it is,' Tegyn said, pointing.

The walls of Valennes were finally visible from their position in the stern of Peyre's ship. It seemed the river would take them directly to the city gates. Liesel stared at the structure, as if it would reveal the secrets of what awaited her inside. Strong, she decided. Yet with an elegance she had not seen in Brasingia. 'Gods,' she muttered to herself. *What stupid nonsense is in your head, Liesel?*

'What's the matter?' Tegyn demanded.

'I'm all over the place,' Liesel admitted. 'One moment, I feel a great freedom, like I am escaping to a new life. Then I am full of trepidation about what awaits me.'

'Oh, poor Liesel,' Tegyn said. 'Off to marry the most eligible monarch in Dalriya and become a queen. How the hearts of every woman must bleed with compassion for your plight.'

'Well, at least I have you for support,' Liesel responded tartly. 'I don't know how I'd manage without it.'

They sat in silence as the boat drew inexorably closer to the city. A great bridge across the river was the next structure to appear. Tegyn didn't seem interested, however.

'What *are* you staring at?' Liesel demanded, looking to the other end of the boat, where her friend's gaze was fixed. 'Duke Peyre?' she asked, scandalised.

'What?' Tegyn said defensively. 'He's not married, is he? And that backside is a pretty fine sight to me.'

Liesel put a hand to her mouth, turning around in case anyone had overheard. 'You're terrible! What about Duke Friedrich?'

Tegyn lifted her palms. 'Are we moving to Thesse? No. We're moving to Guivergne, so that's where I shall conduct my explorations.'

'Your explorations?' Liesel repeated. She thought about it. 'Still. Now I am imagining you and Peyre together. Wouldn't that be wonderful?'

'So you'll help?'

'Help?'

Tegyn turned to look at Liesel, her eyes narrowing.

'Yes,' Liesel said quickly. 'I'm sure, when the chance arises, I could say something.'

When they left the boat, there were so many sights that Liesel struggled to take anything in. It turned out there were two parts of Valennes, one each side of the Cousel. Peyre and his six guards led them through the gates of the walled western half, and they were soon walking through the main streets of the city. Peyre pointed out the cathedral, various shops, and inns—and so many other things that she forgot the previous thing she was told.

The road that took them north from the city centre became quieter after a while. Peyre pointed ahead and to the right. 'The Bastion,' he announced.

It was as ugly—and odd looking—as the rest of Valennes was beautiful. Triangular shaped towers jutted out from the squat structure at all angles.

'It's an interesting design,' Liesel said.

This is to be my home? She asked herself.

'I'll let Esterel give you the tour and history,' Peyre said, as if that was something to look forward to.

As they approached the fort, Liesel could see it was surrounded by a mucky looking wet moat.

'That stinks,' Tegyn said.

'You get used to it,' said Peyre with a smile, guiding them along the drawbridge.

Liesel and Tegyn shared a look. That simply wasn't a smell one could get used to.

They waited in an entrance room Peyre called the Grand Foyer. From a carved wooden balcony above them, the Owl of Guivergne stared down. Its eyes were those of a bird of prey: Liesel found them unsettling and hostile, and wondered why such a thing would be placed in a room meant to welcome guests.

Mercifully, it wasn't long until the man who ran The Bastion came to greet them.

'Lord Sacha of Courion,' Peyre introduced him, giving him a small nod.

Liesel sneaked a quick glance at Tegyn, whose eyes had widened so far Liesel feared they might pop from their sockets. For this man was, by any measure, the most attractive man Liesel had ever seen. Everything: eyes, hair, jaw... body... seemed perfect. Not that perfection was Liesel's type. For some reason, she had found herself attracted to the gangly awkwardness of Tegyn's brother. But that didn't mean she couldn't appreciate what the gods had made.

'Your Grace,' Lord Sacha replied, equally curt.

If not a coldness, exactly, there was a formality between the two men that suggested they were not great friends. Peyre had said nothing bad about Sacha during his lessons on Guivergne. Nonetheless, she felt she should be careful around him for now. And surely, perfect looking people must have something wrong with them.

'Welcome to Valennes, ladies. I am to take you to your rooms,' he said to them.

Peyre raised a hand in farewell, which Liesel returned. She and Tegyn were then whisked away, along corridors and up a flight of stairs. 'The king suggested he should wait to meet you at dinner,' Sacha said to Liesel with a smile. 'He thought a small gathering at top table would work best. Not too many unfamiliar faces but a few other people to help break the ice.'

'Yes,' Liesel agreed. 'That would be most kind.'

'Esterel is the most easy-going and friendly person I know,' he said, with a twinkle in his eye. 'You have nothing to worry about. Is there anyone you would like to attend the meal?'

'Could Tegyn sit with us?'

'Most certainly,' Sacha said, giving Tegyn a warm smile.

'Oh, and Peyre, maybe? Duke Peyre, I mean.'

Sacha's smile cracked at the edges. 'I shall ask His Grace to attend.'

They walked on, and Liesel suddenly wondered whether Sacha had wanted her to ask him to attend. *Oh gods, have I managed to offend and create an enemy already?*

Standing in a line outside a doorway were three maids. Sacha stopped them here.

'I asked these girls to attend to you. Please, ask for anything. If they can't do it, they will come to me with your request. As Royal Steward, I am here to serve you, Lady Liesel. Please ask for me if there is anything you need, at any time. Will Lady Tegyn be sharing your rooms?'

Tegyn had a goofy smile on her face and Liesel felt the need to answer before she said something flirty and embarrassing.

'She will,' Liesel said. 'Thank you so much for your warm welcome, Lord Sacha.'

The steward gave a little bow and left them to it.

The senior maid opened the door to Liesel's rooms, and she and Tegyn entered. It was a suite of rooms—tastefully furnished, with beds and a closet for clothes.

'We should fill the bath tub for you, my lady?'

'Yes please.'

Tegyn let out a whistle. 'It's a far cry from Atrabia, Liesel. And the people are infinitely more likeable than in Essenberg. This place is starting to grow on me.'

LIESEL MET Esterel in the Bastion's hall. The room was similar in most respects to that of her old home, Essenberg Castle. It could hold many more guests than were present this evening. The top table was almost empty: Peyre and Tegyn, the only others who ate with them. The other officials and friends of the court sat elsewhere. Understandably, many looked over towards her, talking in hushed voices. Her arrival was, inevitably, big news. She had done her best, with the help of Tegyn and the maids Sacha had provided her, to make a good impression. They had braided her hair and rolled it up. She wore one of her favourite dresses: red-dyed wool made it look arresting, as well as being warm enough for an autumn evening this far north. Tegyn had insisted she wear a corset to add shape.

'You are beautiful, my lady,' the younger maid had said when she was ready.

No doubt it had been flattery. Even so, Liesel had taken a liking to the girl.

Esterel expressed similar sentiments. He looked pleased with what he saw; or he was an excellent liar.

Esterel himself was exceedingly handsome. It might have been more intimidating if she hadn't met Sacha earlier the same day. He was blond, where Sacha was dark. Where Sacha smouldered, Esterel had a more open face; his smile was big and genuine. He didn't appear to take himself too seriously, either, quickly insisting that they should just call him Esterel. With them both opposite her, Liesel could see some resemblance to Peyre; but it was also easy to see differences in temperament, as well as looks.

'I would like to show you more of Guivergne tomorrow,' Esterel said to her. 'Do you ride?'

'I do. I thought I did when I left Essenberg. But it was only in Atrabia that I learned to really ride.'

'We ride fast in Atrabia,' Tegyn confirmed. 'We taught her to shoot a bow as well.'

'Oh!' said Esterel, looking surprised. 'Well, I wasn't planning on taking Liesel into combat,' he said with a smile.

There was no condemnation in his words, exactly. But Liesel got the impression that he expected her to be more feminine. Girlish laughs and sewing, maybe. That wasn't going to happen.

'Perhaps you should take Liesel hunting one day, brother?' Peyre suggested. 'Test her bow arm.'

'That's a good idea, Peyre. Will you be joining us tomorrow?'

'I think not. I feel obliged to return to Morbaine.' He looked at Liesel. 'I left Lord Russell, my steward, in charge there. Along with my good friend, Umbert. But I feel I should return after all that happened.'

'Of course,' she said. She hid her disappointment. Peyre was so reliable. At the same time, her gratitude to him increased all the more. He'd left his new duchy, threatened by Ezenachi, to come to Essenberg for her. Surely Esterel had other men he could have sent?

'Come on, Peyre. I was going to host a little party tomorrow night to celebrate our betrothal. That is,' Esterel said, turning to Liesel, 'if you are still willing to go ahead? More than understandable if you've changed your mind now you've met me,' he said with a grin.

Liesel blushed. 'Of course, I wish to go ahead, Your Majesty.'

'Wonderful!' Esterel said, smiling at her.

He didn't anticipate any other answer, Liesel could tell.

'How about it, Peyre?' Esterel asked his brother.

'As I say,' Peyre said, looking distinctly uncomfortable. 'I would rather be away. That way, I can return here before winter sets in.'

'Very well,' Esterel said, clearly disappointed.

Ah, Liesel said to herself. *There is his fake smile.*

'Not to worry, Liesel. We will have plenty to entertain us tomorrow. And of course, we need Peyre back in Valennes for the long winter nights. I wish our sister, Loysse, could visit soon. She is the other member of our family you must meet.'

'She is the Duchess of Famiens?' Liesel asked.

'Yes, indeed! My, you really are well informed already, Liesel. I feel ashamed my knowledge of the empire is so inferior. You will have to educate me.' He seemed to catch himself. 'Whenever you are willing to share, of course.'

He has obviously been told something of my background, Liesel noted. *He must know about the current troubles.* But whatever Esterel knew, it seemed he wanted to keep their first meeting light. They flitted from one topic of conversation to the next, avoiding anything too serious. That meant Liesel spoke relatively little, since anything connected to her childhood, family, or recent events was a no-go. Liesel was impressed, and a little relieved that Tegyn behaved so politely. Peyre seemed preoccupied. He had explained why. Liesel thought it must have been a mistake on her part to ask him to attend the meal. No doubt there will be many more mistakes to come.

Still, Liesel felt she survived her first encounter with Esterel without doing irreparable harm.

'So, what do you think of him?' she asked Tegyn when they had returned to their rooms.

She was free of her dress—and corset—and sat by the fire that her maids had stoked for her. The maids had been ready to sleep in her chambers tonight. But Liesel wasn't used to that. She had shared her room with Katrina until her sister had got married; later, with Tegyn. That was enough.

'What do *you* think of him?' Tegyn replied. 'Surely that's the question.'

'I think he is a good man,' Liesel decided. 'A man of action.'

Tegyn made a sexy purring noise.

'Stop it!' Liesel demanded. 'I meant he enjoys riding and fighting and all those things. That is something I might talk with him about tomorrow.'

'Hmm. I'm not sure he liked the idea of women getting involved in those things.'

'You noticed as well? I think that's an idea he might get used to, over time.'

'He'd better. Or else I'll be having words with him.'

THE NEXT MORNING, Liesel went for a ride with Esterel. He took her north from The Bastion, through a small gate in the north of the city walls. A bridge took them across the Cousel. After that, the road was quiet. They were quickly into the countryside. It was a gently rolling landscape, made up of small settlements and plenty of woodland.

Further north, the woods thickened and became the impenetrable forest of the Caladri.

'She's a pleasant ride?' Esterel asked her.

'She's lovely. Taller than I got used to in Atrabia. I can see so far.'

'You ride well. Tegyn wasn't exaggerating. About the archery, either?'

'No,' Liesel said. She resisted the urge to hold up a bicep to prove it. She wasn't about to mention that she and Tegyn had joined the ranks of the Atrabian archers in Thesse, either. Some things could wait until after they were married. 'It's a tradition amongst their women. I never got as good as Tegyn.'

'I was thinking,' he said, 'of our wedding.' He smiled. 'You have a delightful blush when I speak of such things.'

Liesel blushed even more.

'I would like to hold a great martial event for the people of Valennes to watch. It was done in years past. A competition with sword and shield, I was thinking. But what about an archery contest as well? Imagine people's reaction if you were to enter, Liesel.'

'Would they like it?' she asked. 'Maybe the people of Guivergne don't like their women to act like that.'

Esterel shrugged. 'I don't see why not. And it's an area we need to address. Archery, I mean. Guivergne is less well served than many other kingdoms. We were trained to use the bow in Morbaine. I was surprised to learn that it's not common here. It will take us a generation to catch up.'

Esterel seemed willing to talk of more serious matters today. Liesel took it as an invitation.

'Is it the threat from the south that has prompted you to consider this?'

'I would have done it, anyway. From what Peyre tells me, a cohort of archers will not stop this demon.'

'No,' Liesel agreed. Esterel looked at her. 'I was in Thesse when Emperor Coen was killed,' she explained.

'Gods,' Esterel said. 'I'm sorry. It's a threat I struggle to comprehend. Not that I'm totally ignorant of magic.' He looked at her, as if weighing up whether he should continue. 'My younger brother, Sanc. He has magic. I've not seen this Ezenachi, but I've seen my own flesh and blood wield such power. Now, though, Sanc has left Dalriya. His teacher, a Haskan named Rimmon, was killed by Ezenachi. Guivergne is bereft of sorcerers just when we needed them.' He looked at her. 'Your brother has a witch?'

Liesel nodded. 'Yes. Though she has no interest in challenging Ezenachi. She simply advocates submitting to him.'

'Not a plan that can work forever.'

'Agreed,' Liesel said.

'Peyre speaks of gathering the relics from the Isharite Wars. This sorcerer, Rimmon, advised it. A way of holding off Ezenachi and his forces.'

'Those weapons helped to defeat Diis,' Liesel said. 'So the stories say.' She considered it. The more she thought of it, the more it seemed such an obvious thing to try. 'Do you agree, Esterel?'

'I'm not against it. Peyre and I sent a message to our sister and Duke Auberi. Asking them to contact the Krykkers.'

'The sword of the Krykkers,' Liesel said, remembering the stories.

'Yes,' Esterel said. 'The Krykker chieftain, Maragin, is the only champion we know the whereabouts of.' He led them onto a dirt track that wound through the woods. 'Maybe she can give us some direction. At the moment, I don't know what to do for the best.'

'Our role seems only too familiar,' Liesel said, letting the words fall without thinking.

'How do you mean?' Esterel asked.

'It just reminds me of my father, that's all. He held off the Isharites for as long as he could, trusting others to defeat Diis.' She looked at Esterel. 'A thankless role, really.'

'No,' said Esterel. 'I thank him. If that is our role, then I won't shirk it. You were only young when—'

'I was seven,' Liesel said. 'But I remember him.'

'Me too.'

Liesel looked at him with a frown.

'I was seven, I mean. When my mother died.' He gave her a sad smile. 'It was the same year of your father's death. She died in childbirth.'

'I'm sorry,' Liesel said. 'I didn't know.' She struggled to find words of comfort. She'd received few enough in her life. 'It still hurts,' she said. 'Though sometimes I make it worse by pretending my father was perfect.'

'No,' Esterel said. 'Not in my case, at least. My mother was beautiful and clever and kind. She *was* perfect. We carried on afterwards—my father made sure of that. But the joy of life had gone.'

Liesel nodded, understanding. 'We—' she began, then found she couldn't. Her throat was too choked to talk.

Esterel stopped the horses. He took her hand and looked into her eyes. 'Say it.'

'We didn't carry on,' Liesel got out. 'We were lost. We still are.'

'Your brother?' Esterel asked her.

'He can't be emperor, Esterel,' she told him. 'I feel like a traitor saying it.'

'No,' Esterel said, squeezing her hand.

'He is a child,' she told him. 'Scared, cruel, and selfish. Manipulated by Inge. I have lost hope he can change.'

'Then your uncle's plan to make your brother-in-law emperor?'

'I would counsel you to support it,' she told him. 'Ordinarily, you might decide it's none of your business. But with Ezenachi—'

'Indeed,' Esterel agreed. 'I don't have the luxury of ignoring the rest of the world, as my predecessors did.' His face, all serious, suddenly collapsed into a boyish smile. 'Well, Liesel. We have talked of so many things in the first part of our journey that I am worried we will descend into uncomfortable silence.'

He let her hand go and Liesel found she wished he hadn't. 'I don't think so,' she said.

SANC

ARVENA, KINGDOM OF SCORGIA, 675

The days rolled by and Sanc grew accustomed to his new life. He began to identify the supporters of Master Wacho. He learned the man's routines.

Wacho maintained his control over his soldiers through his officers and, like Lenzo, was building alliances among the merchants of the city. Although he was based in the keep, he also spent time in the houses of these merchants—more luxurious settings than the bare stone walls of his home. Sanc discovered nothing incriminating but passed on what he learned to the Prince.

News reached Arvena of events in Scorgia, as ships returned to port, and sailors shared stories in the dockside inns. Lenzo's father, Domizio, had surrendered to Lothar and been taken to Nerisia, to live out his days in captivity. The Nerisians had taken most major towns and cities in Scorgia with little resistance. The only exception, apart from Arvena and the northern marshes, was a territory of mountain and forest in the south-east, called Sinto. Here, a man named Atto had declared himself duke of the region. The word was the Nerisians were inclined to come to some agreement with him rather than chase him across difficult terrain that had little value.

Lothar, meanwhile, had given his ambitions free rein. He was now calling himself King of the Scorgians, as well as of the Nerisians and Gadenzians. Further, there had been a ceremony in a holy place called Peramo. The priests of this temple had given him a new title: Emperor of Silb.

The city council was keen to discuss such developments. Both Lenzo and Wacho attended these meetings, and Lenzo often took Sanc with him to observe. They took place in the Forum, an open-air building in the centre of the city. Over twenty individuals had gathered today. Some were the wealthiest merchants in the city, while others represented the interests of the regular burghers.

'When the envoys of the new emperor come looking for our oaths of allegiance, what do we say?' asked Transamund, one of those who spoke for the many medium-sized businessmen who made their living in the city. 'When they ask us to send him the prince?' he added, gesturing at Lenzo. 'When they ask us to take a Nerisian garrison?'

'Lothar doesn't have our allegiance,' Wacho growled at the man.

'If that is our position,' Nolf spoke next, 'then oughtn't we to feel out potential allies?'

The rumours in Arvena were that Nolf Money Bags was the richest man in Silb. Sanc knew him to be an ally of Wacho's. It didn't help Lenzo's cause that Nolf was the man who had lost his house to the prince.

'This Duke Atto, for one,' Nolf added.

'This would be wise,' Wacho answered, 'even if only for defensive purposes. If Lothar were to threaten one of us, the other could supply aid, or raid the Nerisians and open a new front.'

'Shouldn't this Atto be taking orders from Prince Lenzo, anyway?' Transamund asked, to mutters of approval.

'I'm afraid we need to be realistic about this,' Lenzo intervened. 'When I look at it from his point of view, there is little value to Atto in following our lead. He wants an independent state, and he wants to be the ruler. By all means, let's stay in friendly communication and offer trade deals. But Sinto isn't close. It would be foolish to place too much reliance on an alliance.'

Some deflated at this assessment. There followed another argument about relations with Lothar. Those merchants who traded heavily with the Nerisians were wary of losing their business. Others favoured a more hostile policy: sinking Nerisian shipping and monopolising sea trade; building alliances with other kingdoms.

'I suggest we are wary of provoking Lothar,' came a woman's voice. Amelia the Widow had inherited her husband's interests that stretched west as far as the coast of the Rasidi. By most accounts, she was doing a better job of it than her husband ever had. She certainly didn't shy away from displaying her wealth; jewellery and fine clothes draped over her ample form. She was too clever to commit to any one side, but she had enjoyed plenty of dinners at Lenzo's house. 'Taking Arvena would not be easy for him, but if he feels he must, he could do it. If we can continue without antagonising him, then all the better. I know him well enough. He will soon tire of Scorgia and choose some fresh land to conquer.'

'But isn't that the very point?' Wacho asked her. 'If we allow it, he will conquer all of Silb. Soon he will have no enemies left to distract him from this city.'

More voices weighed in on each side.

'What say you, Prince Lenzo?' Transamund asked, sounding frustrated that the prince had said so little.

'For my part,' Lenzo said, 'the prosperity of Arvena is my priority. Therefore I have decided not to take the title King of Scorgia, as many have asked me to do. It would only serve to antagonise Lothar and draw his ire. If I could avenge my father's defeat, you must all know that I would do it in an instant. As things stand, it seems that Salacus means me to make this city the greatest in all of Silb.'

It was shameless popularity seeking and Wacho openly sneered at the prince's words. But that didn't stop many in the Forum from liking what they heard.

* * *

SANC VISITED at the Temple of Salacus for the fourth time. Outside, the round stone walls made it look more like a small fort. Inside, it was a riot of colour, with giant frescoes running across the walls. Sanc understood they told a story, though he was yet to decipher it. Gigantic figures, some odd looking, mixed with humans, over a varied landscape.

Salacus, god of the Scorgians, was worshipped here. At least Sanc had worked out which one he was. He was depicted in human form riding a chariot, pulled by two creatures. They resembled horses at the front, but their bodies ended in long tails and Sanc lingered on them, drawn to the strangeness but disturbed by it as well.

High-priestess Gamatrude saw him studying the creatures and approached. Her blonde hair fell in two long braids down her chest. She was middle-aged and powerfully built—she looked more like a warrior to Sanc than a priest.

Her approach was a recent development. On his first visit, she had been offended by his presence, demanding to know why he had come. When he explained it was to learn about Salacus, she had scoffed, telling him to go worship his own god. Subsequently, he had been studiously ignored. Maybe now he was trusted enough to learn something.

'What is it you stare at?' she demanded.

'The tails of the two creatures. They are strange to my eyes.'

'Hasha and Ibil. Only they can bear Salacus's great weight, equally well on water as on land.'

'I see. The tails are for travel by sea.' Sanc thought about this. 'Seafaring is important to the Scorgians.'

'Of course,' Gamatrude answered him, a look of disdain on her face. 'Your ignorance is an offence to Salacus and so I must correct it. The Scorgians carried all seven peoples to Silb. We are the greatest shipbuilders.'

Sanc studied the frescoes anew. They suddenly made sense. Salacus and the Scorgians were transporting the seven peoples across the waves to Silb. The other large figures must be the gods of the six other peoples.

'All seven peoples came here together?' Sanc asked.

'Yes. The Scorgians were the leaders of all the peoples. Thus, it was only right that we settled in this region, where the natives had their capital.'

'Irpino, you mean? It was the capital of the native inhabitants?'

'Yes.'

'So you conquered the native people?' Something had been nagging at him for a while and now it seemed he had the answer. 'So, the people with darker hair, somewhat smaller in stature. They lived here first? The Scorgians are the people like you—taller and blonde haired?'

Gamatrude grimaced. 'Yes. But now everyone is in the kingdom of Scorgia and so everyone is a Scorgian. We do not distinguish one from the other as you do.'

'But the Scorgians—I mean, the original ones—they are still the warriors and merchants and priests. The natives are poorer—farmers and fishermen.'

The high-priest shrugged. 'Salacus must will it so.'

'What does Salacus say about the Nerisian invasion?' Sanc dared to ask.

'Salacus doesn't speak to me, foolish outlander. But he will smite the Nerisians for their impudence. I have no doubts about that.'

SANC LEFT the temple for Prince Lenzo's house, who hosted yet another dinner for his important guests. The talk was of trade and politics. Politics, because the rivalry with Wacho was becoming more tangible. The conversation still circled delicately around the idea of a challenge between the two men for control of Arvena. Nonetheless, battle lines were being drawn. Wacho's policy of an aggressive attitude towards Lothar was contrasted with Lenzo's more flexible approach. The prince hoped his guests would see things his way.

Afterwards, the wine flowed and Sanc indulged himself, refilling his goblet as often as Lenzo himself.

'You drink a lot these days,' Gaida commented. He sounded a little disapproving, despite resting a goblet of his own on his ample gut.

Sanc got the impression the man had warmed to him a little, and he didn't mind the tone; it was almost fatherly.

'You try leaving everything in your world behind and learning to get by in a new one. The wine stops me from going mad.'

'Fair enough,' Gaida conceded. He studied Sanc as if for the first time. 'You left family behind, in—'

'Dalriya. Yes. Two brothers and a sister. My father died not soon before I left. My mother died giving birth to me.' Sanc surprised himself by mentioning his mother. He rarely did. 'Now look,' he said, grabbing a wine casket. 'You've made me need more now.' He filled his goblet and drank deeply, ignoring the look between Gaida and Lenzo. It wasn't like he couldn't handle it. He'd been drinking every night since he'd arrived in Arvena, and it now took a considerable amount to make him ill.

The conversation moved on to other things. One of Lenzo's whores took a seat next to him. Sanc was sure he hadn't seen her before. She had the looks of the people the high-priestess had called natives. Petite, slim, with dark brown eyes and hair. She was young and pretty, no doubt about it, and there was something different about her compared to the others. A modesty, perhaps.

'Here,' Sanc said, handing her his goblet. 'You should have some. I think I've had enough.'

'Thank you, Lord Sanc,' she said. When she took it, her fingers gently brushed his, making Sanc wonder if it was deliberate or not. She sipped from the goblet, looking him in the eye as she did. 'Very sweet,' she said. 'And the wine's not bad, either.'

'Ha!' Sanc laughed. He wasn't sure what to say. He knew that if she had spoken like that to him sober, he would have blushed. But the wine lay on him like a blanket of confidence he usually lacked. 'You're flirting with me. Shouldn't you be saying such things to the prince?'

'No,' she said. 'I prefer you. You are my age and prettier than he is.'

Sanc's blanket disappeared. His heart rate and temperature both rose and there was a stirring in his loins. At the same time, an anxiety fell on him. *I have no idea what to do with a beautiful girl like this.* He tried to think of something to say. Tried and failed.

'Oh,' the girl said. 'You don't like me.'

'No, it's not that,' he said. 'I do like you.'

'Then take me to your room.'

Sanc lost the power of speech a second time.

The girl stood, holding out her hand.

Sanc found himself standing and taking her hand in his. It was small and delicate, like her. He began walking towards the rear of the house. He expected some loud ribbing from Lenzo or Gaida, but none came. They left the prince's hall and Sanc took her to the stone stairwell that led upstairs. *Say something, you fool*, he told himself. But the only words that came into his head were wildly inappropriate.

'They say you are an outlander from beyond Silb,' the girl said, sounding almost in awe.

'Yes. A land called Dalriya. What is your name?' *And why am I only asking this now?*

'Tassia. Your room is upstairs?'

'Yes. Would you like to go with me?'

'I've already told you once,' she said, sounding genuinely amazed. 'Is everyone from Dalriya as stupid as you?'

'No. It's just me.'

Tassia smiled at that. 'I don't mind that you're stupid. I still like you.'

'I like you too,' Sanc said. Maybe that was just the wine talking. But he didn't think so. Sanc led Tassia up the stairs to his room.

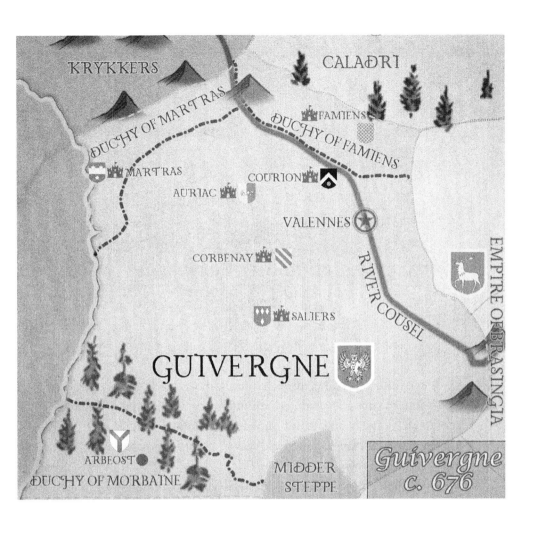

PEYRE

VALENNES, KINGDOM OF GUIVERGNE, 676

Peyre left Morbaine for Valennes. Umbert rode at his side. He didn't plan on returning to his duchy for a while and it would be good to have his friend with him. Umbert's father, Lord Russell, was left in charge of things, and Peyre was grateful for having such a safe pair of hands to rely on.

With them came Peyre's Barissian Guard. Its membership had expanded to forty-eight warriors. Peyre had received many requests, mostly from younger men, to join his troop. He could see it was an attractive post—status, pay, and the excitement of leaving Morbaine for the capital. He'd been able to assess potential recruits and select the best. As it was, Lord Russell had warned him that forty-eight was a large enough drain on his finances. But the fighting in Magnia had convinced him of the need for a core of fighters who were loyal to him and one another. Of course, the new intake meant the name of his troop was no longer accurate—but he still liked the sound of it.

It had been one of the coldest winters Peyre could recall, putting off travel well into the new year. At last, a break had come and Peyre had taken his chance, hoping it would last for the duration of their journey. Melting snow left the ground wet and boggy; huge puddles of water regularly covered the roads and paths they used. Elger organised the Guard, appointing scouts to protect their passage. Peyre and Umbert were given the freedom to talk privately.

Umbert was keen to return to Valennes. He had been a long time away. Peyre was more reluctant.

'It was horrible seeing them together,' he told Umbert. 'I don't know if I can stand it again. And I dread seeing them married.'

'Might do you good,' Umbert suggested. 'Draw a line under it. Once they're married, that's that. You'll have to get used to it.'

'I don't know if I ever will.'

'Remember what happened to your father and uncle? They fell out over a woman. You don't want to repeat that.'

'I know,' Peyre said crossly. 'Logically, I tell myself all of this. But when I am in the same room as her, logic goes out the window.'

'Should you say something to Esterel?'

'Like what? By the way, the woman you're about to marry and make queen? Well, I love her. And I saw her first.'

'Hmm. I take your point. I know what you need. A new woman.'

'Oh gods. Please don't tell me there's plenty more fish in the sea.'

'Not to fall in love with and all that serious stuff. Just to have fun with. A distraction.'

Peyre sighed. 'I'm not much fun to be around at the moment.'

'You can say that again.'

THEY WERE lucky with the weather. The snow returned, but only on their last day of travel. Big fluffy flakes filled the sky in every direction, reducing visibility. Sometimes a gust of wind would blow it straight into their faces, sticking on hair, beards, and eyelashes. It settled on the ground. Before long, hooves were crunching down onto freshly laid snow and the road and most other landmarks were lost in a blanket of white. But ice wouldn't form until the night. All they had to do was reach the city.

Later than expected, they reached Valennes—the city suddenly appearing through the snow as if it had been turned invisible. Great drifts had formed against the city walls. Let in through the south gate, they passed through a city turned white. Valennes had never looked so beautiful. Peyre's new recruits muttered to one another with appreciation—it was certainly a fine way to get one's first view of the capital.

Their customers gone, the traders in the central square had departed and the streets were given over to the youths of the city, who hurled balls of snow at one another and the various targets the city offered. Fifty mounted warriors was not the kind of group one trifled with. But Peyre couldn't help admiring those few who dared to lob their ammunition their way. They did it from hiding—behind a house or down a side street. The snowballs went high into the air, descending on the Barissian Guard from height.

'Tactically sound,' Peyre commented. 'Makes one optimistic that we have a few future soldiers in the city.'

Finally, they came upon The Bastion. It took the guards a while to recognise him, but once they did, they were all ushered inside the fortress. Peyre left Elger to wait with the Guard until Sacha or one of his officials came to see to them. With Umbert in tow, he made his way to his rooms. They caught a maid on the way and begged her to fetch hot water for a bath. Umbert touched his icy hands to her cheeks until she relented and ran off to the kitchen.

Peyre gave him a sideways look. 'You don't waste any time, do you?'

Umbert looked offended. 'Don't be like that, Your Grace. I merely wanted to get you warmed and clean in as timely a fashion as possible.'

EVERYTHING WAS PERFECT. The fire had been lit. Next to it, there was a wooden barrel filled with hot water from the kitchen. The maids were just emptying the last of the water they had carried up to his room, and then Peyre could clamber in and put the days of travelling behind him. If Umbert was lucky, he would get out while the bath was still lukewarm.

Then Esterel entered. 'Why didn't you tell me you were back, brother?' he demanded, a big smile on his face. 'We must have a party tonight to celebrate. Oh, I see,' he said, eyeing the bath. 'That's more important than visiting your king.'

Peyre made a face at Esterel, then rolled his eyes as Esterel began to strip his clothes off.

'I hope you won't deny your monarch his privilege of first bath rights?' Esterel demanded.

'No, Your Majesty,' Peyre said. 'Girls, I think you had better make haste before you get a sight of something you'd regret.'

The maids giggled.

'Oh, they've seen it all before,' Esterel assured him as his hose dropped to the floor.

The maids left, still giggling, and throwing backward glances at the scene.

Fully naked, Esterel let out a groan of pleasure as he sank into the barrel, water slopping out over the side onto the floor of Peyre's room. 'Oh, that's good. Perfect before a party. Don't worry, Peyre, I shan't be long.' His head swivelled to Umbert. 'And you'll want to get in third, I presume, Umbert?'

'Certainly will.'

'Fair enough.' Esterel put both arms around the side of the barrel as the steam escaped. 'A good winter?' he asked Peyre.

'Peaceful enough. Cold, though.'

'It's been bloody cold. Can't have been much fun travelling today?'

'The novelty soon wore off. All things considered, I'm glad to be back in Valennes.'

'It's good to hear you say that Peyre. I must thank you, by the way. I wasn't entirely convinced by your advice on Liesel at first. But I am so glad I listened to you in the end. We've got on like a house on fire the last few months.' He splashed his face with water, going pink with the heat. 'I feel so comfortable in her company. I can't believe it's only been that long. I haven't dared say it to her yet. But I'm in love. Properly in love, for the first time in my life. I don't think I can ever repay you for that, brother.'

The violence of Peyre's reaction surprised him. He pictured

himself shoving Esterel down into the barrel and holding him there until he drowned.

It wasn't that Esterel was older and so got the throne. Peyre was prepared to grudgingly admit Esterel made a better king than he would have. It wasn't that he also happened to be the best swordsman of his generation. Nor that he was universally loved. That everything in life came so easy for him and yet he somehow remained a likeable, down-to-earth clown. It wasn't even that he'd stolen Peyre's bloody bath. He'd stolen Liesel. Stolen the person Peyre couldn't stop thinking about. And now he said he loved her.

And really, Peyre reminded himself, Esterel didn't steal her at all. *I voluntarily gave her to him. Collected her from Essenberg and brought her here. I am angry with myself and that's the worst kind of feeling. Now I must spend my life watching them marry, have children, and rule a kingdom together.*

'Eh?' Esterel said. 'I said I can't repay you, but there must be something?'

Umbert was staring at Peyre, eyes wide, encouraging him to say something.

'Not at all, Your Majesty,' Peyre got out. 'You have already rewarded me with the duchy of Morbaine.' He heard his own dull voice, but it was the best he could do.

'Gods, Peyre,' Esterel said, standing up. 'If you were looking forward to the bath that much, just tell me to get out.'

ESTEREL, Peyre mused, had not yet sealed a place in history. As a king, he didn't have the most conquests; heroic escapades; greatest treasure; the wisest judgements; or any of the usual achievements by which rulers were judged. But he doubted any other king had put on a party like this at such short notice.

It wasn't just the enormous amounts of drink that were served. Or even the musicians and other entertainers that performed for his guests—presumably kept on a stipend to play whenever required. It was his guests themselves. Every young and attractive man or woman in the kingdom seemed to be there, either drinking themselves stupid or dancing like fools—many both. It made Peyre wonder where their income came from if they were permanently ready to carouse the night away at a moment's notice from their king.

Everybody was having a good time. Umbert, who had promised to stay by his side, had disappeared somewhere. Esterel and his friends—Sacha, Miles and Florent—were at the centre of things. Liesel and her friend Tegyn seemed to have made themselves at home in the months he had been away. Liesel talked and laughed with a group of guests, and Peyre certainly didn't begrudge her any happiness. He joined them, determined not to act like a spoiled child at a party his king was throwing for him.

'It's good to see you again, Peyre,' Liesel told him.

He liked that she didn't 'Your Grace' him.

'You will be staying a while now?' she asked.

'I plan to be here for the spring and summer, at least. It depends on what the new year has in store for us.'

Liesel nodded, forcing away an anxious look with a smile. 'Whatever happens, I'm sure we all feel better you are here.'

Dammit, Peyre. This is a party. Save the talk of war and conflict for another time. 'Thank you, Liesel. It's a pleasure to see you again, looking so happy.'

'Would you like to dance, Your Grace?' Tegyn asked him.

Flustered, Peyre allowed himself to be led to the dance floor by the Atrabian woman. 'I can't dance,' he warned her.

'Everyone can dance,' she said. 'Only a few can dance well. Come on.'

Holding his hand, Tegyn began kicking her legs up high to the sound of the music. Peyre wasn't sure whether it was her definition of dancing well. He had no alternative but to join in and found himself grinning despite himself. When the music stopped, they were both out of breath.

'Thank you,' Tegyn said. 'You move well enough. And plenty of ladies looked our way. Now that your brother is getting married, you have become the most eligible bachelor in the kingdom, you know?'

Peyre smiled wryly. 'I've yet to experience women throwing themselves at me.'

'I am in the market, Your Grace,' Tegyn said. 'I suppose I could throw myself at you if that's what you want.'

Peyre was mortified, not knowing what to do. He threw a glance towards Liesel. A mistake, since Tegyn caught the look immediately.

'I knew it!' she said, as the musicians began the next piece of music. She moved in close, putting a hand on his shoulder. 'You are in love with Liesel!'

Peyre put a hand behind her back. 'Please,' he said, on the back foot. 'Don't tell her.'

'She is my best friend,' she said, as they drifted around the floor together.

'I know. But Liesel and Esterel are the two people I am closest to in the world. It would ruin my relationship with them both.'

Tegyn sniffed. 'You are right. And you have been a good friend to Liesel. I won't tell anyone. But neither of them are stupid, you know. They'll work it out, eventually. Or someone else will. You need to stop making it so obvious.'

'Thank you. And I know. I need to do something.'

'And I'm sorry to say that I am in the market no longer,' Tegyn said seriously. 'I can't enter a relationship with you, knowing that you have feelings for my best friend.'

'I see,' said Peyre. 'Well, there are plenty more fish in the sea.'

'Like who?' Tegyn demanded.

'Well,' Peyre said, looking about. 'Lord Sacha is thought to be handsome by some.'

'Of course he is. You think I'm blind? I've not kicked him out of bed once yet.'

'Oh,' Peyre said, taken aback.

'But he is Lord of Courion while I am the daughter of a prince.'

'I see,' Peyre said. 'In which case, let me think on that,' he said, leading her back to the group who stood with Liesel.

'Well,' she said as they approached. 'You two had a lot to talk about.'

Peyre was at a loss for words. 'Indeed,' he managed with a smile. 'Please excuse me.' He left, making his way to the far end of the hall.

Peyre was sure Tegyn would make up some conversation to satisfy Liesel's curiosity. He hardly knew the Atrabian, but she seemed like one of those direct sort of people who are entirely trustworthy.

The doors at the side of the hall were closed against the cold. But Peyre needed to be alone. They opened onto a garden. It was still snowing, though the geometry of The Bastion's walls prevented all but the luckiest flakes from reaching the garden. He paced about, drawing in a breath of cool air, relieved to be alone. The falling snow hid him from the partygoers. He needed to think. Tegyn was right. If he was going to survive the next few months in Valennes, he had to do something.

Footsteps made him turn.

'Not the only one who needed to get away, Your Grace?' came a voice.

It was Sacha's sister. She opened her palms, letting the snow fall on them.

Peyre racked his brain, trying to remember her name.

She looked at him. 'I'm sorry. You wanted to be alone.'

'Not at all, Lady Coleta,' he said. 'Sometimes you just need the right company.'

She gave him a surprised smile. He had to admit, once one got past the resemblance to Sacha, she was very beautiful. Even in midwinter, she had warm coloured skin. And now he looked closely, her brown eyes had flecks of green in them that made them arresting.

'I didn't think you even knew my name, Your Grace,' she said. 'Let alone might value my company.'

'Not at all. Please, call me Peyre. I am just a bit more awkward in company than my brother.'

He held his arm open for her. *What are you doing, Peyre?*

But Coleta wasted no time in linking her own arm through his. They walked away from the party towards the far end of the garden.

'Your brother is more garrulous, that's true. But there are more worthy traits than that. I—I'm sorry. You know about my relationship with Esterel, I assume?'

'I do. Please, you can speak freely.'

'I was an idiot, Peyre. I fell in love with him. Part of me knew he might end up marrying someone else. And Lady Liesel is lovely. But Esterel has dropped me. Doesn't look me in the eye, never mind speak to me anymore. As if he's embarrassed. And that's very difficult to take.'

'I am sure. But you know Esterel. He doesn't have malice in him.'

'Yes. I know you're right. Sometimes it's just nice to confide in someone. Do you understand?' she asked.

They'd stopped walking. Coleta looked up at him and, in that moment, her lips were the most desirable things in the world. She wasn't surprised when he kissed her. Her lips were soft, and they parted as soon as he wanted them to. There was something gentle; vulnerable in the way she kissed him back. He put his hand on her back. She was so thin; delicate. Her hand went to his chest.

Peyre's body was full of desire now. His mind raced with all the things he wished to do. It took all his self-control to part from her. They were at a party, for the gods' sake.

'I—' He looked back at the doors to the hall. 'Someone might see.'

Coleta's eyes were large. She studied his features for a while. 'I'm sorry, Peyre. I didn't mean to—gods, what must you think of me?'

He took her hand. 'Don't say that. I'm at fault. You are in love with my brother. I shouldn't have taken advantage.'

She smiled. It made her face look mischievous, when before it had been sensuous. 'You are a good man, Peyre, Duke of Morbaine. I shall never forget our kiss in the snow. But don't worry. I don't kiss and tell.'

She left, returning to the hall.

Peyre watched her go, then stayed in the garden awhile, waiting until his body had cooled down.

* * *

PEYRE WAS WELCOMED back to the royal council. He resolved to listen rather than speak; get a feel for how things worked under Esterel.

'The Bastion is running low on almost every foodstuff,' Sacha informed them. 'Not to mention ale and wine, Esterel,' he said dryly. 'I propose we move the court elsewhere as soon as the weather allows.'

'If we must,' Esterel said. 'Where is there to go?'

'King Nicolas made The Bastion his permanent home,' Lord Caisin said. 'There is nowhere else in Guivergne set up for hosting the court. Though there are plenty of crown lands that have the potential for it.'

'That is something to work on for the future,' Sacha agreed. 'For now, I was wondering about staying at one of our estates. Courion could manage it. Perhaps Corbenay, Miles?'

'Of course, it would be an honour to host you all.'

'Alright, let's think about it,' Esterel said. 'As long as we are back in time for the wedding.'

'It would help with preparations if we were gone for a while,' Sacha said.

'And how are the preparations going?' Esterel asked. 'I don't need to know every little detail. Tell me about the contests.'

'Contests?' Peyre asked, unable to help himself.

'Have I not told you?' Esterel said, beaming with excitement. 'The wedding celebrations will include a contest of sword and shield and one of bow and arrow. I would like a joust as well, but Sacha pushes back on that one.'

'Expense,' Sacha shrugged. 'Danger. Not to mention the politics of it. The joust attracts only noble lords who then best each other and hold grudges afterwards.'

'Nonsense,' Esterel said. 'It would bring the lords of Guivergne together. Some friendly rivalry and toasting the winner afterwards. Could do wonders.' He looked at Sacha's disapproving expression. 'What do you think, Peyre?'

No. I'm not falling for that one. I kissed Sacha's sister the other night. I'm not going to disagree with him in public. 'Whatever you two decide,' Peyre replied. 'I'll look forward to the other contests either way.'

Sacha nodded at him in gratitude. 'Then there is the question of the empire. We are in the position of having both claimants under the impression that we are on their side. But that will soon be tested. Spring is likely to bring war to Brasingia.'

The doors opened and Jehan, a soldier at The Bastion, entered. He stopped with a bow. 'Excuse me, Your Majesty. I have a messenger for Duke Peyre. She says it's of the utmost urgency.'

'She?' Esterel said, raising an eyebrow.

Oh gods, Peyre prayed. *Please let it not be Coleta.* He shrugged. 'Would you mind?'

'If it's a lady, brother, you must see to it immediately. Then return and tell us all about it!'

Everyone laughed and Peyre forced a smile as he followed Jehan out of the chamber. But his anxiety only heightened when he saw who it was. Syele, who he had asked to look after his sister.

He rushed over to her. 'What is it?' he asked. 'If that bastard Auberi has done something—'

'Whoa,' the Barissian said. She raised a hand, in which she held a letter. 'It's nothing like that. Lady Loysse asked me to bring this to you. If you weren't here, I was told to give it to the king himself. She thought I'd be the best person for the job.'

Peyre took the letter. It was in his sister's handwriting. He scanned the contents. 'I see. Would you come and confirm this with my brother now?'

'Of course. Been wanting to meet the king. Now I can tick the whole family off my list.'

Peyre returned to the chamber with Syele and handed the letter to Esterel. 'It's an urgent matter,' he told the council. 'Good timing, I think, that we are all gathered.'

Esterel read Loysse's letter, then looked around. 'It's from my sister and Duke Auberi. They say they have been contacted by Lord Raymon. He's leading a plot to replace me.'

'Damn him!' Miles said. 'Well, this is the end of the road for Auriac.'

'How much faith can we put in this?' Lord Caisin asked. 'Of course, your sister would not lie. But Famiens?'

'This is his chance to prove his loyalty,' Esterel said. 'So far, he has done the right thing and alerted me.' He turned to Syele. 'Did you have trouble getting through?'

'I was stopped a couple of times,' she answered. 'But they weren't on the lookout for a lone woman and paid me little mind. There's no doubt Lord Auriac and his allies have men out on the roads, alert to trouble. Duke Auberi says Auriac took a risk approaching him and the plot may have already been progressing for some time.'

'You've done us a great service—?'

'Syele.'

'Peyre, I assume you will reward Syele generously?'

'Of course,' Peyre said. 'What are your thoughts? We must wonder who else Auriac has drawn in to this. Saliers, maybe. If needed, I can return to Morbaine and raise a force.'

'As the wiser, or at least older, head, I suggest you don't draw weapons and ride off quite yet,' Lord Caisin said. 'We are ahead of things, assuming Auriac believes we know nothing and still hopes to have Famiens on side. There are several ways to approach it, Your Majesty. You may wish to spend a little time thinking through the options.'

'Thank you, Lord Caisin. You are right. I must respond to a threat like this. At the same time, I don't want to overreact and make it seem more dangerous than it is.'

'That depends on Famiens staying true,' Sacha warned.

'We will learn where his loyalties lie,' Esterel said. 'I would like to think on it alone for a while. But please make yourselves available to me whenever I need you.'

LIESEL

VALENNES, KINGDOM OF GUIVERGNE, 676

I 'm sorry,' Esterel said. 'It means I have to put any intervention in the empire on hold.'

'Thank you for telling me in advance,' Liesel said. The disappointment hit hard, but she accepted Esterel had no alternative. A rebellion by one of his greatest enemies had to be dealt with. She knew that Esterel's father had to face down rebels during his brief reign. Now it seemed the same men had decided to test the son.

Over the next few days, Liesel saw a different side to Esterel. It came as something of a relief. Esterel was kind, fun, and a joy to be around. But over the winter, she had gained the impression that all he cared about was parties and pleasure. Now, he was decisive. He marshalled his lieutenants and forces with strategy; and didn't mind giving out orders that others didn't like.

Esterel would not lead the royal army himself but instead move to Corbenay, from where he could control the centre of the country. Most of the court, Liesel included, would travel with him. Miles, Lord of Corbenay, was given the royal army. He would meet with the forces of the dukes of Famiens and Martras and they had the task of subduing Auriac. Liesel could tell a few at court chafed at that decision. Esterel argued it was a better look for his lieutenants to deal with such a rebellion. Then there was the wedding. It was only weeks away. Esterel was keen to maintain a show of stability.

'The king doesn't need to deal with Auriac personally,' he said. 'Nor does he need to postpone his wedding day. That will show the people of Guivergne my strength more than another personal victory. I've already proven myself on the battlefield.'

Some were left behind in Valennes. Lord Caisin would keep the wheels of government turning. Peyre was asked to remain there, too. He was Esterel's insurance policy: ready to return to Morbaine and raise an army if things went wrong.

Everyone knew their roles, and finally, the royal expedition was ready to leave. They bid farewell to Peyre. Liesel regretted she had seen so little of him. A deeper regret was that they were heading west, when her sister, niece and nephew were to the east and in need of help. *Becoming queen of Guivergne is not so liberating as some might think.*

Leaving the Bastion, Liesel put a hand to her nose as they passed over the moat.

Next to her, Tegyn did the same. 'A few weeks away might be just what is needed to reduce that stink.'

'I hope so. I'm not looking forward to the summer months at this rate.'

They left via the west gate of the city, a long procession of riders and carts. Winter refused to relinquish its grip on the land, and the wind that came from the north was bitingly cold. It felt like they had stripped The Bastion of everything. Everyone's personal possessions were in those carts. Then there were the beds, dismantled for the journey; carpets, tapestries, tablecloths, and other textiles; crockery and dining ware; the royal treasure; the equipment from the stables. All the pots, pans and utensils from the kitchen had to be transported, too.

The benefits of staying in one place were plain. Still, Liesel could see the positives. She was excited at seeing other parts of the kingdom she would be queen of. It was the first time she had left Valennes and its environs.

The lands between Valennes and Corbenay were amongst the

richest in the kingdom. The villages they passed through resembled those in Liesel's native Kelland. Large fields were tended by the whole community; animals and private gardens supplemented the income of the peasants.

Liesel enjoyed their stops when she got a chance to talk with the people. She learned a lot. The people knew Esterel was their king, and he was already well liked; but their knowledge of the events and the world outside their district was often very limited. Esterel was his charming best, winning over the men and women of his kingdom with ease. It was a little harder for Liesel. Brasingians were the national enemy, even if there had been no war between the two nations for forty years. But she won them over in the end. There seemed to be a genuine excitement at the prospect of having a queen: for most, it would be the first time in their lives.

Miles accompanied them to Corbenay and helped them get settled in before he returned to Valennes. His castle home took some adjusting to. It was much smaller than The Bastion and everything seemed more cramped than it had been. Esterel's servants had the worst of it, finding themselves sleeping in every spare space they could find. Rumours came of tensions in the kitchen between the resident servants and the newcomers; so bad that Sacha had to sort things out. It certainly took a few days until mealtimes became reliable occasions. As the first week ended, though, the court began to function properly in its new home.

All this time, it was a waiting game. Miles had taken the army north, but Esterel still waited for his friend's first report. Every day, Esterel took warriors out to patrol the area around Corbenay. He wouldn't let Liesel or Tegyn go with them, worried it was dangerous. In particular, he was nervous of the activities of one Arnoul, Lord of Saliers, whose lands lay to the south.

'Do you regret not leading the army yourself?' she asked him, sensing his frustration.

'Yes. I still think it was the right decision. But waiting for news is disagreeable.'

'What are you worried about most?'

'I wish I knew whether I can trust Auberi. If he stays loyal, there's nothing to worry about.'

At last, Corbenay's first messenger arrived with news. Esterel took the note to Liesel's room to read. It was such a small gesture, really, but it pleased Liesel no end. It seemed Esterel already trusted her as if she were his wife. No. Her father had never trusted her mother like this.

He sighed with relief and handed her the note. 'Miles met with Famiens and Martras,' he summarised. 'Auriac has been forced to retreat into his castle. It's only a matter of time now.'

Liesel looked up after reading the details. 'You must trust Auberi now?'

'More than I did.' He looked at her wryly. 'You have to understand. He tried to kill us all and take the throne. But I think Loysse has somehow won him over. I don't think I've ever been so angry as when father told me about that marriage. But it seems to be working.' He grinned.

It was a look Liesel had come to recognise. She knew what he was going to say before he said it.

'I think this calls for a celebration!'

ESTEREL WAS DRUNK, there was no two ways about it. At one point, he joined his troop of musicians, playing the lute horribly and singing even worse.

Liesel wouldn't have minded in the slightest. Except for his dancing with Sacha's sister, Lady Coleta.

She'd worked out the pair had enjoyed a relationship before she arrived in Valennes. It wasn't hard, between her secretive, sultry looks and his guilty glances over at Liesel. But Esterel had barely spoken to the woman since Liesel had arrived; ignored her, even. And Liesel felt she couldn't ask for any more than that.

Now, though. He seemed to think it was alright to prance around, clinking drinks with her, as she put a hand on his arm and swayed her boyish hips.

'You are staring at them rather a lot,' Tegyn observed.

'Why should I be the odd one out? *Everyone* is staring at them. Then they look for my expression. Does he not see how I am humiliated by it?'

'I don't really see what you have to worry about, Liesel. Compare her stick thin body with your curves. What man would really choose her over you? I am sure it is simply because they are old friends.'

'Don't you get it, Tegyn? He *did* choose her. She is his type and, as you say, she looks nothing like me.'

Tegyn sighed. 'Alright. Hold my drink, love.'

Liesel's friend made her way over to the pair.

Oh gods, what is she going to do?

Tegyn was actually quite diplomatic. If firm. She took Coleta by the elbow and guided her out of the main hall.

Of course, everyone saw it happen. But Liesel decided it was the better of two evils.

THE NEXT MORNING, Esterel was hungover. He made some vague apology about his drinking.

Liesel was in no mood to forgive. She spoke as little as possible and excused herself soon after he came into the room.

If Esterel noticed—surely he did?—he said nothing. Two days of awkwardness followed. Liesel increasingly disliked Corbenay. She longed to return to Valennes. But there she was due to marry a man who refused to apologise for flirting with his old flame.

It was a relief, therefore, when the army of Guivergne arrived at the estate. As tents were pitched outside, its leaders were welcomed into the castle as heroes. There were so many important people in the castle's hall that Liesel felt a little overwhelmed.

Miles stood with the other two leaders of the army, the dukes of Famiens and Martras. They were giving Esterel and Sacha chapter and verse on the siege, which apparently ended with Lord Raymon's surrender at little loss of life. Esterel was keen to hear it all and so

Liesel nervously approached someone even more important. Loysse, Esterel's sister.

Loysse beamed and came over. With shy grins, they embraced.

'I'm so pleased to finally meet you,' Loysse said.

'You too, Loysse,' Liesel said.

She had not realised how much younger the girl was. The fact that she was already married had made Liesel imagine someone quite different, more like her own sister. As it was, Loysse was a stunningly beautiful, poised young lady. The resemblance to Esterel was obvious —the same eyes and hair colour. Liesel looked about the hall. 'Do you think anyone would mind if we disappeared? I have a room upstairs. It looks like they are going to be at it for some time.' She nodded at the group of men excitedly talking war. 'Also, my roommate appears distracted by it all.'

Tegyn stood with the men, nodding vigorously at the descriptions of siege engines. She stood no higher than chest height to any of them, yet her interest in it all saw her included in the group.

Loysse smiled. 'Rather her than me. Of course, Liesel. It's long past time we spoke.'

Liesel led her to her bedroom. Loysse uttered a sigh of relief as she sat on the bed while Liesel fixed her a drink.

'You were at the siege?' Liesel asked.

'I was there for the whole thing. Incredibly dull. Sitting about in a tent or slogging through mud. The enemy simply sat behind their walls until they decided no help was coming. Then they surrendered. I have no idea what there is to talk about, never mind get excited by.'

'Esterel came to regret not going himself. But it looks like he made the right decision?'

'He did, and I will have to thank him for it. Auberi was given the chance to distance himself from Raymon at last. I hope this episode will see his reputation restored in the kingdom.' Loysse looked at Liesel. 'I'm sure you've heard about the rebellion?'

'Yes. Mostly from Peyre. Esterel has talked about it, too. One reason he didn't lead the army himself was to give the opportunity to Auberi and Miles.'

'Nothing excuses what Auberi did. He admits that himself. But he had his reasons. Famiens was the region invaded by the Drobax. His father and other family and friends were killed. The area was laid waste. You know what that was like, Liesel, but in Morbaine, we largely escaped the horrors of that war. It's understandable that the people there are hostile to us—felt abandoned to their fate by the rest of Guivergne.

'Then there was his cruel nickname—Duke of Famine. King Nicolas, my uncle, befriended Auberi. Made him believe that he would have gone to save Famiens if my father hadn't argued against it. My uncle made vague promises that he wanted Auberi to be his heir. When Nicolas died, Lord Raymon persuaded him he had the right to the throne. I can see how he ended up as our enemy.'

Loysse seemed keen for Liesel to gain the same understanding of her husband. Liesel nodded. She didn't know any different. 'So you and Auberi have created a bond of understanding since your marriage?'

Loysse smiled. 'I was so scared. That I was being married to a man who hated me. But he has been a gentleman and, yes, we understand one another. What about you and Esterel?'

'Esterel has gone out of his way to make me feel at home. He has been very kind.'

'I sense there is a "however"?'

Liesel wasn't sure that she should share her worries with Loysse. She seemed lovely. But she was still Esterel's sister.

'It's alright,' Loysse encouraged. 'You can tell me.'

Liesel smiled. 'It's just here in Corbenay that I've noticed it. His relationship with Lady Coleta—clearly, they've had a romance in the past and I'm not sure it's gone.'

'I see. Well, I've spent so little time with Esterel in recent years that I'm not an expert. But yes, when I stayed at The Bastion last year, they were an item of sorts. I found her very sweet, but I totally understand your concerns. I can imagine Esterel being rather clumsy over how to handle it. One of his problems is he is used to everyone doting on him. But I would be surprised if there is anything there to worry about.'

'I thought so, too. But a few nights ago, they were dancing together and everyone was watching.'

Loysse's lips pursed. 'Dancing together? At court?' She shook her head. 'That is unacceptable.'

Liesel felt the need to defend Esterel. 'He'd been drinking. He's never done it before.'

'No excuse! I will be having words with my brother, Liesel, don't you worry!'

Liesel smiled. She got the feeling she had a new ally in her sister-in-law.

PEYRE

VALENNES, KINGDOM OF GUIVERGNE, 676

Peyre spent a full day moping about The Bastion. Part of him understood Esterel's decision making, including leaving him behind. But he also chafed at it. He had proven himself as a commander in Magnia, against a far more dangerous threat than one rebellious lord. But no one in Guivergne gave him credit for that. Instead, Corbenay and Famiens would collect the kingdom's praise for dealing with Raymon of Auriac.

Meanwhile, Esterel and Liesel were busy falling in love in Corbenay's castle and he was left here with the government to run. Well... Lord Caisin was the one running things, but Peyre liked to think he was overseeing the Lord Chancellor's work.

By the second day, Peyre was done with feeling sorry for himself. He sought out Brancat, the castellan of The Bastion. He found him outside, on the training yard his old weapons master had established close by the fortress. It ran along the eastern wall of Valennes. It was not so different from the yard back in Arbeost where Peyre had learned to fight, though it looked a lot drier than Peyre's memories of his time with Brancat.

Brancat had made it a requirement that all soldiers who worked at The Bastion get regular training as well. There was no doubt it had hardened the troop of warriors who worked there. Those that didn't pass muster were transferred to the city guard. Completely trusted by both Peyre's father and then his brother, Brancat had been allowed a free hand in creating an elite unit responsible for the defence of the king and his fortress.

'Not so busy at the moment?' Peyre asked him.

Brancat was supervising a mere half a dozen soldiers, working them with spear and shield exercises. 'No, Peyre. Not with half the guard on service with the king in Corbenay.'

'I have a proposal—a request, I suppose. I'd like to keep my Brasingian Guard hale rather than have them lounging around The Bastion.'

'Of course. You know me. I would enjoy whipping them into shape. Many are boys of Morbaine, no?'

'Yes,' Peyre confirmed. He knew Brancat had a patriot's faith that the men of Morbaine were the stoutest warriors of Dalriya. 'I'd like to join in as well. I need the challenge.'

Brancat grinned. 'That would be good to see. I made you into a fine warrior, despite your occasional objections. It would be useful to have some of my soldiers watch you and your lads in action.'

Peyre shrugged. 'I suppose so. Puts the pressure on, but that's what I need.'

'Anything prompted this desire to put yourself through training again? It's a matter of some personal pride that few men ever request to return to my yard.'

'Ha! I don't doubt it. Alright, I'll let you in on the plan. Esterel's sword contest. If I am to enter, I must acquit myself well.'

'But I wasn't planning on entering the sword contest,' Umbert complained as they made their way to Brancat's training yard.

'No one's forcing you to,' Peyre said. 'But still, you are my close aide, and it is good for you to demonstrate your prowess for my Guard to see. One day you may find yourself giving them orders and they need to respect you.'

'Are you saying they don't respect me now?'

'No. I'm just saying...' Peyre sighed. 'I'm just saying shut up and do what you're told for once.'

Thirty of the Barissian Guard stood around the edge of the training yard, their breath visible in the early morning air. They applauded politely as Peyre and Umbert joined the line. Many had wolfish grins; there was a nervous energy about them, as they waited for their lord to be tested.

Peyre turned to Brancat. 'I was thinking some sword skills to start—'

'Ah!' Brancat said, raising a hand. 'None of you will touch a weapon until your bodies are ready. And your bodies don't get ready by showing off how much you can lift or pull. Movement is the key to soldiering! If your body can't move fast enough, or long enough for what is required of it in war, then all your strength or skill is worthless. Today you will move when I tell you to. As fast and for as long as I tell you. And you will only stop when I tell you. Is that understood?'

'Yes, sir!' the Barissian Guard called out.

Oh gods, Peyre said to himself with bleak regret. *What have I done?*

FIVE DAYS later and Peyre and Umbert walked to the training yard with some reluctance.

'I'd forgotten Brancat was such a sadistic bastard,' Peyre muttered. 'How is it possible to forget that?' He side-eyed Umbert. 'You could have reminded me.'

Umbert looked at him with dead eyes. 'I don't see the funny in any of this.'

They had endured five days of lung-busting pain. At least today they would be holding weapons, if only to push their muscles to breaking. In truth, both Peyre and Umbert had acquitted themselves well. Peyre could feel his old fitness returning—a fitness he hadn't realised he had lost. There were a few in the Barissian Guard faster than he was in a foot race. Quite a few more who could tolerate long distances better than he could. Running had never been his strength.

But he had always moved sharply and had a natural power. Now that they were moving onto strength endurance, he felt confident. That was the kind of pain he enjoyed.

Brancat had them holding weapons and shields out in front, then above their heads. They held heavy weights and lunge-walked; squat-walked. At last, Peyre won the admiration of his Guard. Even the bigger men couldn't match him. His muscles grew and toned, welcoming the intense workouts that he had let slip in recent years.

At the end of the day's session, Brancat asked for volunteers to fight with sword and shield. Peyre was quick to his feet. Most of his Guard didn't even want to take him on, unable to grip or hold up a full weight sword and shield after such a tough day. The few who were given a chance struggled to compete with his movement; were battered aside by his power.

Peyre grinned. *Bring on the contest.*

* * *

THE RETURN of Esterel to The Bastion interrupted Peyre's new regime. The noise of the court returned—larger than usual, with the dukes of Famiens and Martras bringing their entourages with them. Sacha asked Peyre to move the bulk of his Guard outside The Bastion —which he reluctantly agreed to at great expense, finding them rooms in the city.

The only topic the newcomers wished to talk about was the impending marriage of Esterel and Liesel. It all combined to irritate him. For the first time, Peyre began to wonder if spending his time in Valennes was going to work. *Wouldn't I be more content in Morbaine?* he asked himself. *Oh dear. Am I really turning into my father?*

The first item of discussion in the King's Council was the fate of Auriac.

'Surely there's no other option but execution?' Sacha said. 'It has got to the point where the crown looks weak if it doesn't punish this properly.'

Peyre found himself agreeing with Sacha. That happened more often than he was comfortable with.

All eyes turned to Auberi. The size of the Council was a little larger with the two northern dukes present, but that wasn't likely to change the outcome.

'I can't disagree,' Auberi said. 'The matter of the throne was settled by the agreement made between Domard, Bastien, and me. Raymon swore to respect it, like every other magnate of the realm. You've gone out of your way to mend bridges,' he continued, looking at Esterel directly. 'Every lord of the realm would expect such a punishment for treason.' He sighed, shaking his head. 'Such a foolish move on Raymon's part.'

'He couldn't reconcile himself to reality,' Peyre suggested. 'But what about his son, Robert? We have him in the dungeons as well. If his father is executed, his fate becomes important. From my experience, he has been nothing but hostile to us, despite being raised in our father's household and always treated with respect.'

'Caisin?' Esterel asked.

'The law is perfectly clear, Your Majesty. He has committed treason, and the punishment is death. By quite brutal means unless you wish to show clemency.'

'In Robert's case, perhaps clemency could be shown,' Auberi said. 'I know saying as much may not go down well. But I was influenced, too much, by Raymon. Can we not understand a son following his father? Perhaps he should have a chance to make his own decisions? The people may expect some mercy for the son where they expect none for the father.'

'I might agree,' Peyre said, 'if there was any prospect of Robert changing his ways.'

'Then there is the question of his father's lands,' Miles said. 'Leaving Auriac in the hands of the same family to fester with hatred is hardly an appropriate outcome. A rebellion such as this demands changes. Remember, just because we were able to nip it in the bud, doesn't make it any less serious.'

Esterel nodded. 'What are my options, Caisin?'

'Legally, you can do what you like. You can confiscate the lands of a traitor and commute the sentence of execution on Robert, showing mercy. Politically, too, I don't see that it makes much of a difference either way.'

'Then since Auberi has spoken for him, I am inclined to show mercy.'

'Thank you, Your Majesty. If you were to do so, perhaps we should discuss what becomes of him? Should he be allowed his freedom? Could he attach himself to some lord's household? I would offer, but that would not be a good look.'

'I suppose he should be free to serve another lord if they are prepared to have him,' Esterel said.

'I'll take him,' Domard offered. 'He'd be far away from Valennes in Martras, with a chance to build a new life.'

'Thank you, Your Grace,' the king said.

'What about the lands of Auriac?' Sacha asked.

'I have already given that some thought. I would like to reward Florent and make him Lord of Auriac. I need someone with loyalty and tact to sort that place out once and for all.'

Sacha smiled, pleased.

Peyre shared a brief look with Domard of Martras. His brother's friends were advancing once more. But Florent wasn't a terrible choice. And it was Esterel's to make, after all.

'Onto other matters,' Sacha began, 'we really must make the final decisions on the contests to be held.'

'What talk is this of having no knightly contest?' Domard asked Esterel. 'Surely a tourney would be the best spectacle of all?'

'I have to agree,' said Auberi. 'I wouldn't hesitate to enter a tourney. And I've seen Esterel with a sword. No one is going to best Your Majesty in such a contest. There is less excitement when there is a foregone conclusion.'

Esterel smiled, keen to discuss his pet project yet again. 'In Morbaine, we never held tourneys. Please tell me what sort you mean.'

'A proper tourney,' Domard said, 'is two sides who must fight to the end. It begins with a mass charge at one another. Those left seated then continue the fight, taking prisoners for ransom. The best ones last for hours, if not a whole day.'

'With apologies to my role as Chief Downer,' Sacha said, 'but we cannot fit in something so involved. We have already agreed on an archery contest and a contest of sword and shield. The queen and king are entering them, and they cannot be moved. Not to mention the dangers inherent in such tourneys.'

'The queen?' Peyre asked.

'The archery contest was Liesel's idea,' Esterel said. 'She claims to be a decent shot. It will be fascinating to watch her in action, no?'

'Indeed,' said Peyre. It was the first he had heard of Liesel possessing such a skill.

'What about a jousting contest?' Miles suggested. 'Not so difficult to organise and it fits in with the other two.'

'Yes! How about that, Domard?' Esterel enthused.

'That sounds fair. Thank you! Are you in charge of the lists, Lord Courion?'

'I am. And if we are having three concurrent contests, I must insist that no one is allowed to enter more than one of the three. It will be complicated enough as it is.'

'Understood Sacha,' Esterel said. 'But now at least no one can complain they haven't been catered for. I expect to see everyone's name on one of those lists!'

* * *

Once Esterel made his decision on Auriac, he didn't waste time. There was no trial; the word of the King in Council sufficient to establish guilt. As Caisin had suggested, the sentence could have been brutal; but Esterel declared a beheading would suffice. As was customary, it was carried out in public view in the centre of Valennes.

Peyre went alone. He found it distasteful. The citizens enjoyed the event just the same as a royal wedding and the street urchins—some shockingly young—watched with a morbid interest. *But I am here, too, so can hardly complain.*

Peyre had no sympathy for Lord Raymon and regarded it as justice done. Still, he didn't gloat or find any pleasure in the axe's fall. Indeed, a part of him was pleased that Raymon had met his end with courage.

With no reason to stay, Peyre turned to leave the square intending to catch up with Brancat. As he did, he noticed a familiar face.

'Lady Coleta?' Although a hood covered her face, he could still see tears in her eyes. 'You are upset?'

'Peyre?' She forced a smile. 'It's not that I think it was wrong or anything,' she said, as if anxious that he thought her disloyal. 'But it was horrible to watch. I wish I hadn't come.'

Peyre thought about it. 'I have seen some bloody work done on the battlefield in the last few years. You might think me inured to violence, but I agree, it was not pleasant. Why people let their children watch, I can't fathom. Here, let me escort you back to The Bastion.'

He offered his arm, and she took it, just as they had done in the garden at his party.

'The weather is nicer than the last time we did this,' she said, recalling the same event.

Peyre smiled. 'It's fairer. Though there was something about the snow that night.'

'True. It hid us for a while, didn't it? Sometimes it's tiring, feeling like you're being watched all the time.'

'Yes.' They walked along the north road, soon free of the busyness of the city centre. Peyre found he enjoyed Coleta's company. The impending marriage of Liesel and Esterel seemed to weigh on him. He felt frustrated and irritable in their company. His training with Brancat had pushed those feelings away, only for them to return in the last few days. He was sick of feeling like a sad dog.

'You are looking forward to the wedding?' Coleta asked.

'Of course.' *It will be good when the damn thing is done.* 'And you? I know you must have a dress ready. You are always dressed so well.'

'It will be bittersweet,' Coleta admitted.

Peyre felt a twinge of guilt. He knew she adored Esterel, but she didn't know he felt the same about Liesel. Not that he could ever tell anyone else. It was bad enough, really, that Umbert and Tegyn knew.

'There you go, surprising me again,' she added. She gave him a coy smile. 'I always used to think you never noticed me at all.'

Peyre felt his body heat rise. He revisited their kiss in the snow; how he had wanted more. *And why not have more?* he asked himself. How long had he been pining, pointlessly, for Liesel? 'I've noticed you,' he said. He looked straight into brown eyes, flecked with green; studied her warm skin and the shape of her body. 'I'd like to notice you even more.'

'Duke Peyre, you horror!' she said. But she smiled and her arm grew tighter around his.

They entered The Bastion together. 'Let me escort you to your rooms,' Peyre offered. A twinge of guilt hit him, but now he questioned why. He wasn't betrothed to anyone. Neither was Coleta. There was nothing wrong with pursuing her.

'Thank you, Your Grace,' she whispered, as if the words caught in her throat.

They stopped outside her door. 'You can come in, if you wish,' she offered. 'I have it to myself.'

'Good,' Peyre said, twisting the handle.

Coleta smiled as he hurried her inside. By the time he'd shut the door behind them, his lips were already on hers, so soft and sweet. Just like the last time, she opened her mouth, inviting his tongue inside as she leaned against the wall. Peyre put his arms around her, one hand moving down her slim back, the other on her side, then on her hip. She gasped, her arms around his waist as he nuzzled at her neck.

'Gods, I want you,' he whispered hoarsely into her ear.

Coleta moved a hand to his hose, gently caressing. 'Then take me, Your Grace.'

SANC

ARVENA, KINGDOM OF SCORGIA, 676

S anc couldn't stop a grin splitting his face as he walked through
the streets of Arvena. He walked with a strut—a bounce in his
legs he had never had before. He smiled and greeted strangers as he
passed them—didn't mind in the slightest if some ignored him. The
city was beautiful to his eyes; every crack in a wall or pavement
somehow seemed right; the colours of the flowers in the marketplace
were more vibrant than he had ever noticed; the smell of the sea was
invigorating; the endless sky spoke to him of opportunity.

Dalriya had been a cage. In Silb, he was free, and it was intox-
icating.

When he wasn't working for Lenzo, Sanc went to visit Tassia in
her apartment. He had told her straight he didn't want her coming to
the prince's house again in case anyone there got any ideas. He
wanted her to himself.

They made love in the day when everyone else was busy working.
Sanc loved the indolence of it. Tassia's bed was yet another world he
had found, where nothing else mattered—only they existed.

They would talk a little of their past. She was fascinated about the
idea of another world out there. He would make her tell him of her
childhood, even though she didn't like to. She had grown up poor in a

village close by the swamp he had tramped through. She had left for a better life in Arvena as soon as she could and had no interest in dwelling on her past or ever seeing her family again.

'I live for the here and now,' she told him when he wanted more details. 'Isn't that enough?'

'Yes,' he agreed, playing with a strand of her brown hair. He found he always wanted to touch a part of her, as if she might vanish if he let her go. 'I would stay here all day and night if I could. I only eat and drink because I must.'

She laughed at him, a tinkling sound like music. 'You really are stupid.'

'I know. I only ask you questions because I want to know everything about you.' He released her hair and trailed his hand along her neck and over her bare shoulder.

'I must keep some secrets,' she told him. 'Otherwise, you would grow bored with me.'

'Rubbish. Now *you're* being stupid.'

'It's not rubbish. You keep your secrets.'

'I do not! I've hidden nothing from you.'

Tassia looked at him. 'You even hide your eyes from me.'

'I—how do you know?'

'When you are—let's say—lost in the moment. You show your real eyes.'

'Oh.' Sanc supposed that made sense. 'I hide them to protect myself. Not to keep a secret from you.'

'Well, I like them,' Tassia said. 'You don't need to hide them from me.'

* * *

TIME SEEMED TO UNRAVEL, the days floating past quicker than Sanc had ever experienced. It was strange that just as his life now seemed to glow with warmth, the world around him grew colder. Winter began to bite. Arvena was not so pleasant when lashed with storms that came in off the sea. The longer voyages were stopped completely and the smaller ones became less frequent. But even though there was less money coming in, the hundreds of soldiers that had been brought into the city still needed to be fed.

The island city that was the gateway to the rest of the continent turned in on itself. A claustrophobic atmosphere grew as so many ambitious minds, gathered in one place, began to plot. First, one soldier was murdered, then two more. Rumours flew around the city about who was behind it. Even Prince Lenzo grew nervous, insisting that Sanc was with him every single evening and all night, fearful of the assassin's blade coming for him.

He demanded that Sanc give him more information about his rivals. Wacho, especially. 'Seems like you're holding something back,' he said one evening. He was deep in his cups, but it sounded paranoid nonetheless.

'I'm not holding anything back,' Sanc said. *Though I have been spending my days with Tassia*, he admitted to himself. *Perhaps I should have done more.* 'But if I'm here every evening, I can't overhear the important conversations that take place in the houses of his allies.'

'Very well,' Lenzo replied. 'Gaida, you will see to my security for the next few nights. I need to know what's going on, Sanc.'

SANC HAD PERFECTED GAINING entry into the home of Nolf Money Bags. The gates at the back of the property were regularly opened to bring in food and other goods. They were wide enough for Sanc to slip in unseen, using his magic on everyone present. He convinced them they heard and saw nothing as he made his way through the yard and into the house.

The first few times he had dipped in and out, nervous of being noticed and unsure of the layout. He feared getting trapped inside and there were always a handful of brawny guards stood around when Nolf was home. Now, though, he knew his way around. The merchant had a study downstairs he rarely used. Sanc entered the room. Here he could wait a while in relative comfort.

He ventured out once the merchant's guests began to arrive,

listening to the conversation. He heard Master Wacho's voice among them. Good. No Wacho and he would have left. But the general's presence justified further waiting.

Sanc returned to the study, listening to the staff walk back and forth to serve dinner. He had learned after spending time in Lenzo's house that meal times were more formal occasions. It was afterwards that the real gossip would begin.

Only when dinner was over did he re-emerge. He entered the main reception room, taking care of where he moved. He scanned the room. Nolf had over a dozen guests, all drinking—another reason for confidence, since everyone was relaxed and less alert. It was still strange to be walking about, looking at everyone else when they couldn't see you.

Just as well you find it strange, he told himself. *The day it becomes familiar is the day you become blasé and get caught.*

Like Lenzo's evening parties, the room was full of pretty women. He looked for Wacho and found him lounging on a chaise longue. Then he saw her. Sat close to him—too close. Tassia.

Sanc's head spun. For a long time, he fought to keep his self-control, coming dangerously close to losing concentration on his magic and appearing before them all. He felt like he would be physically sick. Then red-hot anger burned through him, and he thought of blasting the pair of them with his magic. Finally, a feeling of loss, and a desperate compulsion to leave and not have to look any longer. Then he experienced it all over again.

All the while, Wacho, Nolf and the other guests were talking and Sanc wasn't understanding a thing. He would catch single words, meaningless on their own, his mind unable to translate the conversation. Gradually, he settled. *You need to know what is being said,* he told himself. *You need to know how deep the betrayal goes.*

'If we can convince my men that Lenzo is behind the killings,' Wacho was saying, his face focused like he was in a battlefield tent discussing strategy, 'then their loyalty is assured. I could order them to arrest him, and they would do it.'

'He has many warriors with him, at all times,' Nolf said, an element of doubt in his voice.

'Twenty at most,' Wacho said dismissively. 'I'm talking about hundreds of my soldiers. We'd surround the house and break in.'

Nolf shuddered. 'And what damage would be done?'

'Nothing you couldn't repair, man,' Wacho said with a sneer.

'And this outlander?' Nolf said. 'He is the unknown factor.'

They turned to look at Tassia.

'How much magic does he have?' Wacho asked her.

'He can change the colour of his eyes,' she said, her voice quiet under the scrutiny of the surrounding men. 'Perhaps he can change other features, too. He told me he was taught how to defend himself from weapons.'

Gods, Sanc said to himself. *She kept telling me how stupid I am. Did I really tell her all this?* Sanc *felt* stupid. Like he was still a child among adults.

'He will not be easy to kill,' Nolf warned.

'Nonsense,' Wacho said. 'He can be poisoned easily enough. Ambushed in one place or another. He wanders through the city like a carefree fool every day. Lenzo is the one who is aware of his own mortality. When the outlander dies, the prince will flee. That is the only problem.' He tapped his cheek with a finger a few times. 'We kill the outlander then move against Lenzo immediately. That is the plan.'

Sanc studied Tassia's reaction. Perhaps he could detect a trace of sorrow on her face. Not enough to warn him he was about to be slain, though. That was for sure.

You've seen enough, Sanc, he told himself. *Don't wait to see her go upstairs with him.*

'I've got the news you wanted,' he said to Lenzo.

The prince put his goblet down and studied him. 'Are you alright, Sanc? You're pale as snow.'

Sanc looked around the room. People were staring. 'Maybe in private?'

'Right.' Lenzo got to his feet. 'Gaida?'

The three of them left the reception room and Lenzo took them into the pantry.

'Cosy,' Gaida commented.

'Well?' Lenzo asked Sanc.

'Nolf's house. Him, Wacho and a few others. Discussed killing you. And me, as it happens.'

'How?'

'They hadn't got to a precise plan when I left. But the idea is that the killings of his soldiers will be pinned on you and his men will be turned against you enough to act.'

Lenzo looked doubtful. 'Wacho is killing his own men to get to me? That is hard to believe.'

'I didn't say that. I missed the first part of the conversation. I can't tell you if they're behind the murders or if they even know who is. But that doesn't matter, really. They will use it to their advantage.'

Lenzo studied him. 'And they intend to kill you? Meaning they know—'

'Yes. They know enough about me.'

'Don't let it upset you, Sanc. Consider it an honour that you're important enough for someone to want to kill you.'

'It's not that. Tassia was there. That's how they know.'

It took Lenzo a moment. 'The whore? Ah. I see. That's my fault. I thought she might do you good, and she did the opposite.' Full understanding dawned on Lenzo's features. 'You like her?'

Sanc felt his cheeks burn. He could see no point in hiding it. 'I thought I was in love with her.'

'Understandable,' Gaida said. 'She's a pretty filly.'

'Maybe she loves you in her own way,' Lenzo said. 'It's not easy to fake those feelings.'

'Loves me? She was sitting there with Wacho when I left. Told them everything she knows about me.'

'Some people can love more than one person.'

Sanc shook his head. 'She's a whore. Why was I so stupid?'

'You think less of her because she gets paid for it?' Lenzo asked him. 'And yet you still fell in love with her.'

Sanc didn't know. He didn't even know why they were having this conversation.

Lenzo shrugged. 'All I'm saying is, let's save our anger for those who really deserve it.'

'Happy to,' Sanc said. 'I don't know when they're planning to do this. I say we should strike this instant.'

'Now?' Gaida asked.

'I know where they are. We're only talking twenty armed men to overcome. They're certainly not expecting anything.'

'Neither were we,' Lenzo muttered. 'I'm half cut. In no fit state for fighting.'

'They're the same. Anyway,' Sanc said, a firmness appearing in his voice. 'I'll do most of it.'

Lenzo looked at him, nodding. 'Do it because it needs to be done, Sanc. Not out of hatred.'

Sanc shrugged. Why the prince had become so philosophical about it all, he had no idea.

'We can trust you?' Gaida asked him.

It was a stupid question really, but Sanc understood it now when he might not have a few hours ago. Maybe if he'd asked Tassia that same question, it would have saved him a lot of heartache. 'Yes. You can trust me.'

THEY ADVANCED through the dark city streets. Lenzo had brought about twenty fighting men with him, the same number as Wacho had. *Too many not to be seen*, Sanc thought to himself, glancing into the side streets and buildings they passed, looking for spies. *But enough that anyone who does see us will think twice about interfering in our business.*

When they reached Nolf's house, Lenzo and Gaida made a series of hand signals to get their men into position. Even if Sanc was confident he could deal with everyone inside, he didn't want soldiers escaping and alerting their comrades garrisoned around the city.

When they were ready, Sanc slammed his magic into the yard

gates, forcing them open. He strode through, Lenzo, Gaida and ten men with him. He looked about the yard, but no one had been posted there.

'They'll all be inside,' he said. 'Keeping warm. But they'll be awake.'

He wasted no time in making for the door, blasting it open. Once he was in, Sanc moved quickly. He went from one room to the next, familiar with the layout. He took no chances with the warriors posted on guard duty. He hurled a blast of magic at them, sending them sailing through the air until they crashed into the nearest wall. Most, he guessed, would survive the assault. Any that still stirred were dealt with by the men who followed behind him, disarmed and their hands tied. Lenzo and the others were dependent on Sanc's knowledge of the house and happy to let him neutralise their opposition.

Sanc told any servants they met to return to their quarters, which they did with no argument. In the main reception room, they gathered Nolf's guests, most of them merchants or prostitutes—both groups well known to Lenzo. The prince hushed them when they raised their voices and Gaida brandished his sword, a mean look on his face.

'No Nolf or Wacho,' Lenzo said.

'Upstairs,' Sanc said.

It was just the three of them who took the stairs up to the next floor. The landing opened onto several rooms, all with closed doors. Only one guard was there, stationed outside one of the doors. He opened his mouth and moved a hand to the knife at his belt before Sanc sent him crashing into the opposite wall. To be on the safe side, he then sent him hurtling down the stairs.

All three of them eyed the room he had been guarding.

'Let us deal with this,' Lenzo whispered.

Sanc nodded. It was probably for the best. He waited on the landing, while Gaida burst the door open and he and Lenzo charged in, knives in hand. There were shouts and grunts, the sounds of struggle. Above it all, Sanc could hear Tassia's screams and he felt like vomiting. He heard anxious voices coming from another room, but he held his position, waiting for Lenzo and Gaida to return.

They dragged Wacho's bloody body out with them, dumping it onto the landing.

Lenzo nodded back into the room. 'She's fine. We'll deal with the rest, Sanc.'

Sanc nodded. Steeling himself, he entered the room.

Tassia was crouched on the bed, a blanket gripped in both shaking hands to hide her nudity. Tracks of Wacho's blood covered the bed, floor, and walls.

Sanc stared at her. He had thought he would be full of anger, but he was wrong. Neither did he feel like rushing over and offering comfort. He was sad for her. Sad for himself, that this would be his last memory of her.

'Did you love him?' he asked her.

She looked up at him. He could tell she was in shock. A few moments passed until she registered who he was. Then a look of fear replaced the shock.

'I—no. Of course not!'

'But you chose him over me,' Sanc said, not caring that he sounded like a bitter child.

'It wasn't like that,' Tassia said.

'What was it like?'

'He threatened to kill me. And worse.' A look of defiance appeared on her face. 'Maybe if you'd done that, I would have spied on him for you.'

'I didn't do that,' Sanc agreed. 'Gods, I thought I loved you. You knew that. And all the time... Would you have warned me? After tonight? Would you have poisoned me? Set me up?'

Tassia's eyes opened wide. Now she knew he knew everything, and she looked terrified. 'I'm sorry. Sanc. Please don't kill me. I'm not a brave warrior like you. I have no magic. No friends or family or anyone to protect me. I should have told you. I was too scared. People like me, we only get bad choices.' She shook her head. 'That doesn't excuse it. Nothing I can say will do that. But please. Forgive me.'

A heavy weight sat on Sanc's chest. He felt his body sway. He was tired. It was partly the magic he had used. But more than that, the happiness he had felt until today had been stripped from him. It left him empty.

'I forgive you. Don't open this door until we are gone.'

He left her. The landing was empty, but he heard noises on the stairs and looked. Lenzo and Gaida had hold of Nolf's arms and were guiding him down.

He followed them. They let go of the merchant in his reception room and he sank to his knees, looking wildly at his captors, then at Sanc as he entered the room and stood facing him.

'I—'

Lenzo held up a hand. 'I will do the talking if you don't mind,' said the prince. He looked at Nolf for confirmation, who nodded his head. 'I blame Wacho for this,' Lenzo said. 'I believe the man has been less than loyal to me. Which is rather irritating, given the situation Scorgia has found herself in. Hence his punishment, which you saw for yourself. As for you, Nolf, it is disappointing to see you caught up in it. But we all make mistakes. And I must remind myself that it was you who generously gave me the use of my house, which is a plus mark on your ledger.' Lenzo gave the impression of considering his options. 'What if we say we forget your part in this little incident?'

Nolf nodded vigorously, still not daring to say anything.

'Of course, there must be certain conditions. Your absolute loyalty in the future being the prime one. Can I rely on that? You may speak.'

'Of course, Your Highness. I will never waver an inch again for the rest of my life.'

'That sounds reassuring. Don't you think, Gaida?'

'I say kill him and be done with it.'

'Yes, well. You are often less forgiving than me, that's true. But I will give you this last chance, Nolf. All I've tried to do since I arrived here is make Arvena a haven. Looking forward, it will be reassuring to have your unconditional support.'

'Yes, Your Highness. You can always rely on me to speak up in Council and offer any other help you might need.'

'Excellent. Because if you don't, you know I'll find out about it. Don't you?'

* * *

SANC HAD TO LEAVE ARVENA. He took Rab to the north of the island, away from the city. He needed time and space to think. He walked the country paths, breathing in the fresh air. Rab, in his element, roamed around, but always came back to check on him.

I got lost, somehow, he admitted to himself. *The thought that someone else loved me made me forget who I was. I didn't come here to spy on Lord Wacho or spend my time with a girl. I came here to save Dalriya. And I have no way of knowing how bad things are there. Rimmon, Jesper, and the Magnians were trying to hold off an invasion when I left. What would they think if they knew how I have been spending my time?*

Sanc thought about the things he had learned about Silb. There were gods, but they didn't dwell among the people in a host body as Ezenachi did. There were champions—magic users like him. Would such people be powerful enough to help him, assuming they could be persuaded to do so? He didn't know. The Scorgians had lost their champion. King Lothar of Nerisia had two: a Nerisian and a Gadenzian. Perhaps it was time to meet this king? As much as he liked Prince Lenzo, he had to focus on who was able to help him. Lenzo, it seemed, could offer little.

When he returned to Arvena, he went to Lenzo's house. He was in his reception room, but there were no guests to entertain this day. No wine. A pile of manuscripts lay on the table in front of him. He looked more relaxed than Sanc had ever seen him. At last, the prince had won complete control of the city and the tensions of the last few days seemed to have disappeared.

Lenzo looked up at Sanc. 'You have red eyes.'

'I've always had them. It's time to stop hiding.'

'Agreed. They suit you. A man with your powers needn't try to blend in. Sit. We need to talk,' Lenzo said, pre-empting Sanc's own words. 'I assume you're going to leave?'

Sanc smiled as he took a seat. The prince was shrewd, he had to give him that. 'I need to find help. And soon. Time is of the essence.'

Lenzo nodded. 'You know, Wacho was right about a lot of things.

We can't just sit in Arvena and hope the Nerisians just go away. We need allies. Together, you and I could play a leading role in that.'

'But you argued just the opposite!' Sanc exclaimed.

The prince shrugged. 'Politics. I need these merchants on side. Many prefer peace to war. But with Wacho gone, and my soldiers taking orders from me, it frees me to do what I want. Here, look.' He stretched out a piece of parchment.

It was an ink drawing of Silb. Sanc studied it, comparing the drawing to the image of the continent he had in his mind. He pointed to one area. 'The Telds? I have heard little of them. Their realm seems small.'

'When the seven peoples came to Silb, the land was divided equally in size and resources. Our unity didn't last long. Human nature, I suppose. People found reasons to fight one another. The Telds had to fight many wars. They have been forced to retreat into the mountains. They were the weakest of the seven realms. Until now,' he added with a wry smile. 'Anyway, my thoughts are leading us here,' he said, putting a finger to the northern tip of the continent. 'The Kassites are the easiest to reach from Arvena. They have lost wars to Lothar in recent years, who has taken territory from them. They are the most likely to agree to an alliance with us.'

Sanc nodded cautiously. 'How does this help me?' he asked bluntly.

'I've seen what you can do now,' Lenzo told him. 'The Scorgians and Kassites need your help. You can demand ours in return.' Lenzo looked at him, his green eyes glittering. 'Of course, you could go see Lothar,' he said, as if reading Sanc's mind. 'But Lothar is winning. He already has two champions and the greatest army in the land. He does not need to make a deal with you.'

Sanc thought about it. He decided that what Lenzo said made sense. 'Alright. Assuming I agree. You'll put me on a boat to the land of the Kassites? How am I to know who I can speak with there?'

'You don't need to worry about that. I would accompany you.'

'You?' Sanc asked. 'Leave Arvena?'

Lenzo shrugged. 'I have control now. Any idiot can run Arvena on my behalf. I was thinking even Gaida could do it.'

LIESEL

VALENNES, KINGDOM OF GUIVERGNE, 676

L iesel couldn't help feeling that her wedding ceremony was defined by who wasn't there. No father to give her away, of course. Her mother, sister, and brother were not there either. She had hoped her uncle might come, but the news they had from the empire was all about the raising of armies. There followed a humiliating search for someone to do the honours. She had thought Peyre would offer, but in the end, Duke Auberi volunteered to lead her down the aisle.

The cathedral was decorated beautifully, and she encouraged herself to find the joy in the occasion. Auberi led her to the stage where the bishop would perform the ceremony. On the front bench on her side of the aisle, Tegyn sat with Loysse and Peyre. It cheered her to see them. Waiting for her, Esterel stood with Sacha. Her husband to be sported a stupid grin. She couldn't help but smile back, relaxing as she did.

It was just a ceremony, after all. She'd already lived at court for half a year. She knew the people here: knew them, whatever their faults, as good people. She was ready to join their family. Ready to be queen? She wasn't so sure about that.

There was a parade through the streets of Valennes, the citizens there calling out her name as she passed. Some came to the door of her carriage, shouting their congratulations. They shoved gifts through the window. Tegyn collected them and placed them on a growing pile: flowers, sweet foods, hand-sewn gifts, even a carved likeness of her.

'You are well loved,' Tegyn noted.

'They don't know me yet,' said Liesel.

'They'll never know you. But they've decided they love you. Don't complain about it.'

It was not long before they returned to The Bastion. The rest of the day was devoted to a private banquet for the guests of the royal couple. Tomorrow the real public celebrations would start, as Esterel's beloved contests got under way.

In the main hall, the guests took their places. The top table was full, Esterel squeezing in as many as he could. Everyone wanted to sit and eat with the newlyweds, but the other tables would have a good time, too. Liesel had been involved in the preparations, keen that everyone should get a taste of the delicacies prepared in the kitchen. Loysse had been an invaluable help, generous with advice on what had or hadn't worked at her own wedding.

Esterel stood and those around him demanded that the hall fall quiet. 'I'm too hungry and thirsty for much in the way of words,' he admitted. It got a laugh. 'But please join me in a toast to welcome my new wife to my family, to The Bastion, and to Guivergne.' Everyone drank and cheered. 'Today is the happiest day of my life,' he said with a grin to Liesel. She knew she was blushing furiously. 'But even more important is what today means to my kingdom. For I believe I have found the perfect woman to be Queen of Guivergne. So please, a second toast, to your new queen.'

The cheering was even louder as fists hammered at the wooden tables. Liesel was not expected to speak, but, feeling like a fool, she rose her goblet to the room in thanks. She was overwhelmed by the welcome and fought off tears.

Thankfully, Esterel was done, and the servants were soon bringing out the first course. There was some silliness at first, with a sharing cup that she and Esterel were supposed to drink from. But Liesel soon forgot that she was the centre of attention and enjoyed the back and forth between Esterel and his two siblings; with Auberi, Tegyn, Sacha, Duke Domard, and a few others close enough to join in from time to time. The food was exquisite, but it was the company she valued the most. They seemed such a young group, in the main. There was some-thing optimistic about that. She was able to push to the back of her mind those that weren't here. Those who were in trouble: her sister, Katrina, fearing for her children while Leopold raised his armies; Idris, still stuck in Essenberg.

When evening came, Esterel's band of musicians made music to dance to and their guests, disabled by so much food and drink, capered about. Liesel resisted temptation. Surprisingly, Esterel did, too. It made her think he must have received his telling off from Loysse about his antics at Corbenay. If so, she was grateful he had listened. She found him talking quietly with Peyre.

'I'm not interrupting?' she asked.

'Of course not,' Esterel said.

'Liesel,' Peyre said, 'you're the Queen of Guivergne now. You might have to stop being so polite.'

Liesel nodded while she stopped herself from apologising. 'What are you two talking about?'

'Serious stuff,' said Peyre. 'After what happened in Magnia, those who survived agreed to search for allies. Specifically, Jesper, a forester from Arbeost—' he frowned, looking at Esterel for help.

'Who also happened to be Sanc's secret protector, a companion of Oisin, King of the Giants, and a veteran of the siege of Chalios,' Esterel provided.

'Thanks for filling me in,' Liesel said with a grin.

'That comes later tonight,' he said with a wink.

'Stop it,' she said, slapping his arm.

'Anyway,' Peyre resumed with a roll of his eyes, 'Jesper arrived back in Valennes with Maragin the Krykker earlier today. I can speak with her tomorrow if you two are busy.'

'*The* Maragin the Krykker?' Liesel asked. Maragin was a legend of the Isharite Wars—the wielder of Bolivar's Sword, one of Madria's relics.

'Yes.'

'I really don't think ignoring her is an option.'

'I'm sure she'd understand,' Esterel offered.

'You know, I don't think she would.'

Esterel smiled. 'Very well. We'll both meet with her in the afternoon. We both have bouts in the morning, Peyre.'

'Don't worry. I have my secret weapon, remember?'

Esterel shook his head. 'Peyre is under the impression that he is going to win.'

'Why not?' Liesel asked. 'We shall find out.'

'Because *I'm* going to win,' Esterel said. 'Just as well you will have some consolation, brother. From what I hear.'

Peyre frowned.

'Oh yes?' Liesel asked.

'Lady Coleta, a little birdie told me,' Esterel said, with a wriggle of his eyebrows.

Coleta? The woman Liesel couldn't help being jealous of. Peyre was seeing her? It seemed every time she needed help, Peyre was there to oblige. 'Oh Peyre,' she said. 'That's wonderful!'

Then she stopped. Peyre's face was like thunder. She had never seen him angry before and didn't understand the cause of it.

'If you'll excuse me,' he said tightly, barely getting the words out through gritted teeth. He stormed off without a backward glance.

'Did I say something wrong?' Liesel asked.

'Of course not,' said Esterel. 'I guess it's my fault. Peyre has always been funny when discussing women. I shouldn't have mentioned it. But don't worry. He'll forgive me.'

Liesel didn't have long to dwell on it. Shouts grew in the hall. Esterel's friends had decided it was time for the bedding ceremony. Sacha, Miles, and Florent led a rowdy group over towards them. Pretending to capture the newlyweds, they led them to Liesel's rooms. Bawdy comments filled the time it took to get there; mainly at Esterel's expense, but still deeply embarrassing.

They burst into the room, a gang of intoxicated fools. Florent lay down on the bed, testing its bounce.

'Alright, alright!' Sacha shouted. 'Everyone out!'

'That's an order,' Esterel added. He shut and locked the door behind the last of the stragglers.

Liesel sat on the bed and, with a smile, he joined her.

'Are you alright?' he asked.

'Yes. I've never done this before, though.'

'Don't worry. I have enough experience for the both of us,' he said with a grin.

Liesel smiled. Maybe that was for the best. But she wasn't nervous. She might be a virgin, but she wasn't some young girl anxious about her first time. Liesel had been friends with Tegyn long enough to know plenty. She wanted sex. She'd been waiting long enough.

'I'm ready for my first lesson,' she said.

He leaned over and they kissed. Her body didn't thump with intense pleasure as it had done when she had kissed Idris. But it was nice.

'How many lessons are you expecting tonight?' Esterel asked her.

She smiled. 'The archery contest doesn't start until the day after tomorrow. I have nothing to save my strength for.'

IN THE AFTERNOON, Esterel invited Maragin to his rooms. Peyre was there, too. Both brothers had won the first bouts in the sword and shield contest, which put them in a good mood. Liesel still detected a tension, but it lay under the surface.

Jesper, the forester, was tall and athletic looking. He had the fair hair and pale skin of the Vismarians. He had come with Maragin and a second Krykker. This one was a man named Stenk. He said little, deferring to his chieftain. She was still strong looking; the famous sword scabbarded at her belt. Her naturally armoured torso gave her a fearsome look. But she had that aged look of wisdom, too. Liesel hoped it was true. She felt like they needed a wise head more than anything.

Jesper handled the introductions, and Maragin congratulated Liesel and Esterel on their marriage. But no one was here for pleasantries.

'You have also seen this Ezenachi?' she asked them as they settled around a table.

'Everyone except me,' Esterel said.

'I encountered him most recently, in Magnia,' Peyre said, then gave Liesel a look.

'And I was in Thesse,' she added. 'When he killed the emperor.'

'He is as powerful as Jesper tells me?'

'Rimmon seemed powerless against him,' Peyre said.

'Inge the same,' Liesel confirmed. 'She is scared. Willing to do whatever he asks.'

'Rimmon and Inge,' Maragin shrugged, as if dismissive of them.

'But who else is there to stop him?' Peyre asked her. 'The great sorcerers of the Isharite Wars are no more. When Belwynn killed Madria, she left us defenceless to new gods.' He looked at her unimpressed expression. 'That is what Rimmon said, at least.'

'There is a lot of nonsense spoken of that moment. For a start, I killed Madria.'

'What?' Liesel asked. The stories of the Isharite Wars seemed the same everywhere. If something so fundamental wasn't true, what else had people got wrong?

Maragin sighed, as if reluctant to share her knowledge. 'I was the only one who stayed with Belwynn after she had destroyed Diis. She knew I understood what others didn't. Madria had her own agenda, just like any god. She didn't destroy Diis for the benefit of the people of Dalriya. She would have the entire world to herself. Belwynn realised the truth at the last moment. Madria had made Belwynn a promise, you see. She could revive one of her fallen champions.' The Krykker looked at each one of them. 'Her brother Soren lay dead. Clarin, too, the man she loved. And what did Madria give her when the time came? Nothing but her own shadow. She said she would take

Belwynn's shadow and place it into one of the corpses. That was the value of her promise.'

Liesel frowned, trying to follow. If this was true, Belwynn's actions suddenly became more understandable.

'We want Ezenachi dead?' Maragin asked them. 'All we need is this,' she said, tapping her scabbard, 'and that.' She gestured at Stenk, who produced a dagger in a leather scabbard, handing it to Maragin.

Maragin drew the weapon. 'Toric's Dagger. Belwynn had Madria put her shadow into the corpse of her predecessor, Elana. She used that animated corpse to strike herself; the blade entering her own head.' The Krykker gripped the hilt of the dagger and thrust downward towards the table. 'Belwynn was dead. Madria was without her host, and she escaped Belwynn's body, looking for a new one. That was when I used Bolivar's Sword to finish the goddess for good.'

Liesel flicked her eyes to those around her. Esterel looked pale. Peyre, confused.

'So Belwynn's shadow—' Liesel began, struggling to get a grip on this new version of events.

'Belwynn's shadow became Elana,' Maragin said. The Krykker noted Liesel's confused look. 'Or Belwynn was inside Elana's body, if you prefer.'

It really wasn't a question of what Liesel preferred. 'So Belwynn—part of her, at least—still lives?'

'If you like,' Maragin said. 'But don't go thinking of finding her. She suffered enough to save Dalriya the first time. Like I say, if these two weapons could kill Madria, they can deal with this Ezenachi.'

'We don't need to find the other weapons?' Jesper asked.

'They would be helpful. But none are easy to get. These two may have to suffice.'

'This can't be right,' Peyre said. 'Rimmon said even if we had all seven weapons, we couldn't kill Ezenachi. He said we needed someone with a power equal to Ezenachi's. Diis was killed by Madria. He couldn't have been stopped without her.'

'Rimmon,' Maragin said with distaste. 'What did he know? What part did he play in the events of which I speak? Madria killed Diis, and Madria was killed by dagger and sword. If we fetch some other god to come to Dalriya and kill Ezenachi, we would still be left with the exact same problem. One god in Dalriya is one god too many. There is no praying for some other being to save us,' she said fiercely. 'We do it ourselves.'

'But Rimmon sent Sanc away,' Peyre said. 'To fetch help from some other world. My brother,' he explained, 'is a sorcerer.'

'I'm sorry for your brother,' Maragin said. 'I can't say what was in Rimmon's mind. Maybe by sending him away, he protected him from Ezenachi. But your brother is on a false mission. If he succeeds, what kind of creature might he bring back?'

* * *

LIESEL LEFT The Bastion in the company of Esterel, Peyre, and Jesper. On the other side of the north road, the fighting arenas had been constructed. A stand had been constructed where Esterel and Liesel could sit as king and queen, along with their guests, and watch the entertainment. They took their seats, overlooking the melee circle. The crowd, gathered to watch, cheered their arrival. Liesel could see the contest was well attended, all seats and benches taken. There was space for shopkeepers to sell food and drink and the atmosphere felt friendly and lively. She had to admit, it was a good idea of Esterel's.

'Well, that was an interesting conversation,' Peyre said as they waited for the next two fighters to arrive. 'I am sorry the Krykker had nothing nice to say about your friend Rimmon, Jesper.'

'I was surprised myself. She said little on the journey here. I don't know what to make of her advice. It flies against everything Rimmon ever said.'

'No offence to Rimmon,' Esterel said, 'but she should know what it takes to rid ourselves of Ezenachi. I'm certainly ready to give it a try.'

'But what did she mean, exactly?' Liesel asked them. 'A few people head south with the sword and dagger, find Ezenachi and kill him? Having witnessed exactly what he can do with my own eyes, I just don't see it.'

Peyre and Jesper nodded in sombre agreement.

'I'm sure that's not what she means,' Esterel said. 'No doubt she wants an army to head south with her. But we need to discuss strategy with her. There must be a way to get our hands on more of the weapons as well.'

'I intend to travel to Halvia next,' Jesper said. 'I am the one with the best chance to persuade Oisin to return.'

Liesel didn't know the forester well, but she detected a loneliness about him she wished she could help with. His friend, Rimmon, had been killed—by his own arrow. His other friend, Herin, had no sooner been rescued from Ezenachi's control than spirited away to some distant land. Then there was Sanc. She had never met Esterel and Peyre's younger brother. But they had told her how Jesper had been there for him—a silent protector—for years. It seemed he felt the boy's absence more than Sanc's own brothers.

'You will take part in the archery contest before you leave?' she asked him.

'I have little interest, Your Majesty,' he admitted.

Liesel still wasn't used to that title. She looked to Esterel for support.

'There's a prize not to be sniffed at,' her new husband said. 'Besides, the point of the archery contest is to encourage take up of the skill in Guivergne. There are so few archers to call on here compared to Morbaine. The queen and I hoped the contest would encourage people to see the bow as the equal of the sword or lance.'

'If you think my participation will help, then, of course,' Jesper said.

'Wonderful,' Liesel said. 'Perhaps you could accompany Tegyn and I tomorrow?'

'Of course, Your Majesty.'

'You may regret this, Liesel,' Peyre suggested. 'Inviting Jesper may harm your chances.'

'I'm sure it will,' she admitted. 'Not that I have a chance of winning. I just hope I don't make a fool of myself.'

'You won't,' Esterel said. 'Oh. Here come the next combatants. Is that Jehan?'

'Yes,' said Peyre. 'I have an interest in all these fights. I'm excited to see them.'

'Jehan is a guard at The Bastion?' Liesel asked, thinking she recognised him.

'That's right,' Esterel said. 'He had the dubious pleasure of escaping with Peyre and I from The Bastion a few years back. Swam across the moat with us.'

'Oh gods!' said Liesel, horrified at the thought.

'He fights Inhan,' Peyre said. 'One of my Morbainais recruits in the Barissian Guard. Young, but lots of potential.'

'Ah!' Esterel said. 'Your man against mine. I say Jehan will take it.'

'Quite possibly,' Peyre admitted. 'Jehan has had more time with Brancat, after all. But let's see.'

The two men raised their swords to the crowd and to the royal box. Then they began. Liesel was fascinated by the skills on display, never having seen a contest like it. Esterel and Peyre commented throughout. She learned to observe more than just the swords— blunted for the contest, but still potentially dangerous. The shield, which she had assumed was purely for defence, was used as much in offence. The footwork, speed and agility of the combatants were as important as raw strength.

Peyre's man, Inhan, started the aggressor, full of energy. Jehan fended off these early attacks, and the fight became more even. In its later stages, he looked the stronger, finally battering the younger man to the ground in an exhausting finale. He raised his sword arm, with some effort, to his king. Liesel joined in with the applause for his efforts, but was grateful to see Inhan get back to his feet and watch the two combatants leave the circle together.

'Pass on my approval to your man,' Esterel said to Peyre. 'He fought well.'

'He'll appreciate that. This next may be the pick of the first round,' Peyre said, excited.

Two very different looking fighters emerged next. One was small in stature, compact, with an easy grace. The other was a huge bear of a man, clad in furs, looking nothing like the Guivergnais Liesel had met so far.

'Gosse, Lord of the March!' Esterel said, indicating the latter. 'Another of Peyre's friends,' he said to Liesel. 'Can he use that sword?' he asked Peyre dubiously.

Gosse carried an enormous sword one-handed, with a much larger reach than his opponent.

'The sword is his preferred weapon,' Peyre confirmed. 'He defends our border with Brasingia, Liesel,' he said with a smile.

'If they all look like him, no wonder you have kept the empire out,' she said. 'He looks terrifying.'

'He is fighting Ragonde, Domard's man,' Esterel said. 'The duke speaks highly of him. I think skill will still win out over brawn in the end.'

The two warriors raised their swords to their monarch and began.

It was clear Gosse would be the aggressor. He came for Ragonde, trying to land a hit with his weapon. The smaller fighter was in and out, left and right, unpredictable in his movement. It was strength against speed, a contest easy enough for Liesel to understand. Then it was all over.

Ragonde had, perhaps, been too fixated on that huge blade. Gosse moved fast—faster than Liesel thought him capable. It was his shield that caught Ragonde out, clattering him with huge force, unbalancing him. After that, Gosse didn't let up. The shield came down again, three or four times, at least as fast as sword blows. By the end, Ragonde was sprawled out on the ground.

Gosse checked on his defeated opponent, getting him back to his feet. He then waved up to the royal box, a big grin on his face.

'I was wrong,' Esterel admitted.

'He's going to be hard to stop,' Peyre added. 'Strength, speed, aggression.'

'Unusual style,' Esterel said. 'Though now everyone has seen what he can do, the element of surprise has been lost. What's this? Umbert is next?' he said, looking down at the two new fighters. 'Is every fighter related to you in some way, Peyre?'

'I believe Sacha put them all in this section so they wouldn't have to fight me,' Peyre said. 'Maybe he thought they wouldn't try as hard against me, though I doubt that's true. They're actually in your half, brother. You'll meet someone from this session in the last four. If you get that far.'

'*If I get that far*,' Esterel repeated as if there were no question of it.

Liesel wasn't as confident. She didn't like the idea of her new husband getting bashed by the great beast of a man they had just watched.

Umbert's fight turned out to be one-sided. His opponent, from the west of the kingdom, lacked the skills of Peyre's friend, who progressed into the next round without breaking much of a sweat.

The final bout caught Liesel's attention immediately. Syele, another character known to Peyre, was the only female warrior in the competition.

'She's a Barissian,' he told her. 'Part of my Guard originally, but she serves Loysse now.'

Syele faced another guard from The Bastion. He was good, as all the warriors trained by Brancat seemed to be. Liesel feared for Syele in the first few exchanges, absorbed in the contest in a way unlike anything she had experienced before. It felt like she was the one wielding the sword and shield against an opponent who was stronger —more weight in his shield shoves, more power in his sword strokes.

But Syele was tricky. She avoided contests of strength where she could. She dodged away; counterattacked when she saw an opening. Her sword strikes were unpredictable: down at ankle height as often as anywhere else. She broke up her opponent's rhythm, forcing him to defend when he didn't want to, and Liesel could hear him grunt in frustration as he moved his shield from one position to the next.

Like the first contest they had watched, the longer it went on without Syele's defeat, the more she got into the fight. Each of them took blows as they tired. The guardsman began to lose discipline— going for a big strike that wasn't on, then using up energy on a series of blows that Syele simply took on her shield. Whether it was exhaustion or laziness, Liesel couldn't tell for sure, but his shield wasn't lowered far enough and Syele finally got in a wicked looking strike on his ankle. Reeling, he lurched to defend the next strike, but it was a feint. In and out, Syele's next blow caught him on the back of the head. If he hadn't been wearing a helmet, it might have been a killing blow. As it was, Umbert and Gosse had to return to the fighting circle to carry him off.

Syele raised her sword to the cheers of her audience.

'Well done!' Liesel shouted, still caught up in the moment. She could feel the sweat on her own skin from the tension of the combat.

Peyre, Esterel, and Jesper were also pleased at her victory.

'A shield maiden in the last sixteen,' Esterel said, 'and who knows what tomorrow's archery contest will bring?'

Whatever happens, I will be as fearless as that woman, Liesel promised herself.

* * *

THE NEXT DAY was the busiest of the royal contest. The archers and swordsmen would be reduced to eight participants; the horsemen to four.

In the morning, the archers kicked things off. The rules were simple enough. Anyone with their own bow could take part. The straw targets were eighty yards away. Each archer shot five arrows and scored according to the accuracy of their hits. They had three rounds, and their biggest score would count.

Liesel walked with Tegyn, Jesper, and seven other hopefuls to the range. They were the second group to shoot: ten scores were already in, and when they lined up, Liesel was already shaking with nerves. A sizeable crowd had gathered to watch—and of course, all eyes were on her. At that moment, Liesel didn't care about where she placed. She just cared about not showing herself up. She had taken part in similar contests in Atrabia. But she hadn't been the centre of attention then.

The first round was a nightmare. She rushed her shots. The wind didn't help, either. It gusted about, taking arrows away from the targets. Even Tegyn swore under her breath as one of hers went completely wide of the mark. Nonetheless, she outscored Liesel, while Jesper was ahead by a distance.

Liesel did her best to control herself in the second round. *It's a good thing we have an audience*, she tried to convince herself. *The whole point is to encourage more people to take up the weapon. Even if I lose, I have done my job.*

Her shaking stopped, and she slowed down. But she wasn't relaxed, instead over-thinking every shot. Her score was more respectable but wouldn't trouble the leaderboard.

She saw Peyre arrive to watch them. He caught her look and gave her a quick thumbs up, indicating he had won his fight. Esterel would be waiting for his turn. Maybe it was just as well they had been scheduled for the same time.

'You need to account for the wind,' Jesper said, quiet enough that only she could hear. His gaze was fixed on his target; his hand pulled back to his cheek as he aimed and fired.

'How can I?' she demanded, not intending to sound quite as grumpy as she did. 'It's gusting back and forth all over the place.'

'It's coming from the west,' he said. 'When it blows, adjust your aim to account for it. When it's gusting back and forth, wait until it's steady again.'

She took his advice. It worked. She held her string, struggling with the effort, until a strong wind came. She had been avoiding the wind at its strongest, waiting for it to calm; but in fact, when it blew hard, it was more predictable. When she got one shot on target, she adjusted her aim by the same amount and each time her arrow hit satisfyingly close to the bullseye.

The crowd cheered her last shots excitedly. She'd finished behind Jesper and Tegyn, but she'd scored well in the end. She'd have to wait to see if it was good enough for tomorrow's final.

'Come,' she said to Tegyn. She was keen to get back to The Bastion and change, so that she could watch the sword contest. 'We might still catch Esterel's fight.'

PEYRE

VALENNES, KINGDOM OF GUIVERGNE, 676

Peyre loitered beside the fighting pit. There was a break in the proceedings after Esterel's victory. The king and queen would return shortly, in all their finery, to watch the final bouts.

Despite his own success, Peyre was unsettled. He and Esterel had made the last eight. On opposite ends of the draw, they could meet in the final. Peyre found he had a desperate desire to face his brother and defeat him. Ever since Esterel had humiliated him—mentioning Coleta in front of Liesel, to make himself look better at Peyre's expense—this anger-fuelled obsession had settled on him. Esterel needed to be put on his backside for once in his charmed life.

But his brother had enjoyed another easy contest today and tomorrow's offered little threat. Elger, head of Peyre's own Barissian Guard, would fight him. Elger was skilful; tricksy and experienced; but he had nothing to worry Esterel.

He caught sight of Corbenay heading over from the list field and intercepted him. 'What news from the jousts?' he asked.

'No great surprises,' Miles said. 'Both dukes are into the last four. That should keep all sides happy.'

Martras and Famiens had been keen for a tourney, so Peyre wasn't surprised to learn they rode well. 'Anyone stand out?'

137

'Florent is the best rider I know. But the joust seems pretty even to me. Makes me regret picking the melee contest,' he said wryly.

'You wish you were jousting? But you won your fight today!'

'I prefer the melee. But I'm up against Sacha tomorrow.' Miles shrugged. 'That's as far as I'll get.'

'He's that good?'

'I've never beaten him. He and Esterel are a cut above the rest of the field. No offence intended, Your Grace.'

Peyre *did* take offence, but he tried to hide it. 'What makes him so good? Sacha, I mean. I know all about my brother.'

'They're two peas in a pod. Speed and skill. They can do things with a blade no one else can.'

'And who used to win their fights?' Peyre asked.

Miles shook his head. 'They were a sight to behold. Esterel usually got the better. When he put his mind to it.'

Peyre nodded. 'I look forward to your fight with Sacha. I'll be cheering you on.'

Miles smiled. 'More to see Sacha lose than me win, I believe.'

'Of course,' said Peyre, giving his own smile. 'I don't mind him, really.'

'Good. Because he has cause to dislike you as well.'

'What do you mean?'

'The talk is you have a dalliance with his sister. He is protective of her.'

It had never crossed Peyre's mind. Strange that it hadn't. He instantly imagined his own feelings if Sacha was having pre-marital relations with Loysse, and the entire court knew about it. He would be apoplectic with rage.

Peyre looked at Miles. He had nothing to say.

'Anyway, that's your business,' Miles said with a frown, as if he had not intended to mention it. 'Are you watching the last bouts?'

'Yes,' Peyre answered, finding his voice. 'Let's take our seats and wait for the royal couple.'

It wasn't long before Esterel and Liesel joined them. Peyre felt his usual tug of jealousy at seeing them together. It was a sore that refused to heal. No matter what his mind said, his heart wouldn't change.

As soon as the king and queen arrived, the penultimate fighters of the day came out to the recognition and applause of both the royal stage and all the Guivergnais, of all stations and ages, who stood around the edges of the pit. Peyre's friend Gosse, recently given the title Lord of the March by Esterel, brandished his impossibly large sword, though all now knew that his shield arm was equally dangerous. Against him, Jehan the guardsman looked smaller than he really was.

Jehan knew his task. He must avoid both blade and shield. But knowing what one must do is not the same as being able to do it. Gosse's shield shunted forwards, and the sword came at the guardsman in thunderous swings. Jehan's focus was on defence: moving out of the way, blocking with his shield. He offered little offensive himself. The outcome seemed inevitable.

Perhaps tired of giving ground, Jehan sought to gain the initiative by leaping towards the big man, shield braced for impact. Gosse was up to it, bringing his own shield in. They came together with a thunderous crack and Gosse, his full weight behind him, shoved the lighter man over onto the ground. His sword came down quickly. Jehan raised his own, trying to defend the blow. His weapon was torn from his grip. Peyre could imagine Jehan's numb arm after that blow. He had no choice but to yield.

Gosse bellowed out a cry of victory before helping his opponent up.

Peyre turned to study his brother's face as everyone on the stage applauded the combatants. 'Starting to worry yet?' he asked Esterel.

'He's good,' Esterel admitted. But there were no signs of worry on his face. 'Let's see him properly tested first. Who does he fight next?'

'The winner of the last bout,' Liesel said. 'Syele against Umbert.'

'You are following the contest closely?' Peyre asked her.

'I am cheering for Syele,' she told him. 'No offence intended to your friend.'

'Umbert doesn't offend easily. And I am neutral on the outcome.

But I think Umbert will win. He's a great warrior, even though I would never admit as much to his face.'

Umbert and Syele appeared, and their fight began. It was a cagey contest. They circled one another, prodding in and out, testing one another's moves. Umbert was a careful fighter, and he took precautions against Syele's flicked blade strokes towards his ankles. When they clashed, it was no surprise that he had the greater strength, forcing Syele to give way. He did not press his advantage, however, too willing to return to a neutral position. *Come on Umbert*, Peyre said to himself. *It's clear that you must be the aggressor.*

There were a few mutterings from the crowd. It was not as thrilling as the previous encounter. Peyre turned to the rest of the stage, but here there was nothing but concentration. Liesel, in particular, seemed absorbed in the contest. Her eyes were fixed on the combat, mouth slightly open. Peyre smiled as he saw her arm move in and out, mimicking Syele's strike. She probably didn't even know she was doing it. He caught Esterel looking at him and turned back to the contest.

Umbert had Syele on the back foot, twisting away from his advance. He used sword and shield together, restricting her options. An opening came, and he struck—a blow to the shoulder. Peyre saw Syele grimace, but she carried on, feinting a swing before stepping out of reach. Umbert let her go, returning the bout to neutral.

'He could have had her,' Esterel muttered.

He was right. Umbert was drawing this out longer than necessary. 'I think he fears hurting her,' Peyre admitted.

'It's a combat. No one asked her to enter,' Esterel retorted.

'It's honourable on his part not to want to hurt her,' Liesel said.

'He'd be better just getting it over with,' Peyre said. 'Syele will not yield unless he forces her to. Dragging it out is no kindness.'

'It's honourable,' Liesel repeated.

Peyre and Esterel shared a glance but said nothing else.

Eventually, Umbert got close enough to Syele to knock her to the ground. He pinned her down with one foot, and pointed his blade at her face. She yielded and Umbert pulled her up, a look of relief on his face rather than triumph.

'He's good,' Esterel admitted. 'Not sure he's ruthless enough to defeat Gosse. But he'll give him a test.'

* * *

PEYRE WOKE EARLY the next day. He was full of excitement. Esterel's contest, which he had first seen as an extension of his brother's marriage to Liesel—an event to be endured—now consumed him. He took an interest in every result. But most of all, he wanted to win.

He arrived at the archery final before the contestants themselves. Liesel and Tegyn had surprised him by making it to the last eight of the competition. There was obviously something the Atrabians did with bow and arrow that the Guivergnais needed to learn.

He had to give his brother credit for identifying the deficiency and attempting to correct it. Peyre knew well enough what part of the problem was. Not a single nobleman had entered the contest. Those who had were either foreigners or common folk, who had learned the skill as woodsmen and hunters. What effect Liesel's participation might have, it was hard to say. He had his doubts that one contest, however famous it might become, could really change behaviour and custom. But it might help.

Alone with his thoughts, he considered his own contest, the melee. The four fights were scheduled last and Peyre's fight would be the first of them. His opponent was Benoit, son of Arnoul of Saliers. He'd heard he was a rare talent. Peyre had a few years on him, and he thought that might be enough. But he wasn't going to underestimate him.

Benoit's father would ride in the jousts that followed the archery. They were a military family and Arnoul had demonstrated an intelligence to match his physical prowess. Captured after the battle of Corbenay, he'd persuaded Peyre's father that he could be trusted and was released. He'd not put a foot wrong since—refusing to get drawn into subsequent rebellions. His presence in the contest, and that of his son, would help him recover his standing in the kingdom. Esterel wasn't one to hold grudges. But the man was a snake. Not to be trusted, and dangerous with it.

The three sides of the archery field began to fill. The citizens of Valennes were coming early to get a good spot to see their new queen. Food vendors rolled up, and the smell wafted in the air. Peyre was forced to buy a meat pie to keep his energy levels up. When he returned to his spot, guards from The Bastion had appeared. They were stationed along the row where the competitors would stand, ready to protect Liesel should anyone get ideas.

The crowd grew, several rows deep now. Small children sat on their father's shoulders; older ones tried their luck at pushing in. Before long, the eight archers appeared, marching to their positions. A cheer rose as people recognised Liesel. However she performed today, Peyre realised, she had become a favourite with the people.

The first shot was taken, as each archer took their turn to aim for the straw targets a considerable distance away. The final was enjoyable to watch, but it lacked the tension Peyre had hoped for. Liesel was out of the running, having to settle for seventh in the end. It became a shoot-out between Tegyn and Jesper, but Jesper was always far enough ahead of her that Peyre was never in doubt about the outcome. He had seen Jesper shoot his friend, Rimmon, from a much greater range. The distance set for this competition was no challenge for him.

Esterel appeared for the ceremony at the end. He awarded Jesper the main prize of a bag of coin, with smaller amounts for the second and third place finishers. Jesper looked embarrassed by the whole affair, while Tegyn held her bag aloft in triumph. Last, each finalist received a specially designed silver brooch to commemorate the competition. When Liesel consented to Esterel fixing her brooch to her top, the crowd roared with approval. Peyre was the only one amongst hundreds of spectators who took no joy from the moment.

As the crowd slowly dispersed, Peyre found Umbert, and they went for something to eat. Umbert faced his own test later today—combat with the giant Gosse—and they both shared an unspoken desire to distract themselves from what was to come. They made their way to the list field where two jousts were due, to decide who would face one another in tomorrow's final.

The field had raised seating on the two long sides. With nowhere else to go, the crowds were filling in already. Peyre and Umbert took their seats and watched as an acting troupe performed for the crowd. It was the old story of Will of the Forest, who proceeded to outwit the nobility of Guivergne when they clumsily tried to catch the heroic outlaw. Will was never without his trusty bow and Peyre realised just how ingrained the culture of combat was in Guivergne. The bow was the weapon of the commoner; the nobleman made war from horseback. There was a rigidity to it he hadn't witnessed elsewhere in Dalriya.

There was a stir when Esterel and Liesel arrived to watch, taking the royal seats. A small group of guests were with them. Loysse was there; and Coleta. Peyre looked away, preferring the solitary company of Umbert today. The actors finished their performance, and the tension was palpable as everyone waited for the first two knights to arrive.

One of the actors made the announcements, his voice loud enough to be heard above the muttering of hundreds of spectators. First was Domard, Duke of Martras. He had spared no expense on his appearance. His mail outfit was painted gold and purple, the colours of his house. The same colours decorated the barding of his stallion. He was a powerful and muscular bay who strutted about the field, tossing his head at the noise of the cheering crowd. Next came Florent, the new lord of Auriac. Even if Florent didn't have the income of his opponent, he too arrived in splendour. He had given his lordship of Auriac new colours of green and gold with ivy leaves and the images adorned his armour and that of his horse, just like the duke's. His mount was slimmer—a dun colour, and Peyre had never seen a more beautiful looking beast.

As they paraded about the field, settling at either end, Peyre appreciated the popularity of the joust. If the melee was the ultimate contest for the purist, this was a feast for the eyes that everyone could enjoy.

Each horseman looked like a metal clad monster, with their great helms hiding their faces from sight. It was a spectacle where the combatants fought in a manner most people could never emulate: a true celebration of nobility, with all its trimmings of wealth, power, and display.

The crowd seemed evenly split in their support. Florent was better known in Valennes; he was young and handsome, too. Domard had his supporters from Martras; and he was a duke, only beneath the king in status.

Each man had a squire, who now appeared, dipping under the railings that kept the crowd from the field of combat. They handed their masters their lances, blunted at the end to reduce the chance of injury. *Nonetheless*, Peyre thought, *this sport seems most dangerous. To strike one another at full charge requires some balls.*

Both men spent some time getting their lances into just the right position, couching them under their armpits so that their grip was secure. The lances they used were long and not easy to hold still. The rules said they should strike their opponent on their shield or chest. If they dipped lower or higher, they could cause serious, if not fatal, injury. It was for this reason that Esterel had been strict on who was allowed to enter the competition. To reduce the chances of an accident, only the best knights had been accepted.

When both men raised an arm, it was time. A horn blew, and they began their charge.

It was a long field, but even so, it took time for a horse in armour with a heavy rider to build up speed. This was where the mounts made their impact. Chosen for power as well as speed, they steamed forwards, throwing up clods of dirt as they accelerated. As they neared, the crowd held its breath. Peyre found himself both fearing and wanting the clash. The long lances passed first, and then the riders were past each other.

'They both hit?' Peyre asked, making his voice heard above the cheering.

'Yes,' Umbert replied. 'Florent's lance glanced off his opponent's armour. Domard, I think, hit Florent's shield.'

'That scores points?'

'I don't think so. His lance must break, signifying a true strike.'

Peyre nodded. He didn't fully understand the rules, but it hardly mattered. He observed the two opponents as they prepared to go again, from the opposite ends to the previous time. Their horses were breathing hard from the exertion. He wondered how many times the animals might be asked to charge back and forth until a winner was declared.

The horn blew a second time, and the knights charged. They came together, and a crack reverberated around the field. Martras was thrown into the air by the impact, landing yards away. Florent remained seated, riding to the other end of the field, holding a lance that had been snapped in half.

The cheering gave way to murmurs of concern. The Duke of Martras lay unmoving. Peyre got to his feet to watch as figures ran over to check on him. Florent dismounted, pulled off his helmet, and clunked across towards his opponent.

Peyre heard his brother's voice, shouting down for information. The figures about Martras gave hurried signals and a group of four men dashed towards them, carrying a stretcher between them. This didn't look good. But from his position, Peyre could hear no details of what the injury might be. He had seen for himself, however, how far Martras had been thrown. The landing could easily have broken bones or damaged skull or spine.

Florent stood, metal encased hands on hips, as Domard was gently lifted and lowered onto the stretcher, before being carried off.

'Quiet!' Peyre demanded of those around him, as the actor turned host tried to communicate with Esterel.

The crowd settled.

'Duke Domard is dazed, but awake, Your Majesty. He can talk, but is somewhat confused. Do you wish us to continue with the tournament?'

'It is what the duke would want,' Esterel decided. 'I will visit him after the joust and make sure our best people treat him.'

'That's a relief,' Peyre murmured. He couldn't help recalling his father's injuries after the Battle of Corbenay. He had never properly recovered. Hopefully, Domard only suffered from a blow to the head.

Florent departed the field to muted applause. It was a shame for him, but he had performed well and was into tomorrow's final. After a while, his potential opponents emerged. No doubt they had seen Domard stretchered out. Peyre wandered how much that would affect them.

First came Duke Auberi. Of course, Peyre recognised his colours from the battlefields on which his family had faced him. The silver lattice on a field of azure. They looked like a hero's colours, but the Duke of Famine didn't get a hero's reception. He was roundly booed and Peyre was neither surprised nor sympathetic. Even if he was now his brother-in-law and forgiven for his rebellion, it had still led to numerous deaths, and many in the crowd made their feelings known.

Auberi waved a hand, responding to the smaller number of cheers and ignoring the insult. He led his grey coloured mount to the far end of the field, while his opponent arrived. Lord Arnoul of Saliers was encased in black armour and rode a black stallion. His house colours of crimson and silver accentuated the dark colours. The crowd made a collective groaning noise. Here was another villain who had fought against the royal family at Corbenay. What was more, he had embraced the role with his raiment. The crowd had no one to cheer for.

'It's a shame they couldn't have changed the order,' Umbert suggested.

Peyre shrugged. 'I suppose that would have been more popular. But this is a jousting contest, Umbert,' he said, chiding his friend for his frivolity.

As before, the horn blew to start the first pass. Famiens and Saliers rode at pace, but neither one touched the other. Perhaps the fate of the duke in the previous encounter weighed on them because several passes followed and still there was no result. Umbert scored it one point apiece, since each of them had broken their lance once. The crowd muttered, growing tired of the impasse, while the two mounts panted and dripped sweat.

On the next pass, Saliers scored when his lance hit Duke Auberi's shield square on and splintered from the impact.

'Two-one,' Umbert said. 'The pressure is on Famiens now.'

Peyre knew it would now be like an oven inside those great helms. Meanwhile, he doubted Auberi could see very much through the narrow eye slit.

Both men hefted their lances and went again. The sound of cracking wood rang out around the field once more. For a moment, Peyre thought Auberi had clawed himself back into the contest. Then he realised both men had scored at once, meaning Saliers had his three points.

Esterel led the crowd in applause as both men dismounted and embraced on the field, their hair soaking wet and their faces red.

'So, Auriac against Saliers tomorrow,' said Umbert. 'Both dukes are defeated.'

'Yes,' said Peyre, feeling his insides drop. 'But I am full of nerves now, since I am the next to fight.'

'How do you think I feel?' Umbert asked him. 'I have to fight that brute, Gosse.'

If Peyre could have argued, he would have. But there was no doubt that Umbert had the worse draw.

PEYRE

VALENNES, KINGDOM OF GUIVERGNE, 676

Peyre strode out into the pit, a mix of dirt and sand. The crowd encircled him, bigger than it had been in his last fight. Liesel, Loysse, Auberi, and others looked down from the royal box. Esterel was waiting in the fighters' quarters, ready to come on next.

Peyre raised his sword, and the crowd cheered wildly for him. Of course, fighting Benoit, son of the traitor Saliers, he had known he would be the people's favourite. The acclaim felt good, but the truth was Peyre already felt good. Sword in hand and shield strapped to arm, his body brimmed with energy, eager to start. Training with Brancat again had helped more than he had anticipated. He hadn't realised how a few years away from the weapons master had affected him: he'd got too heavy and become a pace too slow. Now he felt fit and strong, and that made him a problem for anyone.

Benoit looked confident, practising his sword strokes. His hair was dark, his face angular, looking like nothing if not the son of his father. Peyre knew his opponent was quick and skilful with a blade. He couldn't let his own confidence defeat him. If he had to wait for his opportunity, he would. At this stage, winning was everything.

He raised his sword, and Benoit followed suit. They showed them to the crowd and to the queen. Then they began.

Peyre let Benoit come to him, the younger man's sword sizzling in and out, fast as a viper. Peyre made sure he had plenty of space in which to defend. He blocked and moved, his feet not stopping—not allowing Benoit to pin him down.

Once Benoit slowed, he went on the offensive. Unlike his opponent, Peyre led with his shield, waiting for the younger man to react. As soon as Benoit moved, Peyre swung his sword at him, putting force into the blow. Benoit had no choice but to block with his shield. Peyre rammed his own shield at him, but Benoit escaped by inches, darting away. Nonetheless, Peyre had shown him what he could do.

Peyre now faced a more defensive opponent. He let Peyre come at him, then counterattacked at speed. He was not so fast that Peyre couldn't stop him. But as the fight wore on, with neither man landing a blow, it became a battle of stamina. Peyre still thought he could get through such a test. But he became frustrated. This wasn't the fight he had wanted.

He glanced up at Liesel, looking down on him. Waiting for her husband's fight. And that was what Peyre needed. An injection of emotion—of anger—to put fire in his belly. He was being too careful, and if he wanted to beat the likes of Esterel and Sacha, he would have to show more than he was offering now.

He pressed forward again, then a skip, and he was launching himself in the air towards Benoit. It was too good an opportunity for the young man to resist—his sword snaked out and Peyre, ready, chopped down with his own, neutralising the strike. He landed, shield on shield, the weight of his body driving Benoit backwards. He let his anger surge, not content to let the young man escape. His sword punched forwards, his shield following, one after the other, too fast to avoid, too strong to ignore. His options diminishing, Benoit rammed his hilt towards Peyre's gut, aiming to wind him.

Seeing it in time, Peyre turned side on, the blow striking his hip instead. He twisted forwards, his shield driving at Benoit. The young man met it with his own shield, good enough to absorb the blow. But Peyre now had a free sword arm, and he smashed his hilt into his opponent's helm. It was a clean connection and the young man collapsed to the ground. Peyre had enough control to watch for the sword strike, which came at ankle height. He lunged forward, stepping onto Benoit's forearm, pinning his arm to the ground. Then his own blade was at the younger man's neck.

'Yield,' Benoit said quickly, soundly beaten.

He released his sword and Peyre offered him a hand, pulling him to his feet. He then raised his sword, meeting the crescendo of noise. He smiled, satisfied. He had won through. It was now up to his rivals to do the same.

He and Benoit left the pit together, through the door into the wooden building where the other fighters waited their turn and doctors and servants waited in case they were needed.

'You fight very well,' he told Benoit. 'I feel I should call you the viper from now on, due to the speed of your sword strike.'

He was pleased when Benoit grinned. It was a slit of a smile, but the eyes told him it was genuine enough. 'Then I should call you the bear,' Benoit answered. 'I've never taken blows as hard as that.'

'The bear,' Peyre said, smiling. 'I like that. Though I wonder if Lord Gosse would claim that name.'

Benoit shrugged. 'Maybe. I've watched him. He's a big fellow. But I doubt his blows land harder than yours. Anyway, good luck in the next bout. If you win again, it makes me look better.'

Peyre laughed. 'I intend to.'

He entered the fighters' quarters to get changed. Both Esterel and Elger were there waiting, sitting on separate benches. He said nothing to either, knowing that interruptions weren't welcome at this point. Anyway, it was his king and brother against the leader of his Guard, and he didn't know what to say either. They were soon called out to get ready for their fight. Peyre rushed, trying to make himself as presentable as possible. He did his best about the smell, splashing himself from a bowl of rosewater. He put clean clothes on and left, making his way out to the royal stand. Tegyn offered him a seat next to her and he stared down into the pit. It was empty.

'Where are they?' he demanded.

'Esterel's won already,' Tegyn told him, a wry smile on her face. 'Congratulations on your victory, by the way.'

'Yes, congratulations Peyre,' Liesel said next to her, and the rest of the company joined in.

Peyre gave his thanks, though he didn't think congratulations were in order. He'd expected to defeat Benoit; it would have been a humiliation if he hadn't. It was his next fight that mattered.

After a wait, during which Peyre stewed over his brother's quick victory, the two fighters entered the pit. It was the winner of this bout he would fight next, and according to one of the fighters—Miles of Corbenay—it was a foregone conclusion. Miles had admitted to Peyre that he'd never beaten Sacha. Peyre was more than interested to see just how good the Lord of Courion was.

The first moves of the fight were cagey, considering the two must have sparred so often in the past. Both men displayed solid skills in defence and offence. They moved well and when their shields came together, there seemed little difference in physical strength. Sacha's dominance came imperceptibly. He began to move and attack to a unique beat. His sword went through one combination after another —it could come from left or right, high or low, feinting here, an unorthodox angle there. Just when it looked like Miles was coping, the shield came in to put him on the back foot.

As for Miles, he showed no weaknesses. It was just that while he struggled to predict what attack would come next, everything he did seemed to be anticipated by Sacha. It was no surprise that the confidence of one friend soared, while that of the other sank.

When Sacha rattled off another series of sweeps, stabs and slashes, Miles appeared to be stuck in position, his sword and shield wafting at ghosts. He didn't follow Sacha's move to the side, nor did he avoid the shield to the head when it came. So, Sacha could also be brutal when necessary. As Miles staggered, Sacha pulled him backwards, sticking out a leg that sent him crashing to the ground. He avoided a wild sword swing, Miles now totally disoriented. With a backward flick of his sword, Sacha struck his friend's gauntlet, and Miles dropped his weapon. It was over.

The crowd applauded appreciatively. Sacha raised his sword to the royal stand, where Esterel had arrived for the last part of the fight, sitting on the opposite side of Liesel to Tegyn. Annoyingly, he looked like he hadn't broken a sweat.

Peyre had to admit, Sacha made the melee contest good to watch. And there was an uncanny similarity to the way Esterel fought. Peyre had watched his brother countless times. With a two-year age difference, Peyre—like all the boys his age—had witnessed his brother's skills blossom open-mouthed. Many in the training fields of Arbeost had tried to emulate Esterel and none succeeded. Peyre had managed, with Brancat's invaluable help, to come out of his brother's shadow by developing a style that suited him. He had to hope he had seen enough of Sacha to implement a plan that could work.

Peyre noticed those around him looking his way, as thoughts turned to tomorrow's contest. Esterel had one eyebrow raised.

'He's good,' Peyre admitted, feeling the need to say something. But that was all he was prepared to say. Let people say Sacha was the favourite to win tomorrow. He didn't think that would do his cause any harm.

'Well, I for one will cheer you on tomorrow,' Esterel said.

'Because you hope to face me instead of him?' Peyre asked.

Esterel shrugged and gave a coy smile. Peyre fixed a smile of his own on his face. How he burned with desire now. One more fight and he would face Esterel in the pit. There was nothing in the world he wanted more than to win this contest.

'What of our final fight?' Esterel asked him, perhaps sensing his stiffness. 'No one knows Umbert better than you.'

'Umbert's best quality is the ability to adapt to his opponent. He'll have a plan to contain Lord Gosse. As for Gosse, we've all seen what he brings.'

'It will be intriguing,' Esterel said, as the pair made their way out to the pit.

Gosse paced about, intimidating. Umbert didn't flinch, an impassive expression fixed on his face. For the sake of the contest, Peyre wanted Gosse to win. Of the two, he was the more dangerous to

Esterel. But now he saw his friend down there, he couldn't help but wish him victory.

Umbert's tactics were clear within moments. He moved around the edge of the pit, drawing Gosse onto him. He defended and moved away. The same thing, every time; not even once offering an attack of his own.

Gosse threw himself into his attacks but faced either an impenetrable wall, or a shadow that was gone before his sword swing arrived. The border lord growled with frustration as the fight wore on. The crowd, too, disliked Umbert's tactics, shouting at him to fight. Umbert showed nothing. That same, blank face looked out, concentrating on his task. He seemed prepared to do it all night. And he was asking Gosse an interesting question: how long could he continue without tiring?

'Fight me!' Gosse exploded. 'Are you a coward?'

It was an obnoxious insult to throw at someone fighting a much larger opponent and Peyre prickled with resentment. Some in the crowd repeated the accusation. But Umbert said nothing; not a frown or even a smile came to his face. It was as if he hadn't heard it at all. Instead, he offered the same look of concentration, ready to turn aside anything the bigger man offered.

Gosse threw himself into another attack. This time, after his shield and sword were turned away, he lunged at Umbert with one leg, aiming to kick him square in the chest.

It was a crude move and Umbert did the right thing in punishing it. He moved to Gosse's sword side and struck out for the first time, slashing at his unbalanced opponent. Gosse only just fended him off, getting his sword in front of enough of the strikes until he could bring his shield in. Perhaps Umbert should have thrown everything at his opponent in those frantic moments.

Because afterwards, Gosse was a different fighter.

Perhaps he only now realised he was in a real contest. He set himself for the long haul with no more complaint. He worked at Umbert, probing his defences, but no longer committed to an all-out attack. It made Umbert come at him more often and the fight became more even as they traded blows. Gosse matched Umbert's concentration, refusing to give his opponent an opening. The fight continued, the longest of the tournament by far. The crowd settled, appreciating the commitment and stamina of each man. As the contest lengthened, the stakes seemed to get even higher. Because after all this effort, one of them would still lose at the end.

The end seemed innocuous at first. Umbert didn't quite meet Gosse's shield barge with enough power. Suddenly, he was being pushed back. He threw himself forwards and Gosse took a step to the side, before swinging his blade into his midriff. Umbert doubled over in pain and Gosse's shield came down hard. Umbert crumpled to the ground.

Peyre stood and stared at Umbert's prone form, concerned after what had befallen Domard earlier in the day. But Umbert was alright, helped to his feet by Gosse, who was now all smiles. Everyone applauded them both when Gosse raised a tired sword arm to the sky.

'Umbert's done me a favour there, tiring him out,' Esterel declared.

Wishful thinking, Peyre suspected. Gosse had shown himself to be far more than a powerful brawler. *Looks like we both have our work cut out for us tomorrow, brother.*

PEYRE

VALENNES, KINGDOM OF GUIVERGNE, 676

Peyre woke late the next day. He felt the need to save his energy
for his fight with Sacha and kept to himself during the morning.
Esterel was in a private meeting with the Krykker chieftain, Maragin.
Peyre was interested to know what was being decided. But for now,
his king was keeping things close to his chest, as was his right.

He sought Umbert out at midday, and they took lunch together.

'How are the bruises?' he asked his friend.

Umbert grimaced. 'Always hurts more when you've lost.'

'That's true. Still, you impressed a lot of people last night.'

'That makes me feel a bit better.'

'The aches will be even worse tomorrow,' Peyre advised his friend,
in case he got too comfortable.

PEYRE ASKED ELGER, the captain of the Barissian Guard, to observe the
jousting final for him. He reported back with news of Arnoul of
Saliers' victory.

'Was it a good contest?' Peyre asked.

'Three strikes to one for Saliers,' Elger replied. 'It was enjoyable to
watch. I heard some talk afterwards that people thought Lord Auriac

was a little hesitant after what happened to the Duke of Martras yesterday. It's hard to say whether that's true.'

'And what news of the duke?'

'It's said he has a brain commotion. He was sick in the night and remains dizzy and disoriented. But he is conscious, and it's hoped he will recover.'

'How did you find your contest with my brother yesterday?'

'It was an honour to fight with the king, though I wish I had lasted longer. At no point did I feel comfortable against him. If you wish, Your Grace, I could try to give a more detailed analysis for you.'

'Not now. My head is full of Sacha today. If I win, I can talk with you. If I lose, there is no point.'

THE TIME TO fight came soon enough. Umbert and Elger helped him put on his armour. Unlike the plates of mail worn by the jousters, chain mail over a padded gambeson was the order of the day for the melee. One had to accept the risk of broken bones so that freedom of movement wasn't restricted.

They accompanied him to the pit. The biggest crowd he had yet seen awaited him. As he passed through well-wishers and entered the wooden building, the excitement reached him and he felt his adrenaline rise. When he saw Sacha was already waiting on a bench, it surged further. *Yes, just as well I've had a relaxing day.* He'd learned, from the fighting in Guivergne and Magnia, that the wait before battle could be as exhausting as the combat itself. He needed all his strength and energy now. Sacha didn't look his way, and Peyre didn't mind. *I'll play mind games if I have to. But it's not my style.*

They were called out. Sacha went first, still ignoring him. A wall of noise greeted them as they entered. Peyre's eyes were drawn to the royal stand. Esterel wasn't there—readying himself somewhere for his own bout. But otherwise, it was full of onlookers. He saw Liesel, wearing a garland of flowers around her head. He even saw the Krykker, Maragin, looking down at him. For a moment, Peyre wondered how she might have fared in this contest, wielding Bolivar's Sword. But then he scolded himself. *By the gods, focus Peyre!*

At last, Peyre and Sacha looked at one another. Peyre liked to think his expression was nearly as cold as his opponent's. There had never been any love lost between them. But none of that mattered. He had his plan. He had to stick to it, whether it worked or not. If he implemented it as best he could, he'd have nothing to regret. He let the passion—the controlled anger he needed to be at his best—take him.

He raised his sword, and Sacha did likewise. Another wave of noise roiled from the crowd and Peyre was surging forwards.

He'd learned a handful of things from observing Sacha's fight with Miles. He liked a leisurely start; warming up and allowing his strokes to flow as his confidence grew. Well, he'd get none of that from Peyre today.

He was immediately onto Sacha. He hurried and harried. He forced him to defend; got as close as he could. It came at some cost, as Sacha got a strike in on his thigh, but Peyre would worry about that later. He was going for a quick win—wasn't about to fight on Sacha's terms. He would lose a test of skill. That was plain. But Sacha would get no time or space from Peyre, just a grappling, bruising encounter. He punched with shield and sword, not attempting to deploy classic strokes. As soon as Sacha moved, he followed him, giving him no respite; no time to think or breathe. Peyre's own lungs were soon burning, but he knew Sacha would be the same.

They came together, Sacha only just pulling away in time to avoid Peyre's head-butt. Sacha snarled in disgust, then grabbed onto him. 'You think to fuck me as well as my sister?' he said in Peyre's ear.

But Peyre had anticipated a taunt, and he barely heard the words, never mind let them affect him. They pushed each other, pulling apart. There was nothing Peyre wanted more than a few moments to gain his breath. His heart strained with the effort, and his limbs felt weak and shaky. But he didn't allow himself even one. He forced himself to go again; was rewarded with the look of dismay that briefly flitted across Sacha's face. It encouraged him, helped him to re-double his efforts. *I'm going to win this!*

Sacha feinted, then moved to the side, finally buying himself some space. Peyre wasn't having it, coming after him like a dog with a bone. He didn't even try to block Sacha's strike—knew Sacha was too good for that. Instead, he braced himself. It struck his chest, a painful stab that ran up and down his torso. But he took it and had both sword and shield ready. Shield met shield. He turned his sword wrist so that the weapon was horizontal, and then rammed it into Sacha's neck.

It worked. He saw Sacha's eyes bulge as he staggered backwards, defenceless, but somehow stayed on his feet. Peyre suffered a moment of indecision as victory suddenly appeared before him. This was his chance, but he didn't want to hurt the man. He twisted, leaned his weight into his shield and shoulder barged him. Sacha nearly got out of the way, but not quite. Peyre clipped him and it was enough to knock him off balance and send him to the ground.

Sacha dropped his sword, putting a hand to his neck. He was choking. Peyre waved a desperate hand to the doctors in the building, and they hurried over. With the battle over, his rage gone, a feeling of dread stole over him. He didn't want to have killed the man. Suddenly, the whole contest, that he had desired to win so much, lost its appeal.

The doctors rolled Sacha onto his side. Gradually, painfully slowly, Sacha regained control of his breathing, until he was drawing in large lungfuls of air. He rubbed the water from his eyes and turned to Peyre.

'Sorry,' Peyre said, kneeling next to him awkwardly.

Sacha lifted himself up to a sitting position, knocking away the helping hand of a doctor.

'You won,' he said to Peyre. 'Fair and square.'

Relieved, Peyre offered him a hand and pulled him to his feet. 'I'm sorry about your sister, too,' he said.

'That's a conversation for another day,' Sacha said. Obviously, Peyre wasn't off the hook for everything.

They picked up their swords and waved them to the crowd and the royal box. It was only now that Peyre noticed his reception was more muted than he would have expected.

So, they don't like the way I won. No doubt, they'd have preferred me to receive a gallant defeat. That's not my way. They might as well learn it now.

He turned, tramping away. They'd get their gallant hero next. And yet. He did wonder how Esterel would fare against Gosse.

Peyre and Sacha changed in awkward silence but made their way together to the royal stand where they were quickly found seats on opposite sides. No one spoke to either of them, perhaps wary of offence. There was still some wait for Esterel and Gosse to arrive, the organisers perhaps building the tension for the final event of the day. As conversation warily restarted around him, he noticed Maragin shuffle towards him.

She lent in. 'I like the way you fight,' she offered.

'Thank you,' Peyre said, with genuine gratitude. He had won against the odds yet felt like a pariah for it. He made a gesture at the crowd. 'I don't think it entertained everyone.'

'Fighting is not for entertainment,' Maragin said, letting her distaste show. 'It is for survival.'

Peyre nodded. She was probably right.

The crowd stirred once more, excitement and anticipation rekindled, as Esterel and Gosse entered the pit. This was the kind of contest they loved, Peyre thought sourly. The hero and the monster. And the hero must win.

The noise built to a crescendo as they began. It wasn't lost on Peyre, that this was essentially a rematch of his own fight. Gosse was all over Esterel, trying to make it physical. Esterel was all movement and counterattack. His brother had started sharper than Sacha had. He feinted, his feet appearing to go in one direction and his body in another. More than once it left Gosse looking slow and ponderous.

Before long, Esterel was putting more venom into his sword blows as well. Somehow, he was able to dive out of the way and land a strike at the same time. He feinted to use his shield but usually withdrew it, not wishing to get involved in a shoving match. Losing his temper, Gosse charged him. Esterel sidestepped, swinging his sword high. The crowd gasped.

'He caught him in the face,' Tegyn said.

'Good job these blades aren't sharpened,' Peyre said.

Gosse seemed taken aback by the blow. Disheartened, maybe. He backed away from Esterel. 'Come on, arsehole,' he shouted at his king, gesturing for Esterel to come to him for a change.

Many in the crowd booed his words. Esterel smiled. Peyre recognised that smile. It didn't bode well for Gosse.

Esterel moved on to the attack, targeting Gosse's shield side. Blow after blow came, never from the same angle twice. Gosse moved his shield up and down with his opponent's strikes, his sword ready to retaliate as soon as he had the chance.

Esterel paused to take breath. Gosse launched his blade in an overhead strike. Peyre knew Esterel was faking. Maybe Gosse did too, but it had been just too tempting a sight. As the blade came down, Esterel was leaping. Again, it seemed like Gosse moved in slow motion compared to the king. Esterel's blade followed Gosse's and struck the big man on the hand.

Gosse grinned. His blade lay on the ground. He knew he'd lost, but he wasn't yet defeated. He charged at Esterel with his shield, trying to tuck him up, maybe even grab him. Gosse aimed his shield for Esterel's sword to deny him use of it. Then, the sword was gone and Esterel was spinning in mid-air as Gosse moved into the empty space. As Esterel's spin ended and he came back to earth, his shield struck the back of Gosse's head. The border lord's momentum carried him stumbling forwards, then his balance was gone, and he landed heavily on the ground.

'Yield,' he grunted as Esterel's blade hovered above him.

Esterel groaned as he got the big man back to his feet. He then took in the crowd's applause, holding his sword aloft. His big goofy smile broke out and he approached the royal stand, where he blew a kiss to Liesel. The queen got to her feet and Peyre watched as she took the garland from her head and flung it down to him. Esterel speared it with his blade, and it slid down the length of the sword to his arm.

Tegyn cried out as she got to her feet and applauded. Everyone in the box followed her lead. Reluctantly, Peyre did the same. The crowd around the pit was cheering wildly. It was a clever gesture, Peyre supposed, to celebrate the marriage and win over the people with the romance of it. The shouting and cries of delight just wouldn't stop, and Peyre felt a blackness leaking into his heart.

* * *

PEYRE WOKE the next morning with a sense of guilt. He had been dreaming of today's fight. The details of his dream hovered beyond his mind, unwilling to be seen. But he knew he had killed Esterel.

He washed and dressed, following his usual routine, but something was missing. That potent desire to win Esterel's contest had gone. Why, he didn't know. He had never given less than his all in a fight. Didn't think he could when it came to it. But he couldn't help thinking it would be better for everyone if he lost today.

He went down for breakfast, choosing to sit alone in a corner of the hall. He had a long day ahead of him with nothing to fill the time until the fight with his brother. It occurred to him that leaving The Bastion and its environs for a while would do him good. Without wasting more time, he left the hall and made his way past the guards and out of the fortress.

He drew attention as he passed the pit, the archery field and the list field, from stares and whispers to friendly shouts. The contest had consumed the city in the last few days and a final between royal brothers was perhaps the biggest talking point of all. Peyre wondered what people would do with themselves when the structures were taken down and the fields returned to grass.

He felt a lessening of tension as he left it all behind and walked through the centre of the city. There were shops and stalls here, but he wasn't in the mood. Instead, he made for the east gate of the city. The untamed eastern part of the city always drew him. He passed through the gate and walked along the bridge over the Cousel. He had been warned, plenty enough, not to go into the eastern half of the city alone. He had an entire guard back at the Bastion, paid for from his own pocket. Yet here he was, about to do just that.

Until, walking along the bridge towards him, he saw a face he knew. Two faces, in fact, but one held him. It was the face of Farred, the companion of Duke Walter of Barissia. It held such a sadness that Peyre knew instantly what had happened. Next to Farred was a lanky spearman, whom Peyre recognised as the friend of Lord Gosse but whose name escaped him.

When Farred spotted him, recognition came to the man's face, but the expression became even more grim.

'Lord Farred,' Peyre said. 'Sul,' he said, nodding to the spearman, remembering his name just in time. 'It's Walter, isn't it?'

'He's dead,' Farred confirmed. 'I've come to give the story to your brother, the king.'

Peyre struggled to imagine what he must be going through. 'Of course. Esterel is at The Bastion. I will take you there immediately.'

ESTEREL MET with Farred in his council room, with what one might call an extended council. Liesel was there. She sat ashen faced, in shock. Then there was Caisin, Sacha, Miles, Loysse, Auberi, and Peyre. Maragin the Krykker stood against one wall. Lord Gosse had also been summoned, presumably because his man, Sul, was there. The pair stood solemnly by the other wall as everyone listened to Farred's account.

'I woke to find him still lying next to me, his throat cut, the bedding red with blood. I sensed a presence in the room.' Farred's eyes spoke of horror, but his voice was dispassionate, as if telling a story he had already told hundreds of times. 'I knew it was Inge. I grabbed a sword intending to strike her down. But I couldn't see or hear her.'

'You're sure it was Inge?' Maragin asked him. 'Not Ezenachi, or some other?'

'Yes, I'm sure. It is typical of her to spare me. I saved her life once, at Burkhard Castle. Only Inge could have such a twisted sense of honour that led her to spare me while she murdered Walter in his sleep.'

'Killing in such a way bears no resemblance to the way Ezenachi has behaved up to now,' Peyre added.

'And you believe Duke Leopold authorised this?' Esterel asked Farred.

Farred looked at him. 'Inge does what she likes. But does he know and approve? Of course. He will now claim the duchy as Walter's heir. It will give him the four duchies he needs to claim the imperial title with legitimacy. It may be enough to break the will of his opponents.'

Peyre momentarily closed his eyes with the pain. He supposed his time living with Walter in Coldeberg had not been very long. But it had been an important time in his life and Walter had been like a father to him. When he opened them, he found Esterel studying him. Esterel then looked at his wife, Liesel, whose uncle had been slain. Finally, a glance at Maragin.

'We cannot let this stand.' His voice was quiet and controlled, but there was steel in it. 'Duke Leopold has had the queen's uncle murdered. If he becomes emperor through this act, Brasingia will become a direct threat to Guivergne. I see no alternative but war. I intend to raise the royal standard and ask all those who owe me service to raise their forces. Does anyone advise me against this?'

Esterel had complete mastery of the room and of his kingdom. No one said a word, whatever their private thoughts.

Peyre felt a wave of gratitude and loyalty. Walter's death didn't really mean very much to Esterel. He was doing this for Liesel. For Peyre, even. At last, Leopold would get the justice he richly deserved. The empire would no longer sit cravenly and turn a blind eye to the danger on its southern border. He felt a wolfish grin come to his face.

Esterel saw it and smiled. 'I am sorry, brother. Our bout will have to wait. I must ask you to leave for Morbaine and raise an army.'

Peyre returned the smile, offering his hand, which Esterel took in the warrior's grip. 'Another time, Your Majesty.'

PART II
THE PRICE OF WAR

SANC * PEYRE * LIESEL * JESPER *
BELWYNN

JESPER

VALENNES, KINGDOM OF GUIVERGNE, 676

King Esterel's messengers travelled to all parts of Guivergne. An invasion of the empire seemed inevitable.

But this meeting is more important than any of that, Jesper told himself. *Whether the king believes it, I'm not sure.*

The meeting, held in Esterel's private chambers, was certainly exclusive. No officials were present to have their say. His brother and his new queen were there: Jesper saw them both as allies. Peyre and Liesel had witnessed Ezenachi's power and seemed to understand the urgency of stopping him before it was too late. The only others present were the Krykker, Maragin, and Farred. As veterans of the Isharite Wars, their advice was crucial.

'Collecting more weapons seems to rest on finding the where-abouts of Gyrmund and Moneva,' Peyre said. 'Since you and Gyrmund were close friends, we thought you might be able to help with that, Farred?'

Farred shook his head. 'I wish I knew.' There was still a rawness to the man's voice. He mourned Duke Walter deeply. That was clear. Jesper had suffered his own losses recently and sympathised with the man. 'I would very much like to see Gyrmund again,' Farred said. 'But as far as I know, Gyrmund and Moneva told no one where they were going. That was the point. And knowing Gyrmund, he found some-where so remote that their seclusion could last forever.'

'Then we are at a dead end,' Esterel said, unsatisfied.

Jesper knew the king disliked this talk of magic and legend. He wasn't as hostile as his father had been; but he shared the same beliefs.

'Maragin has the sword and dagger,' Esterel continued. 'Jesper might cross the Lantinen and find the spear. Three of the seven weapons. Will that be enough?'

'We are not quite at a dead end,' the Krykker chieftain said. Jesper had witnessed Maragin's authority in her homeland. It seemed to extend here, because every time she spoke, people made an extra effort to listen. 'There is Belwynn. She had the power to communicate with those close to her.'

'Belwynn?' Jesper repeated. 'I thought you were set against involving her in this?'

Maragin closed her eyes with a deep sigh. 'I've been thinking otherwise. I've held onto Toric's Dagger all this time. It allowed Belwynn to forget her past. To start a new life. But maybe she needs to be told what is happening. Make the choice for herself. And if Guiv-ergne and Brasingia are truly about to go to war,' she continued, a rebuke in her tone, 'I can hardly rely on their help to deal with Ezenachi. It wouldn't be a bad thing, in these circumstances, to gather as many of Madria's weapons as we can.'

'Where is she?' Jesper asked. It was the question on everyone's lips. After the Krykker's revelations about Belwynn Godslayer, they all shared the same rapt look.

'Elana returned to her family.'

'Yes, but—' Farred began. 'It wasn't Elana.'

Maragin shrugged. 'Who was it? That is not a simple question to answer. Who is she now, after all this time? If there is a part of her that is still Belwynn, perhaps she can help us. I believe she is our best chance of locating more of the weapons.'

'Her family home being Magnia?' Esterel asked. 'And you would be willing to go there now?'

'Aye,' said the Krykker. 'I will send Stenk back to my people to explain my absence.'

'Who will go with Maragin?' Esterel asked.

Farred shook his head when eyes turned to him. 'No. I would return to Barissia. My experience is in war, not dark magic such as this. My future lies in avenging Walter. But I wish you well.'

And so, everyone looked to Jesper.

I can't very well let her travel to Magnia alone, he told himself. *Even if that's what I would prefer.* Jesper had spent enough time with Rimmon and Sanc to lose his fear of magic. *But I am scared witless at the thought of meeting Belwynn's shade.*

* * *

Jesper and Maragin rode south with Peyre and his Barissian Guard. Peyre would raise his forces in Morbaine and then march them to join with the army of Guivergne. They passed through the territory conquered from the Middians. It was a familiar route, one they had all taken plenty of times over the last few years.

All except Maragin. Jesper assumed this was the farthest south she had ever been. Not that she seemed in the least bit awed by the experience. Some of Peyre's younger warriors would gawp at her and she would stare straight back until they looked away.

Jesper wondered at her resilience. She was not young anymore—she'd seen off one threat to her people already, when the Isharites had taken the lands of the Krykkers. She'd led the resistance, hiding underground with her rock walkers, attacking her enemies where they least expected it. Then she had taken Bolivar's Sword and served as one of Belwynn's champions. Still, Jesper considered, looking at her. She didn't seem to have lost any of her strength. The tough, bark-like skin of the Krykkers covered her torso: it gave her a natural armour that weighed nothing and needed no maintenance.

'You have a question?' she asked, noticing his look.

'I had thought you might have passed the sword on by now,' he admitted. *Perhaps not to Stenk*, he said to himself. *Loyal and brave, but not of Maragin's stature.* 'To a younger warrior.'

Maragin frowned at the idea, gripping the hilt of the weapon as if for reassurance. 'This sword belongs to me,' she said in a fierce voice. 'No one else can be trusted with it.'

She was clearly possessive of the great weapon. A thought struck Jesper, and it made him smile.

'What is funny?' the Krykker demanded.

'I was just wondering about when Rabigar returned from Halvia. Whether you ever let him hold the blade again? After all, he was its previous owner.'

'No I did not,' Maragin answered. 'And he knew not to ask.' She sighed. 'I do miss him, though.'

When Jesper had reached the realm of the Krykkers to fetch Maragin, he had learned of Rabigar's death some four years ago. Such news had been hard to take.

Rabigar had been the catalyst for Jesper's adventures. He had arrived at their home with Gunnhild and Stenk, half-dead after an attack from a white wyrm. But it had not stopped the Krykker from completing his quest to locate the Giants' Spear. Too ill to make the return journey, Jesper had taken his place. Now Rabigar was gone. Rimmon, too. He had heard nothing from Sanc and Herin and feared the worst. Tadita was gone; even Rab, the foolish dog, had jumped at Sanc and disappeared to whatever other land the boy had been transported to. Jesper had never felt so alone.

'You, too, miss others,' Maragin said, observing him.

'Yes,' Jesper admitted. 'I miss my dogs, as well as my friends.' *Though I shall refrain from mentioning that Rab is named after Rabigar. That might not go down so well.*

'It is about time you took a female to marry,' Maragin advised. 'You are past the ideal age already.'

Jesper nodded. 'I'll bear that in mind.'

* * *

THEY LEFT Peyre in Morbaine and continued their ride south through the duchy. Jesper was known well enough in these parts to be given passage through people's estates without question, despite his unusual companion. Many knew him as the archer who had shot dead his friend, the sorcerer Rimmon. The episode seemed to have given him a certain mystique and the people he spoke with on their journey were perhaps less surprised to find a Krykker in his company than otherwise.

Some glanced at Maragin's sword, buckled at her waist, guessing what she carried. But when Jesper explained he was on the business of the king and the duke, no one questioned it. Even those who hadn't gone to Magnia with Peyre last year had heard all about it. Ezenachi was a name on everyone's lips—a dark threat to discuss over a pint on an evening, or to threaten youngsters with. Some even looked reassured to learn their rulers were sending people such as Jesper and Maragin south. The threat seemed so much closer in Morbaine than in the rest of Guivergne.

Once in Magnia, it felt even more real. An uneasy peace had come to the kingdom since the battle with Ezenachi's forces last year. The god had declared a truce based on a new border and the Magnians had no choice but to accede. Still, no one expected the peace to last. The question everyone asked one another was when the enemy might return.

For several reasons, Jesper thought it right that they first visit with Elfled and the new king, Ida. They were directed to the chain of castles from where the Magnians had issued and fought Ezenachi's invading force. These fortifications had been built during the Magnian civil war. They now represented the southern border of a reduced Magnia. A few miles south of them was the expanded land of the Lippers. A people who had dwelt on the margins of Dalriya for generations—almost forgotten. Now transformed by Ezenachi into the greatest danger Dalriyans had faced since the Isharites.

I wonder if such threats will ever end? Jesper asked himself. *Or is life merely a never-ending cycle of one group brutalising another? After all, it's said the Magnian realm was created by invaders who stole this land from the Lippers. Are we unable to live in peace?*

Ida was directing his kingdom from one of these castles. When Jesper explained he had business on behalf of Guivergne with the new king, he and Maragin were allowed inside and taken to wait in a small reception room. Jesper had no doubts Ida and Elfled were busy. The government must be stretched. Thousands of refugees from the conquered south had to be cared for, while they had to prepare for war, whenever it returned.

It was sad to see the Magnians brought so low. Rimmon had given much of his life to keep this kingdom protected. He had lost his life in its defence. *It isn't right that my friend's efforts are in tatters. I must have faith that our joint project will pay off. And somehow, Sanc must find a way to help us all.*

Elfled and Ida arrived. Jesper had always admired the sun-kissed beauty of the Queen of the Magnians. Now he was shocked to see her look so weary. It was as if she carried the weight of the world on her shoulders. Her son looked no better—he seemed adrift in a new world of responsibilities he had no experience of. He looked blankly from Jesper to Maragin, allowing his mother to do the talking. Jesper hoped they presented a better face to their people. If not, Magnian unity could quickly disintegrate.

'We are honoured by your visit, chieftain Maragin,' Elfled said.

'We come with King Esterel's approval,' Jesper explained. He glanced at the Krykker. 'Maragin believes we might find Belwynn here.'

Ida's eyebrows rose in surprise. Elfled's didn't. *She knows something.*

'What of aid from Guivergne?' Elfled asked. 'We sorely need it here.'

'Esterel is raising his armies,' Jesper told her. 'He plans to invade Brasingia.'

'Invade the empire? How will a war help us?' Elfled looked distressed. 'Guivergne is a wealthy land, and they are wasting their resources on this?'

'It may not be so unhelpful. If Duke Leopold takes the imperial title, the empire will not lift a finger against Ezenachi. We know Inge's position on that. Dalriya needs someone else on the throne.'

Elfled shook her head, unconvinced. 'We will see what comes of it. I still say it is madness.' She sighed. 'As for Belwynn. She made her home here after the Isharite Wars. Edgar always believed she had earned her peace; her anonymity. What do you want with her?'

'The weapons,' Jesper said, unable to keep the surprise from his voice. He tried hard to avoid an accusatory tone. 'You argued yourself, that is what we should focus on. Belwynn could help us collect them.'

Elfled sighed again. 'I don't know how much help she will be. I hope you are not expecting the old Belwynn.'

'Maragin told me her story. Even so, she has knowledge and powers no one else does.'

Elfled nodded. 'She returned to Kirtsea. The village Elana was from.'

'How did I not know this?' Ida asked, sounding astonished.

'Your father and I wanted her left in peace.'

'But I am king now!'

Elfled grimaced. 'You are right, Ida. I'm sorry. I should have told you, but with everything else—'

Ida looked at Jesper and Maragin. 'I don't know how much longer Magnia will last. By all means, see what aid Belwynn can offer. She is a Magnian, after all. She has a duty to help.'

There was something Jesper needed explained. 'She returned to Kirtsea... as Elana?'

Elfled nodded. 'She returned as Elana. To Elana's family.' The queen looked uncomfortable, eyes refusing to meet Jesper's. Ida looked shocked.

Jesper let out a whistle. It was the strangest thing he had heard.

'Try to imagine everything she went through and everything she lost before you judge her,' Maragin said.

'Of course,' Jesper agreed. 'I'm just glad I've been warned of it.'

* * *

KIRTSEA LAY due west and Jesper and Maragin wasted no time in heading for the Magnian coast. It had now been a relentless week of travelling. Jesper had lived through worse before and the Krykker's stamina seemed unbreakable. They pushed on, expecting as much from their mounts as they expected of themselves.

Kirtsea lay in a remote spot, accessed by a dirt track. It was the most ordinary looking fishing village one might find. Strange to think that Madria had spoken to Elana, a fisherman's wife, of all the possible candidates she could have selected. It was just more evidence that the games the gods played were beyond his comprehension.

Jesper made sure he asked for Elana rather than Belwynn. He was directed to a simple wattle and daub house. It faced the sea and was set apart from the nearest dwellings. As he and Maragin led their horses over, he found he was full of nerves at what he might find.

They stopped outside the house. She was sitting in a wicker chair, looking out to sea. Blonde hair so fair as to be almost white; piercing blue eyes; and a face and body that said she was still in her twenties. Impossible, of course. Jesper had never met Elana—she was dead before he had arrived in Dalriya. To see her body risen from the grave, looking as alive as anyone else, made his skin crawl.

Belwynn looked at them, no surprise showing on her face. 'I knew someone would come eventually,' she told them. 'After what has befallen Magnia. I didn't expect you, Maragin.' She stood. 'Come, your horses need looking after. Then we can talk.'

Inside, Belwynn's house was as simple as it was from the outside. Part of Jesper felt it strange that the greatest hero of Dalriya had ended up here. Another part wasn't so surprised. And after all, for someone with Belwynn's fame, the only way she could have escaped the world would have been to assume another person's identity. He wondered whether that had prompted her to make her fateful decision.

She sat them down with a fish supper and mugs of ale. *Simplicity can taste good*, Jesper reminded himself. 'You are not joining us?' he asked the Magnian.

Belwynn gave him a small smile. 'I rarely eat. I don't need food or water.'

Jesper tried to control his reaction, deeply uncomfortable with the comment. 'I see,' he muttered.

'I remember you, Jesper, in case you wondered,' Belwynn said. 'You came over from Halvia with Oisin the Giant.' She smiled at a memory. 'How is Rabigar?' she asked Maragin.

'Dead these four years.'

Belwynn's head dropped. 'I'm sorry. I shouldn't be surprised by it. But time has flown so fast the last few years, I find it hard to keep up. Rabigar dead. At least tell me his last years were good.'

'Very good. The best of his life, he would tell me.'

Belwynn nodded. 'That makes it easier to bear. There are so few of us left now. That little group who set out from Magnia to take back Toric's Dagger. We paid a heavy price. Just as well we had no idea what we were letting ourselves in for.'

A silence settled on them.

'You have the dagger?' Belwynn asked at last.

'Here,' said the Krykker. 'You wish to see it?'

'Of course.' Belwynn took the weapon, pulling the blade from its sheath.

The weapon that had killed two gods. It wasn't so special to look at, Jesper decided. The only thing that set it apart was the runic inscription on the thin sliver of a blade.

'I have been thinking of it more and more, lately,' Belwynn explained. 'It could be the only thing in the world that sets me free,' she added with a bitter smile.

Is that how it works? Jesper wondered. *She is simply a shadow that doesn't age or die?* It didn't bear thinking about. He wished Rimmon were here to deal with such matters.

'I suppose you plan to kill this new god?' she asked.

'Aye,' Maragin said. 'You've not thought to get involved yourself? You're closer to these events than me, after all.'

'I've done my part,' Belwynn said. 'As you have done yours, Maragin. It's time for others to do theirs.'

'You have family here?' Jesper asked Belwynn.

She looked at him, as if suspicious of some hidden barb. 'Yes. Two daughters and their children. I look after the bairns often. They have not rejected me, if that's what you are asking. Even though I now look like their sister rather than their mother. Perhaps I don't have long left. When they grow older than me, things will change, I am sure.'

'Your husband?' Jesper asked, aware he was treading on thin ice.

Belwynn gestured to the door. 'Lost at sea. Eight years ago now.'

'I'm sorry.'

'No need. He always used to say his time on the waves was loaned to him. Sooner or later, the ocean would call in its debts. He was right. And I don't think he ever suspected, like he surely would now. So you see, If I hadn't come back here, Elana's daughters would have been orphans. No one can tell me I made the wrong choice.'

'I wouldn't presume to pass judgement,' Jesper said quickly.

Belwynn made a face as if she didn't believe him. 'Soren warned me about Madria. Warned me I would lose myself to her. And I came very close. If I hadn't escaped her when I did, I wouldn't have escaped her at all. Now, no doubt, people are asking, "What did Belwynn do? She left us defenceless." I disagree. I showed them the way. Here,' she said and gave Jesper the dagger. 'You have the dagger and the sword. That's all we needed.'

'Agreed,' Maragin said. 'But Ezenachi has an army, just like Diis had. It wouldn't hurt us to have the other weapons.'

'What do you want from me?' Belwynn asked.

'I want the whereabouts of the others. You can still contact people telepathically?'

'Maybe. Or maybe not, now Madria is gone. I've never tried, and I have no intention of doing so. Belwynn is gone. Can you not see that?'

'Moneva and Gyrmund,' Maragin said, persisting. 'They have the right to decide for themselves if they wish to help.'

'They made their decision,' Belwynn countered. 'They've gone. If they wanted to return, they would have. Take my advice, Maragin. Pass the sword and dagger on to others. Let the next generation play their part. You've done everything expected of you. Once you accept that, you can find peace.'

'But your daughters and grandchildren,' Jesper argued. 'This place is perilously close to the Lipper border. The next push and it will be lost. Do you know what he does to his victims? Turns them into mindless slaves. Herin was one such. He told us after he was released from it. He had memories of doing terrible things. Don't you want to save your family from such a fate?'

'Herin still lives?'

'Yes. He has left Dalriya to find help.'

'How was he released from this slavery?'

'A lad called Sanc who has gone with Herin. He has magic. He found a way to free him.'

'Then there is your answer, Jesper. This Sanc and others like him. They are the ones who must find a way. It will be a different path to the one Soren and I trod. And that is how it should be.'

'He's gone with Herin,' Jesper said. 'Until he returns—if he returns —it's still up to us to do what's right.'

'What's right,' Belwynn repeated. 'You can take my advice or leave it. But I won't be lectured to. I won't be persuaded. It's been a long time since I've been swayed against my better judgement. Those days are gone. Feel free to leave whenever it suits you.'

SANC

TYRIAN GULF, 676

Sanc and Lenzo were given the use of a fast ship and its crew for their crossing by Amelia the Widow. It sped west across the Tyrian Gulf, cutting through the waves. Rab whined for the most part of the first day, before he was sick all over the deck. After that, he seemed to settle, to everyone's relief.

The captain turned north, hugging the coast. The worst of winter was over, but the sea was still choppy, and he took no risks. Sanc saw sandy beaches and spiky grass; forbidding, tree-lined cliffs; and they passed the occasional fishing village, which looked no different to those he'd seen in Scorgia. He had to rely on Lenzo for any understanding of what the interior was like.

'There are no cities this far north,' the prince told him. 'Most settlements are small, but even many of these have earth and wood fortifications. Raiding each other's lands has become the way of life on this border. It's only recently that the Nerisians have deployed larger armies for conquest. The Kassites weren't ready for that.'

They sailed on until they came to a cove which the captain was sure lay in Kassite territory. There was a larger settlement here and more ships than Sanc had seen since they'd left Arvena. Their ship had no space for bulky goods, but Sanc wasn't surprised to learn that Amelia had given the captain a stock of precious items: jewellery, spices, fragrances, and other items that would fetch a high price. They docked and Sanc wobbled along the pier, trying to find his land legs. He and Lenzo bid the captain farewell and made their way into the settlement.

The Kassites they passed stared and muttered at Rab as he walked dutifully beside Sanc. For his part, Sanc got his first sight of Kassites. They looked little different to the Scorgian ruling class or the Nerisian warriors he had fought. Tall, often broad; men and women grew their hair long and braided it to be manageable. Almost all were blue eyed, pale skinned, and there were even more shades of blonde and red hair here than in Arvena. Their clothes were woollen, designed for warmth in a cold climate. Sanc knew there were a dozen things that made him an outsider.

He let Lenzo do the talking. For a while, he assumed the Kassites the prince spoke with had a different language. Only gradually did he pick out individual words—their accents so thick that it seemed everything was pronounced differently.

Lenzo did nothing to hide the truth behind their visit. When asked bluntly why he had no bodyguards, he told them he had Sanc. The Kassites eyed Sanc with interest. They weren't hostile—far from it. So close to the Nerisian border, these folk must have been involved in the recent years of war. Allies from across the sea seemed welcome.

A young man, about the same age as Sanc, agreed to take them to the hall of his chieftain for a few coins from Lenzo's pouch. His beard and eyebrows were as blonde as his hair. He looked more fisherman than warrior, but he had a long, thick knife at his belt that looked like it could do some serious damage. For more coin, three horses were found. They were a bit on the thin and straggly side, but Lenzo was assured it wasn't far to their destination.

'What about your creature?' the Kassite asked, gesturing at Rab.

'He can keep up,' Lenzo assured him.

There was a path out of the Kassite settlement, but it was nothing more than a slick of mud and their guide ignored it, leading them cross country. Large swathes of territory lay uncultivated—plains at first, that were gradually interrupted by the curves of hill and valley and the appearance of woodland. They passed some isolated settlements: single farms and hamlets. Several were abandoned. Perhaps it was the time of year, but it seemed a hard landscape to Sanc—difficult to make a living from. The recent conflicts with the Nerisians had doubtless made existence here even harder.

The chieftain's hall sat on a high hilltop overlooking the surrounding area. It looked down on muddy fields, presumably already sown with grain. Other fields contained livestock. A wooden enclosure circled the settlement. It lacked the strong stone walls of a castle, but it covered a large space, big enough to bring in animals and the local population. Slabs of stone had been used to make a crude set of steps, and they dismounted to lead their mounts up.

The gate was open, and their Kassite guide did the talking for them as he led them towards the hall. There were a dozen other wooden buildings inside the settlement. The hall was the dominant feature, however, and as they walked towards it, a crowd of interested onlookers formed outside. Then, half a dozen figures emerged from the hall.

'Which one is the chieftain?' Lenzo asked their guide.

He pointed to the man at the front of the group. He was big—wide as well as tall, with huge shoulders, arms and legs, and a gut that protruded above his belt, where he carried a hand axe. His hands were empty save for a half-eaten leg of bird in one. His hair and beard were flaxen, his facial hair so overgrown that it covered the lower two thirds of his face. Ice-blue eyes studied them from beneath a prominent brow ridge.

'Chief Grindan,' their guide said as the two groups met. 'I bring Lenzo, Prince of the Scorgians, to your hall.'

'I have heard what has befallen your realm,' Grindan said to Lenzo. He glanced at Sanc and Rab, a look of interest appearing on his face before it was replaced by a cold demeanour. 'Now you come to our lands for help, I don't doubt. When the Scorgians never lifted a finger to aid us against the Nerisians.'

The Kassites murmured their agreement at their chieftain's words. Sanc looked around. The people weren't hostile, exactly. But suspicious, certainly. He wondered about Lenzo's wisdom in coming here. A common enemy didn't necessarily make them allies. He was reminded that despite all he had learned about Silb in the last few weeks, there was still plenty he didn't know.

'I won't pretend otherwise. The Scorgians have been guilty of hiding behind our walls. Now we have paid the price. Our king is a prisoner, our champion lies dead, our capital taken, our people conquered. Lothar has broken us,' he admitted.

'If you are so broken, why bother coming here?' Grindan demanded. 'You can offer us nothing. Or did you just come for some sympathy? You'll find that in short supply.'

'May we speak in your hall?' Lenzo asked, nodding in the direction he wanted to go.

'That is not the Kassite way,' Grindan told him. 'We have not made kings to rule over us. We always speak before our people,' he said, gesturing at the men and women around them. 'Not hide from them.'

Lenzo looked at Sanc. Sanc gave him a nod.

'I can offer you something,' Lenzo said. 'Another champion. This outlander I have brought here. He is prepared to work with the Kassites. As well as having the largest army in Silb, Lothar has benefited from having two champions at his disposal. Now, at least, we can match him in that area. With time, I hope to bring the other peoples of Silb against the Nerisians. Lothar broke us, I have admitted that. But I haven't given up hope.' He looked around at his audience. 'Have the Kassites?'

There were unhappy murmurs at this. Lenzo wasn't making friends. But he'd laid down a challenge.

Grindan sneered at the prince. 'The Kassites never give up, Scorgian. We are already planning our invasion of Nerisia.' He gestured at Sanc. 'Maybe this outlander can help.'

* * *

GRINDAN BROUGHT Sanc and Lenzo to the Kassite war meeting. There they learned the plan to invade Nerisia was indeed already well advanced. Five Kassite chieftains spoke together by an ancient oak, their supporters listening in as was the way of this people. Sanc learned these men represented all five tribes, who had not all fought on the same side in generations.

'The Nerisians have forced us to unite,' Grindan had explained to them as he led his small band from his settlement north to a meeting place closer to the centre of Kassite territory. 'Now we will be graced by the presence of Rinc the Black and Tredan Late to Battle.'

All five chieftains had a nickname for one another. In Sanc's opinion, Rinc the Black had come off best: his epithet simply referring to his coal black hair, on head and face, that was unusual amongst the Kassites. He was the quietest, but when he spoke it was with purpose.

Tredan Late to Battle had a dishonourable sounding moniker, apparently earned from arriving to war after the worst of the fighting was over. He was powerfully built, with rotten teeth and a face covered in gold: rings of the precious metal in his beard, ears, nose, and eyebrows. He scowled every time his nickname was used—it didn't stop the other four from using it frequently.

Grindan Won't Stop Eating had a well-deserved nickname which he seemed to take pride in. He was also keen to remind the northerners how much his tribe had suffered from the depredations of the Nerisians, citing the loss of land, men, and resources.

Holt Slender Legged had come from the far west. Sanc couldn't help studying his legs, which he supposed were on the thin side, but then he was a very tall man. His chest and arms were muscular, which Sanc conceded made his body look a little out of proportion.

Finally, there was List the Castrator, in whose lands they met. Half of his face had been burned, the skin leathery and puckered. His teeth had been filed down into sharp points and he stared at Sanc with small, nasty looking eyes. He was terrifying, but Sanc did his best not to show his fear. Like Grindan, List had been in the thick of the fighting with the Nerisians. That was where he had earned his sobriquet, from his preferred method of punishment for his enemies.

Given equal status with the chieftains was the Kassite champion. Mildrith was young, surely only a little older than Sanc. She was blue eyed, flaxen haired and athletic looking, dressed in the leathers of a Kassite warrior. But some sense told Sanc she had magic. He found it reassuring to meet someone like him. It was a connection when he had little in common with most other people in Silb. For her part, Mildrith treated him with the respect of a peer, which encouraged the chieftains to accept him.

'The trouble we have,' she explained, for the benefit of Sanc and Lenzo, 'is the chain of forts Lothar built on the Kassite lands he has taken. Even though his main army is far away in Scorgia, he has left many men in those forts to hold down the territory. We could attack them directly. But they would send warning to Count Erstein in Obernai. He has a force there he would bring to reinforce the forts. Enough to hold us off until Lothar returned with his main army.'

'We can circumvent all of that by bringing our army west,' said Holt Slender Legged. 'There are paths through the White Forest that can take us deep into Nerisian lands undetected. We could emerge close to Obernai and catch them unawares. If we take that town, we will have freedom of manoeuvre. Lothar's forts could be attacked from north and south.'

'We wouldn't be so far from Mournai,' List added, referring to the Nerisians' capital.

'That would be sweet revenge,' Lenzo muttered.

List curled his lips at the prince, revealing his pointed teeth. 'Your new champion can help us. But what will you do, Scorgian?'

'We have a chance to bring more people into this war. Arvenan merchants sail across Silb, as far as the Rasidi in the west and the Egers to the south. Those are places the Kassites cannot reach. If we convince them to invade Nerisia, we could defeat Lothar for good.'

'So,' said Tredan, 'while the Kassites fight and bleed, the Scorgians will talk. Is that it?'

'The Scorgians can fight as well. Think about it. If Lothar is invaded from north, east, south, and west, he can't stop us. His army can't be everywhere at once.'

'Let the Scorgian go do his talking,' Grindan said as he chewed. 'The Kassites have never relied on help from others, anyway. So long as his champion is ready to stay and fight with us.'

'I am,' Sanc said. 'But I have my conditions. I am not here to help the Scorgians or Kassites from the goodness of my heart. If I help you defeat Lothar, I want something in return. You must give me your word that you will send help to my lands. We, too, face an invader that must be defeated.'

'What help?' asked Rinc the Black, his dark eyes full of scrutiny.

'Mildrith's,' Sanc answered, with a nod at the champion.

Rinc pursed his lips. 'You must show us your worth first, before we would ever agree to such a thing. And the Nerisians must be totally defeated. Mildrith cannot leave while we are still at war.'

'I understand,' Sanc answered him. 'That is fair. What would you have me do to prove my worth?'

'You and I will be the first to pass through the White Forest,' Mildrith told him. 'We will prepare the way for our army.'

Sanc glanced at Lenzo, who nodded at him. So Lenzo would return to Arvena, while Sanc was left here to fight with the barbarous Kassites. But what choice did he have? 'Alright,' he agreed. 'Rab and I will come with you.'

'Rab?'

'My friend,' Sanc said, gesturing at the dog. 'He can sniff out trouble while I can move unseen. We'll show you how much we are worth.'

Mildrith allowed herself a smile. 'Then it is agreed, outlander. You and your friend are coming with me.' She looked at the five chieftains of the Kassites. 'No reason to wait any longer, I say. If you can raise your warriors and follow us in five days' time?'

'I cannot return to my people, raise a force and bring it to Holt's lands all in five days,' complained Tredan.

'Don't worry, Late to Battle,' said List with an ugly smile. 'You will head south and wait with Grindan. When the time is right, you can help us win back our lands from the Nerisian robbers. You'll be ready for that, won't you?'

'You'll see how ready we are,' Tredan said, loud enough for all those gathered at the old oak to hear him clearly. 'We will feed the stolen Kassite lands with Nerisian blood. We will make a red river that will flow all the way to Mournai.'

LIESEL

VALENNES, KINGDOM OF GUIVERGNE, 676

In the quiet moments, grief threatened to overwhelm Liesel. Losing her uncle Walter, a rock of honour and strength amongst the weakness of her family, felt unbearable. But Liesel grieved for her people, too—for Kelland and for Brasingia. For it was now clearer than ever that her brother Leopold, and the witch Inge, would stop at nothing to seize the imperial title.

Only the use of force could stop them. And that meant war—war between Brasingians; war between her new kingdom of Guivergne and the empire. It was the innocents who would suffer the most, and yet Liesel saw no alternative. Because Leopold and Inge's bloodthirsty ambitions would never stop; would never be sated.

It had taken so long for everyone to understand this. Even Walter himself had argued that Inge should be respected; that Brasingia needed her magic. And she had killed him while he slept, in the most cowardly and despicable way possible.

At least things were so busy that quiet moments were few and far between. Her marriage celebrations in Valennes had been cut short—the ceremony seemed so long ago now, even though it had only been a few days. Most of the guests had rushed away to raise warriors for their king. Peyre had left for Morbaine; Auberi and Loysse for

Famiens; Domard, not even fully recovered from his fall in the joust, for Martras. Sacha, Miles, Florent, and many other noblemen to their estates. More sacrifice, Liesel knew. Young men and women who would be ordered to fight in a foreign land over the death of someone they didn't know.

That left fewer people to plan the campaign. Lord Caisin and his team of clerks were busy organising the supplies. Brancat, the castellan of The Bastion, advised them on what exactly was needed. The clerks had long parchments covered in inky black scrawl listing the numbers of fighters expected; how much food they would bring; how many carts, horses, craftsmen, and various other miscellaneous items had to be sourced before the army was ready to march.

In Esterel's council chamber, more parchment was spread over the table: maps of Brasingia held open. Liesel's new husband fine-tuned his strategy. He questioned her, Farred, and Tegyn about the empire— a realm he had never visited himself. How many soldiers could each duchy raise? How did they train and fight? What was the temperament of each leader? What was the terrain like in Barissia? How strong were Coldeberg's defences? Where were the river crossings? Where were the major towns? What were the roads like?

He sucked information in like a sponge. He asked questions Liesel would never have thought of. All with the aim of leaving as little to chance as possible. She couldn't imagine Leopold doing the same. But she couldn't help dwelling on the unfairness of the situation. Leopold had Inge. Sometimes it made her feel that Esterel's numbers and strategy were meaningless.

'You must make sure you are protected at all times,' she told him.

Esterel rolled his eyes and gave her a hard stare. Liesel had to admit he was laid back most of the time. But he disliked such talk, especially in front of others. He felt it was unmanly to talk of his own safety.

'Yes, yes,' he said, as if she were an overanxious mother. He prodded the map he studied with a finger. 'Here is our problem. Rotelegen. I foresee few obstacles to our entering Barissia and meeting up with the forces of Thesse and Gotbeck. But Rotelegen is isolated, its army is small, and Guslar is very close to our enemies. But if we were to send help, it would involve splitting our forces.'

'We *must* provide help,' Liesel said at once. 'My sister, niece and nephew are there.'

'I know,' Esterel said. 'We will do something. I'm just not sure what. Sending men to sit in Guslar doesn't particularly help.' He stared at the map as if it was a puzzle waiting to be solved. 'I need to send someone to Guslar to speak with Duke Jeremias. We need to cooperate.'

'I will go,' Liesel said. 'It's my family who are there.'

Esterel, Tegyn, and Farred all stared at her with the same expression. As if she had gone mad.

'What?' she demanded.

'You are the queen of Guivergne,' Tegyn reminded her. 'You can't go wandering around Rotelegen.'

Liesel didn't know what to say. She hadn't got used to her new status, that was for sure. Would she spend the rest of her life treated as a precious treasure, unable to do anything? She looked at Esterel, a small smile playing on his lips. Well. Wasn't that exactly how she had just treated him? 'Sorry,' she said.

He grinned. 'I know how you feel. But it can't be us. Farred?'

'Of course. So long as I am back for the invasion of Barissia. I have no intention of missing that.'

'Agreed. You are too useful not to have with us for that. But we won't be leaving until Peyre returns with the Morbainais and that's still weeks away.'

'I'll go with him,' Tegyn said.

The other three looked aghast at the idea.

Tegyn jutted her jaw out. 'I've lost as much to Leopold and Inge as any of you. You'd better have a damned good reason to say no to me.'

No one dared to argue.

* * *

WITH TEGYN AND FARRED GONE, it felt even more lonely in The Bastion. It made Liesel appreciate her Atrabian friend anew—she had left her home for Liesel, and the last few months would have been so much more difficult without her.

Her thoughts turned to Tegyn's brother, Idris. The old, painful feelings of guilt returned. She'd had a soft spot for him which he had shared and in different circumstances, who knew what might have happened. Now she struggled to remember exactly what he looked like. What would he think about her marriage to the king of Guivergne while he languished in his room in Essenberg Castle? While part of her hated the thought of war coming to the empire, she also welcomed the chance it would bring to right so many wrongs.

Esterel chafed at having to wait for his forces to arrive in Valennes. But their marriage and the war had brought them closer together. Barely a night went by when he didn't visit her room.

Liesel's jealousy over his relationship with Coleta, Sacha's sister, was all but forgotten. Whatever had happened in the past, it seemed that the woman was interested in Peyre, now. And anyway, all she had done to cause offence was dance with Esterel. Liesel even decided that with the top table in the hall now so empty and the atmosphere so quiet, Coleta and her friend Aizivella should dine with them. It was becoming an insult to keep her away. She was able to speak with the two girls in a friendly way and thaw some of the ice between them. She struggled to find much common ground with either. *Perhaps it's my fault. Though it doesn't help that Coleta is so damned attractive. Couldn't she wear something plainer or put on a few pounds?*

At last, the Guivergnais warriors began to arrive in the capital. Some came from the royal estates; others with the great noblemen of the kingdom, a new unit every day. First Sacha, then Miles, Florent, Arnoul of Saliers, finally Auberi and Loysse from Famiens. The hall was full again at meal times; the Bastion was full; the city was full. With no room left in the old city, Auberi stationed his force in the eastern half of Valennes. Esterel's council was full, as he explained his plans to his captains.

'You're not going to try to leave me behind in Guivergne, are you?'

Liesel asked him as they lay in bed together. They would leave any day now, and she knew he would be making his final decisions.

'It's safer here,' Esterel said, putting an arm around her as if he was protecting her even now. 'Besides, someone must run things from here in my absence. It's vital that we get support from Guivergne while we're in hostile territory.'

'I know that, Esterel,' Liesel said, pushing his arm away. 'But it doesn't have to be me. I'm Walter's niece; Leopold's sister. If I'm in Brasingia, it gives your presence there more legitimacy; makes you look less like an invader. I know the people. It would be stupid not to take me.'

Esterel sighed. 'Maybe that's true. But I can't afford to lose you. War is horrible, you know. Anything might happen.'

'Don't treat me like a frail old lady, Esterel. You married me because of who I am. Don't throw that away.'

He looked into her eyes, a small frown on his face. Then he put a hand to her cheek. 'That's not why I married you, Liesel. I married you because I love you.'

Liesel got to her knees, then put her hands to her husband's neck, pushing down with her weight. 'Then do what I say!' she demanded.

'Alright,' Esterel conceded, unable to stop a goofy smile coming to his face. 'You win.'

* * *

THE LAST PIECES of Esterel's preparations fell into place. The forces of the Duchy of Martras arrived from the farthest corner of the kingdom. On the same day, Farred and Tegyn returned, unharmed, from Rotelegen. Liesel was invited to a meeting of the royal council—nearly twenty people, crammed around a table designed for far fewer. Esterel was ready to announce his decisions.

'Duke Jeremias is on board?' Esterel checked with Farred.

The Magnian nodded. 'He knows how vulnerable he is. He has claimed the imperial title for himself. He's convinced Leopold won't be satisfied until he's dead. And he's sure the Luderians, Griennese, and Trevenzans will do what Leopold tells them.'

Esterel nodded. 'Thank you, Farred and Tegyn both. Your Grace,' he said, turning to Auberi. 'I've decided intervention in Rotelegen is crucial. The goal is to keep Jeremias in power and divide the enemy's forces. Having Rotelegen against them makes life difficult for our enemies.'

Auberi nodded. 'What would you have me do, Your Majesty?'

'Lead your force into Rotelegen and rendezvous with Jeremias. March into Kelland and take Burkhard Castle. I'm told it's deserted. It's not the fortress it once was, but hold it as best you can. One more thing for our enemy to worry about.'

Auberi nodded his consent, phlegmatic. But Liesel couldn't help noticing the reaction of Loysse, who'd gone white as a sheet. Esterel had sent her husband on a dangerous mission, into Leopold's own duchy. Many would say, Liesel knew, it was the price he had to pay for his treachery.

'Your Grace,' Esterel said, now talking to the other duke, Domard of Martras. 'My wife has persuaded me to take her with me. It means I need someone to manage the kingdom in our absence. I ask that you and your force stay in Valennes and govern. Be ready to bring your force into Barissia or Rotelegen should we need it.'

'If this is because of my injury, Your Majesty, I can assure you I am fully recovered. I would be shamed to sit here while all others go to fight.'

Domard looked around the table for support, but no one here was going to argue with Esterel. Florent stared at the floor, embarrassed, since he was the one who had accidentally inflicted the injury in their joust.

Esterel looked genuinely sympathetic. 'I have no one else of your stature, Domard. Can you not see that? I promise, next time we will ride to war together.'

Next time, Liesel thought to herself. *That's a revealing statement.*

Domard had no choice but to accede to his king's wishes.

'My Lord of Saliers,' Esterel continued. 'The rest of us shall march to your estate, if that is acceptable? We shall await my brother and the army of Morbaine. From there, we shall head south-east and cross into Barissia.'

Liesel noted the excitement in the air at these words. The Guivergnais had long been the rivals of Brasingia, forced to accept their enemy's greatness in recent times. Now they were ready to invade once more. *And I am invading with them. May the gods forgive me. I'm sorry, father, that it has come to this.*

BELWYNN

KIRTSEA, KINGDOM OF MAGNIA, 676

Footsteps along the beach. A man and a woman, she guessed.

Belwynn drew her gaze from the ocean and watched as Elfled of Magnia approached. With her was a bodyguard. He stopped, a respectful distance away, as Elfled drew near.

'I'm sorry about Edgar,' Belwynn said.

Elfled acknowledged the words with a slight tilt of her head, while her mouth twisted with some emotion.

Belwynn sighed. No doubt Edgar's wife blamed his death on Belwynn's inaction. That was a hard lesson she had learned. *When you're a hero, every tragedy becomes your fault.* She got to her feet. 'Shall we talk inside?'

Elfled nodded.

'Sit here,' Belwynn said to the Magnian warrior, gesturing at her chair. 'It's a pleasant view.'

The man took her up on her offer and she and Elfled entered the house. She showed Elfled to a chair. 'Drink or food?'

'No thanks, Belwynn.'

'You're here because of Maragin?'

'Yes. I've come to ask you to do more. I'm struggling without him, Belwynn. I'm doing my best to help Ida grow into his father's role. But

193

time is against us. If Ezenachi comes a second time, Magnia is finished.'

'What is it you want?'

'What can you do?' Elfled replied, her voice sounding sharp. 'What can you do beyond sitting on your arse and looking out to sea? There are people who can help us. Moneva, Gyrmund—'

'I won't be giving them up.'

'You *do* know where they are!'

'I know. They're someplace safe. They don't have any of the weapons. There is no special help they can give that someone else couldn't.'

'Ask them, Belwynn,' Elfled said. 'Tell them what's happening and ask them if they wish to help. If they don't, so be it.'

She could do it. She knew where they were. Living a simple life amongst the Sparewaldi tribe, in a remote corner of Luderia. Raising their family in peace. More than that, she could speak to them if she wished to. Her link to others hadn't disappeared, despite the death of Madria and of her own body. Some part of Belwynn remained, in her mind, that could still do those things. But she wouldn't. 'I'd be asking them to give their lives and I'm not doing that.'

'Edgar lost his life. Along with thousands of others. Why do they get a pass?'

'I lost my brother,' Belwynn bit back, buried feelings of anger and despair resurfacing after so many years. 'I lost Clarin. I lost myself. We've all lost people, Elfled. Your grief is raw but not unique. Some need to live. Otherwise, what's the point of it?'

She'd imagined the scene countless times. Moneva and Gyrmund, hearing her voice in their heads after so many years. Their first instinct is to find each other. When they do, they share the same look. *It's over.* Then they argue about who should go, both insisting the other should stay with the children. Of course, they can't agree. That night, Gyrmund sneaks out of bed into the stables. He saddles a horse. He will go. Ride north. When Moneva wakes, he'll be gone, but she'll be safe. The doors to the stables close behind him. He is locked inside.

He shouts her name. *Don't do it, Moneva,* he begs and pleads. But she is gone.

'Belwynn?' Elfled said.

Belwynn returned to her house in Magnia. 'I'm not doing it.'

Perhaps Elfled had seen something in Belwynn's face to make her finally believe it. 'Alright,' she conceded. 'But what about you? You are the best chance we have of getting the weapons back.'

'For how long must it be Belwynn?' she asked. 'What happens the next time? And the next? You want the weapons, you get them.'

'I can't. I'm needed.'

Now it was Belwynn's turn to twist her mouth. 'Is that what you tell yourself?'

'I can't,' Elfled insisted. 'Maragin and Jesper are going. But it is just the two of them. Surely, you will not let them go while you just sit here?'

'If no one in Magnia is prepared to go with them, Magnia doesn't deserve to survive,' Belwynn said. 'No one lives forever. No realm lasts forever.'

'How profound,' Elfled said, her voice dripping with sarcasm. She shook her head. 'You know, Soren came to Magnia when he was looking for the Cloak of the Asrai. We put him up and fed him. Every day, Morlin would ride with him down to the coast. Soren would go out, searching the ocean for a people and a place that most of us thought was a myth. Morlin waited for him and brought him back, exhausted.'

Belwynn envied Elfled that time with Soren. Time they had been apart, when Belwynn had been in Kalinth, playing the role of Lady of the Knights. It seemed she'd always been given a role to play by others. Even now, it had been decided she must be the saviour of Dalriya once more.

'Soren never gave up. He found the Asrai. He'll always be remembered for that. Maybe he couldn't have done it without our help, providing enough support so he could go out and look one more time. Ordinary folk like Morlin and I don't pretend to be heroes. We're nothing special. But everyone has their own part to play. And I understand that your part is the hardest. Maybe you never asked for it. Or maybe you have grown tired of it. But only a few get to choose their role in life. And you are Belwynn Godslayer. You're not Elana the fishwife.'

Belwynn Godslayer. Was such a name meant to inspire her? The weight of it crushed her. She had been Belwynn, sister of Soren the wizard. That had always been enough for her. It had only been when Elana lay dying in her arms that her life had taken such a course.

But Elana had been a simple fishwife before Madria had made her a priestess. She couldn't recall her friend ever complaining about it.

'Alright,' she said, the word sounding like a hammer blow. 'I will help find the weapons. But there is something you can do.'

'What's that?'

'You can get the cloak from the Asrai.'

Elfled frowned. 'How do I do that?'

Belwynn shrugged. 'I have no idea. You and Morlin can work it out, I'm sure. Everyone has their part to play. Don't they?'

* * *

MARAGIN AND JESPER had been waiting for her in Kirtsea, a spare horse and supplies ready for her in case Elfled was successful in her mission.

Belwynn said nothing as she mounted her horse.

Wordlessly, Maragin passed her Toric's Dagger and with a grim expression, Belwynn put the weapon on her belt.

'We'd planned to head north through Guivergne to the land of the Krykkers,' Jesper said, breaking the silence. 'From there, I can travel to Halvia. I don't know where you intend to start.'

'Kalinth,' Belwynn said with a heavy heart. 'I will start in Kalinth.' *I can't believe I'm doing this.*

'I will go with you,' Maragin said.

Belwynn nodded. *Perhaps the Krykker thinks I'll get cold feet.* 'We can pass through Guivergne without problems?'

'Aye,' Jesper said. 'I have lived in Guivergne the past ten years. They know me.'

'Very well. Let's get moving.'

They journeyed north through Magnia. Belwynn saw the effects of the war for herself. South Magnians—her people—had fled north. The lucky among them had found new homes. Plenty hadn't, the authorities overwhelmed with numbers. She thought of the places that had been lost—her family's estate at Beckford; Ecgworth, the old home of Toric's Dagger. It had been easier, in Kirtsea, to shrug it all away. *Maybe I'm doing the right thing.*

On the second day, they crossed into Morbaine. Belwynn had traipsed all over Dalriya in her younger days, but this land was new to her. The old kingdom of Morbaine had been claimed by the kings of Guivergne and it had an unkempt feel to it, as if the Guivergnais had paid it little attention since.

'You said you've been living in Guivergne?' she asked Jesper.

'Aye. Here in Morbaine most of the time.'

'And this boy who is with Herin. Sanc, you called him.'

'He grew up here in Morbaine. Third son of Duke Bastien.'

'Bastien still rules here?'

'No. Bastien is dead, but his sons rule now. Peyre is the new duke and his eldest, Esterel, is king of Guivergne.'

Names Belwynn didn't know. She had allowed time to run unchecked in Kirtsea. *What other changes has time wrought on the world,* she wondered. 'And you told me that Sanc and Herin left Dalriya? Where to?'

Jesper made a face. 'I don't know. Rimmon sent them to fetch help. To some other world, he said.' He looked at her blank expression. 'He was a Haskan sorcerer. Apprentice to Pentas, once.'

'Was?'

'He's dead. Ezenachi killed him.'

Belwynn sighed. The efforts of the Dalriyans had been worse than she could have guessed. *Some wizard has sent Herin and a boy away somewhere and then got himself killed. That's left Maragin and Jesper to search for the weapons. No wonder Ezenachi has found his conquests so easy.* 'What's so special about this boy?'

'He was born with red eyes,' Jesper told her, his gaze holding hers. 'The birth was the same day Pentas was killed.'

A shiver ran down Belwynn's spine. 'Madria replaced Pentas,' she murmured. 'Then I killed Madria. Did Sanc inherit Pentas's powers?'

Jesper shrugged. 'I'm not an expert on such matters. But Sanc is powerful. Getting more powerful each day, Rimmon said.'

If Soren were here, he might have something to say about this young sorcerer. But he's not, and I don't see what I can do about it. 'We must lay our hands on the weapons,' she said. 'Then see what must be done.'

Maragin patted Bolivar's Sword at her side. 'Sword and dagger,' the Krykker said gruffly. 'All we really need.'

Belwynn hoped her old champion was right.

Jesper led them north through Morbaine into Guivergne proper. He chose where to stop and rest and where to stay the night. The innkeepers he selected knew him, and they were left in peace. Even Maragin attracted little interest. As for Belwynn, no one knew who she was, and that was how she liked it.

They learned that a great army had been raised by the king and had left for Brasingia. According to Jesper, it was to intervene in a succession dispute over the imperial title, caused by the death of Coen. The Guivergnais were opposed to Leopold, son of Emperor Baldwin.

'That's a shame, given this threat from the south,' Belwynn said. 'While I didn't agree with Baldwin on everything, he was a strong leader when the empire needed him. I'm surprised his son is disliked so much. What prompted this conflict?'

'Oh, many things,' Jesper said. 'Leopold's adviser is a witch named Inge. She wants the Brasingians to submit to Ezenachi. But it was her murder of Duke Walter that brought things to a head.'

'Walter is dead?' Belwynn asked, shocked.

'You know him?'

'Yes, he saved us once. We were close to being caught by Gervase Salvinus and dragged back to Coldeberg. Walter protected us.'

'Hmm. Well, Salvinus is another one of Leopold's advisers.'

'Then I know whose side I'm not on. Who wears the imperial crown now?'

'No one. They couldn't agree. Walter supported Jeremias of Rotelegen against Leopold. Seems it's a contest that can only be settled by war.'

Belwynn shook her head and shared a rueful look with Maragin. 'We saved the world not so long ago. It hasn't taken long to turn rotten.'

'Humans,' Maragin said dismissively. 'What else did you expect?'

THEY REACHED the far north of Guivergne, following the Cousel towards its source. Their mounts left behind, they climbed, following trails that wound their way around mountains. The terrain only got more difficult once they crossed into the lands of the Krykkers. Not that her companions slowed their pace much. Maragin had made such journeys all her life and led the way despite her advanced years. Jesper seemed as fit as they came.

As for Belwynn. Well. Elana's body simply did as she asked of it. It reported no aches or pains. No tiredness. It simply obeyed her instructions. Revived by Madria's magic, it hadn't aged a day since, even though the goddess was gone.

There was no inn with warm bed and hot meal that night. Not that such luxuries mattered much to Belwynn. They were in the land of Maragin's clan, the Grendals. Even so, the best she could offer was a cave to shelter in.

'We're still a few hours from the nearest settlement,' the Krykker explained.

Belwynn thought it strange that the chieftain sounded almost apologetic. It wasn't like her. For her part, Belwynn wasn't surprised to see nothing but rock. It was one reason Maragin's people had survived for so long, when they were outnumbered by human kingdoms. What army would march this way, simply to capture acres of unproductive, mountainous terrain?

Jesper and Maragin busied themselves making a fire. Belwynn let them work. Memories came, unbidden, of her old friends doing the same thing. Gyrmund in charge; Clarin and Rabigar carrying bundles of firewood; Moneva complaining about the cold and wet and insects and anything else she could think of. Soren reading, his eyes squinting. Belwynn reading to Lyssa...

She pushed those memories aside. They only made her melancholy, and she had learned, over the years, to send them away.

'I'll take first watch,' Jesper offered, as he nibbled on his dried meat. He'd offered some to Belwynn, then looked abashed when he realised what he'd done.

Belwynn gave him the same small smile as she had then. 'You get some sleep, Jesper,' she told him. 'I'm the perfect lookout. I never fall asleep.'

He gave her a wide-eyed stare before looking away. Belwynn found it amusing that someone who had spent so much time around wizards was constantly shocked by her. *Am I so monstrous? I suppose I am.*

She turned her gaze to look at the night sky. So many stars were visible from this vantage point. It wasn't as peaceful as sitting by the sea. *But maybe it's time for a new vista.*

SANC

KASSITE/NERISIAN BORDER, 676

Sanc and Mildrith rode west on well bred horses, Rab keeping pace with them. The Kassite warriors would not be following for days. Mildrith let him know when they passed into the lands of Holt Slender Legged. It wasn't long before they entered the edges of the White Forest. They turned south, following trails deeper and deeper into the woodland, until the sun was all but hidden from view.

It was thick, ancient woodland, not unlike the Forest of Morbaine. Rab seemed to feel at home in it, bounding around as if it was playtime. Mildrith laughed at him, fascinated by the dog. Silb had so many similarities to Dalriya that sometimes it was easy for Sanc to forget he was in some other world. That no one here had seen a dog before helped remind him of the strangeness of it all. He had come to this world but didn't know where it lay in relation to his own. Without Rimmon, he didn't know how to return. Sanc stopped himself from continuing down that route. The more he thought about such things, the more overwhelming his quest felt. Better to concentrate on the here and now; take one step at a time.

'Which of the Kassite tribes were you born into?' he asked Mildrith.

'I'm from the north. Rinc the Black was my lord. But I cannot be seen to favour any one tribe. I am the champion of all Kassites. I have lived amongst the southern tribes for the last three years. That is where the fighting has been.'

'Why didn't the northern chieftains help until now?'

'They weren't directly threatened. Maybe they even thought they could profit from it. Only last year, when Lothar conquered Kassite lands and made Kassites his subjects, did they understand what was happening. I hope it's not too late for us.'

'It sounds familiar,' Sanc admitted.

'You are talking about your people?'

'Yes. Ezenachi controls the southernmost parts of our continent. Only those closest to him have felt threatened. Now he has grown in power and people are slowly realising that it affects everyone.'

'Then people are the same everywhere,' Mildrith said. 'You came here by magic. How?'

'My teacher found this world. He helped me to come. By tele-portation.'

Mildrith studied him. 'Moving with magic?'

'Yes. You don't do that in Silb?'

'Short distances, I can. I suppose I've never really tried to move farther. Who is this teacher you had?'

Sanc described Dalriya to Mildrith. How, until recently, there had been many sorcerers from different realms. Then how the Isharite Wars had led to the near annihilation of magic users as one after another was consumed by the wars. 'This is why there are so few left to stand up to Ezenachi, who has come from another world and taken a human form.'

Mildrith frowned as she took in this information. Sanc studied her face as she did. She seemed serious and tough, but he couldn't help noticing how attractive she was—piercing blue eyes and high cheek-bones. *Not that I'm at all interested in women*, he told himself. *Ever again.*

'Then what do you hope to achieve from coming here?' she asked him. 'Here there are only ever seven champions. None of us come close to the power of a god in human form. I never had the luxury of being trained to use my powers like you did. The Scorgian is dead.

The Nerisian and Gadenzian are our enemies. Who in Silb can save Dalriya?'

'I didn't know any of that before I came here,' Sanc admitted.

'Huh,' Mildrith said, the kind of noise that tells you exactly how stupid you are without the need for words.

They stopped to make a camp in a natural glade. Sanc had learned enough from Jesper to know what he was doing, and Mildrith knew more.

'We can build a big fire. There is no one else around for miles,' the Kassite said.

That was reassuring. Sanc peered into the gloom of the forest. He couldn't see beyond a few feet, but he heard odd sounds.

'No humans, I should say,' Mildrith clarified. 'There are many night creatures who would like nothing more than to eat us up. The spiders paralyse their victims with poison, then eat them alive.'

Sanc couldn't tell whether she was joking, but after that he didn't stray far from the fire. 'Stay here,' he told Rab, not keen on him wandering off.

The dog was tired enough that he wasn't inclined to disobey, and he lay between them while they ate supper, each of them offering him bits of food from their packs. He rested his head on Mildrith's leg, and when she petted him, he licked her hand.

'He seems to like me a lot more than you,' she observed.

'He can just taste the food on your fingers,' Sanc said, a little miffed.

'Huh. You can sleep first. I'll wake you when it's your turn.'

Sanc felt he should be the one to take the first watch, since he was the man. But when he thought about it, that didn't make a whole lot of sense and he had the feeling Mildrith would strongly disagree. Or worse, laugh at him. 'Alright. Make sure you wake me.'

'Don't worry, I will.'

Getting to sleep wasn't easy. Sanc felt vulnerable and the strange noises of the White Forest at night didn't help, even if he knew there was a champion close by watching out for them. Mildrith would poke the fire every now and again to keep it burning. Sanc was a little annoyed with Rab. Even with the fire, it was cold, and he could have done with sharing the dog's body warmth. Instead, Rab was flopped over Mildrith.

He must have got to sleep, because Mildrith was waking him. He sat up, freezing cold, and put his hands to the fire. 'Come here, Rab,' he said and pulled the dog onto his lap, giving him a hug to warm himself.

Mildrith lay down next to him and closed her eyes. Right next to him. It made sense to share body warmth, but he had only known the Kassite for a day. *Suddenly you're a prude?* he asked himself. *After sleeping with Tassia within minutes of meeting her?*

He stared into the fire. The truth was, he didn't know what to think of his relationship with the girl in Arvena. It had hurt him badly. But already, it seemed like a long time ago. *Perhaps I should put it down to being in a strange new world,* he told himself.

He would have liked someone to talk to about things like this. Peyre had always had Umbert to discuss such matters; Esterel his friends; Loysse at least had Cebelia. He had briefly talked to Lenzo about it, who had tried to make him understand Tassia's perspective. But Lenzo was so much older and had doubtless forgotten what it was like to be Sanc's age.

He glanced at Mildrith, who looked asleep. He quickly looked away. It wasn't right to look at people while they slept. And if she caught him doing it, he would be mortified.

For some reason, he looked again. Her blonde hair, tied up in plaits, fell about her face. Her chin poked over her blanket. At rest, she seemed so much younger than when she was awake.

The screech of a bird gave him a fright, and he jerked away, gazing back into the fire once again.

Just concentrate on staying awake, Sanc, he told himself. *Let's get through the night without being paralysed by spiders.*

* * *

SANC WOKE Mildrith when dawn came. They were both cold and tired, eating breakfast in silence. Sanc knew that once they got moving, they would regain some energy. But Mildrith had other ideas.

'I think it's time we test each other's magic,' she said. 'I want to see what you've got before we get closer to our target.'

It made sense. The Kassites only had Lenzo's word that Sanc was a sorcerer, after all. 'Alright. But first, let's see what you've got as a fighter. It'll warm us up. You carry that handaxe around. Can you use it?'

'Of course I can use it!' Mildrith growled, taking the weapon in hand.

Sanc drew his sword with a grin, and they approached one another. Mildrith's weapon had a long wooden handle with a single axe head attached at the top. The sharp blade was long, curved, and deadly looking, but Sanc had always thought of axes as clumsy weapons. They were popular among the Kassites, though.

He wafted his sword at her, tempting her to knock it away. Mildrith moved to the side, her footwork calm and assured.

Sanc sliced at her; she moved out of the way then flashed the axe towards him. It whistled past, not close enough, but Sanc got a sense of the damage it could do if she did land a strike with it. She tried to get in behind his defence, but he blocked her with his blade. *Maybe the axe is more dangerous,* he admitted to himself, *but I have more control.* He shoved his hilt towards her face, and she blocked, a hand on either end of the axe's shaft. They pushed at one another; with two hands on her axe, Mildrith was strong enough to keep him at bay. They separated warily, watching out for any attempts from the other to get in another strike.

'You're pretty good with it,' he admitted.

'I've been taught to fight well enough for my needs. But come now, Sanc. Anyone would think you were stalling.'

'Very well,' Sanc agreed, and he laid his sword on the ground. 'Ready?'

Mildrith launched a blast of magic at him, making it green and brown to blend in with the surroundings.

Sanc stopped it easily enough. She tried again, and this time he took the attack and returned it at her. She blocked with a shield of magic.

'My teacher, Rimmon, told me that defence is easier than attack.'

'He sounds so wise,' Mildrith said. 'Did he teach you this?'

For a moment, Sanc stood waiting for whatever threat she referred to. Then he was grasped. Roots twisted from the ground to hold his legs, and branches wound their way around his arms. He tugged, but he was held tight. He desperately tried to think how best to deal with his predicament, having never been attacked by a tree before.

Mildrith gave a satisfied smile and wound up for an attack.

Sanc couldn't move his hands. He knew he didn't *need* to use them; but he was so used to relying on them he worried whether he could get his magic to work without them. He pulled at his sword, sending it flying towards Mildrith, blade first.

With a gasp, she saw it coming just in time, sending it spinning back to the ground. Meanwhile, Sanc brought heat to his limbs, flame running up and down his arms and legs. The tree loosened its grip, and he pulled himself free, blocking Mildrith's blast just in time.

They stood facing one another, panting from their exertions.

'You're pretty good,' Mildrith said with a grin. 'That tree got you, though.'

'I've never seen that before,' Sanc admitted. 'You learn that yourself?'

'Yes. But I could learn a thing or two from you. It wasn't easy fighting alone against two champions.'

'I can imagine. How old are they?'

'Temyl, the Nerisian, must be in his forties. The Gadenzian, Guntram, about ten years younger.'

'Much more experienced,' Sanc said. 'And they can learn from each other as well. I'm impressed you survived against them.'

His compliment was rewarded with a smile. 'Yes, well. I couldn't hope to defeat them. When they came for me, I ran.'

Sanc nodded. It reminded him of what Rimmon had told him. Whenever Ezenachi had come for him, he'd run. And then Sanc had run as well, teleporting away from the Red Fort in Magnia. *Am I even running now, so far away from Ezenachi's clutches in Silb?* He didn't like the thought of that. *I hope Rimmon is alright.*

'Are you alright?' Mildrith asked him.

'Yes,' Sanc answered, realising he had disappeared into his own thoughts. 'Well, we're a team now. We can take on Timbi and Gunter.'

'Temyl and Guntram.'

'Yes. Them too.'

THEY CHANGED COURSE, riding eastwards. The White Forest thinned as they travelled, until by midday they had escaped its clutches, emerging into lands worked by man. They were in Nerisia now—deep into the lands of their enemies.

'We are travelling along the old border between Nerisians and Kassites,' Mildrith explained to him. 'There are many Kassites here, now serving Nerisian lords. Few would give me a second glance, but you stand out. Rab, too. You told me you could move unseen?' she said.

'Yes. I will show you. But I don't think it will work from horseback.'

'Then we will leave the horses. We can walk to Obernai from here.'

Mildrith took their mounts to an isolated farmstead, owned by a Kassite family. Sanc and Rab waited in a patch of trees until she returned. 'Well?' she asked.

Sanc put a leash around Rab. 'Look away,' he told her.

When she turned away, Sanc used his magic to create the illusion that neither he nor Rab were there. 'Alright, you can look now.'

Mildrith's brow creased in a frown when she turned to find they had vanished. 'Impressive,' she murmured. Then she shouted. 'Rab? Where are you? Good boy!'

Rab pulled at the leash, desperate to get some attention from the Kassite. When Sanc held him still, he whined with displeasure.

'Ah!' Mildrith said with a victorious grin. 'I see you!'

Sanc sighed and allowed his treacherous hound to get a petting.

'It's not perfect,' he admitted. 'But it works well if no one suspects I am there. Better if I don't have a stupid dog to worry about.'

'Oh, I am sure,' Mildrith said, serious now. 'It's perfect for what we need to do. Come.'

They joined a rough dirt track that led to the town. Sanc didn't waste energy on using his magic all the time, only deploying it when they neared other travellers. As they got close to Obernai, he found he had to use it more frequently. It was clearly the locus of Nerisian activity in the region. As they arrived at its outskirts, Sanc saw one reason why. Occupying a large plot, barrack buildings had been constructed inside and outside its walls, capable of quartering thousands of warriors. They explored the buildings outside the town, finding them deserted. They slipped inside one of them, a safe enough place to talk.

'Lothar took surplus troops to Scorgia,' Mildrith explained. 'But there will still be a large force inside the town.' She pursed her lips. 'Erstein and several others will recognise me. I had thought we could burst in and take him by surprise. Maybe at night.'

'But it's far better if I go in alone,' Sanc said.

'You don't have to. I'll go with you. I'm no coward.'

'I know,' Sanc said. A covert assassination would give them a much better chance of escaping Obernai unharmed. Sanc and Mildrith made a powerful team, but they weren't invincible, and there were still hundreds of Nerisian warriors stationed here. 'I'll do it. Will I meet you here?'

'Yes, why not? I'll look after Rab for you. But we need to work out how to get you inside first.'

Back outside, Mildrith leaned against the wall of the building, staring at the town's open gates. Sanc stood next to her. It would not be easy. Even if they were some distance from the fortified border, Obernai was still a military town and the guards who allowed entry were thorough. There wasn't space for Sanc to squeeze past unnoticed.

'I could teleport,' he suggested. 'But I would need a safe place to end up in.'

Mildrith shook her head. 'Seems too risky. I've a better idea.'

THE MEN JUMPED from their stuck wagon, inspecting the muddy ground that gripped the wheels tight. Unbeknownst to them, they were held fast by roots that had broken through to the surface.

Sanc deployed his magic as he climbed onto the back of the vehicle, persuading the men they heard nothing untoward as he did so. When he was safely ensconced behind a pile of timber, the wagon came loose.

The wagoneers resumed their journey to the gates of the town. The guards knew the group, but still insisted on inspecting their goods. Sanc peered at them from his hiding place, content that his magic would prevent them from spying him. When they were done, the wagon was allowed through.

As they rolled into Obernai, Sanc got the chance to look around the place. It was teeming with armed warriors, out enjoying the spring sunshine. Some were engaged in games and sports, boisterous shouts filling the air. Stallholders tempted others with their wares. No doubt the soldiers had endured a long winter stuck here while the main Nerisian army was winning glory against the Scorgians. Sanc could imagine that after so many weeks of boredom, such men would be more than eager for action. Like chasing down a Kassite champion and her outlander ally. *I must be careful.*

The wagon was led towards the barracks area. *I'm not keen on waiting around for a dozen soldiers to start unloading while I'm stuck here,* he thought. His decision made, Sanc exited his hiding place and eased to the rear. A light jump and he landed softly in the dirt. He departed quickly, not looking around to see if anyone had noticed. He kept moving, no idea where he was going, turning left and right past one building and the next, until he'd travelled enough distance to feel confident he was safe.

He paused and tried to get his bearings. Mildrith had told him what she knew of the town plan, but this was not especially helpful when Sanc wasn't sure of his current location. *There's nothing else but to move and look around,* he told himself.

Slowly, taking care not to be seen, Sanc put together where he was. He'd moved off in the wrong direction, heading towards the edge of town, where the barracks met private housing. He needed to be in the centre of town, where the primary buildings were located. That was where he was most likely to find the count.

Having gained his bearings, Sanc moved towards his target, still using his magic to mask his progress. Only now did he fully register the smell of the place—too many people living in the same space for too long. Not enough attention given to hygiene. *My father would not be impressed*, he thought, and he allowed himself a wry smile. He put his fingers to the hilt of the dagger his father had given him on his thirteenth birthday. He wondered what his father would have made of his curse of a son skulking about a town in some distant world, invisible to the eye. He couldn't decide if Duke Bastien would have been surprised or not.

Sanc arrived at the central square, surrounded by the buildings one would expect in a town this size: a church, two inns, workshops, and a hall, from where he presumed the count governed. All were built from the same rough wood, functionality clearly the concern over style. It still had the hallmarks of a border town, even if the Nerisians had pushed the border north in recent years.

The doors of the hall were wide open. As he approached, Sanc saw a reception room was busy with people stood about in groups. Some were dressed in warrior gear, some were townsfolk, while others had the fine clothes of noblemen or merchants. It was so busy, he had little fear of being seen or heard.

He got inside, finding a space against a wall. There were so many conversations taking place he had a hard time tuning in to them. The nearest group was the largest and as he listened, he found it comprised merchants from out of town discussing business with a range of individuals. Finding nothing for him here, he slinked over to a group of half a dozen soldierly looking types. They were older than the average warrior, grizzled looking, and as Sanc listened, he learned they were veterans with some sort of authority in the Nerisian army.

Much of their conversation was personal—banter around drinking, gambling, fighting, or women. But then they would discuss other things—news from the invasion of Scorgia; speculation about the next war with the Kassites. With no better options available, it was enough to keep Sanc listening for now, in case he heard something more useful.

Then, out of nothing, it happened.

'So, where is his lordship anyway?' one man asked, an element of sarcasm in the use of the title.

'In with the quartermaster,' another answered, nodding his head in the direction of the hall's interior. 'Working out how else they can reduce our rations.'

'Bollocks to that,' a third man said. 'We're gonna have good men leaving if this carries on much longer. It's past time we go and pay the Kassites a visit. What's the point in keeping us sat here like this?'

'Erstein ain't gonna make that call without the king's agreement. He's waiting on a royal order.'

The debate continued amongst the men. Sanc had a location for the count, but nerves gripped him for a moment, his legs refusing to move. He had killed men in battle before, but nothing like this. He realised he wasn't breathing and made himself take a long, quiet breath, in and out.

Come on, Sanc, he told himself. *Get a grip.* He left the reception area, making his way deeper into the hall. The next room was the banqueting hall. It was full of tables and benches, but empty of people.

With the quartermaster, the soldier had said. Sanc took that to mean the two of them were in a private room somewhere. Such rooms were usually located on the upper floor. He found a set of stairs leading up. Pressing himself against a nearby wall, he waited as a maid descended the rickety wooden structure. Every. Step. Squeaked. The servant continued towards the back of the hall, where the kitchen rooms would be located. Sanc, meanwhile, glared with hostility at the stairs. There was no way he could get up there without being heard.

He ran through his options. *To hell with it,* he decided, feeling a rush of energy. He sprinted up the stairs.

Yes, the noise is horrific, he reasoned as he reached the top. *But at least it's over quickly.*

He was in the middle of a corridor with various rooms coming off it. It might have been hard to say which one the count was in had there not been an armed guard stationed outside the door at one end, turning to look in Sanc's direction with a frown.

Who knows how many more armed adversaries there are around here? But I've made my choice, Sanc told himself. *I've gone for speed.*

'Who—' the guard began.

That was all he got out. Sanc stopped hiding himself. As he did so, he pushed both hands out and yanked at the Nerisian with his magic. The soldier came flying towards him, then Sanc pushed him away, all the way to the other end of the corridor, where he crashed against the wall and slumped to the ground. Sanc was already running for the door he had been guarding, keen to take the initiative. The longer this went on, the more trouble he'd bring on himself.

He reached the door and swung it open. Two men were inside. They had been seated at a table, but one had stood and was facing Sanc. The man's appearance told Sanc this was the count in an instant. He wore a woollen cloak over a long tunic and wherever there was an opportunity—clasp, belt, scabbard, fingers—jewellery proclaimed his status. Russet hair hung in curls to his shoulders. Erstein's hand went for his sword.

Sanc threw a blast of magic. The count raised a hand in a vain attempt to protect himself, but was sent flying into the far wall of the room.

Sanc marched towards him. With a hand on the hilt of his dagger, he turned to the quartermaster. 'I suggest you leave.'

The second man, more simply dressed, shook as he got to his feet. Once up, however, he wasted no time in vacating the room.

Sanc inspected his victim. He still lived, but his eyes were unfocused, and he let out a pained groan. *I must finish this,* Sanc told himself. He took his dagger in hand and struck it with force into the count's chest. He pulled it out and watched Erstein die. It was a swift death, at least.

Sanc wasn't sure how long he had stood in the room, staring at the weapon his father had gifted him. His gaze returned to Count Erstein. *It was so easy.*

What would father make of me now, he asked himself.

What right did I have to take this man's life? The Nerisians were the aggressors in this conflict. That was clear enough. But Sanc thought back to his first taste of war—the invasion of the Midder Steppe. His father had taken the lands of the Middians, even if the campaign was against his better judgement. If a Middian had assassinated Duke Bastien, would it have been justified? Perhaps so. War seemed to have a way of obscuring the difference between right and wrong.

Sanc wrestled with what he had done. *I've killed so many people already. I used to know why. Killing a Nerisian because I want the Kassites help against Ezenachi. Have I done the right thing? Have I committed some terrible crime?*

Sanc wiped his blade clean on the expensive cloak of his victim. He stared into the metal and a pair of red eyes stared back at him. *Now I see what father saw when he looked at me.*

'Am I a monster?' he asked out loud.

No one answered. But then he heard shouts and the sound of running feet. *I must get out of here.*

He moved to the window of the room and looked out. The height gave him a clear view of the town. He could see the wooden wall encircling Obernai and beyond it the empty barracks where Mildrith and Rab would be waiting for him. He fixed his gaze on a precise location.

Sanc teleported away.

PEYRE

GUIVERGNAIS/BRASINGIAN BORDER, 676

The army of Guivergne approached the border with Brasingia.
Peyre didn't think there was a soul who didn't understand the
significance of it. It had been forty years since the two great nations
had fought, but still, everyone knew the Brasingians were the enemy.
For the last hundred years, it was the Brasingians who had the upper
hand in Dalriya. Times were changing.

Peyre had to hand it to Esterel, for unifying his subjects in so short
a space of time. He had raised the largest army Guivergne had seen in
generations. *And I deserve some credit for that*, Peyre told himself. The
Morbainais were second in size only to the forces of the king himself.
They were also the most experienced, having seen action in Guivergne and Magnia. Once he had rendezvoused with the rest of the
army at Saliers, Esterel had given Peyre the honour of vanguard,
leading their forces south-east. He, in turn, had given Gosse the job of
directing them through the rocky borderlands. His fur-clad warriors
rode ahead, scouting the area and deciding on the best route to take
such a large force.

Peyre reckoned they numbered well over twenty thousand in all.
That wasn't even the total might of his brother's forces. Domard held
the army of his duchy in Valennes as a reserve. Auberi, meanwhile,

was marching his force into Rotelegen to support their ally, Duke Jeremias. Peyre had been absent in Morbaine when Esterel had devised this strategy, but he liked it all the same.

'It's always wise to consider the point of view of your enemy,' he had advised Umbert when they discussed the plan the other day. Leopold and his advisers had as many options as they had enemies —they could attack Rotelegen, Gotbeck, or Thesse; or face the Guivergnais in Barissia. But wherever the Kellish might go, they would leave their duchy open to attack from another direction. *I wouldn't like to be in Leopold's shoes right now,* he thought, without sympathy.

Peyre spied two figures riding towards him. They were easily identified. Gosse was a giant of a man and his second-in-command, Sul, stood even taller. Only the strongest of horses could bear their weight.

'News?' he asked as they pulled up.

'You're about to pass into Barissia, Your Grace,' Gosse said. 'Thought you'd like to know.'

'Of course,' Peyre said. A shiver ran up his body and he smiled with pleasure. 'Do you know who I think should be the first to enter?' he said, raising his voice for those about him to hear. 'The Barissian Guard!'

His Guard cheered their approval, and he nodded at Elger to organise it. They had started out a ragtag band from the streets of Coldeberg, who had joined him on the promise of pay. Now they were one of the most well-trained units in Guivergne and a source of considerable pride to Peyre.

'Come Umbert,' he cried. 'Gosse, Sul. My guard will follow on. But I can't wait any longer.'

Gosse and Sul turned about and led them at a good pace towards the border. Giant rocks dotted this landscape; black caves gaped uninvitingly, and streams trickled underground. It was unlike anywhere else in Guivergne, and Gosse and his people were unlike anyone else. Raw and untamed, it was like passing through another world to get to the empire. Brasingia, for all the mutual enmity between their peoples, was more like his homeland. During his time there, Peyre had found people to hate and to love.

'Here,' Gosse said, waving a hand to point out an expanse of rock no different from that through which they had just travelled. 'Barissia. The empire.'

'Hmm,' Peyre said, looking for somewhere that wasn't rock. 'Over there.'

His three companions didn't question, simply rode with him towards a patch where grass had managed to take hold. Peyre dismounted and dug into the ground. The soil was thin, but he gathered a handful of dirt.

The Barissian Guard, nearly fifty men strong, approached on their mounts, looking down at him. Some wore puzzled expressions.

He held his prize aloft. 'The soil of Barissia,' he explained. 'Here, Inhan, take it. Deliver it to the king and tell him he has won his first piece of land in the empire.'

* * *

IN BARISSIA, Farred took over from Gosse. The Magnian had helped Walter rule the duchy for nearly twenty years, and he knew where he wanted to send scouts. Peyre gave him the use of the Barissian Guard, many of whom had the local knowledge and contacts to glean information about the enemy. For now, their destination was clear: Coldeberg, capital and stronghold of the duchy. As the day wore on, the scouts brought in news about the city. By the evening, Peyre and Farred agreed they had enough corroborated information to update the king. Leaving Umbert in charge, they made their way to the centre of the camp.

The royal tent, dyed blue and decorated with the owl of Guivergne, was by far the largest amongst the sea of canvas that was erected as the army made camp. Not that every soldier was lucky enough to have a roof over their heads. Plenty slept in the open, woollen blankets their only protection from the elements. But spring was now turning to summer, and it was a mild enough night ahead.

Inside, Esterel had to host and feed the great men of his kingdom every evening. As Peyre entered, a trestle table was already being laid out with food.

'Come on Farred, let's get some sustenance.'

'Should we not wait?'

'No.' Peyre guided Farred over. 'Here, get some ham. I brought this from Morbaine, so we can hardly feel guilty about eating it. The fresh food will all be gone soon enough, so we might as well enjoy it now.'

Peyre helped himself while Farred continued to hesitate.

'Getting in early, I see,' came a familiar voice.

Liesel approached them, with Tegyn at her side. Both wore the same expression—part amused, part disapproving.

'Why not?' Peyre asked once he had swallowed his mouthful. 'Esterel won't mind.'

'No,' Liesel agreed. 'But in the empire, we are used to a blessing before we eat.'

Tegyn and Farred both nodded in agreement.

Peyre knew that well enough. Brasingians worried over religious rites far more than was necessary. 'Yes, well—ah. I was about to say we aren't in the empire. But of course we are. Still, this is Guivergnais food. Tastes just as good without a blessing.'

'I think you're missing the point, Your Grace,' Tegyn ventured.

'Am I?' Peyre answered with a smirk. With studied nonchalance, he broke off a chunk of cheese and popped it into his mouth. He gave the Atrabian a cheesy smile. 'Perhaps we disagree over what the point of food is.'

'Yes. Of course, you are correct as always. Your Grace.'

'Glad you appreciate that. Now, if we had some Cordentine red to wash it down, I would be willing to praise the gods.'

The red wine of Cordence had always been a luxury. With the kingdom conquered by Ezenachi, it had become an extravagance. There was little prospect of new supply and so wine drinkers across Dalriya hoarded their last bottles of the stuff. Tales abounded of barrels being sold for astronomical prices.

Esterel arrived and soon the other lords joined them—Corbenay,

Courion, Auriac, the king's three good friends. Gosse, Lord of the March, who, to Peyre's satisfaction, was increasingly included in the king's inner circle. Saliers, the odd man out in so many ways. While Esterel's friends laughed and joked, Saliers just watched them, revealing nothing of himself. The bastard caught Peyre looking at him and turned his dark, detached eyes his way. Peyre held his gaze, and it was Saliers who looked away first.

That's right, you lizard. You've been taught your place.

'Do we have any news, Morbaine?' Esterel asked him.

'We do. Not necessarily good. Farred is best placed to tell it.'

'Thank you, Your Grace,' Farred said. 'Leopold has acknowledged Mixo as the new duke of Barissia. Mixo is in his thirties, from a well-connected noble family. He was always loyal to Walter. Able and well-liked. I imagine he'll have support from many who approve the idea of a true Barissian as their duke and who won't like the idea of foreigners invading their homeland.'

The news had been more than a surprise to Peyre. He vividly remembered his very first meeting with Leopold, when the bastard had crowed about how he would one day inherit his uncle's duchy and rule three of the seven duchies of Brasingia. He had seemingly given up that ambition. At first, Peyre had interpreted it as a sign of weakness. The Kellish didn't think they could hold Barissia. Now he was less sure. Was it a sign of flexible thinking? Had Leopold won the Barissians over to his side, despite Walter's murder? He wondered whether their invasion of the empire might be more of a challenge than he first thought, despite the size of his brother's army.

Esterel made a pained expression. 'I see. Sounds like a clever move on Leopold's part.'

'Or Inge's,' Liesel added.

Esterel nodded his head at her in acknowledgement.

'I'm afraid so,' Farred said. 'Mixo isn't powerful enough to be anything but a yes man to Leopold. But he'll fight to keep his new title and I think he'll persuade enough people to support him to make our lives difficult.'

'Do you agree, Liesel?' Esterel asked his wife.

'It sounds like it could be a problem for us,' she conceded. 'Not everyone will fall for it. Plenty know what Inge did to Walter, and no one trusts Essenberg. But if Mixo presents himself as a defender of Barissia against Guivergne, he'll have some willing fighters.'

'Alright. Peyre, take extra precautions from tomorrow. Look out for enemy activity, or potential ambushes. I'd rather we go slower than get caught out. Miles, we need to get in contact with our allies.'

'I'll head south tomorrow.'

'Anything else?'

'I have a request,' Liesel said.

Everyone turned their attention to their new queen.

'We all know what happened to my uncle,' Liesel said. 'Some might say you can't stop a witch, even so, I think it's best to be prepared. Lord Gosse, I would ask that you serve as my husband's bodyguard while we're in Brasingia. I don't need to spell out the consequences for us all if the king should fall.'

Peyre didn't know where to look. Esterel looked embarrassed. Gosse wasn't sure what to say. The last thing Peyre wanted to do was meet eyes with Farred, who had been in the same bed as Walter and hadn't been able to stop Inge. He looked at Liesel. She was aware of the awkwardness, but held her chin high, regardless. It was her husband's life she was protecting, Peyre supposed. Not for the first time, he wondered whether his brother fully appreciated who he had married.

'The last thing I want is the queen worrying about me,' Esterel said. 'Lord Gosse, if you would fulfil such a role, I would be grateful for you putting her mind to rest.'

Gosse punched a hand to his shoulder. 'Your Majesty, I would be honoured. I would gladly lay down my life for the king or queen.'

'Nobly said, Lord Gosse,' said Sacha, patting the man on the back. 'Well, I think this calls for a celebration. Your Majesty, I took the liberty of packing a barrel of Cordentine red. I thought it might come in for a special occasion. Perhaps this is as good a time as any?'

Peyre noticed both Liesel and Tegyn staring at him, and he recalled his earlier promise with a smile. 'Praise the gods,' he declared.

Esterel raised an eyebrow. 'Well, since my brother is so enthusiastic, I suppose I'll have to agree. Though I would have thought taking Coldeberg would be a more appropriate moment.'

'Don't worry, Your Majesty,' Peyre said. 'The wine cellar in Coldeberg Castle is extensive. Mixo won't have time to drink it all.'

* * *

THEY MARCHED SOUTH-EAST FOR COLDEBERG. Peyre witnessed the terrain transform from rocky wilderness to rich agricultural land. They passed one prosperous village after another, joining a road that would take them straight to the capital. Peyre gave out strict orders that the Barissians should not be molested, issuing a range of punishments to deter anyone who thought they might ignore him.

Farred continued to direct the scouts. Peyre wasn't surprised to learn they had detected an opposition force ahead of them. Their numbers were estimated at a thousand, not nearly enough to trouble Peyre's force, let alone the entire army. But Esterel had given him a direct order to take extra precautions and so Peyre had Umbert take a cavalry unit and ride parallel to the main force, with orders to engage any threats. He gave Farred extra scouts. Unsurprisingly, the Barissians didn't try anything, retreating before them.

It was the middle of the afternoon when Farred returned. 'We are approaching the town of Schilling. It sits on the road to Coldeberg. It has wooden walls and a keep. We could go round it.'

'Sounds like a good base for us to take,' Peyre said.

'I would have thought so,' Farred agreed.

'Alright. Let me speak to the king.'

Peyre rode back down the line of the Guivergnais force until he reached the royal troops. They wore new uniforms, in azure and silver, with the charge of the owl of Guivergne displayed on their tunics and banners. The colours were still vibrant and arresting. But Peyre thought he preferred the worn in look of his own soldiers. He said a few greetings to those he recognised, including Jehan, now an officer in the army.

He found Esterel riding with Liesel, Tegyn, and Gosse. The big warrior looked a little depressed, so far from the action.

'Schilling is up ahead,' Peyre said. 'Farred says it's sizeable enough to be useful to us as a base. It's also kind of in our way.'

'Any opposition?'

'There's an army out there. We reckon between one and two thousand. They may be operating out of the town. Best guess is they'll continue to retreat rather than try to hold it against us.'

'You advise taking it?'

'Certainly. Who knows how long Coldeberg may hold out? It could prove very useful to us.'

'Alright. Take it.' Esterel seemed to think for a moment. 'Use Saliers as well.'

'Saliers?' Peyre repeated, bemused. 'We don't need his help.'

'I know that. But it's good to have everyone play a role. Share the glory out.'

Peyre would rather have anyone than that treacherous lizard. But Esterel had given him an order. 'Very well.'

'THE WALLS DON'T LOOK capable of holding off an army our size for long,' Peyre commented.

He rode with Farred, Umbert, Elger, Sul, Arnoul of Saliers, and the latter's son Benoit, towards Schilling. They were close enough to get a good look at the town now, which straddled the road to Coldeberg. It was sizeable. The walls were wooden, not stone, making them more susceptible to an attack. With designs on Coldeberg, they had brought plenty of siege engines that would make quick work of the defences. The delay would be in getting the engines ready in the first place.

'Maybe if this elusive army had decided to defend the town,' Farred said. 'But the numbers on the walls look small.'

Peyre had arrayed the Morbaine army in full view. The townsfolk knew they were there; had an indication, if they didn't already know, just how many warriors Esterel had led into the duchy. He imagined those sheltering inside Schilling were more than a little worried right now. The lack of guards on the walls certainly suggested they didn't have the numbers to hold off a concerted attack.

'The stone keep is a different story, though,' Saliers warned them. 'It has stood since the last war with Brasingia. A small force might hold it against us for some time. Better to persuade them to surrender than have to dig them out of it.'

Peyre grunted. He didn't need the snake's advice. And anyway, how did Saliers know how long this keep had stood here? *If he's trying to impress with such knowledge, I'm not exactly speechless with fascination.*

Peyre glanced at the man's son, Benoit. He'd fought the boy in Esterel's contest. It seemed so long ago now, but Benoit had certainly shown promise. *Perhaps his words of wisdom are for his son's benefit.*

'Let's see what they say,' he said.

They stopped outside the gates of the town, closed and barred to them. Half a dozen guards stood on the wall walk and stared down at them. Sul shouted up, demanding they fetch someone of importance. Eventually, that someone appeared.

'I am Krin, mayor of this town,' the man declared.

'Krin. You know me,' Farred shouted up.

'Aye, Lord Farred.'

'This is Peyre, Duke of Morbaine and brother of King Esterel,' Farred said with a gesture towards Peyre.

'Your Grace,' Krin shouted down. 'I wish I could have made your acquaintance differently.'

Peyre tried to take the measure of the man they spoke with. He spoke like a merchant, but wore the breastplate of a noble warrior. Which would he be when push came to shove?

'King Esterel has come into Brasingia to punish the murderers of Duke Walter,' Farred continued. 'And I support him. He asks that you open Schilling to us.'

Krin gave a pained look. 'Aye, well. I have every sympathy over the death of Duke Walter. But Mixo is the new duke of Barissia, and we have all sworn oaths to him. He has ordered us to defend the town against uninvited foreigners.' He gave an awkward shrug. 'I can't betray Schilling to you.'

Peyre's hopes sank. Seemed he was looking at a long and drawn-out siege.

'May I?' Saliers asked him.

Peyre sighed. What harm could it do? 'Be my guest.'

'Mayor Krin,' Saliers shouted up. 'If you do not open your gates to us, we will take your town. No one will be spared. Your menfolk will have their eyes gouged out; their noses, ears and hands will be severed. Your women and girls will be taken and used by our warriors and made to sire bastards. We will set up metal spikes and place your children on them, giving them a slow and painful death. Schilling will serve as a lesson to the rest of Barissia not to resist King Esterel. No other town will make the same mistake. Is this what you want?'

Krin had visibly paled. It was a sickening threat, one that Peyre doubted Esterel would ever carry out. It might work. If it didn't, and they didn't follow through with such threats, would it do more harm than good?

'I will speak to the town council,' Krin replied. He sounded shaken and wasted no time in leaving.

'It's important,' Saliers said, now talking to his son, 'to deliver the threat in a calm, controlled voice. That way, they believe you intend to carry it out. Shout and scream it, and they may interpret it as empty bluster.'

SCHILLING OPENED its gates to them. Esterel gave the town to Saliers. His soldiers manned the walls, and he took the keep for his own residence. When Peyre told Esterel of the man's threats, he laughed them off.

Peyre wasn't sure what to think. He disliked the man. But he had won the town for them, without the loss of life. *This is war,* he told himself. *Men like Saliers have a use in war. And for all Esterel's goofiness, he has an ambitious side to him. He's come to Brasingia to win. He's prepared to do what it takes. And if the result is the defeat of Leopold and Inge, I'm all for it.*

Leaving Saliers and Schilling behind, the army marched on,

getting closer to Coldeberg with every footstep. Peyre's Morbainais still led the way and Farred continued to manage the scouts. They took just as much care as before, but after Schilling, Peyre knew everyone had come to the same conclusion. The Barissians weren't going to challenge them in the field. They would put all their efforts into holding Coldeberg. The city would not fall easily.

It was close to midday when Miles returned, accompanied by Friedrich, the new duke of Thesse. The army rested awhile and Esterel ordered his tent put up so he could talk with the duke in some comfort and with privacy. He and Liesel spoke to Friedrich alone for a good while before Peyre and the other leaders of the army were invited in.

Friedrich had arrived with his chamberlain and a handful of nobles, and they all mingled good naturedly as food was brought in. After a while, Liesel grabbed Peyre and introduced him to Friedrich.

'Welcome, Your Grace,' Peyre said. 'I hope my brother hasn't put you off our alliance?'

'Not at all. And I appreciate what you are all doing.' He gave Liesel a look. 'What Inge did to Walter was a violation. It cannot stand unanswered.'

Peyre nodded. 'I am sorry for the loss of your father, too.'

'Thank you.'

'I witnessed what Ezenachi did to Edgar of Magnia. Horrible.'

Friedrich's eyes looked raw with emotion for a moment. Peyre understood. Watching his father collapse at dinner had been bad enough. He could imagine how hard it had been for Friedrich to see that happen.

'Indeed. And ridding ourselves of Inge is a step towards ridding ourselves of that monster to the south.'

Peyre nodded his agreement, even if he struggled to see how one might lead to the other. Defeating Ezenachi didn't seem to be a matter of raising armies and crowning emperors. That was a job for others. He thought of Jesper, gone to search out the weapons of Madria. He thought of Sanc, gone to some other world. He tried to remember the last time he had thought of his brother. But what did thinking of him achieve, anyway? Sanc was on his own and Peyre had to trust he was alive and well and making progress with his strange quest.

Esterel gathered everyone together and went through the strategy he had agreed earlier with Friedrich. It consisted of the Guivergnais laying siege to Coldeberg, while the armies of Thesse and Gotbeck sat on the Great Road. Should the Kellish march to relieve Coldeberg, Friedrich would march on Essenberg. Like everyone else, Peyre nodded his agreement. It was no different to the strategy Esterel had laid out before they had left Guivergne. But the Thessians seemed happy with the arrangement, and they left with promises to keep their end of the deal.

'What do you think of Friedrich?' Liesel asked him as they watched the Thessians depart.

'He's earnest. Seems like a good man.'

'By which you mean he's naïve. I worry about him a little. We knew each other as children. He was always a gentle boy. Different to Leopold.'

Peyre shrugged. 'I didn't say he was naïve. But if he is, he'd better learn quickly. These aren't times for innocents.'

Liesel gave him a look. 'You were a sweet boy when we first met.'

Peyre looked back, unsure what she meant by it. *She doesn't mean anything, Peyre.* He put a hand to the scar that Leopold had given him. 'I wasn't a duke then, though. Was I?'

'No. He has to realise no one else is on his side.'

Surely, he's learned by now that Leopold and Inge aren't on his side? In which case, who is she talking about? He gave Liesel another look. *Who else can she mean but Esterel?*

BELWYNN

THE LANDS OF THE KRYKKERS, 676

Belwynn and Maragin stood on the shoreline, watching as a Vismarian vessel pulled out to sea. Jesper stood on deck, beginning his journey back home to Halvia. Accompanying him was Stenk, chieftain of clan Dramsen. Once in Halvia, they would have to search its wild lands for Oisin, the King of the Giants, and the spear he carried. Perhaps not the easiest of tasks, but it was one Belwynn would have infinitely preferred to the one that she faced.

'Well,' Maragin said, her voice as hard and heartless as her mountainous homeland. 'We have prevaricated enough. Time to go.'

Indeed. It is time to face up to my past.

They set off north for Kalinth. A kingdom that had once been home to Belwynn. It had been a brief part of her life, but the most important. There she had become a disciple to Elana and, in the end, her replacement. There she had become Lady of the Knights and had nearly become queen. There, she had become the lover of Theron and had come close to becoming his wife. There she had become a mother to an orphaned girl named Lyssa and then abandoned her. There she had killed not just one god but two, and in so doing had killed herself, becoming the half-woman she was now. It was a place she had run from and never wished to return to. Yet a part of her knew she had unfinished business there. The truth was, Belwynn Godslayer feared returning to face the people she had left behind.

The endless mountain passes, the peaks and valleys of the Krykker lands, became a torture. Not physically, for Belwynn no longer felt physical pain. But the long, hard days prolonged her agony. Knowing it was coming, she wanted her reckoning done. Instead, it felt like they crawled towards their destination and the longer it took, the more time Belwynn had to dwell on what was to come.

It's alright for you, she told her dead brother, Soren. *You died a hero, your life's purpose done. I'm left here to stew over my decisions, to constantly wonder what might have been. Forever.* She put a hand to the small scabbard at her belt that contained Toric's Dagger. *Well. Not necessarily forever.*

Maragin was a mixed blessing as a companion. Belwynn knew she would get no comfort from the hard as nails Krykker. She was a woman who simply did what she thought right and didn't even consider the alternative. But her implacable nature didn't allow Belwynn to question their destination. They were going to Kalinth, and that was that.

At last, they descended, and the Kalinthian Plain opened below them. Apart from the Dardelles range that spiked across the centre of the kingdom, Kalinth was flat. Here, the skilled horsemen, the Knights of Kalinth, were dominant. They had withstood the greatest power in Dalriya and survived. Part of Belwynn didn't want to discover how things had gone since she had left almost twenty years ago. She'd allowed herself to imagine a kingdom bathed in success and happiness after its tribulations. Now she was here, she recognised that real life wasn't like that.

They passed Chalios, the great fortress that had seen the climactic battle with the Isharites. Old memories stirred at the sight of it; lyrics to a song came to her throat, tongue, and lips, asking to be sung once more; emotions that Belwynn had buried. She fixed her gaze ahead. Maragin, matching her stride for stride, did the same.

They continued due north, knowing that Chalios would be empty. Their destination was the High Tower of the Knights. It was where Leontios, Grand Master of the Knights, governed. Belwynn would always remember him as a young man, asking her to bless his sword before his first battle. Now he would be middle aged, a veteran of the Isharite Wars. She sighed, a feeling of bitterness overcoming her until she pushed it to one side. *You have enough enemies,* she told herself, *without picking a fight with the irresistible passage of time.*

Belwynn supposed she shouldn't be surprised that a pair such as them would be spotted. They didn't get much past Chalios before a group of half a dozen riders approached them. They were young knights, no doubt given patrol duties that would cover a wide area. Belwynn was relieved at their age. It meant they wouldn't recognise her or Maragin.

'Clan chief Maragin?' one of them ventured.

Belwynn gave her old champion a look. *I suppose I shouldn't be surprised that Maragin has kept up relations with her allies. But she could have said something.*

'Is Grand Master Leontios at the Tower?' the Krykker asked.

'He is.'

Maragin looked at the horses the knights rode with distaste. 'Can you take us?'

THE FACE of the Grand Master of the Knights of Kalinth crumpled in confusion. It amazed Belwynn, how someone who had witnessed dark sorcery plenty of times in his past could still be so surprised by it. It was as if some people's minds could put their experiences to one side and protect their safe, narrow view of the world. 'Lady Belwynn?' he uttered, getting down on one knee before her.

'Sort of,' she admitted. 'I'm what's left of her, anyway. Please, Leontios. There's no need for you to kneel.'

'Of course there is,' he said, but he got to his feet. Not as nimbly, she noted, as he once would have done. For a moment, he visibly dithered. It seemed he had many questions to ask, and Belwynn could hardly blame him for that. But his years of discipline kicked in and a look of composure returned to his face. 'How can I best serve you?'

His simple loyalty touched her. The boyish looks were gone and the hair, once long, was now cropped short. But the big brown eyes remained and something of his devotion to her clearly did, too.

'I need to speak to Theron.'

'You can't simply—' he put two fingers to his head.

'Maybe I could still speak to him like that,' she admitted. 'But it would be an invasion to turn up in his thoughts after all this time. I should speak to him the conventional way.'

'I see. I will have a brigade of knights—'

'Leontios. I want as few people to know about my visit as possible. I have my reasons.'

'Of course, Belwynn. Well, if you want as few as possible, then Maragin and I can escort you to Heractus alone.'

'Thank you.'

* * *

THE THREE OF them set off the next morning, on fine horses. It was another day of memories for Belwynn. The High Tower had been the place where the rebellion of the Knights had begun, a chain of events that had led to old King Jonas being deposed and Theron taking the throne. They followed the road that rebel army had taken, to the capital.

They crossed the Pineos, the river where they had fought the army raised by Siavash. The Lord of the Isharites had killed many close to her, his shadow wearing their bodies as a disguise. How he had repulsed her. How ironic that she had become the very same thing. It was in that battle that Siavash had slain Pentas. According to Jesper, a boy from Morbaine had been born with red eyes who could wield magic like him. She wondered what it meant; wondered if it meant anything at all.

Soren would have had an opinion. How she wished the likes of Pentas and Soren were still alive. They would make the decisions and all she need do was follow them. Now it was up to her to decide what to do. *I have no instinct for what is right. I don't even know whether this journey is a terrible mistake.*

Inevitably, her thoughts turned to Theron and their imminent reunion. The man she had fallen in love with, more completely than anyone else. The same man whose ruthless ambition had fractured the trust she had put in him.

'You still get on well with the king?' she asked Leontios, wondering what kind of man Theron had become since she last saw him.

'Of course. The Knights of Kalinth have returned to their role as the tool of the monarchy and the servants of the people. Those days when the Knights fought the throne are long gone. Praise Madria.'

It hadn't escaped Belwynn's notice that the faith of the people in Kalinth remained as true to Madria as it had been when Elana had been engaged in her missionary work. She wondered what Leontios and others knew of her and Maragin's role in the death of Madria. *People believe what they want to believe,* she reminded herself. *No doubt the faithful believe Madria still lives and protects them. And I can hardly criticise since I was one of them for a while. Life is so much easier when you have a god to believe in.*

Leontios got them rooms in an inn, in a small town that lay in the shadows of the Dardelles mountains. It was impossible for them to avoid attention. But their tactics seemed to work. Belwynn hid inside a deep hood, while the presence of the Grand Master of the Knights and a chieftain of the Krykkers took attention away from her.

They woke early to begin the last leg of their journey. There was more traffic on the road to Heractus—farmers, merchants, and other travellers attracted to the capital, carts bulging with produce and other goods to sell. They served as a distraction for Belwynn. Before she knew it, the morning had gone, and the walls of the city appeared in the distance. Grey and uninviting, as they had always been. Yet long ago she had learned there were hidden qualities to the city and its people. Many lives had been lost when the Isharites had sacked the city, killing any foolish enough not to have escaped south. But the evidence told Belwynn Heractus had recovered. She had expected nothing less from Theron and she was grateful to see it.

Amid the horrors of the war against Ishari, she had built a life in Heractus. There had been Theron and there had been little Lyssa. But the city meant something else to her now. It was the place where she had confronted Siavash for the last time; where Diis had fought Madria; where Soren and Clarin had been killed. When it was done, she had wanted to run far away and never return. Even now, she wished to turn around and retreat to Kirtsea; to sit by the sea and watch the waves come in and out. Instead, she followed Leontios to the gates of the city.

He was quick to get what he wanted from the soldiers on duty. They were soon moving under guard the short distance to the castle. It was a route Belwynn had travelled many times, but never in circumstances like these. The people of Heractus were Elana's people. If they caught even a glimpse of her, their efforts to keep her arrival secret would be done. The news would spread like wildfire and the second coming of the priestess would be declared. Belwynn held her hood closed, fearful that it would blow open and Elana's features be revealed.

When they passed into the castle courtyard, she relaxed a little. Once inside the building, there were fewer things that could go wrong. Leontios was quick to dismount and offer his help to her. They waited for Maragin—Belwynn had yet to see a Krykker dismount a horse gracefully—and then hurried inside. Belwynn thought she might recognise a face or two amongst the servants of Heractus Castle, but she didn't. Times had changed. Leontios had Belwynn and Maragin taken to a private chamber and then set off to find the king.

He soon reappeared, his face grave. 'The king will see you alone,' he said to Belwynn.

'Is he alright?'

Leontios shook his head. 'I think he is in shock. But he needs to see you for himself.'

. . .

231

'COME IN.' Theron's voice.

Belwynn felt sick. Steeling herself, she entered the King of Kalinth's private apartments.

He was alone. She studied him. The years had not been unkind. Those dark brown eyes she used to gaze into hadn't changed, while his brown hair was only beginning to turn grey. She was not surprised to see he had maintained his physical strength. There was, however, a melancholy fixed on his features. Belwynn supposed she shouldn't be surprised by that, given everything he had lost.

He studied her back, a frown creasing his features.

She had tried and given up on preparing something to say. No choice of words would make this any easier. But as the silence lengthened, she knew she should be the one to break it. 'I'm sorry.'

'You're sorry?' he repeated.

She could detect the slew of emotions in his voice, even though he strived to control them.

'What are you sorry for, Belwynn? If, as Leontios tells me, it's truly you.'

'It's me. I'm sorry for leaving and letting you think me dead. And sorry for returning. I swore to myself I never would.'

Theron nodded slowly. 'I understand why you did it to me. I let you down. But Lyssa?'

Straight to the point, then. Her greatest crime. 'You want to know why I abandoned her?'

'Yes. I do.'

'Then try to understand how broken I was. Soren and Clarin were dead. I killed Madria, my goddess, by stabbing myself with Toric's Dagger. All that was left of me was my shadow, inside the body of Elana, my old friend. For years I've blamed myself for what I did, but would anyone be in a fit state to make good decisions in my place?'

Theron shrugged. 'I don't know. I don't pretend to understand what you went through.'

'I was in no state to be Belwynn anymore. I wasn't even sure if I was Belwynn. I couldn't be Belwynn for the Madrians. Or you. Not even for Lyssa. How could I explain to her what I had become? I thought it best if everyone thought me dead. Because in a way I was. I could have ended it, Theron. I didn't. I don't even know why. I left for Magnia. I found Elana's family. I have lived as her all this time.'

'With her husband?' Theron asked, unable to hide his revulsion.

'Yes. Though he has been dead for a while now. Her daughters are married with families of their own.'

'So that's why you've returned?'

Belwynn smiled at him. 'No. Maragin and others found me. Insisted—persuaded me, I suppose—that I still have obligations. I presume you have heard about Ezenachi?'

'Yes. He's taken half of Magnia, so I'm told. Another god to kill?'

'I suppose so. It seems I am expected to play my part in defending Dalriya once more. Maragin and I are looking for the weapons. Many of them were left here. I ask for your help with that.'

'I see. Not a personal call, then.'

'No. And I'd be grateful if you kept my presence here a secret. I don't want Lyssa to find out.'

'Well. I agree with that. But if word gets around that Belwynn has returned from the dead, she will hear it.'

'I intend to keep myself hidden from view. How is she, Theron?'

'She is well.' He couldn't help a smile coming to his features, and the sight of it did Belwynn more good than he would ever know. 'She and Evander are married. One child and another on the way.'

Belwynn sighed with relief. 'I am so pleased. I always believed she would have a good life here, but it means so much to hear it. I heard you adopted her?'

'Yes. I have made them my joint heirs.'

'Joint? They will rule together?'

'Yes.'

'And if they disagree with one another?'

He grimaced. 'I know. But that's how they wanted it.'

Belwynn allowed herself a little smile at that. 'What about you, Theron? You have no queen?'

'No. I was celibate before I met you. I have found it no hardship to resume that life.'

'I'm sorry. I wish things had turned out differently for you.'

'My people suffered terribly at the hands of the Isharites. Too many of my friends died young. Companionship is the only area where I have missed out and I am wise enough to recognise that I have enjoyed a blessed life. There is no greater honour than ruling as king. Lyssa is giving me grandchildren. I certainly don't want your sympathy, Belwynn. Or your apologies.'

Belwynn bowed her head. 'Then on to business?'

'Aye. On to business. I will fetch Maragin, and we can talk about this Ezenachi.'

'JESPER HAS SET sail for Halvia. To find Oisin,' Maragin explained to Theron.

They sat together around a table, three cups of wine left untouched. Belwynn was more than content to let the Krykker do the talking.

'I have the sword, and Belwynn has the dagger. We know Gyrmund returned the bow to the Jalakhs. We need to know the whereabouts of the remaining three weapons.'

'That's not so hard,' Theron said. 'I thought they should be returned to their rightful owners. The Asrai came to retrieve their cloak.'

He seemed to shudder at the memory. Belwynn gave a little nod. Where else could the cloak have gone?

'The shield, we returned to the kingdom of Persala. I delivered it myself to King Zared. The Blood Caladri made a claim on the staff. Their king, Lorant, has it. News from those lands is scarce, but I have heard he has used it to win victories against the Shadow Caladri.'

Maragin sat back and allowed herself a drink. 'Then all that remains is how to persuade them to part with these weapons.'

'That won't be easy,' Theron said.

'The Asrai could be the most difficult,' Belwynn warned. 'I have asked Elfled of Magnia to carry out that task. She witnessed Soren do it. One of our problems is we have no one with the powers to repeat what he did.'

'I may be the best person to speak with Lorant,' Maragin said. 'He has been a willing ally in the past.'

'I am best placed to ask Zared if we can borrow the shield again,' Theron admitted. 'Though I must warn you, here in the north we do not lie awake worrying over this Ezenachi. It's Gansukh and the Jalakhs that keep us up at night.'

'And I suppose that's the task left for me,' Belwynn said.

'Pointless,' Theron said. 'The khan will never part with the bow again. It has helped him win his empire, and he is eager to expand further. Why would he give up his personal weapon?'

'I don't know,' Belwynn said. 'But I suppose I have to try.'

'He'll kill you.'

Belwynn allowed herself a wry smile. 'He can try.'

SANC

KASSITE/NERISIAN BORDER, 676

Sanc and Mildrith wasted no time in retracing their steps, vacating the area around Obernai. Sanc was sure the soldiers of the town would be out looking for him as soon as the count's body was found. Mildrith retrieved their mounts, and they rode for the safety of the White Forest. Rab kept pace with the horses, who seemed to have got used to his smell.

Sanc's mood didn't improve. His mind kept returning to the corpse of Count Erstein, the wound in his chest he had inflicted. *I didn't even speak to the man*, he realised. *Didn't find out if he was good or bad. I just killed him. It's wrong.* When he mulled it over some more, he found the counter arguments. *The sooner I defeat Lothar, the sooner I can leave Silb for Dalriya. I don't have time to question every action.* He shook his head. The truth was, he was becoming lost in this world, unsure of his purpose.

Mildrith looked across at him. 'I would have gone in with you.'

'I know. It's not that.' He sighed, looking at her as he debated what to say. *Why not tell her? I trust her as much as anyone else I've met here.* 'I just don't know if I did the right thing. It was right for you, I suppose. For the Kassites. But what business did I have in killing him?'

Mildrith looked at him, thinking. 'I must admit, I hadn't really thought about it. All I can say is thank you for taking our side. And just to let you know, I'll keep my promise. Once we've defeated the Nerisians, I'll help you. You believe me?'

'I do,' Sanc said. He'd told himself to stop trusting people so easily after Tassia. But there was something about Mildrith that he liked. 'It's defeating the Nerisians that seems the hard part.'

Mildrith gave him a little smile. 'Don't tell anyone I said so. But you're right.'

* * *

BACK IN THE WHITE FOREST, Sanc knew he could relax a little. There was no evidence they were being followed. He and Mildrith had carried out their part of the plan. Now it was time for the Kassite warriors to join in.

Once they crossed into the lands of Holt Slender Legged, they soon found the Kassite army. The warriors from three tribes were gathered under the forest canopy, waiting for their return. They had made a clearing, stripping the felled trees and building siege equipment.

Holt, Rinc the Black, and List the Castrator spoke with them while their followers listened in.

'Erstein is dead,' Mildrith told them. 'Sanc entered his hall and killed him.'

'You saw him dead with your own eyes?' List asked her. He gave a suspicious sneer, revealing his sharpened teeth.

'No. But I have no doubts.'

'He could be lying,' List said. 'Could be working for the Nerisians for all we know. Could have warned them of our plans.'

Sanc met eyes with the chieftain but said nothing. A denial from him would carry little weight.

'If you didn't trust us, why did you agree to the plan?' Mildrith demanded, her voice rising in volume.

'Thought you'd be with him, didn't I?'

'You never asked for that,' Mildrith said. 'We did what was agreed. Erstein is dead. There's a good number of soldiers, near a thousand I'd say, stationed inside the town walls. The barracks outside are empty. They'll have their guard up. But from what we know, there isn't a ready-made leader to replace the count.'

'You've done well,' said Rinc the Black, publicly siding with Mildrith. 'By the time we reach Obernai, my guess is they'll no longer be so alert. In disarray, we can hope.'

'Not expecting an army, that's for sure,' said Holt.

'I overheard some of his officers talking,' Sanc volunteered. 'Complaining that the count was reducing rations. Sounded like they were on their last supplies and keen to move into Kassite lands.'

'Bastards want to come and raid us again,' List said. 'Steal whatever they didn't take last time.' The Kassites gathered around murmured darkly at this.

'Keeping that number of fighters fed over the winter ain't an easy task,' Rinc said. 'Especially with the bulk of Nerisian resources sent into Scorgia. This might work out well for us.'

'Then let's find out,' Holt said. 'I'll lead us through the forest and take us to Obernai. We got killing to do and vengeance to mete out.'

* * *

SANC AND MILDRITH travelled with Holt's men, traversing the forest paths on foot this time. Behind them came List's crew, while Rinc's force took the rear. Each chieftain had brought around a thousand warriors, meaning they easily outnumbered the force at Obernai. The only problems Sanc could foresee were getting spotted and getting past the walls of the town.

Once clear of the forest, they made sure to only travel at night. They kept north of the city, travelling through the lands the Nerisians had recently conquered from the Kassites. Sanc was used to an army reducing in size over time, as deserters slipped away when they'd had enough of military life. Instead, their ranks swelled as rebel Kassites appeared in small groups to help overthrow their new masters. No one could say for sure they hadn't been seen by the enemy. But they got within range of Obernai and there was still no evidence they were expected.

They made a basic camp with some rudimentary defences. It was a place to retreat to should the worst happen. Sanc decided to leave Rab behind with the small force who remained. He would use magic in the attack on Obernai, and the dog wouldn't be able to follow where he went.

Mildrith gave Rab into the keeping of Sweterun, a friend of hers, insisting that on no account should the woman allow him to be eaten. The instruction almost made Sanc change his mind. But Sweterun took a liking to Rab, and Sanc judged he'd be better off with her than on his own or in the battle to come.

They waited until dusk had settled to resume their march. The Kassites wore their strongest armour and sharpened their weapons. Axes abounded, as well as spears and swords. Some carried wooden shields, others didn't bother. There was little discussion of tactics compared to what Sanc had got used to in the army of Guivergne. No one expected a pitched battle. This was to be a raid, albeit on a size-able settlement, and it seemed the Kassite warriors knew what they were about without the need for orders.

Holt's force took a circular route, past the southern entrance to Obernai until they stopped to the west of the town. List's warriors moved to a location opposite them, to the east. Finally, Rinc led his fighters to the south. The Kassites would attack the walls from three locations, making life difficult for the defenders.

Sanc and Mildrith waited with Rinc the Black. There was little light in the sky, but they could just make out the walls of Obernai. Sanc could see a few patches of light from the town, probably braziers that offered the night guardsmen a little warmth. Otherwise, it was hard to make out anything else that might give them clues as to the preparedness of the defenders.

Then, more lights appeared to the east and west. Holt and List were taking their warriors to the town walls, their torches visible against the night sky. Shouts carried to them. Sanc could see some torches fly over the wall, the Kassites hoping to spread fire and create panic.

'Let us try the gate first,' Mildrith said to Rinc. 'Give us some time to get it open.'

Rinc's dark hair and pale skin made him look like a ghost or some other denizen of the night. 'How long should I wait?' he asked her flatly.

'Count to one hundred twice.'

He sighed. 'I can't count that high.'

'Do your best,' Mildrith advised. 'Come, Sanc.'

They crept towards the south gates of the town. As they neared, Sanc took Mildrith's hand and used his magic to hide them. He tried to ignore the tingle of excitement he felt at the contact, silently berating himself for not being able to concentrate fully on the task at hand. The details of the structure came into view and atop it, he could make out half a dozen soldiers, peering warily into the night. They knew their town was under attack from two directions and would be foolish not to suspect more.

'Ready?' Mildrith whispered.

Sanc nodded. He felt himself being lifted. He stood on his toes and then his feet were dangling in the air, Mildrith carrying him higher.

They drifted up the wooden wall, only a few feet from the gates. Sanc concentrated furiously on his own magic, hiding their advance, while looking at the Nerisian soldiers to see if they'd been spotted. Mildrith gently deposited them both onto the wall walk, where there was just enough width for them to stand comfortably beside one another. Once his footing was secure, Sanc reluctantly let go of her hand and drew his sword.

The movement and sound drew attention as the Nerisian guards turned to see them, both now visible. Eyes widening, some shouted a warning, others drew weapons. One of them threw an axe at Mildrith, but Sanc had now put up his defensive magic and the weapon clattered into his magic shield and fell to the floor.

Sanc charged them, sword at the ready, Mildrith close behind. They had to be quick and ruthless. As the nearest warriors came at them, Sanc blasted two with his magic, sending them flying over the wall into the inner courtyard. Mildrith blasted a third, sending him over the other side, where he landed with a crunch outside the town. Sanc waited for a warrior to jab his spear, then moved in. His sword cracked into his opponent at chest height and the man lost his balance, tumbling over the wall after his two comrades.

Mildrith moved ahead of him. Her axe strike was blocked by her opponent's shield. She pushed with her magic and her opponent went sprawling backwards, clattering into the man behind him. They landed in a flailing mass of limbs and Mildrith was onto them. Her axe fell again and again, the sounds of the men's screams mixing with the noise of armour being pounded, bones shattered, and flesh lacerated. At last, to Sanc's relief, she stopped, her gory work done.

'Down here,' she said, gesturing with a bloody arm to a set of stairs ahead of them that led off the wall.

She turned and Sanc followed her. They moved quickly, not waiting for more Nerisians to discover them. The stairs took them down to the courtyard that lay in the shadow of the gates. The area was deserted, save for the bodies of the Nerisian warriors. They lay in the dirt where they had landed after falling from the wall walk.

Elsewhere, Sanc could hear the shouts and crashes that came from Holt and List's attack on the walls. Their warriors had made crude ladders and battering rams in the forest. Enough to cause the defenders problems, but not necessarily enough to break through. He looked at the wooden gates in front of him. Opening them would surely do the trick.

'Come on,' Mildrith said. She had her hands on one end of a wooden bar that was slotted through huge metal hooks.

Sanc grabbed the opposite end, and they lifted the bar off and dropped it to the ground.

Mildrith pushed at one of the gates. 'Locked,' she said, pointing to the keyhole in the centre of a metal plate.

Sanc opened his palm and aimed at the plate. He sent a blast of magic at it. It rattled with the impact and the surrounding wood scarred black from the strike. Mildrith aimed her axe head with care and gave the plate a hefty strike. It fell to the ground, and she peered at the inner mechanics revealed. She gave the gate another push and Sanc joined her. With a shudder, they forced it open.

Mildrith gave Sanc a smile and raised her arm. She let forth a blast of fiery coloured magic that sizzled high into the night sky. 'Hopefully Rinc sees that,' she said. 'And stops trying to count.'

* * *

WHEN RINC'S warriors entered Obernai, there was only going to be one winning side. The defenders were overwhelmed, Holt and List's men soon getting inside the town. The Nerisians made a last stand in the count's hall. But the Kassites didn't shy away from using fire to flush them out.

What followed was the most brutal reprisal Sanc had ever seen. List's men were the worst, and their chieftain lived up to his nickname by cutting body parts from captured warriors. But Rinc and Holt didn't hesitate to join in with the murder. Few Nerisians were spared. Some of the women and children were taken as slaves.

When the Kassites ran out of people to kill, they flattened the buildings. It was clear nothing would be left of the town. Seeing enough, Sanc had to leave, walking through the gates he had helped open, towards the Kassites' camp. He needed to find Rab—needed to distract himself from the massacre he had enabled.

Footsteps behind him made him turn. It was Mildrith.

'I'm sorry,' she said. 'But it's nothing compared to what the Nerisians have done to our people in the last few years.'

'I don't doubt it,' Sanc said. He resumed his walk, and Mildrith strode beside him. 'But how can they kill unarmed men and women? And where will all this bloodshed end?'

'It must end when Lothar is defeated. You know what he's done to the Scorgians and to us. He won't stop until all the peoples of Silb have been crushed.'

Sanc believed her. He'd had to kill Lippers, Caladri, Cordentines, and Magnians in Dalriya. Men and women. Innocent victims of Ezenachi, who had turned them to his bidding. But that had felt different, somehow. They were the god's slaves, impossible to reason with. Nerisians and Kassites were so alike to his eyes he couldn't tell them apart. Why were they killing one another?

'What I don't understand,' he said, 'is how it got to this. When I was in Arvena, I visited a temple there a few times. I learned something about the history of Silb. The high priestess there taught me how the seven peoples came to Silb together and conquered this land, dividing it up equally. So how did you become enemies?'

Mildrith looked at him. 'Human nature, Sanc. Greed. When the natives were defeated, there was no common enemy. The rulers and warriors began to covet the lands and wealth of their neighbours. Petty disputes escalated. Though what Lothar has done is worse than anything that has gone before.'

'Why?'

'I don't know. The Nerisians, Scorgians, and others desire one ruler. A king. It is a recipe for aggression. We Kassites belong to our tribes. We don't need more than we have.'

'Your tribes are too busy quarrelling with one another?'

'Perhaps. But you see how we act, Sanc. We don't place our chieftains on a pedestal above us. They must consult us; make decisions for the good of the tribe, not just for themselves. When I look at the other peoples, I don't see this. Thousands of Nerisians have fought and bled to take our lands from us. All for the benefit of Lothar and his henchmen. He won't stop until he is king of the entire world.'

Sanc considered this. He wondered whether Mildrith would be equally critical of Guivergne and the other kingdoms in Dalriya. She probably would. But where was the solution to what he had witnessed in Obernai? Was humankind simply doomed to fight, kill, and enslave their enemies? Forever, until the end of time?

He sighed. 'I need to find Rab and forget all this for a while.'

Mildrith nodded. 'I'll leave you alone.'

Sanc wondered whether the Kassite champion wanted to come with him. By the sounds of it, she had experienced far worse than he had. Maybe she needed some time apart as well. But by the time he thought to ask her, Mildrith had turned around and was making her way back to the town.

SANC

KASSITE/NERISIAN BORDER, 676

There was no reason to stay in Obernai. The town had been flattened. The Kassites took whatever supplies they could find, but as Sanc had warned them, the Nerisians had been running low.

Still, it was enough to keep their army in the field a few more days. The next part of the plan was to head north, for the chain of forts Lothar had built to control his newly conquered lands. The garrison in Obernai had been the reserve force for those forts. Now it was destroyed, the Nerisians on Kassite soil were dangerously exposed.

Sanc was included in the meeting of the warlords again. List still sneered at him, but there were no more accusations of treachery.

'We need to send word to Grindan and Tredan,' Rinc the Black said. 'It will be best to time our assault on the forts, so we attack together. If we strike from north and south, they won't stand a chance.'

'Aye,' agreed List the Castrator. 'Tredan Late to Battle needs plenty of warning to get to the fight on time.'

'Then perhaps our champions should go?' Holt suggested.

'I suppose so,' Mildrith agreed. 'Can't see we're needed much here anymore.'

'No,' said List. 'I think we can manage walking a bunch of bloodthirsty Kassites to a meeting with a bunch of murderous, rapacious Nerisians.'

No one could argue with that. Mildrith and Sanc took a couple of horses and rode ahead, taking Rab with them. Sanc was pleased to leave the Kassite army behind, still sickened by their barbarity in Obernai. He had to trust in Mildrith's knowledge of the local terrain —where the enemy forts were, and how far their garrisons patrolled.

Grey clouds filled the sky, depositing a steady drizzle that reduced visibility. It was uncomfortable, but Sanc supposed it benefited them. The Nerisians were more likely to stay hunkered up in their forts than go out in this weather. The terrain they passed through was a mix of woodland and long grass. The ground was wet underfoot, but not so bad as to slow their mounts' progress.

Sanc had few worries, even though they were passing through enemy held territory. If they were to have an encounter, he trusted that his and Mildrith's magic would be enough to keep them safe, preferably by hiding rather than a fight. They didn't want to alert the Nerisians to their activity.

When they heard the riders, they were so close that Sanc had little time to react. The worst part about it was the noise came from the woodland to their right, where Rab had padded to go exploring.

Mildrith gave him a sharp glance.

'We need to hide,' he said, offering her his hand.

'What about Rab?'

'He'll run off and hide,' Sanc said, trying to assure himself as much as her. Rab was no longer the foolish pup he'd once been. If he smelt men and horses he didn't recognise, he'd make himself scarce. The only reason he'd stay was if Sanc was threatened.

Mildrith took his hand and Sanc covered them both—and their horses—in his spell of illusion. It told anyone looking their way that they saw and heard nothing.

It wasn't long before the four riders came into view, exiting the woodland via the path Rab had entered. Sanc felt his stomach constrict in worry for his dog. A part of him wanted to go charging into the situation and ensure Rab was safe. But he knew he had to accept that these situations would occur. He hadn't wanted Rab to come with him to Silb. But he had, and that meant the dog would get into danger from time to time. He had to accept that and keep his head.

The four Nerisians rode in the opposite direction to Mildrith and Sanc. Sanc assumed these warriors were patrolling the perimeter of their territory.

'What *was* that?' he heard one of them ask.

'Badger?'

'That looked nothing like a badger.'

'Well, you got the best sight of it. You tell me.'

'That's what I'm saying. It looked nothing like anything I've ever seen.'

Sanc and Mildrith exchanged looks. They'd seen Rab. But obviously not for very long. Sanc felt a little better.

'It'll be some creature that only exists in these forsaken Kassite lands. Wait 'til we get full control of the place and then we can hunt them down properly.'

'Nah. Once we conquer the Kassites for good, I'm going home. Not spending one more day in this hole than I have to.'

'Are you mad? The king will give out land to his soldiers. We'll all get our own estate with Kassite slaves to work on it.'

'And spend the rest of my days getting rained on? No thanks. Wait, what's this?' One of the riders was peering at the ground. 'Hoof prints.' He turned to look in Sanc and Mildrith's direction. 'Two horses heading that way.'

Sanc gave Mildrith an apologetic look. It hadn't crossed his mind that they had left a trail in the wet earth for the Nerisians to follow.

The Kassite champion made a grim face and put a hand to the throat of her axe.

Sanc sighed, looking at the Nerisians. All four of them were now looking in their direction. It was only a matter of time before they were seen. He gave her a reluctant nod, and they released hands. The Nerisians saw them instantly and their hands went instinctively to the weapons at their belts.

Sanc and Mildrith released their magic. Their first strikes both hit the same victim. Their second strikes felled two more, one warrior sent flying from his mount, which promptly turned and galloped away. The last warrior, eyes wide in terror, turned his horse around to escape, but Sanc's blast of magic took him in the back of the head.

Before Sanc had time to take it all in, Mildrith was kicking her mount and setting off in pursuit of the departing horse.

Sanc dismounted and approached the Nerisians. He examined their bodies one at a time to make sure they were dead, taking care not to agitate the three remaining horses. He had to lower one corpse from its mount, pulling a booted foot from its stirrup.

I'm getting used to dead bodies, he thought. *That's not a good thing.* Together, he and Mildrith were deadly. He wondered just how many warriors they could deal with, just the two of them. The thought made him look around, back into the trees. He knew his thought had been arrogance. It would have taken just one archer, hidden in the undergrowth, to take him out with his back turned. It was one of the things he feared most about his magic—letting the power of it get to his head. *Once that happens, I don't reckon I'd last much longer.*

Having assured himself the Nerisians were dead, Sanc began shouting for Rab. He walked towards the woods, wondering if he should follow the path and start searching before Mildrith returned. Then the dog burst from the undergrowth, ears bouncing up and down, pelting along faster than Sanc had ever seen him. He only just slowed down enough to avoid crashing into Sanc, who rewarded him with a rub while he got slavered on. 'You've been hiding somewhere, have you? Clever boy!'

Rab barked, releasing the tension of his encounter with the Nerisians, but Sanc had to tell him off or else he'd scare the horses. Turning around to check on them, he saw Mildrith returning, holding the reins of the recovered Nerisian mount.

'He's alright?' she asked.

'Yes. What are we going to do with them?' He gestured at the fallen Nerisians.

Mildrith dismounted with a casual grace. 'Strip them of their armour and weapons. Then we'll take the loot and the horses north with us.'

Sanc made a face. It was bad enough killing these men. Taking possessions from a corpse seemed low, adding insult to injury.

Mildrith looked straight back. 'These are decent items, Sanc.' She tapped at a breastplate. 'Hardened leather. It could make the difference between life and death for one of our warriors.'

Sanc sighed. He couldn't argue with that. They unbuckled straps and took anything of value, tethering their haul to the four horses they had acquired.

'Drag the bodies into the trees,' Mildrith said when they were done.

'Could this get any grimmer?' Sanc wondered. But he did as asked, grabbing the first warrior under the armpits and dragging him into the woodland. When they were done, they had four bodies laid out in a row.

'Maybe we should cover them with something?' Sanc suggested. 'They'll be found by anyone looking for them.'

'I'll deal with it,' Mildrith said. 'Stand back.'

She held up both hands and cast her magic. The ground around the bodies churned and tree roots broke to the surface. Rab barked, and Sanc couldn't silence him. The roots twined themselves around the four bodies and then dragged them down, burying them. When the magic was done, bodies and roots were gone. All that was left were chunks of earth, which Mildrith flattened down with her boot. She caught his look. 'Well?'

'Something tells me you've done that before.'

'I'm sorry, Sanc.'

'Sorry? What—'

'Sorry I'm not the kind of girl who spends her time sewing, or milking cows. I didn't ask for this. Of all people, you should know that.'

She stomped off back to the horses. Sanc thought better of shouting after her. 'What did I say?' he asked Rab.

Rab tilted his head to the side, apparently as oblivious as Sanc.

*　*　*

Sanc and Mildrith didn't talk as they resumed their journey north, passing between two of the Nerisian forts. The Kassite champion didn't even want to look at him. Maybe silence wasn't a bad thing. Riding two horses and leading four more, Sanc felt more vulnerable than before, worried they'd be that much easier to spot. He didn't think he'd be able to hide them all if the need arose.

Despite this concern, he couldn't stop wondering what had upset Mildrith. He knew he'd been moaning about the dirty work they'd had to do. And then he'd said something about her magical burial of the Nerisian warriors. She'd clearly taken it personally. All he could come up with to explain it was that she seemed to care what he thought of her. Someone caring about his opinion of them was such an unfamiliar experience that he hadn't given it a single thought until now.

He glanced at her. The annoying thing about it was, he really liked her. She was strong and beautiful, and they shared a bond—their age and magic—something he hadn't experienced before. *Trust me to mess it up.* Well, he'd be more careful from now on. He'd make sure he let her know how much he thought of her in future. Best to let her cool down first, though. *I think if I start apologising or talking about it, I'll just make things worse.*

When evening came, they had to stop and make a camp. They had six horses to see to now, and the constant drizzle looked like it might get worse instead of letting up. It seemed like they were in for a miserable night.

When they were done, Sanc sat against a tree with Rab and did his best to cover them with his blanket. To his surprise, Mildrith sat next to him. Sleeping next to one another and sharing warmth seemed to be something that was second nature to her. For Sanc, her proximity always made his heart beat fast and his mouth go dry. He offered her his blanket, and she moved in even closer.

'It's cold,' he muttered, just for something to say. He could feel her next to him, could smell her damp leathers, could see her wet hair at his shoulder. 'Do you know where we are?'

'Right on the new border between the Nerisians and Kassites.' She didn't move, so all he saw was her hair, not her face.

'Hmm. So all the land we passed through today was taken from the Kassites?'

'Yes.' There was a pause. 'Look, I'm sorry about before,' she said. 'I'm sick of this rain and I lost my rag with you. You did nothing wrong.'

'I was whingeing like a child instead of just getting on with it,' Sanc admitted.

She turned, looked up at him, and smiled. He looked into her blue eyes, feeling lost in them. 'Maybe a bit,' she said. 'But this is all new to you. You're entitled to have a gripe without me acting up.'

Come on, Sanc, he told himself. *Tell her how much you think of her.* He hesitated. 'Well,' he made himself say, 'I'm glad we're talking again. Because we make a good team.'

'We do. It's nice to have someone to work with. You've no idea how lonely it is being the only one.'

'I do,' Sanc said.

She said nothing, just looked at him. Sanc looked at her lips, desperate to kiss her.

'Mildrith—'

'Yes?'

'When I was in Arvena, I met this girl called Tassia. At the time, I thought I was in love with her. She betrayed me and I realised I hadn't been in love with her at all.'

'And you're telling me this because?'

'Well, I think I might be in love with you. But I've got it wrong before.'

She smiled, leaned into him, and they kissed. Sanc put a hand to her back, one on her waist. He wanted to touch her all over, had to stop himself from moving too quickly.

Mildrith put a hand to his chest. It slid down to his stomach and then lower. 'It's alright,' she said, her voice breathy. 'You don't have to fall in love with me, Sanc. Just keep me warm tonight.'

* * *

THEY WOKE early and readied all six horses. The weather hadn't let up all night and every piece of equipment was soaking. Despite his discomfort, Sanc had to stop himself from allowing a goofy smile to appear on his face. He cast the odd, furtive glance at Mildrith when she wasn't looking. He thought he caught a little smile at the corner of her mouth, but then wondered whether he'd imagined it.

Their journey felt a bit more relaxed, since they were travelling across territory still owned by the Kassites. Mildrith led them northeast, into the lands of Grindan Won't Stop Eating. They came upon the settlement where Sanc and Prince Lenzo had first met with the chieftain. Now it was surrounded by a military camp. Kassite warriors huddled on the sodden ground, looking miserable. When Mildrith and Sanc appeared, a crowd of them followed them as they climbed the stone steps, before passing through the gates and stopping before Grindan's hall.

Grindan emerged with a piece of bloody meat skewered on his knife, his flaxen beard slick with grease. With him came Tredan Late to Battle, who had obviously defied his nickname and travelled south with his tribe's warriors. Gold still hung from every available space on his face, while he eyed their spoils of war with interest.

Mildrith presented the four horses and the armour and weapons they had taken to Grindan. The crowd of Kassites who observed the meeting murmured appreciatively, and Grindan beamed with delight.

'These are well received,' he said, patting one of the beasts, which trembled nervously. 'Ymer knows, we need as much armour and weaponry as we can get. But what news from Obernai? We have sat on our arses for days now, waiting to hear from you.'

'Obernai is taken,' Mildrith declared, her volume rising for all to hear. 'We stormed its walls and killed its soldiers. None escaped, while the town itself is a ruin.'

Cheers rang out at this. Their news had turned the mood amongst the Kassites full circle.

'The warriors of Holt, List, and Rinc are now heading north for the Nerisian forts,' Mildrith continued. 'There is no Nerisian force left to relieve them. If you march south, your warriors can join in with the slaughter. At last, it's our chance for revenge on the invaders. We can sweep them all from our lands.'

Grindan and Tredan shared the same greedy, grisly looking smiles.

Sanc could feel the hunger for violence amongst the gathered Kassites. Mildrith gave him a look, almost apologetic. Obernai was only the beginning. More bloodshed was coming, and Sanc couldn't see an end to it.

LIESEL

COLDEBERG, DUCHY OF BARISSIA, 676

The stone walls of Coldeberg reared before them. Thick and tall, built on a hill, they looked more than a match even for an army of the size Esterel had led into the empire.

Liesel had been to the city once before for her uncle's inauguration. She had only been a child and remembered little of the place. She did vividly remember seeing the strangers who had come, however. There had been a queen of the Blood Caladri. She had seemed both beautiful and terrifying with her clawed feet. Then there had been the Krykkers. Not quite so alien looking, but the tough hide on their chests had marked them as different. One of those Krykkers had been Maragin, an important chieftain even back in her father's day. She spared a thought for the Krykker and for Jesper, sent on a quest to assemble the weapons of Madria that had saved Dalriya before and, she had to hope, would do so again.

She liked to think this invasion of Brasingia was linked to that quest; that their efforts had a shared goal—the defeat of Ezenachi. But she knew this conflict had become very human. Her husband had committed himself to victory and anything else would be a humiliation from which he might not recover. For her brother Leopold, too, having the imperial title denied to him would be unthinkable. Somewhere in Coldeberg Castle, Mixo, the newly proclaimed Duke of Barissia, had cast his dice and tied his colours to Leopold's mast. Liesel knew he would hold on to the capital at all costs.

Everywhere, in Guivergne and Brasingia, there were men and women whose fates would be changed by the outcome of this war. Sometimes, she wondered if she should have tried to stop it. Instead, she had encouraged it. *I suppose the gods will judge me.* But she thought of Walter, Idris, and so many others. *If wars are ever necessary, then this is one.*

Liesel wasn't sure whether war was necessary, but she soon learned it could be deathly dull. Not for Esterel, of course. He talked of nothing else. He arranged the positioning of his forces to within a yard, taking personal interest in every minor detail. There were his own soldiers to organise, and then those brought by his magnates: Peyre, Miles, Sacha, Florent, Gosse, and half a dozen other lords with the right to raise their own units. Esterel had a nose in every pie, interfering until he had a complete investment of Coldeberg. No one was getting in or out of the city. From now on, the citizens and Mixo's soldiers had to live off their food stores.

Esterel hadn't sent a single messenger to the city. It was pointless, he told her, to hope the defenders might submit at this stage.

'Silence serves a better purpose. To sow fear and doubt,' he explained.

Instead, his messengers went out into the country to find support amongst the people. They told the Barissians about Inge's murder of Walter; claimed that Mixo was a mere puppet of Essenberg; and justified the Guivergnais intervention.

'We don't even need them to give us more soldiers,' he told her. 'If all we get are some towns and villages willing to sell us their produce, it will be worth it.'

Her husband was a ball of energy, certain about every single decision he took. But he wasn't nearly done. Liesel had imagined the Guivergnais would assault the city walls and force their way in. Esterel told her that would leave thousands dead. Instead, his next step was to begin the construction of double fortifications. Not just facing Coldeberg, to defend against a sortie from the Barissian army. But facing out as well, in case the Kellish army should arrive to break the siege.

'How long?' she asked him, doing her best to sound patient.

'We should have the basic structure ready in a few weeks.'

Liesel nodded and smiled politely. 'Wonderful.'

'A FEW WEEKS?' she demanded of Tegyn when they were out of earshot, walking a circumference of the camp. For her safety, Esterel had told her she wasn't allowed outside the fortifications. She could hardly complain after making such a fuss over his own welfare. 'How long are we going to be stuck here? Meanwhile, every day the camp turns more and more into a quagmire and the stink from the latrines gets worse and worse.'

'Mm. It's almost as if we're living in an army camp. Wait 'til the dysentery starts going round.'

Liesel gave Tegyn a fearful look. 'I don't want to wait for that.' She imagined her new subjects watching her shitting blood into a muddy trench and shivered at the thought. 'I think I made a mistake coming here. I should have stayed in Valennes.'

Valennes, where she had her own room and a huge, soft bed. The stink of the Bastion would be nothing to her after this. 'What is the point of me being here? I imagined I might be useful, to encourage the nobility of Brasingia to side with Esterel. I imagined meetings over dinner where I persuaded men to support my husband and desert my brother. I certainly didn't imagine this. And in all seriousness, I'd stick it out if I thought it would help. But I'm a spare part.'

'So what?' Tegyn asked. 'You can always return to Valennes.'

'I could. But I want to do something useful.'

'Like what?'

'I don't know. That's what I'm asking.'

'Oh. What about a meeting with Duke Friedrich to discuss strategy? It could be held in Lindhafen, in his castle.'

Liesel's eyes narrowed at her friend. 'Is that suggestion just so you can fish for a marriage proposal?'

Tegyn's eyes went wide with fake innocence. 'No! The thought hadn't crossed my mind.'

Liesel thought about it. 'Actually, that reminds me of an idea I had. Maybe there is something to be gained from going to Thesse.'

'Fine. I mean, you're married to the King of Guivergne, but don't concern yourself with the fact that I'm a spinster.'

Liesel sighed. 'Friedrich is camped out with his army on the Great Road. He doesn't have time for flirting.'

Tegyn made a face. 'It might help him take his mind off things,' she mumbled.

* * *

IT WASN'T until late evening when Liesel could grab some alone time with Esterel. They had a small meal of dry army rations, Esterel insisting that he should eat the same food as his soldiers. He enjoyed the hardship, she realised. He was playing war with his friends and the terrible food and general discomfort were all part of the fun.

'How do you think it's going?' she asked him.

'Well enough. It's going to be much harder for the Kellish to disrupt our position from now on.'

'Do you think they'll try?'

Esterel shrugged. 'I would have done. I wouldn't want to leave my ally isolated and vulnerable. But who knows what Leopold, Inge and Salvinus think? You know them far better than I.'

'They certainly won't be losing sleep over Mixo,' Liesel told him. 'He's just an expendable tool to them.'

'Well, so far, they've done nothing. It's not like they don't have options. If not west against us, they could strike north against Rotelegen, or south against the Thessians and Gotbeckers.'

Liesel frowned. 'All three of them are erratic—hard to predict, in their own ways. But they won't be sitting there doing nothing. Don't underestimate them, Esterel. They'll be up to something.'

'I won't,' he assured her with an easy smile.

'I wanted to discuss my own role with you.'

'Oh?'

'I'm not much use sitting here waiting for Coldeberg to starve.'

He looked at her, then shrugged. 'True. But I enjoy having you here.'

She smiled, put a hand on his. 'Thank you. But I was thinking of travelling to Thesse. I have an idea, you see,' she said quickly, sensing he immediately disliked the idea. 'We've discussed before the need for Guivergne to develop its archery. But training archers in sufficient numbers is such a long-term project.'

Esterel gave her a wary nod.

'Well, the Cordentines use crossbows. I saw them in action against the forces of Ezenachi. They are deadly. Most of the Cordentines who escaped Ezenachi's invasion are living in rough camps. Since Coen's death, they are seen as an unwanted burden. But I see potential. I want to bring some of them to Guivergne. In exchange, we can learn how to build their weapons. They require far less training than the long-bow. You just point and release the trigger.'

Esterel puffed out his cheeks. 'Would you not prefer a pet to occupy you? I could get you a puppy?'

'Stop it, Esterel.'

'Sorry. But even if it's a good idea—'

'If?'

'Alright. It sounds like a good idea. But now? When I have this siege to worry over? I can't worry over you as well.'

'You think I'm safer in the middle of a siege than travelling to Thesse, miles away from the fighting?'

'If you're here, I can look after you.'

Liesel gave him a look. 'Let me do this, Esterel.'

He held his hands up. 'If you're going to insist. But I'll have to send someone with you.'

'Tegyn and I can go.'

'No,' he said firmly. 'If you're leaving, you're going with a full complement of warriors.'

'Alright.' Liesel could tell she would have to agree on this condition.

'I think Miles.'

'Miles? He's your marshall! Surely he's needed here.'

'*I'm* in charge here. Besides, Miles has met with the Thessians. He'll know who to speak with. And after all, your mission is a military one. He should be involved too. You can work together.'

'Very well.' Liesel had got what she wanted. She could hardly complain.

* * *

MILES, Lord of Corbenay, Marshall of Guivergne, was not impressed with his new task. That much was plain. He had picked out twenty of his own warriors to escort them south from Coldeberg, towards the border with Thesse. He was scrupulously polite to Liesel, and no doubt did his best to hide his frustrations. But he was the most straightforward of Esterel's friends, and not the sort of man who was very good at concealing what he felt.

'He's not married,' Tegyn murmured, riding next to Liesel as her eyes bored into Corbenay's back. 'He has a nice estate and is easy on the eyes as well.'

Liesel considered Miles. He was, indeed, conventionally handsome —physically strong, square jawed, tidily dressed, with chestnut-coloured eyes and hair, and tanned skin. He was wealthy, responsible, and amongst Esterel's closest advisers. It was also a far more realistic match for Tegyn than the other noblemen she had considered. Atrabians were of little interest to Guivergnais from a purely political point of view, but as the daughter of a prince, Tegyn's status easily matched his. In addition, if she married Miles, Tegyn would always be close. Liesel didn't want to lose her friend.

'I have to admit,' she whispered, 'I think he'd make a splendid match for you.'

Tegyn's eyes sparkled. Before Liesel knew what was happening, her friend had nudged her horse forwards and fell in with Corbenay, striking up a conversation. Liesel stared at Tegyn, open-mouthed. *I suppose it shouldn't surprise me anymore.*

In theory, one could argue they were travelling through enemy territory. But it didn't feel like it. There were those Barissians who supported Mixo, and those who supported Walter. The vast majority either didn't care or didn't understand what was happening. But they had heard that a mighty Guivergnais army had entered their duchy, and no one thought it might be a good idea to waylay Corbenay's contingent of well-armed warriors. They found accommodation in the towns and villages that lay along their route and the journey was easy enough. Liesel was grateful to be travelling in the fresh air, liberated from the stench of the Guivergnais camp.

The well organised fields of the Barissian villages gave way to the equally well organised fields of the Thessians. The road they took swung south-east for Thesse's capital, Lindhafen. Liesel hadn't returned to these parts since Emperor Coen's ill-fated campaign to the border of Cordence. Everything seemed to have gone wrong at once. A darkness had entered her soul, and the truth was she'd not been able to get rid of it.

It had begun with Coen's execution by Ezenachi. Then, Inge and Salvinus had captured Liesel, Prince Gavan, and Idris when they returned to Atrabia. They'd killed Gavan in his prison cell. She had no idea how Idris fared, whether he was even alive. The guilt she felt over their fates was never far away. She'd had to distance herself from them in Essenberg, carefully building the trust of Inge and her brother.

Even then, it was only the intervention of Esterel and Peyre that had allowed her to escape to Guivergne. Esterel had made promises of an alliance with Leopold—promises which he had now broken. She could guess how much hate they would have for her husband now; how her brother would be raging and cursing both his sisters for their treachery. There was no going back, she knew. A victory for her brother was unthinkable.

When they arrived at Lindhafen, Miles proved his worth. He negotiated his way into the ducal castle, arranging to have his men quartered. Otto, chamberlain of Thesse, soon gave them an audience.

'Your Majesty. Lord Miles. I did not realise you were coming,' the man explained, rubbing his neck. 'Duke Friedrich is still positioned on our northern border, as agreed.'

'We haven't come to see the duke,' Miles said. 'We've come—' he trailed off. 'Perhaps you would like to explain, Your Majesty?'

'Yes,' said Liesel. 'I don't want to bother Friedrich. I've come to offer shelter to some of the Cordentines who have fled here. On behalf of Guivergne.'

Otto's hand travelled from his neck to his head. 'You... want to take some Cordentines with you? To Guivergne?'

'It's the least we can do,' Liesel confirmed. 'But I don't want to bother you, sir. I know you must be very busy with the war effort.'

The chamberlain squashed his lips together and said nothing for some time. His face looked very much like a frog's. Liesel smiled sweetly at him.

'Well, you're quite welcome to do so,' he said at last. 'There are a significant number now living in the city. And I can have some officials take you to the camps to the south. I suppose you can take your pick.'

'You are most kind, sir. We shall offer them a fresh start and a warm welcome.'

'Well,' said the chamberlain, then coughed. He glanced at Miles, who stared at the floor. 'That is quite the act of charity, after everything that's happened. I hope they appreciate it. I do wonder—without wishing to sound rude—if your goals are purely philanthropic. It's my job to know exactly what's going on in Thesse, you understand.'

'You've caught me out, Lord Otto,' Liesel admitted. 'Crossbows. I love crossbows, you see.'

PEYRE

COLDEBERG, DUCHY OF BARISSIA, 676

The sun baked the ground. Peyre left the Morbainais zone of the siege works and walked through the dried mud towards Esterel's tent, for yet another meeting of the leaders of the army. He wondered what the point was. Whatever he said, Esterel maintained the same strategy.

Peyre had lost count of the days. The siege of Coldeberg had gone on for weeks, with nothing to show for it. The warriors of Morbaine were restless. He'd had to have a dozen of them flogged for fighting already, and things were only going to get worse. They simply weren't used to this kind of warfare. Marching, pillaging, pitched battles—that was their experience until now. Hard and brutal, maybe—but not so tedious as this. These were young men used to action and all they'd been asked to do so far was sit tight.

Two figures ahead of him stopped and waited for him to catch up. Sacha of Courion and Florent of Auriac. It didn't help that they automatically agreed with everything his brother said. And what other voices did the king hear? Miles had been sent south on some harebrained quest with Liesel. It had reached the point where Peyre wished Saliers were here. Yes, he was a snake, but he would have spoken his mind by now.

'How are things?' Florent asked him politely.

'All well,' Peyre told him. He wasn't about to admit his soldiers had needed to be disciplined. 'Quiet.'

Florent nodded. 'Same.'

The three of them strode past the trio of guards posted outside and entered Esterel's tent. His brother waited for them, with only Gosse in attendance. The big man was slowly getting used to his new role of royal nursemaid, looking less awkward each time Peyre saw him.

'Sit,' Esterel said, wafting a hand at the seats made ready. He poured them each a cup of wine. Peyre sat and sipped. He gave a heavy internal sigh. The Cordentine red was long gone, and his brother insisted on drinking the cheapest stuff they had.

'What news?' Esterel asked, still standing.

The three of them shared a look.

'Just the same, Your Majesty,' Sacha spoke for them.

Esterel studied them. 'Good.' He caught Peyre's expression. 'And before you start, Peyre, that means our force remains at full strength and well provisioned, while those inside Coldeberg have gone four weeks without being resupplied. Each day that passes tips the odds in our favour.'

Everyone in the tent looked at Peyre, expecting a counter argument. *Well, it would be a shame to disappoint,* he told himself wryly. *Still, better to deploy the right words and arguments if I want them to listen.*

'Things are going fine,' he admitted. 'I would just argue now is the time to begin the use of our siege engines. Give the defenders something to worry about. Keep them awake at night; fray their nerves.'

'I understand,' Esterel said quickly. 'But as soon as we do that, we risk casualties, even if only from a catapult malfunctioning. And the reality is, we're not going to break through those walls. We'll run out of projectiles before we do any serious damage. Only starving them out is going to work.'

'I think it would be good for morale, though,' Peyre responded. 'Give the men something to focus on. They're doing very little day after day. I think they'd be happier, even if we do get a few injuries.'

Esterel nodded slowly. 'Aye. I see that. If only we knew what was going on inside the city. I would like those inside to turn on one another. Assaulting their walls might unite them against us.' He grimaced. 'Sacha? Florent?'

'I see little harm in some long-range siege work,' Sacha ventured. 'Still keep everyone well away from the walls. We have catapults and trebuchets in position. They could fire at specific targets, out of range of the enemy archers.'

'Hmm. Before we do that, we should approach the walls and go through the formalities of asking for a surrender. Give them promises they'll be well treated. Some warnings of consequences but nothing gory like Saliers did at Schilling. I want the citizens to see us as the defenders of Barissia against Leopold and Inge. Not the aggressors.'

'I'm sure we can come up with some suitable words,' said Florent.

'Sul has a loud enough voice to deliver the message,' Peyre said, with a wink at Gosse. Gosse grinned back, though there was disappointment in his eyes, too. Peyre knew the march lord would like to be the one doing the shouting.

'Your Majesty?' A guard had poked his head inside the tent. 'Lord Ragonde asking to enter.'

'Of course,' Esterel said at once. 'Show him in.'

Peyre frowned. Ragonde? He was the stocky warrior who served Martras. If he was here, the duke must have sent him from Valennes.

The warrior entered. He was red-faced and tired looking. He marched in and quickly got to one knee. 'Your Majesty.' He reached into a pack slung about his shoulder and produced a leather pouch. 'A message written by Duke Domard.'

He offered it to Esterel, who took it. Esterel pulled the parchment from the pouch. 'Stand, Ragonde. You know what this is about?'

'Yes, Your Majesty.'

'Then give us the gist.'

'The duke has received more than one report. The Middians are on the rampage. Their army is said to be in the thousands, comprising many tribes. At least one of our steppe forts is taken, the town raised to the ground, the people killed or fled.'

Peyre and his brother exchanged a quick glance, before Esterel read the details of Domard's letter.

'The Kellish,' Peyre muttered. 'They've encouraged this. They let us sit here outside Coldeberg knowing the Middians would revolt.'

'We're not breaking the siege,' Esterel answered him. He read to the end of Domard's letter and threw the pages to the floor. 'Damn it!' he shouted, loud and raw. Peyre watched with concern as his brother clenched one hand into a fist. The pressures on Esterel were substantial enough already, without this. 'Martras wants us to a send force west while he marches south. Catch them between two pincers.'

'Does he not have the manpower to deal with it himself?' Florent asked.

'The enemy outnumbers us, at least two to one,' Ragonde said. 'He wouldn't have sent me if he thought we could handle it alone.'

'He's right,' Esterel said. 'We can't risk a defeat. It would leave Guivergne defenceless. Then I *would* have to leave, tail between my legs.' Esterel looked at them, thinking. 'Peyre,' he said at last. 'It has to be you.'

'Me? With how many warriors?'

'With the men of Morbaine.'

'That's a quarter of your army!' Peyre reminded him.

'I'm aware. But that still leaves us with enough to keep the siege going. And it gives you enough to deal with the Middians. It needs to be quick, and it needs to be decisive.' Esterel fixed his gaze on Peyre. There was no warmth in his look. Only an iron-willed monarch who wanted a job done.

'I understand,' Peyre said. 'Your Majesty.'

* * *

PEYRE GAVE the orders for his warriors to break camp and they were soon marching west for the steppe. 'This is what I get for complaining about the lack of action,' he grumbled to Umbert, as they rode near the front of their column. Elger and his Barissian Guard had the job of scouting the area ahead. Farred had not offered to join him, even though Peyre could have done with his knowledge. The man was intent on getting his revenge for Duke Walter's death, and Peyre understood that.

Most of the Morbainais marched on foot, restricting the pace at which they could travel. Horse pulled carts and wagons followed behind, full of supplies. Even if Peyre's goal was to defend the newly won Guivergnais territory from the Middians, the reality was his army would invade Middian land and he would need all the materials, food, and weapons the carts could carry.

Ragonde, Domard's man, had ridden ahead, keen to return to his master. Peyre had written some brief notes about his thoughts on the campaign, but there was little to say at this point. He did not know where the enemy was, its precise size or composition. But surely, if his army pushed west and Martras pushed south, the Middians would find themselves in trouble.

On the first night, they made their camp outside Schilling. Arnoul of Saliers invited Peyre and Umbert for a private meal in his new keep.

'Ragonde stayed here and explained the basics,' Saliers said. 'Did the king ask anything of me?'

'No,' Peyre answered, 'but don't be surprised if he wants you to move your force to Coldeberg. It's a sizeable chunk of his army I'm taking away.'

'Indeed. And the most battle-hardened troops he has. It's a gamble, but I understand his thinking.'

Peyre nodded, worried at the words. If Leopold led his army against Esterel, and the Barissians in Coldeberg sallied out, his brother would have his hands full. 'I will put down this revolt as soon as I can and return.'

'It won't be easy,' Saliers warned him. 'The Middians have the option of retreating south out of your way. I have a feeling they are well informed about this war. They may think they can simply outwait you. Return north as soon as you've left.'

Peyre gritted his teeth at the unasked-for advice. 'I can handle the Middians.'

'I don't doubt it, Your Grace.'

Peyre saw no signs of sarcasm on the man's face, but who knew what Saliers was thinking.

'I would ask a favour of you. My son, Benoit, would benefit from experiencing this campaign more than sitting here in Schilling. Would you be willing to accept him in your entourage? I would be grateful to you.'

Peyre could think of no reason to decline. Benoit had certainly shown promise as a fighter in their melee contest. 'I could use someone of his talents. But it will be dangerous.'

'Of course,' Saliers said. 'That's what he needs.'

'Alright then. Maybe Umbert will keep an eye on him?'

Umbert shrugged. 'Of course.'

'Then it is settled,' Saliers declared. 'I will tell him to be ready to join you tomorrow.'

THE NEXT DAY got them to the border between the empire and the steppe-lands. At first, Benoit had ridden with Peyre and Umbert, but they had got little conversation out of him. Peyre gave him to Elger and had him working with the scouts. They made a new camp amongst the tall grass, dried out from the recent spell of fine weather.

As the sun set, Peyre walked by himself and stared out across the grasslands of the Midder tribes. Dull greys warred with pinks and oranges in the sky, a sky that was so much larger here than anywhere else. Inevitably, memories of his father's campaign in the steppe returned—his first taste of war.

I was a foolish boy in those days, he admitted to himself. *But not so stupid that I didn't learn a thing or two about war from my father.* The endless grassland before him was a very different challenge to Barissia. Take Coldeberg, and Esterel had conquered the duchy. There was no city to take here. The Middians travelled from one place to the next. His army could walk across miles of territory and get nowhere. That was why his father had built his forts. He'd cut the land into pieces; transformed it to resemble the civilised world. Peyre would have to do the same.

I don't have half the patience my father had, he admitted to himself. *But I need to win. So that is what I will do.*

After a night on full alert in case of enemy attack, Peyre marched his enemy into the steppe. They were in Middian lands, not those conquered by his father and uncle four years prior. Elger told him they were the lands of the Black Horse tribe, but that left him none the wiser about his enemy. He could only guess, from the information Ragonde had passed on, that this tribe was one of many who had joined in with the attacks on their forts. That would place them far to the north and west, in no position to stop the army of Morbaine from marching through their territory.

Peyre figured half a day's march was the best place to stop. As his warriors made a protective camp, his craftsmen began construction. A new fort. He hoped it would give the free tribes of the steppe pause for thought. Did they really want to risk losing more land to Guivergne?

He was woken in the night by warning shouts. As he stumbled, bleary-eyed, from his tent, a figure emerged from the darkness. It was Inhan, a warrior from his Barissian Guard.

'What's going on?'

'Arrows fired into camp.'

'How many?'

'Few. Elger estimates twenty archers. He thought you'd still want to know.'

'Of course. Take me.'

'Elger said if you wanted to see, you'd need armour and shield.'

Peyre sighed. 'I suppose. Come, help me, will you?'

Once Peyre was suitably protected, Inhan led him to the west side of their camp. Peyre eyed the sky nervously. It was too dark to see arrows coming before it was too late, and he held his shield above his head. But no missiles came. Elger had a score of warriors lined up along the timber palisade. They had weapons and shields at the ready.

Peyre joined his captain. 'Well?'

'They've stopped. But I can take the men out if you wish.'

'No. It would be foolish to go chasing them in the darkness. Inhan says you estimate their numbers at twenty?'

'Aye. No reason to think there's any more than that.'

'In which case, the bulk of their manpower is probably still far from here. I'll keep watch for the rest of the night. You get some rest.'

'It's alright, Your Grace. I've got this.'

'I'm awake now,' Peyre said. 'Go on.'

Elger nodded and left him to it.

Peyre spent the rest of the night on guard, but no new attacks came. It gave him time to think about his strategy. He didn't know what was happening to the north. But he had to assume Duke Domard was following the enemy's movements while avoiding an engagement until Peyre's force arrived. The Middians knew his army was here now, and the news would soon reach their leaders. Peyre had close to five thousand warriors with him, similar numbers to the Middians, according to Ragonde. He was building a fort in Middian territory. He couldn't envisage many scenarios where the Middians wouldn't head south to challenge him.

By morning, he'd made his mind up. He kept his army in place, directing a thousand soldiers to help with the construction of the fort. He wanted it up and functioning as soon as possible. He sent Umbert out with a cavalry force to see if he could find signs of last night's attackers or anything else of interest in the vicinity.

Otherwise, he played a waiting game. *Let the Middians spend energy marching back and forth across the steppe. They'll come to me,* he told himself. *They could have half a dozen tribal leaders, all keen to demonstrate their daring to one another. They're not going to sit and wait while an army occupies their land.* He paced about his camp, waiting for Umbert to return, while the noise from the building site filled his ears. *Surely,* he told himself, *they'll come to me.*

Umbert returned. He'd seen no sign of the Middians. They were out there somewhere, of course, but this was their territory. They could hide and move about with far more confidence than the

Morbainais. *I must accept they have the upper hand in that regard,* Peyre told himself. *I'll not win by chasing them through the grass.*

That evening, he made sure his warriors had well organised rotas for guard duty. The Middians attacked in the night once more, but their numbers meant it was no more than an irritant.

'I wish we had enough archers to see them off,' Peyre grumbled to Umbert. 'Even a company of two hundred could be sent out to return fire and neutralise them.'

'Maybe if Liesel's mission works, we'll have crossbowmen in our ranks by next year.'

Peyre gave a dubious grunt. 'Ever the optimist, eh Umbert?' Though, truth was, a unit of crossbowmen would be more than welcome.

Peyre gave his men the next day to finish the fort. 'It needn't be perfect,' he instructed. 'But it needs to be done.'

Umbert rode out once more. He reported back with no signs of an enemy army. Peyre knew he shouldn't be surprised. His loose grasp of geography told him that even the mobile Middian warriors weren't likely to reach them that fast. Still, doubts wriggled their way into his thoughts. What if Martras had engaged the enemy and lost? What if the Middians were riding on Valennes while he sat here like an idiot? There was no way to know for sure. And while he might be tempted to send scouts out across the steppe to find out what was happening, the risk of them getting captured was too high.

There was no attack that night. But in the morning, he ordered his army to pack up and move out. He wavered over who he should choose as the fort commander. It needed to be someone who could think for themselves and, with some regret, he picked Elger.

'It's a useful refuge for us should things turn sour,' Peyre told him. 'But if the very worst should happen, it's a half day's march back into Barissia. Get your men safe if you have to.'

'Will do, Your Grace. Good luck.'

Peyre moved the rest of his army out, heading north-west. A westerly wind bent the grass, but otherwise the dry spell continued, which made the going easy enough. The tramp of so many feet and hooves kicked up a cloud of dust that he knew would be visible for miles around in this flat landscape.

Peyre led the vanguard, thinking through his options. He had enough materials to build a second fort if necessary. Surely, the Middians wouldn't stand for his provocations much longer.

With Elger left behind, he had Umbert ride ahead with the scouts, the young Benoit by his side. They did not have an easy task. They had to give ample warning if the enemy army was closing in. But it was highly likely that small groups of Middians might be waiting for them to deliver an ambush.

They had only advanced two or three miles when Umbert and Benoit returned. They rode at pace and that told Peyre they had news.

'We've spotted them,' Umbert said. 'A huge cloud of dust. They're coming this way at some speed.'

'Numbers?'

'Comparable to ours. All of them must be on horseback.'

Peyre nodded. That was the element he most feared. The Middians were renowned horsemen and out here, in the open, their mobility could be deadly. But his own cavalry, if smaller in number, were battle hardened. *Archers*, he said to himself. *Liesel and Esterel are right about that. That could make all the difference.*

'Alright. Umbert, I need your help to get us in a decent position. Wooden stakes and whatever else we can set up in time. Benoit, get back out there. I need constant updates on their progress.'

'Yes, Your Grace,' Benoit said, an excited grin on his face as he pulled his horse around.

Peyre wished he still had that boyish enthusiasm for the fight. He felt sick to his stomach.

PEYRE HAD his infantry lined up in three divisions. He was sorely in need of commanders he could rely on and now deeply regretted leaving Elger behind at the fort. But there was nothing for it. He gave Umbert the centre, and Benoit and Inhan the much smaller divisions on each side. They were good warriors and could at least lead by example. But Inhan and Benoit were young and inexperienced. He just had to hope they'd cope.

They had fixed sharpened stakes around their positions. All they had to do was hold their ground should the Middians attack. Peyre gave himself command of the cavalry. They numbered in the hundreds against the thousands of the Middians. He placed them further to the rear than he usually would, allowing himself more options. He had considered the possibility that the enemy would ignore his infantry and target his cavalry. If they did, he would withdraw, as far as Elger's fort if he had to.

A half dozen Middians approached on horseback, one of them carrying the white flag of truce.

He took Umbert and Benoit with him for the meeting. The Middians had put up a tent for the occasion. They were welcomed inside, where there were five chieftains waiting for them. Each looked at them with varying degrees of hostility. They shared food and drink while the introductions were made. The most angry was probably Cuenin, chief of the Black Horse tribe on whose lands they stood.

'There should be no talk until you leave my territory,' he said. 'How dare you build on the land of my people?' Like all the Middians, he was dark skinned, his long, black hair tied up in a ponytail. He was also powerfully built and tried to intimidate with his size. But Peyre had no interest in such games.

'Have you not just come from Guivergnais lands?' Peyre asked him. 'Where you have killed my people and destroyed our settlements? And you dare to complain about my actions?'

'They are not your lands,' retorted the chieftain named Jorath, who ran Cuenin a close second in his hostility. He represented the northern Middians, who had lost much of their homeland four years ago. Perhaps, Peyre mused, he was slightly less angry because he had at last reaped his revenge on the Guivergnais. 'They are Middian lands you took from us.'

'I don't deny it,' Peyre said. 'Though those were the actions of a king who is now long dead. I was there, and I know full well that my father's army didn't harm a single Middian.'

'Maybe,' Jorath answered. 'But Nicolas did. And that's beside the point. We both know it was a war of conquest and you can hardly complain that we have taken back what was ours.'

'You could have spoken with my brother. Looked for a peaceful resolution. Instead, you strike when we are at war elsewhere. Thinking, no doubt, we were in no position to defend ourselves. Well, you calculated wrong. Here I am, with an army at my back.'

'An army we will destroy,' said Frayne, with a humourless grin. Frayne was the oldest of the chieftains and the least emotional. He had a certain presence about him and, if not the leader of the Middians, at least the one the others seemed to respect. Peyre worked out his tribe was from the southeast corner of the steppe. He had little to gain from this conflict, and that was a fact worth bottling away and using.

'I don't think so,' Peyre answered him. 'The Morbainais have faced worse than anything you can throw at us. Then there are the reinforcements arriving from the north.'

'You are thinking of the warriors of the duchy of Martras?' Frayne said with a smirk. 'They are no more.'

Peyre kept a straight face, though he saw Benoit start at the suggestion. *That's a bluff*, he thought. *Has to be.* 'Not at all,' Peyre said. 'They are right behind you.'

Frayne continued to smile at him. 'You are on our ground. You don't stand a chance.'

Peyre sighed. 'Say you're right. Say you kill every last one of us. You'll force my brother to break off his siege of Coldeberg, march here and punish you.' He gave Cuenin a cold look. 'You're upset about one fort? He'll build a hundred of them, right across your miserable territories, until there isn't a corner of the steppe without a garrison to watch over it. You've had your fun. Time to come to your senses.'

Frayne laughed.

Cuenin growled. 'There's no deal until that fort comes down.'

'I've just built it,' Peyre retorted. 'It's not coming down.'

Cuenin's hand moved to his belt.

Lightning fast, Frayne put a hand on the man's arm. 'Looks like we've had enough talk.' He jabbed a finger at Peyre. 'You've got some balls, Duke of Morbaine. You've shown us that. But I suggest you leave now and have a think. Show us you've got a brain as well. Otherwise, we'll cut your force to pieces, too fast for any help to come.'

'WHAT DID YOU MAKE OF THAT?' Peyre asked as they trudged back to the waiting infantry. Most were resting on the ground, the sun beating down on them. Far from pleasant conditions and it would only get worse.

'They didn't seem very happy,' Umbert offered.

'But they're not attacking,' Peyre noted.

'The one called Frayne,' Benoit said. 'He'd be the one to cut a deal.'

Peyre eyed the young man. He was sharp—sharper than Peyre was at his age. 'Give it a little while, Benoit, then go back and see if you can find him. See if he'll come and speak to me, man to man.'

'DUKE PEYRE,' Frayne greeted him. They had both come alone. The Middian still had a smile on his face, as if he was enjoying himself. Either he was a good actor, or he was someone who'd been in worse situations than this. Peyre believed it was the latter.

'I thought we could talk honestly,' Peyre said. 'We both have bigger enemies than one another. My king is at war with Kelland. If I'm not mistaken, your people border the realm of Ezenachi. I've seen what he does. I'm terrified, and my lands are not nearly so close to him as yours.'

The smile left Frayne's face. 'Of course, I know my tribe is in great danger. That is why the Middian tribes must act as one. I must support the other chieftains if they are to support me.'

Peyre nodded. 'I understand that. And I sympathise. But with all respect to the prowess of your warriors, you will need support from beyond the steppe. I fought with the Magnians against Ezenachi. King Esterel also wants to fight. That's why he's invaded the empire, to remove Ezenachi's collaborators from power. We'll not see progress until Leopold and Inge are out of the picture.'

'Oh, *that's* why your brother wants to conquer Brasingia,' Frayne said, the sarcasm heavy.

'We are not conquering Brasingia. Most of the dukes are our allies.' Peyre paused. Frayne looked unimpressed. 'If I were to guess, I'd say Leopold funded your war.'

Frayne's smile returned as he spread his hands. 'Our warriors need the best equipment if we are to match the warriors of Guivergne.'

'Taking their money means you're doing Ezenachi's work.'

Frayne sneered. 'All you offer is words. But look at the actions of Guivergne, here and in the empire. You are as guilty of aggression as Ezenachi.'

'I fought with the Magnians against the Turned!' Peyre declared, offended. 'Lost good men.'

'You did. I know that. But you don't sit on the throne, Duke Peyre. Your brother does. And his interest is in power. He's had enough time as king to talk to the Middians. He's ignored us. We are just savages to him, with more land for him to take.'

Esterel's government had done little to build alliances outside Guivergne. That needed to change. 'I see how that might look to you,' Peyre said. 'We have been busy with our internal problems for a while now. But it's not true that the king covets your land. I can prove it to you now if you're willing to come to an accord.'

'The fort you have built east of here? Clever, on your part. But I know that would give us something you don't even want.'

'Of course I don't want it. I don't want to be here. But I can keep it if I have to. It is garrisoned with five hundred men. They can be spared if need be.'

Frayne whistled. 'How many men do you command? It is unfair.'

'What forts did you take to the north?'

'I don't know their names. Two of them, the third and fourth in your chain from Morbaine. They have been raised, most of the warriors killed.'

'Then for a truce, I will give you that land. And I will remove my new fort and vacate the steppe.'

'You will give up that land?' Frayne asked, suspicious. 'That would cut your conquests in two.'

'I will agree to that for a truce. I will speak to Esterel and persuade him to meet with you to find a more lasting peace between our realms. I don't have the authority to give you more at this time.'

Frayne studied him. 'I can sell that to the other chieftains. It is enough to satisfy Cuenin and Jorath. I am trusting you, Duke Peyre. You seem a man worth trusting. I would like to believe what you say about Ezenachi. But know this. If you betray my trust, you will have made an enemy of me.'

Peyre held out his hand. 'Agreed.'

The Middian took it, and they shook on their deal.

Thank the gods, Peyre thought, as relief flooded him.

BELWYNN

KALINTHIAN/HASKAN BORDER, 676

Leontios insisted on accompanying Belwynn on the first part of her journey. From Heractus, they travelled north east, until they reached the border with Haskany. Here stood the fortress of Masada. Belwynn had been a part of the Kalinthian army that had captured it in the Isharite Wars. When she saw it, Belwynn found she could only recall the faces of those who were gone. Sebastian, Prince Dorian, Rabigar, Elana. She urged her horse on and Leontios, judging her mood, said nothing.

A new town had grown in the shadow of the fortress, a testament to the recent peace between the two countries. Leontios had kept his tongue to this point, but he now became quite insistent.

'You'll need escorts to get you to Samir Durg,' he said. 'Haskany isn't Kalinth.'

'I think I can manage,' Belwynn replied, wondering why Leontios still saw her as a lady who needed protecting after all that had happened. That said, the powers Madria had given her were long gone. She was hard to kill, true enough. But all she had to defend herself was Toric's Dagger and the spectral strength of a body inhabited by a shadow. It wouldn't take more than a few determined men to make her life difficult. And women travelling alone could attract the wrong sort.

Thus, when Leontios insisted he would not leave her side until he knew she had company, she relented.

'What makes you think we'll find some Haskans who can be trusted?' she said doubtfully.

Leontios made an appalled face. 'I think nothing of the sort. There are a few Kalinthians I know who make a living here. One is a former knight. He will lead the mission for a reasonable payment.'

'I don't have money.'

Leontios shook his head. 'The Knights of Kalinth have money and I am the Grand Master, remember?'

Belwynn smiled at him. 'I remember. Thank you.'

ALCANDER WAS THE NAME OF LEONTIOS' contact. He quickly accepted the mission and payment, recruiting three others: another Kalinthian and two Haskans, who promised they would get her to the northern border safely. Before long, they had set off, riding in the shadows of the Dardelles mountains.

The Haskans had offered her two routes. The direct one was on the west side of the mountain range, through rough terrain. The second was longer but followed the major arteries of the kingdom east, then north. Belwynn chose the former. She wanted as little attention as possible and had no fears of roughing it.

Belwynn remained aloof from her companions. She didn't want to give away anything about what she was doing or who she was. The men respected her privacy—had no doubt been told to by Leontios— even though they must be curious why a woman would travel alone to the Jalakh Steppe. The weather was dry, and the terrain was not as difficult as she had imagined. They weren't troubled by the locals. Belwynn didn't know if it would have been any different had she been alone.

In the evenings, they made a fire and the four men sat around talking. Belwynn sat apart from them. After a while, they stopped encouraging her to keep warm by the fire. She knew she was strange, but they were getting paid well for easy work and they seemed content to let her be.

She listened in to their conversations. The closer they got, the more they talked about the Jalakhs. They didn't hide their fears. Khan Gansukh had destroyed the remnants of the Isharites and all the Drobax. It was said not a single member of either race had been left alive. Belwynn might have felt pity for her old enemies once, but not now. The men feared for Haskany. It seemed inevitable that Gansukh would try to add it to his empire. The only thing that had stopped him so far was Haskany's defensive pact with Kalinth and Persala. When war came, it would consume the north.

When they were done with their talk, her companions took turns to keep watch. Belwynn wasn't expected to help. So she lay down, closed her eyes, and pretended to sleep.

* * *

AT THE BORDER, Belwynn's escort said their muted farewells. They seemed keen to leave and Belwynn felt a relief at being alone once more. The remaining part of her journey was straightforward. The old Isharite fortress of Samir Durg was due north. It was now capital of the Jalakh Empire and where she was most likely to find its khan.

She travelled through wasteland, thin soil supporting only the hardiest of plant life. The sun beat down relentlessly. Belwynn rested and watered her horse regularly.

She reckoned she was half way to her destination when the patrol found her. There were only three of them, two men and a woman. Their clothes were bright and colourful, over which they wore light, lamellar armour. Their mounts were much smaller than her own—stocky and hardy looking. When they pulled up, Belwynn saw they had curved swords at their belts. The looks they gave her were more inquisitive than hostile.

'What are you doing out here alone, woman?' one of them asked, sounding almost cross.

'Travelling to Samir Durg. I am come to see the khan.'

'For what purpose?'

'I have been sent by Theron, King of Kalinth.'

'Why would the Kalinthians send just you?'

'Because there is no need to send anyone else.'

'Huh. What do the Kalinthians want? Are they ready to bend the knee to Gansukh?'

'My message is for the khan's ears.'

'Huh.'

The three Jalakhs looked at one another. The woman gave a shrug. 'Ride with us,' she said. 'Do you carry a weapon with you?'

'Only this,' Belwynn said, tapping the scabbard of Toric's Dagger.

'Ha. You can keep that little thing.'

SAMIR DURG CAME INTO VIEW. Belwynn had never seen it from the outside. It didn't seem to belong in the otherwise barren landscape. The wall sparkled wherever the sunshine hit the diatine crystal embedded within. It carried on and on, a straight line of stone longer than anything else in Dalriya. Behind it was the fortress proper, giant towers stationed in every corner and along every wall. Then, to the east, the other parts of the giant complex. There were the mines that the Isharites had worked with slaves. She supposed the Jalakhs now worked those mines and it wouldn't surprise her if new slaves had been found.

Soren had visited with the Jalakhs and come away with their bow. He'd described them as purely nomadic, with no permanent settlements. She had thought Gansukh would tear down Samir Durg. She wished he had. Instead, he'd taken it as his own. It was a perversion of his people's way of life.

They dismounted and waited outside the gargantuan double gates for entry. Eventually, a door within one of the gates was opened, still large enough for them to walk their horses through. She followed the Jalakhs along a roofed walkway that led towards an entrance to one of the giant corner towers.

'Here,' said one of the men. 'I will stable your horse.'

Belwynn handed him the reins and then followed the woman into the tower.

GANSUKH GREETED her in the throne room of the palace. Belwynn had been here once before. She remembered its vaulted ceiling and the way the dome at the top bathed the room in a golden light. Erkindrix, Lord of the Isharites, had sat in the chair the khan now occupied. What did Gansukh's use of this room symbolise? Was he the vanquisher of the Isharites, or their successor? Was it simply that he had found a ready-made setting that sufficiently stroked his ego?

Warriors, curved swords at their belts, stood to attention on either side of the throne. Perpendicular to this row stood four men who eyed Belwynn with suspicion. They were probably the khan's advisers, or generals.

Opposite them, seated on an array of colourful rugs, blankets, and silk cushions, was a frail looking old woman. Her gaze was fixed on her knitting, as if oblivious of her surroundings. But Belwynn knew better. This was Bolormaa, mother of Gansukh. For all the khan's military prowess and his use of the Jalakh Bow, only fools believed Bolormaa had not played a key role in the rise of the Jalakh Empire. She added wisdom to her son's strength. And Soren had told Belwynn something the woman preferred to keep secret. She was a witch—one of the last humans on Dalriya with magic.

Gansukh had his legs spread wide and his chin raised high. The bow—the weapon Belwynn had come for—rested against one arm of his chair. 'Why does a woman come to my court?' he demanded. 'I have enough concubines.'

His four advisers grinned.

'Not an ordinary woman,' Bolormaa muttered, eyes still fixed on her knitting.

Gansukh's eyes narrowed at this. 'My scouts say you came here from Kalinth.'

'Yes. Though my journey began in Magnia. I trust Your Majesty has learned of events in the south. A god named Ezenachi has come to Dalriya. He has killed the kings of Magnia and Cordence; killed the emperor of Brasingia. All Dalriyans must unite to defeat him, as we did against Diis and the Isharites.'

Gansukh waved an impatient hand. 'The Jalakhs care nothing of this. If anything, the arrival of this Ezenachi is good for us. It keeps the southerners from meddling in the north. State what it is you have come to ask me.'

Belwynn pointed at the khan's weapon. 'I have come for the Jalakh Bow. It is needed once more. All seven weapons must be gathered again to defeat Ezenachi.'

Gansukh gave an incredulous laugh, and his advisers joined him. The khan took the Jalakh Bow in his hands. 'Do you know how many Isharite shamen I killed with this weapon? You came here all the way from Magnia, believing I would hand it to you?'

'When it is no longer needed, I will return it. Gyrmund returned it to you the last time, did he not? You destroyed the Isharite menace, and for that you will go down in history. But now there is a new menace to defeat.'

Gansukh studied her. He looked to his advisers, then across to his mother, then back to Belwynn. 'If the kings of Kalinth and Persala want the use of the Jalakh Bow, then they know the price I ask in return. The Jalakhs claim Haskany. Allow us to take it and I shall lend you the bow.'

Belwynn didn't know what to say. The three northern kingdoms had stayed true to their pact for a reason. Should one fall, it would not be long before Gansukh turned his sights on the others. 'I'm not sure they will agree to that.'

'That is up to them. There is nothing else you can offer me that would make me relinquish my people's weapon a second time. Should they decline, then this Ezenachi will continue with his conquests. And I will take Haskany, anyway. It will be a great war, for I will defeat Persala and Kalinth as well.' He pointed at Belwynn. 'Zared and Theron both know I have the army to do it.'

Gansukh's advisers nodded their agreement.

Belwynn looked at the weapon in the khan's hands. She was so close to her goal. And if she tried to take it? There were a dozen men with swords. There was a fortress full of warriors. And there was Bolormaa.

As if reading her mind, the old woman finally raised her head. Belwynn met her gaze.

'The khan is right,' the witch said. 'I have read bones, the stones, and the stars. Gansukh will take Haskany. I see you are more than you appear. Fate guides you as it does my son. To gather all seven weapons together, a price must be paid. You already know that.'

JESPER

HALVIA, 676

Even before the Vismarian ship docked, Jesper felt the yearning for home. The view of the Halvian shoreline filled him with emotions long buried. A single decision, to leave his home in the far west of the continent, had changed his life forever. It was natural, he told himself, to wonder what he had missed—to have a deep longing to return home to his family. But he had things he must do.

He and Stenk alighted in a Vismarian village that hadn't existed when they were last here. The Vismarian lands had been a wasteland, ravaged by the Drobax. The survivors had sheltered with the Krykkers until the war was over. Now, there were wooden buildings, a central street, and a dock with ships both large and small. There was also an inn, and this seemed the best way to gather the information they needed.

They kept to themselves at first, ordering food and drink and getting a feel for the place. Jesper had wondered whether a Vismarian and Krykker might be an unusual combination, but he found it was the opposite. The two races shared tables everywhere, their time as allies obviously forming a lasting affiliation. It gave him the confidence to ask his questions.

'We've come over from Dalriya,' he explained to the folks on the table next to theirs. 'We're looking for King Oisin.'

Interested heads turned their way.

'I can tell by your accent,' a Vismarian said.

Jesper hadn't realised his accent had changed since he had been away. But he supposed it must have.

'I thought I recognised you,' a Krykker said to Stenk. 'You're the one who wielded Bolivar's Sword. Who went west and found Oisin.'

All heads had turned their way now.

Stenk looked a little embarrassed. 'Aye. I am Stenk, chieftain of the Dramsen clan. I was one of those who went west. And I carried Bolivar's Sword, but only to pass it from the hands of Rabigar to Maragin.' He nodded Jesper's way. 'Jesper and I returned with King Oisin. Now we are returned to Halvia, on a mission from Maragin. We must find Oisin a second time. Bolivar's Sword and the Giants' Spear are needed once more.'

The Krykkers in the room fell over themselves to give Stenk the information they needed.

'Up north.'

'Where the Nasvarl begins.'

'You'll need a guide. And something warm to wear. It's so cold your piss turns to ice on its way to the ground.'

'Keep walking till you can feel the frostbite, then walk some more.'

'Watch out for the bears. They grow big up there.'

Stenk exchanged a look with Jesper and gave a little smile. It seemed everyone knew where Oisin was. 'Thank you, cousins,' he told his people. 'But worry not. I remember the way to the Nasvarl.'

* * *

JESPER AND STENK heeded the advice they got, buying themselves fur-lined hats, gloves, and boots. Their new purchases weren't needed for the first few days. Their journey through Vismaria was downright pleasant.

Last time they were here, it had been crawling with Drobax. There had been the talking ones, too—those who had the cunning to plan ambushes. They'd had to fight their way through to the Krykker lands, relying on Oisin and his spear to get them past their enemies. Now, the Vismarians had reclaimed their land. It was still a wild place, but hamlets perched on hills and nestled in the valleys. The Vismarian people were busy hunting, fishing, felling, and raising their families. It was good to see.

They were a friendly lot, and Jesper and Stenk were soon brought up to speed with the goings on in Halvia. Not that the news they heard differed significantly from the rumours that had come out of Halvia in the past few years. While it was the Jalakhs who had cleansed Dalriya of the Drobax, in Halvia, it had been the Vismarians. Led by Oisin and his wife—their old companion, Gunnhild. There had been bitter fighting for years, every yard of soil fought for. Eventually, the tide had turned. The Drobax had been pushed further north, at greater speed, as their numbers dwindled. Some storytellers said that Oisin had won the aid of a monster in those final days. Whatever the truth of that, Oisin and Gunnhild's work was done. The Drobax were no more, and the pair had retired to the north.

As they neared the Nasvarl, the warm clothes were needed. The morning frost became ice and then hung around all day instead of melting away. The world through which they trudged turned increasingly white. Once they reached the river, their clothes no longer kept out the chill. It numbed the extremities; entered one's bones and refused to leave; even stung your teeth when you opened your mouth. 'I don't remember it being this cold,' Jesper complained to Stenk. 'Perhaps one forgets the pain after a while.'

'We were younger then,' Stenk said.

'Thanks. Now I'm depressed as well as frozen half to death.'

'Sorry,' the Krykker said. Stenk was always ready to apologise. He had a humility to him, and it seemed becoming the chieftain of his tribe hadn't expunged it. He reached into his cloak and pulled out a clay jar. 'Here. This will help.'

Jesper took it. His hand was too cold to grip the stopper, so he pulled it out with his teeth. The smell alone was enough to perk him up. Arak. He took a swig, savouring it in his mouth for a while. His tongue pickled, and he let the liquid slide down his throat. It warmed him—first his chest, then his stomach. Even that small amount was enough to give him a warm glow. 'That's better.'

'Aye. But don't drink too much.'

Reluctantly, Jesper handed the jar back.

The effect of the drink didn't last long. They were beyond the Nasvarl now, and this was where things might get complicated. They'd been told to head due north, but no one seemed to know the precise location of Oisin's home. He'd chosen a remote location for a reason—he didn't want to be found. Rocks and ice lay in every direction. They were climbing, getting steadily higher. In the distance lay an implacable looking mountain range. This wasn't the kind of place to wander in. It wasn't the kind of place to get lost.

Stenk stopped. 'What's that noise?' he asked.

Jesper stopped to listen. His ears didn't pick it up at first, telling him it was the icy wind whining through the rocks. But no, it was a little more musical than that. It was a whistle—a very loud, deep whistle. He turned to the Krykker. 'Oisin?'

'Sounds like it.' He pointed. 'I think it's coming from over there.'

Stenk led Jesper along to the beginnings of a copse of tall spruce trees. An animal track took them up through the trees. Through the shade, Jesper saw a great figure lumbering towards them. If it hadn't been for the whistling, he would have thought it a bear. Even with, he stopped walking, anxiously trying to assure himself it was instead a giant.

'No!' boomed a voice as the figure rounded the corner and stopped before them. It had green skin, decorated with blue tattoos, and towered above them, twice the size of Jesper. Oisin carried no spear. Instead, a bundle of cloth was strapped to his chest. From the top of the bundle, a face peered at them from a fur-lined hood.

A second figure descended a few feet behind Oisin. Not nearly as tall as the giant, but larger than any human. Apart from her size, in looks, she resembled any other Vismarian woman. She stopped slightly behind him. It was Gunnhild, with a huge bump that nearly reached her husband. 'Don't tell me!' she declared.

'Our old friends, Stenk and Jesper?' Oisin asked, as if unable to believe it was true. 'What a wonderful surprise!'

OISIN AND GUNNHILD took them back to their large log cabin. Once unstrapped and out of its bundle, Jesper learned the face belonged to their son, an energetic three-year-old named Donal. He wasn't far off the size of an adult human. Despite her immense bump, Gunnhild told them she was still a few weeks away from having their second. She sat the two of them down at an enormous table.

'I swore never again,' she declared, gesturing at her son. 'Have you any idea what it was like getting that thing out of my minky?'

Jesper shook his head. 'No.'

'Still. They say it's easier the second time,' Gunnhild said, perhaps trying to convince herself it must be true.

The couple explained they shared the cabin with Gunnhild's brothers and their families. But they had gone north on a hunting expedition, while Gunnhild was in no condition to make the journey. 'You found us on one of our little walks. It's all I can manage these days. A far cry from the old days, eh?'

'Aye,' said Stenk. 'But you'll be back to full strength soon.'

'True,' Gunnhild said.

Oisin placed vast bowls of steamy broth at the table. Jesper's mouth watered. He had yet to warm up, even though he was inside the cabin and broth was just what he needed. Oisin and Donal joined them at the table and with no ceremony, they all tucked in.

Gunnhild eventually broke the sound of slurping. 'So. You're here for a reason other than a social call.'

Jesper nodded. She wasn't stupid. Why else would they be here but for Oisin and the spear? He felt more than a little guilt at bringing his news to this young family. But he could hardly keep it to himself now. He told them of events in Dalriya; of Ezenachi, his conquests, and his turned followers. He told them of his meeting with Belwynn and how it had been agreed that the seven weapons of Madria needed to be gathered once more.

Oisin wore a grim face during the telling. 'Haven't I saved the world enough times?' he asked when Jesper was done. 'I've sworn to Gunnhild that I'm done with all that.'

'I'm sorry, Oisin. Truly,' Jesper said. 'It's the spear we've come for, really. But—'

'But no one can wield it, save for me,' Oisin finished.

Jesper looked at Stenk, who gave a helpless shrug. That seemed to be the situation.

'And you expect me to abandon my pregnant wife and return to Dalriya with you?'

Jesper had rarely seen Oisin angry. It was frightening to witness. 'No, of course not. We had no idea about Gunnhild's condition.'

'Would it have stopped you?' Gunnhild asked him sharply.

He would not start lying to them. He gave a heavy sigh. 'No. I'd have come, anyway.'

SANC

KASSITE/NERISIAN BORDER, 676

A five-tribe army marched south on Mournai, the capital of the
Nerisians. The mood was confident. The Nerisian forts had
been dispatched with ease. The first few had shut their gates and tried
to hold out against the horde of Kassites that had descended from
north and south. But no relief had come, and each had fallen. No
warriors were spared. The Kassite philosophy was simple. Kill them
now, and they wouldn't have to fight them a second time. The last
forts they reached had already been abandoned, news of the devastation reaching their garrisons. The Nerisian warriors had fled, no
doubt with dire warnings of the menace that was coming.

Sanc, Mildrith, and Rab ranged ahead of the main army. She hid it
well, but the Kassite champion didn't share the confidence of her
countrymen. 'Lothar has had time to bring his army from Scorgia,' she
said as they peered south from a rise.

It was a good spot to get early warning of movement from the
south. The city of Mournai was too far for Sanc to see from here, but
he could make out the blue ribbon of the river Dogne on which it sat.
The river turned northeast in its final stages, entering the Gulf of
Nerisia.

Mildrith's words brought Lenzo to Sanc's mind. They had heard nothing from him. The prince would be pleased to learn Lothar was leaving Scorgia. Was that all he had wanted? Did he have any intention of fulfilling his vague promises of bringing the other peoples of Silb into the war? Sanc liked the man. But he wouldn't put such a betrayal past him. *My days of blindly trusting people are long gone.*

The light faded and still they saw no sign of activity to the south.

'Time to get back?' he suggested. The Kassites would soon call a halt to their march and make a night camp.

Mildrith shrugged, then blew a stray strand of blonde hair from her face. 'By the time we get back, it will be nearly time to set off again. Why don't we stay here? It will give us an early lookout tomorrow morning.'

Sanc was quick to agree. He was infinitely happier alone with Mildrith. They could be themselves when it was just them. Sometimes, he even forgot about wars and magic and gods.

A fire would be seen from miles around, and so they huddled under their blankets. Sanc held her close. Mildrith had said he didn't have to be in love with her. But he was pretty sure he was. He didn't even mind if she didn't feel the same.

* * *

THEY WOKE early and packed their things, ready to return to the Kassites. Then, Mildrith saw the Nerisian army. Her face went pale. They watched as the ranks of the Nerisian infantry marched in their direction, sunlight glinting off armour.

'So much iron,' Mildrith whispered.

'I remember Lenzo saying the same thing,' Sanc said.

'They have so many mines and metalworkers. It is the source of their power.'

With the infantry came hundreds of cavalry—huge warhorses, as well armoured as their riders, who wielded long lances.

'Gadenzians,' Mildrith explained. 'Fighting on horseback is their speciality. The combination of the two peoples makes them a formidable enemy.'

Sanc nodded. The Nerisians alone would have been a handful. 'Why do the Gadenzians serve Lothar?'

'They found themselves caught between the Nerisians and the Egers. Lothar helped them defeat the Egers in exchange for their loyalty.'

'What does the Gadenzian god think of that?'

'What do you mean?'

'His people now serve the Nerisians. Doesn't he care?'

Mildrith shrugged. 'I know nothing of that.'

'Then what about Ymer?' Sanc persisted. When it came to the gods of Silb, he felt like Rab worrying at a bone that was mostly buried in the dirt. 'Does he want you to defeat the Nerisians?'

'Ymer wants his people to be independent.'

'But you are his champion. Does he speak to you?'

Mildrith looked at Sanc and then back to the approaching army. 'Ymer is not among us. Come, we need to go. Lothar himself must be leading that army, and that means Temyl and Guntram are with him.'

She sounded worried, and so Sanc did as she asked. They rode north to warn the Kassites. It took the full morning until they connected with the scouts who ranged ahead of the main Kassite army. The number of mounted troops in the Kassite force now looked pathetically small. Even their infantry, who Sanc had until now seen as a bloodthirsty, rampaging horde, looked like a ragged band of rebels.

Grindan Won't Stop Eating led his warriors in the vanguard, the other four tribes spaced out into the distance. Sanc noticed how the chieftains always kept their fighters separate, as if worried they would start fighting each other given half a chance. *The Kassites like to fight,* he thought. *But they lack the professionalism of their enemy.*

Sanc and Mildrith pulled up at the front of the force, where Grindan rode with a dozen of his closest followers. Sanc couldn't help but feel sorry for the man's stallion, whose eyes seemed to ask why he had been chosen to bear the weight of the chieftain.

'You've spotted them?' Grindan asked.

'Half a day's ride away. The full army,' Mildrith told him. 'Maybe eight thousand fighting men, plus their cavalry approaches two thousand. We need to meet and decide on our course of action now.'

Grindan waved a hand in the air. 'Alright, alright. First, let's talk together, just us three.' He pulled away to the side, leaving his followers behind. Such a move seemed to go against everything the Kassites had claimed pride in—decisions taken in full view of their people. But Sanc joined Mildrith in following the man over for his private talk.

'Let's just think about what we want to say to the others about this,' the chieftain suggested.

'I'm not telling the others anything different from what I saw,' Mildrith said.

'I'm not suggesting that, by the Irgasil,' Grindan said, wiping sweat from his forehead. 'It's what we do about it that I care about. Look at us. When will we ever again have an army of all five tribes at our disposal?' He gestured at Sanc. 'When will we again have two champions to pit against Lothar's? This is our one chance to take the Nerisians on. Yes, you could advise a retreat. We could hide in the woods and marshes of our homeland. But what will happen if we do that? Rinc and Tredan will take their armies north. When Lothar comes, he'll have the luxury of taking us on one at a time. My people, List's people—they'll be conquered for good, added to the Nerisian empire. Maybe Holt's, too. Rinc and Tredan won't lift a finger until they're threatened, and it'll be too late by then. Fuck running and hiding. This is our only chance.'

Sanc and Mildrith shared a look.

'I'm not asking you to lie,' Grindan said, almost pleading. 'Just show our people some bravery.'

THE FIVE CHIEFTAINS and two champions met in a circle, surrounded by their people. Grindan made his case to stand and fight.

Rinc the Black was the most doubtful about the wisdom of it. 'Out here in the open?' he asked, gesturing at the plains they had walked across. 'Gives the Gadenzians an advantage.'

'There's a perfect place to make a good stand nearby,' List argued. 'Jackdaw Hill. Where our ancestors defeated the Nerisians. Ymer will surely bless our arms if we form our shield wall there. What about you, Late to Battle?' he asked Tredan. 'Not thinking of turning tail, are ya?'

'I say we fight,' Tredan declared, loud and clear. 'We've still got more killing to do.'

List's burned skin creased as he gave a vicious smile.

Sanc suspected the constant goading of Tredan had made him more bellicose than he would have been otherwise. But whatever the reason, that was three chieftains in favour of fighting. Mildrith was on the fence. Eyes turned to the other two.

'On condition we use Jackdaw Hill,' Holt said. 'We need to neutralise those horsemen.'

'O' course, Holt,' Grindan said quickly. He turned to Rinc, one eyebrow raised.

Rinc sighed. 'So be it.'

* * *

THE CARTS and wagons were led away to the north, along with any non-combatants. With them went Rab and Sweterun, and Sanc was relieved to see his dog leave the army.

For everyone else would fight at the site chosen by List. Sanc was under no illusion that it would be anything other than a bloodbath.

JACKDAW HILL WAS steep on all sides, with thick woodland covering a good third. It was a tight squeeze to fit the warriors of all tribes into the space. Four of the tribes each had a side to defend, while Rinc had his force at the very top, held in reserve.

Mildrith was nervous about the upcoming contest with Lothar's champions. Her nerves transferred to Sanc. He'd used his magic in battle before—he and Rimmon had fought Ezenachi's turned Caladri sorcerers at the Red Fort. But he didn't want to let her down.

It wasn't a long wait before the Nerisian army approached, a morning crispness still in the air. Sanc stood with Mildrith and Grindan. They watched as the Nerisian soldiers were halted and the leaders studied the Kassite position. It was a while until they acted, bringing their warriors into position facing Grindan's force.

'They're not readying their cavalry,' Grindan said in a pleased tone. 'We're too dug in here.'

The Kassites had placed wooden stakes about the bottom of the hill, making it difficult for the Gadenzians to charge them. Sanc still wondered if Grindan wasn't over-confident. He recalled the battle of Corbenay, when Auberi's cavalry had pressed his father's force hard, the men on horseback enjoying a height advantage. *But I am no expert on such matters,* he admitted to himself.

Meanwhile, two heralds approached the hill on horseback. Both wore the finest clothes. The older had russet hair and beard. He gazed at the Kassite army with a mix of disdain and displeasure. The second seemed about the same age as Sanc and Mildrith. He was the tallest man Sanc had ever seen. Taller than Holt Slender Legged; taller than Peyre's friend Gosse back home in Guivergne. His long, blond hair fell straight to his shoulders, and he wore a longsword at his belt. Despite his size, the way he held himself gave the impression he deferred to the first man.

'Temyl and Guntram,' Mildrith hissed.

The champions of the Nerisians and Gadenzians. It was good, Sanc supposed, to put faces to the names at last. 'Are all Gadenzians so large?' was all he could think to say. Most people he had met in Silb were tall, save for the native population, like Tassia. But this was something else.

'Aye,' Grindan acknowledged. 'They are the tallest of the peoples of Silb. The best horsemen, too. But don't give them too much credit. They are the first of the seven peoples to give up their independence to another.' He spat on the ground, perhaps to emphasise what he thought of the Gadenzians.

'I bring a message from Emperor Lothar,' Temyl said, his voice carrying to the Kassites on the hill, far louder than normally possible.

'He's no emperor!' Grindan shouted. 'I shall stick his head up his own arsehole!'

The other Kassites joined in, suggesting various other things they might do to Lothar's body parts.

Temyl listened to it with nothing more than a slight sneer on his face. 'You have committed heinous crimes in this insurrection. The emperor gives you this ultimatum,' he said, once the noise had died down. 'Lay down your weapons and surrender. All may return to their homeland, save for the chieftains who have led this rebellion. If you do not, we will give battle and take this hill. Of those captured, half will be executed, the other half hobbled.'

'Hobbled?' Sanc murmured.

'They break the feet and ankles so you cannot walk,' Mildrith explained.

The Kassites loudly rejected the Nerisian terms. This, Sanc could see, was where the Kassite way of leadership worked well. The chieftains included their people in their decisions and fought side by side with them. Sanc had learned enough about these people to know they wouldn't give their leaders up.

'Ah, Mildrith,' Temyl said. He had spotted her, and an unpleasant smile came to his face. 'I see you are here, too. It's going to be difficult for you to escape from this mess.' With that, Temyl turned his horse around. Guntram did likewise, and they returned to the Nerisian force.

'They don't know we have two champions,' Grindan said, sounding triumphant.

Sanc felt less confident than the chieftain. Temyl had delivered his master's terms, but he hadn't seemed either surprised or disappointed that they were rejected. Lothar had all his Kassite enemies in one place, and Sanc couldn't help wondering if they had made a grave mistake.

SANC

JACKDAW HILL, NERISIA, 676

The Nerisians moved their units across the battlefield at a leisurely pace. They were in no hurry and there was little the Kassites on the hill could do except watch and sweat as the sun rose high in the sky. The Gadenzian cavalry circled around, to the opposite side of the hill, where Tredan's warriors faced them. They were placed some distance from the hill, cutting off any attempt at retreat.

The infantry, formed up in wide ranks of warriors holding spears, shields, and axes, marched towards the base of the hill. Grindan readied his warriors, while Sanc and Mildrith studied the ranks of the Nerisians, looking for Temyl and Guntram. To their right, List's warriors shouted obscenities at the enemy, and on the left, Holt's band waited amongst the trees.

At last, the battle began. The Nerisians were exhorted to advance, as their officers reminded them what the Kassites had done to Obernai and the forts.

'A helmet full of gold coin to anyone who brings in the head of a chieftain!' Sanc heard someone shout, and the Nerisians, encased in metal armour and helmets, gave a loud cheer.

The first clashes began. Spears struck armour, and shields crashed together. The Kassites stood behind the defensive stakes and had the height advantage. The Nerisians advantage in numbers meant little in the tight space around the hill. Sanc observed their line moving past Grindan's warriors to the flanks, but List and Holt's forces were waiting for them there. The Kassites held. The breathless, brutal fighting continued for a while longer until the Nerisians pulled back, having gained no ground. The wounded on both sides were helped away and fresh warriors came to replace the warriors in the front line.

It was ferocious, gruelling work, and both sides rotated their warriors at regular intervals to give them a chance to recover. Warriors on each side fell, hacked at, until they stopped moving. The ground on which they fought became slick with blood, but the engagement continued. Grindan's Kassites refused to give up an inch of ground. Sanc and Mildrith toured the hill, watching out for Temyl and Guntram, but they were nowhere to be seen. It was tempting to use their magic to help with the fighting, but Mildrith insisted they would need all their strength.

The morning crawled its way towards midday, and the Nerisians couldn't break through the Kassite defences. The impasse perhaps prompted their change of tactic. A rumbling noise brought Sanc and Mildrith to the far side of the hill where Tredan's warriors defended. The Gadenzian cavalry were coming, and Sanc could sense the two champions were with them, even before Mildrith warned him.

Tredan had ensured sharpened wooden stakes embedded in the ground would prevent the Gadenzians from simply rolling up the hill. Despite that, their arrival was a frightening sight: their horses were huge and ferocious looking—and, encased in armour, would be very difficult to stop. When the Gadenzians reached the barrier, the front row dismounted and tried to pull the stakes from the ground. When the Kassites moved in to attack, a blast of magic came for them.

Sanc intervened immediately, putting up a protective barrier.

Mildrith joined with her countrymen in trying to throw back the dismounted Gadenzians, but they, too, were protected by magic. A test of strength followed, as Sanc and Mildrith pitted their powers against Temyl and Guntram. Win, and they would allow the Kassites to lay into the attacking Gadenzians. Lose, and the Gadenzians would be free to pull apart their defences and ride unimpeded into Tredan's warriors.

What followed was a draining battle of magic, and of wills. Temyl and Guntram must have assumed that Mildrith, alone, would not have been able to stop them. Now they knew she had an accomplice. But they still seemed determined to win, pouring their magic into the contest. For Sanc's part, accepting defeat wasn't an option. Temyl and Guntram would be in the ascendancy, and the enemy would run riot. The Kassites were defending admirably, but he knew their situation still had the potential to turn into a slaughter.

Sanc was reminded of Rimmon's advice. Defence was easier than attack and after a while, it seemed clear they were in a deadlock. Neither pair had the power to force the other aside. His only fear was that he or Mildrith would run out of stamina; but there was no reason why they would have less than their enemies. Time seemed to stand still as they strained against their opponents, the Gadenzians and Kassites inches away from one another, yet unable to engage. The shouts and screams of combat continued on the other sides of the hill, the fighting fierce, but Sanc couldn't afford to lose concentration on his own contest.

At last, the Gadenzians remounted and rode away from the hill. Temyl and Guntram stopped their assault, unable to achieve their breakthrough.

When Sanc stopped his magic, he staggered, lightheaded. He had never cast so much for so long and he worried, both for his own power and for Mildrith. 'Are you alright?' he asked her.

She had her eyes closed, but when she opened them, she looked fine. She even allowed herself a smile. 'That's the first time I've ever held them off. Thank you, Sanc.'

He nodded, pleased at her words. He looked up at the sky. It was after noon. 'Come,' he said, turning to the crest of the hill. The fighting had continued unabated elsewhere, and they needed to learn how things stood. Already, as the two of them climbed to the top, Sanc could see a difference.

'Rinc and his warriors are gone,' Mildrith said.

Which meant Rinc had been forced to enter the fray with his fighters, shoring up the defences.

The top of the hill groaned. It was full of the injured, in all states of suffering. Some lay unconscious, or dead. Others sat leaning against trees, mumbled or cried out, pressing ripped up bandages to their sides, soaked red. Men had lost digits, limbs, teeth, ears—any part of the human body that could be hurt, damaged, or destroyed, had been. A woman lay gasping, her mouth just a red hole, the lower jaw completely gone. Sanc looked from one to the next, overwhelmed by what he saw. His heart hammered in his chest, and the urge to run away gripped him.

Mildrith grabbed his arm and directed him to a group of warriors seated around a prone figure. Sanc immediately recognised who it was. The huge gut told him it was Grindan Can't Stop Eating, even if the rest of him looked mostly unrecognisable.

One of his warriors looked up. 'They surrounded him. Eager for the reward. We couldn't stop them striking him down. It was all we could do to stop them dragging his body away. Rinc the Black came in the end, but it was too late then,' he said, a note of reproach in his voice. That last statement was more than likely grief turned to anger.

When Sanc looked down the hill, he saw Rinc with his warriors, fighting at the same spot Grindan had held. He shared a look with Mildrith. They'd held off the Nerisian champions, but the Kassites were being worn down and there were still hours of daylight left.

Sanc felt a rumbling beneath his feet.

'Temyl,' Mildrith gasped, her arms held out wide as the ground shifted.

The crest of the hill collapsed in stages. Those who could move ran from one spot to the next, desperately trying to keep their feet. Those who couldn't were swallowed by the earth, as the hill collapsed in on itself.

'Protect me,' Mildrith called to Sanc.

He did as she asked, putting a sphere of magic around her. He looked about. Somewhere, Temyl was directing this attack, perhaps drawing on Guntram's power. But neither was visible.

Meanwhile, Mildrith was busy strengthening the hill. He could see tree roots moving through the earth. They overlapped, to create a lattice of wood, stabilising the hill.

A few arrows came their way, but Sanc's magic held them off. Then, a blast of magic struck the spherical shield he had placed around Mildrith. Sanc was quick to trace the origin of the strike. The tall form of Guntram was visible amongst a unit of Nerisian warriors. Sanc threw a blast of magic back at him. The Gadenzian champion blocked it with ease. He stared up at them for a few moments, as if weighing his response. Evidently, he decided Mildrith had foiled them again, because he slunk away. The hill stopped moving, and Sanc withdrew the spell of protection from Mildrith.

He took stock of the situation. It had been the centre of the hill that had taken the brunt of the attack. The victims were mostly the injured who had gathered there, fallen into the churning earth, and buried. At the bottom of the hill, the situation continued as before. The four remaining Kassite chieftains marshalled their warriors. The Nerisian generals still urged their men on, despite the casualties they had taken.

'Lothar must believe he can win a great victory here,' Sanc muttered, as Mildrith joined him.

Mildrith studied the battle. She looked tired after her efforts. 'Aye. I fear we let Grindan talk us into making a mistake. We were in the ascendancy after clearing the Nerisian forts. We've thrown it all away. This could be a disaster.'

Sanc had to agree. Every Kassite warrior worth their name stood on this hill. If they all died here, their people were done. Lothar would take another step—and a big one—towards his goal of ruling all Silb. 'Then we have to fight on,' he said, putting a hand to the hilt of his sword.

'Conserve your magic,' Mildrith said. 'Temyl and Guntram are still a threat.'

Sanc nodded. He had no intention of using it where he didn't have to. He still held on to the hope that they might yet escape. 'Stay in touch.' With that, he drew his sword and descended the hill to stand with List's men. Of all the chieftains, he liked List the least. But his warriors had seen more fighting than any other and needed the help.

List's armour and axe were bathed in blood. He welcomed Sanc with a grisly smile, revealing his teeth, sharpened to points. 'Grindan?'

'Dead.'

'Then Ymer demands revenge!' List shouted, his voice a jagged rasp.

List's men met the oncoming Nerisians with a howl and Sanc fought with them, shoulder to shoulder. Fighting with blade instead of magic felt good, and for a while he lost himself to the carnage.

SANC TOOK A TURN TO REST. His chest heaved, and he was parched. His shoulders ached, and he had pulled muscles in several places. But he had avoided serious injury, and that made him one of the lucky few.

He staggered up towards the top of the hill, glaring at the sky. He cursed it. For even though evening had come, the sun refused to set. Darkness seemed their only hope of respite now, a faint hope that it might cause the Nerisians to stop their attacks. But even if they did, then what? A sleepless night, then it would start all over again.

He found Mildrith fighting with Holt's warriors. It was Holt who spotted him. The chieftain grabbed Mildrith and walked her over for a meeting.

'Well?' Holt demanded. Blood dripped from his helmet, which had taken a massive dent.

'Not sure we can carry on for much longer,' Sanc said, barely able to get the words out, his mouth was so dry. 'Not sure the Nerisians will stop, even when it gets dark.'

"Course they won't,' Holt said bluntly.

Mildrith just looked at them. Sanc could see exhaustion had taken hold of her. She had little left to give, at least physically. He hoped she had some magic left.

'I'll try to teleport us away,' Sanc said.

Holt looked at him quizzically. 'How would that work?'

'I don't have the power to send us far. Beyond the hill,' he said, pointing east, where Holt's warriors still fought. 'It will take them a bit of time to realise where we've gone. Then everyone escapes under cover of darkness.'

Holt and Mildrith looked at him wordlessly for a while, trying to process the idea. Perhaps they were weighing it against some other option, but Sanc would be surprised to hear there was one. Making a break for it seemed the only path open to them.

'What do you need?' Mildrith said at last.

'Magic from you if you've any to spare.'

'I have enough.'

'What else?' Holt asked.

'It helps when everyone links hands.'

Holt scrunched his face up. 'I'll send word to Rinc, List, and Tredan. They can give the men their orders. We'll have horns blown eight times to signal it. The Nerisians will think it a signal to attack. With any luck, they'll stand back, waiting for us to come to them. Then—'

'—Then they all rush up the hill,' Sanc said. 'Mildrith and I will be waiting. I'll take as many as I can, as far as I can. After that, I'll have nothing left. It'll be every man for himself.'

SANC TASTED EARTH. He lay face down on the ground, exhaustion overwhelming him. It masked his aches and pains; masked the sickness in his stomach. All he wanted to do was give in and sleep. But someone kept pulling at his shoulders.

He forced himself to get up, his body protesting, while Mildrith yanked unhelpfully on one arm.

He looked around. In the twilight, he could make out the silent figures of the Kassites he had teleported from the hill. He had successfully evacuated somewhere near three thousand warriors. Those left on the hill were doomed. Those he had taken away had a fighting chance of escaping north to the lands of the Kassites. But many lay ill on the ground.

Those able to walk were staggering away in different directions.

Holt's tribesmen, who were perhaps the largest group, veered to the west. Others aimed for the lands of List, or Grindan. They had to keep quiet, but that meant there was no organisation to the retreat. They walked in ones and twos, in small groups—concerned only for their own safety, or at best that of their close friends. The Kassite army was breaking up before his eyes—defeated, but not yet destroyed.

Mildrith pulled on his arm, and they began walking. He focused on her face. Her pupils had expanded in the darkness, and she looked like a night sprite, too beautiful to be human. He could see she was tired, too. He had been careful not to take too much magic from her. His own was depleted. It meant there would be no hiding from the Nerisians. He made himself walk faster, anxious to get her to safety.

She looked at him and he saw relief on her face that he was picking up the pace. Warmth rose in his chest. Of all the people here—her people—it was Sanc she had chosen to drag to safety. *Yes,* he told himself, *she needs my powers. Just as I need hers. But there is more to it than that. Surely, I haven't imagined it this time?*

They walked on, heading for the border. Sanc looked around but saw no faces he recognised. Grindan was dead, of course. But he was sure List and Rinc had escaped. Maybe Tredan too, though he hadn't seen him since the Gadenzians had attacked the hill. The Kassites nearby began to murmur and Sanc cursed them for ill-disciplined fools. Then Mildrith was turning him around. She pointed into the sky.

There was a mist. It bathed the hill on which they had fought in a swirling blue light, so that Sanc could just make out figures on the crest. Then he realised it was moving. It was coming in their direction, a ghostly shroud that would reveal the fleeing Kassites to their enemies.

'Guntram,' Mildrith whispered.

'He can do that?' Sanc asked her.

'I have never seen him make one with lights in it before.'

Of course it was the Nerisian champions. They were looking for the Kassites, maybe for Sanc and Mildrith in particular. And they had a spell with which to find them.

Sanc and Mildrith wasted no more time. They resumed their journey, except now they jogged through the grassy Nerisian plain, the threat posed by Guntram's mist giving them the energy of fear. The other Kassites did the same, trying to make their tired bodies move faster. In the half-light, with tired minds and bodies, Sanc knew there would be twisted ankles and other injuries. But what choice did they have? There was nowhere to hide in this landscape, and it was miles before they would reach the relative safety of the Kassite lands.

Sanc kept going, keeping to the same pace as Mildrith. They passed Kassites, doubled over, gasping for breath. Sanc needed to do the same, his lungs in burning agony, but every time he looked behind, he could see the mist matching their pace. They veered to the east, desperate to get out of its path.

Then there was a noise, barely audible at first, but growing in volume. The ground beneath them shook.

Sanc and Mildrith shared a look, but no words were needed. The Gadenzian cavalry was coming for them.

LIESEL

DUCHY OF THESSE, 676

I can teach you how to shoot them easy enough,' the woman said. She shared a shack with another family in one of the Cordentine camps that had sprung up in Thesse after the invasion. There were eight children in all, and no men. She was small herself, no bigger than a child to Liesel's eyes.

'I can help you build them, too. My husband used to repair cross-bows. I know exactly how they work; how to make them release with power and accuracy.'

It was said with some desperation. *And why shouldn't this woman be desperate to leave this hovel?* She could be lying about her expertise, of course. 'You can come,' Liesel told her, just as she'd told most everyone she'd spoken with in the camps.

She felt Miles stir with dismay a few feet away. He sank into a greater gloom with each addition Liesel made to the company of refugees she had recruited. She still insisted it was all done to strengthen the Guivergnais military. But everyone knew otherwise. This had now become a mercy mission, as much as anything else.

No one in Thesse cared about these people. Liesel stopped short of blaming Friedrich for it. He had lost his father and some of the Cordentines had been to blame for that. But someone should have stepped in to help. Many were hopelessly vulnerable. She had heard countless stories of men coming to take children away from their families; even of parents selling their children or giving their daughters as child brides. It turned Liesel's stomach. But she had gathered as many as they could cope with. More, in all honesty.

Tegyn led the woman and her children to the carts, where they'd have to share a small space on the journey north.

'I think we're done now,' she said to Miles.

'Done? As in finished?' he asked carefully, as if not quite daring to believe it was true.

'Yes. We have no room left on the carts for anyone else.'

'We had no room left three days ago,' the lord marshall said. 'But I'm pleased to hear you say so. We might just get these people safely to Guivergne with no trouble.'

THE JOURNEY NORTHWEST was painfully slow. These were not soldiers on the march. The Cordentines did their best, walking by the carts to give the horses a rest. But they carried infants, and they were malnourished after months of hunger. There was nothing for it but to carry on and hope that once they reached Lindhafen, Otto, Friedrich's chamberlain, could be persuaded to help. At the very least, Liesel thought, he could feed the refugees properly and give them the energy to complete the journey. They were taking hundreds of dependents off his hands, after all.

Miles chafed at the delay, muttering to himself and barely speaking to anyone. Liesel could tell his patience was close to breaking. Tegyn spoke with the Cordentines, children and adults, sharing a joke and keeping spirits up. Liesel was grateful and wondered how she would have coped without her friend.

When they neared the capital, a company of twenty cavalrymen arrived to escort them. Their presence sped things up a little, the soldiers happy to sit a child in front of them. Outside Lindhafen, they were asked by the guards on duty to keep the Cordentines outside the walls. The Thessians didn't seem to hate the Cordentines, Liesel mused. But they didn't trust them. As she, Tegyn, and Miles entered the city, she felt better about what she was doing. Those she had gathered would have a better life in Guivergne.

Otto was waiting for them in the ducal castle, an anxious look on his face. When Liesel made her demands, she was surprised to find he was quick to accede to every one without a fight.

'I have bad news,' he said when she was done. 'The Luderian army has invaded Gotbeck.'

'Under Salvinus' command?' Miles asked, coming alive at the mention of military matters.

'Yes. Duke Friedrich has sent messengers here and to King Esterel. He asked me to consult with you as soon as I could and send him your thoughts. Archbishop Emmett has taken his army into the duchy to defend it, while Friedrich has kept the Thessians in position on the Great Road. But he wonders if he should support our allies in Gotbeck instead. He knows Esterel wanted him to put pressure on the Kellish, keep them pinned in Essenberg.' The chamberlain gave a little shrug as he looked at them all. 'But he wonders whether this changes things?'

Otto looked uncertain about how to proceed, and it seemed Friedrich was as well. Liesel had to admit she wasn't sure what was best. It would do no good to let Salvinus defeat the Gotbeckers. But she knew Esterel's main objective was Coldeberg, and he wouldn't want his plans changed unless it was necessary. She gave a nod to Miles, allowing him to speak for them.

'If Friedrich takes his force into Gotbeck, it leaves the Great Road Open for the Kellish,' the marshal said. 'They could reach Lindhafen in days, or follow him into Gotbeck, trapping him between their force and the Luderians. My advice is to stay put for now, and hope that Emmett can hold Salvinus off. If the full Kellish army comes south, Friedrich must retreat. Their forces are superior. If he has to, he should come here and wait it out. Coldeberg will fall before Lindhafen does.'

Miles and Otto looked at Liesel. She nodded her approval. Miles' words made sense, but she still felt a chill in the pit of her stomach.

Military logic was all well and good, but it didn't factor in Inge. The witch had yet to act in this war, but Liesel knew she had the power to turn logic on its head. She felt a sudden eagerness to leave Thesse and return to Esterel.

* * *

MILES INSISTED they should return to Coldeberg as soon as possible, and Liesel feared that if she refused him, he might explode. Tegyn assured her she could handle the remainder of the journey to Guivergne, and Miles put half of his men under her command. With a little reluctance, Liesel accepted it all, and they set off for Coldeberg at speed.

Two days of hard travel saw them to the earth and wood fortifications that surrounded the city. From the outside, it appeared nothing had changed since they had left. But once admitted inside, Miles was quick to notice a development. He gestured to the walls of the city.

'They've got inside!' he cried.

He was right. The gates of Coldeberg were open, and soldiers walked back and forth from the city to the Guivergnais fortifications encircling it. Liesel noticed it was less crowded, suggesting that some of their units had been stationed inside the city. Desperate to learn what had happened, they raced towards the city. As they neared the gates, Liesel saw Peyre and Umbert exiting them. When Peyre noticed them, he gave a big grin.

'You'll have to tell us what happened, Your Grace!' Miles said excitedly. 'Gods, why did I miss this!' he added, momentarily oblivious to any offence he might have given Liesel.

She forgave him, for it was indeed wonderful news.

'Don't worry, not as exciting as you might think,' Peyre told them. 'For starters, they still hold the castle against us, and it's not easy to get into, that's for sure. Anyway, as you know, we began bombarding the city walls. Seemed to do the trick, because three nights ago a group of citizens opened the gates for us. Told us in no uncertain terms they took Duke Walter's side and didn't want Leopold to profit from his murder. We snuck through the city to the castle, but the soldiers there are loyal to Mixo, and we couldn't break in. Come, we'll find Esterel. Pretend I told you nothing. He'll want to tell the full story. You know what he's like.'

Esterel had commandeered an inn in the city called The Boot and Saddle and was in high spirits when Liesel arrived. He held court in the main lounge of the inn, and it seemed they had liberated a cellar full of ale. He made a show of welcoming the return of his queen and then recited at some length the events that Peyre had summarised in a few sentences. Liesel was a little surprised by the tone of the celebrations. Coldeberg Castle was a monstrous fortification, and they seemed no closer to ejecting Mixo from it. But she supposed that, after all these weeks of monotonous siege, it was a relief to have some success.

At last, it was her turn to tell her story. She told them about the caravan of refugees slowly heading their way. She was disconcerted to see so many concerned faces.

'Ah,' Esterel said. 'We've had problems on our western flank. I had to send Morbaine into the Steppe.'

'A revolt of the Midder tribes,' Peyre explained as Liesel and Miles turned to him with questioning looks. 'Inge was behind it. I expect she thought it would cause us more difficulties than it did. I hope I've settled things down there, for a while at least. But it's hardly a safe journey for Lady Tegyn to be making.' He turned to Esterel. 'Perhaps I could send Umbert with a small force to ensure the safe passage of these refugees? It would put everyone's mind at rest.'

'Of course,' Esterel said. 'Would that be agreeable, Umbert?'

'I will gather a force and leave immediately, Your Majesty.'

'Good man.'

'Thank you, Umbert,' Liesel said.

Umbert bowed and left to get on with it, much to Liesel's relief. 'Did you receive a messenger from Duke Friedrich?' she asked Esterel.

'Yes. Salvinus has entered Gotbeck. Not great news, but overall I believe we are still in good shape. Friedrich still holds the Great Road, while the last message from Jeremias was positive. Famiens has taken

Burkhard Castle and the Kellish haven't moved against either of them. The Kellish have shown no signs of interfering in our siege, either. If we can take Coldeberg without a serious loss elsewhere, we shall be in the ascendancy.'

* * *

WHEN THE KELLISH CAME, it wasn't with an army. A score of riders only, carrying the flags of Kelland and Brasingia, and the white flag too. The Kellish had come to talk. It wouldn't have been threatening in the least, if Leopold's envoy had been anyone other than Inge. And she wanted to speak with Liesel.

Liesel only had a few brief moments to talk with Esterel before he met with his other advisers. She hoped it was enough for him to see sense. The Guivergnais were acting as if they had won a victory over their Brasingian enemies when they hadn't even taken Coldeberg castle yet.

The royal council met in a room in the inn, while Inge was made to wait outside the siege fortifications, hundreds of warriors monitoring what she did. The witch's presence had changed the mood— more sombre. Edgy.

'I don't see how we can allow her into the city,' Sacha said.

'If she'd come to kill us, she wouldn't have announced her visit,' Liesel said. She sighed, eyeing the worried faces. 'She's come to talk. I'm not afraid.'

'You can't be serious,' Peyre said, eyes darting from Esterel to Liesel and back again. 'What if she kidnaps the queen? Holds her for ransom?'

'If she did that,' Esterel said slowly, 'would she expect me to return meekly to Valennes? She'd be finished. The people of Guivergne would never rest. I agree with Liesel. She's come to negotiate and that might not be a bad thing.'

'There's no negotiating with her,' Farred said. Liesel could see he struggled to contain his emotions. 'Her word can't be trusted. I say we

311

agree to a meeting, and I put a dagger in her chest. When she's dead, the war will be all but over.'

'You think she'll let you, Lord Farred?' Liesel asked him.

'She's not so powerful,' Farred said. 'She's dangerous, but let's not overestimate her.'

Liesel shook her head. She didn't agree and feared Farred was letting his desire for revenge cloud his thinking. 'When she killed my uncle, she did it without warning. Yes, we need to be careful. But look at her actions. She raised the Middians against us, hoping for a proxy war. Only now has she freed Salvinus to invade Gotbeck. The Kellish army hasn't been used at all. I think she's come to find a deal, before this turns into a full blown war.'

'What sort of deal?' Miles asked her.

'I can only guess,' Liesel said. 'Perhaps she'd be willing to give up Barissia.'

'For what in return?' Esterel asked her.

Liesel shrugged. 'Leopold wants to be emperor. Maybe she thinks you'd concede that if they acknowledged your ownership of Barissia.'

Farred stirred. 'You can't agree to that!' he cried. 'This alliance is built on removing Leopold and ensuring Jeremias is made emperor. He was the man legally elected in Guslar. No one else.'

'Be careful how you speak to the King of Guivergne, Lord Farred,' Sacha said. He spoke softly, but there was steel in how he said it. 'He doesn't answer to you.'

Esterel held up a conciliatory hand. 'I'm not agreeing to anything. I'm talking, and in so doing we may get an insight into what our enemy is thinking. Liesel will go. Peyre, will you accompany her? Don't allow Inge to get within touching distance of my wife.'

Peyre nodded. 'Of course.'

'Lord Gosse,' Liesel said, relieved at her husband's decision. 'Please stay with the king at all times. And I hate to say it,' she added, looking at Farred. She remembered, like it was yesterday, the Magnian risking his life to rescue her from Witmar, and their journey to Atrabia. 'But someone needs to keep an eye on Lord Farred while Inge is here.'

'Walter and I governed in Coldeberg for seventeen years,' Farred said, turning a stern look on her. She recalled how much she had been nervous of him as a child. 'Now you're keeping me a prisoner?'

'You can keep Gosse and I company during Inge's visit,' Esterel said mildly.

Liesel threw her husband a grateful look. He had listened to her advice and spoken sense, taking his council with him. Despite his propensity for vainglory, he made the right decisions when it mattered.

INGE HAD COME ALONE, not even giving the pretence that anyone's opinion in Kelland mattered save hers. She gave one of her knowing smirks at the length of table that kept her apart from Liesel and Peyre.

Let's not overestimate her, Farred had said. But that was the problem. Inge took care not to reveal exactly how powerful she was. But Liesel had seen her do things. In Witmar, she'd sent Peyre flying with a mere flick of her hand. And Farred himself had told how she'd infiltrated this very city, got into the castle with no one knowing, and killed Walter in his sleep. *Let's not underestimate her is better advice*, she told herself.

'How does the siege go?' Inge asked Peyre, as if trying to make polite conversation.

He raised an eyebrow and almost let loose a smile. 'The castle is holding out. We'll take it eventually, though. They'll be eating their horses soon, if they haven't started already.'

Inge nodded absently, not really interested. She turned to Liesel. 'I sent you to Guivergne to get King Esterel's support for Leopold. You haven't done a very good job.'

'You and Leopold haven't done a very good job of winning anyone's support,' Liesel countered. 'He shouldn't become emperor. If you've really come here to negotiate, give that ambition up.'

'So, now you're a queen, you're telling everyone what to do. You were ever an ungrateful child, Liesel.'

'Grateful?' Liesel demanded. She stopped herself from reacting too much. That's what Inge wanted, of course. 'What should I be grateful for?'

'Before he left, your father asked me to look after the three of you. I've tried to do that. Katrina is a duchess. You are a queen. Leopold is a duke twice over. Do you think Baldwin would have been disappointed with that? And what terrible things have been done to you, Liesel? Only *you* could sit there, pampered queen of the richest kingdom in Dalriya, and ask why you should be grateful.'

This was what Inge always did. Twisted things, made Liesel feel guilty and ashamed. But Liesel wasn't going to fall for her games anymore. She said nothing, waiting until the witch was done.

'What's the end game of this invasion you've encouraged?' Inge said. 'Take Essenberg next? And what will you do with Leopold, then? A hanging? Beheading? He's your little brother, for the gods' sakes.'

That one hit home. Liesel had thought she was strong enough not to let Inge hurt her anymore, but she was wrong. She remembered Leopold as a little boy. Remembered how scared he had been when their father had died; when they'd had to flee Essenberg. And ever since, Inge and Salvinus had dug their claws into him, turning him into the twisted man he'd become. *If father really entrusted us into Inge's keeping, why? Did he not know her at all?*

'Queen Liesel's little brother was quite happy to give me this scar,' Peyre said, gesturing to his face. 'And I'm not the only one to feel his knife. So let's skip the sympathy plea and all the other bullshit. What have you come to offer?'

Liesel gave silent thanks to Peyre for his intervention. He'd cut through the nonsense, reminding everyone who had done what to whom. Peyre had risked his life to get Liesel away from Inge and Leopold. He'd witnessed it all, and Inge's words were meaningless to him.

'Very well,' Inge said. 'Contrary to what some have said, Leopold had no intention of taking Barissia for himself. He admits it may have been a mistake to acknowledge Mixo as the new duke. He's willing to recognise Esterel as duke of Barissia in exchange for Esterel's support of his rightful claim to the imperial title.'

Peyre shrugged. 'Not much of an offer. I've already told you we're going to take Coldeberg, anyway. Meanwhile, Esterel understands that the other dukes of the empire don't support Leopold. That's why you killed Walter.'

'I did no such thing.'

'Even if you didn't, Inge,' Liesel said, 'we were both at Guslar for the vote. Leopold doesn't have the support of the rest of Brasingia. Why pursue it? It's this relentless need to make Leopold an emperor that threatens him. That's led us to civil war. If you pull back, Leopold will keep Kelland and Luderia. There will be peace. That's the part I still don't understand.'

'Ezenachi,' Inge said. 'I need Leopold to be emperor to keep Ezenachi happy. To keep him from destroying us all.'

'Why?' Liesel demanded. 'Because Leopold does what you say? Give me a reason I can understand.'

'You *don't* understand. Leave such things to me. Your job is to push out babies for your new husband. Stick to that.'

They spoke a while longer but got no further. They left after telling the witch they would pass on her offer to Esterel. It seemed to Liesel that Inge had come all this way to offer them nothing. Until Peyre spoke.

'We need to work together on this,' Peyre said. 'Persuade Esterel to reject a deal.'

'That won't be hard. You said yourself, we'll soon take Coldeberg. Esterel will have the duchy to do with as he sees fit. What did Inge offer that Esterel wants or needs?'

'You need to see things more from his point of view,' Peyre warned her. 'Esterel is doing this partly for you, partly for the glory of war, partly for the territory and riches he can gain. But it comes at a price. A year of his life to take Coldeberg. He's spending and borrowing eye watering amounts of money. And for now, the nobility of Guivergne are all for it. But they'll tire of it soon. The glamour of a new king and a war against the old enemy will fade. Do you really think he wants another four years of attritional war against the Kellish? And then there's Ezenachi to worry about, while Guivergne and Brasingia tear lumps from one another. Inge's offering him a win and an easy way out. Don't be surprised if Esterel finds that idea more than a little appealing.'

'Four years? It won't take that long.'

'Maybe. Maybe not. A deal with Leopold means he doesn't have to worry about it. He returns to Valennes having defeated the empire and taken Barissia. He'll become a legend. Set for life.'

Liesel had to admit that what Peyre said sounded all too true. But that would leave the empire in Leopold's hands. And she had no faith that her brother would let things lie—wouldn't take his revenge on Jeremias and Katrina and the other dukes. And how much would Esterel care then, back in Valennes with his parties? *I would have my own children to care for. Being a mother changes people. I've seen it.* No, Peyre was right. They needed to see this through. They'd not get another chance.

'I'm glad I have you as an ally, Peyre,' she said, meaning it sincerely.

'I agree. We're in this together. We both know what Inge and Leopold are—Esterel's only heard it second hand. And we were the ones in the meeting, after all.'

Peyre pulled a face she couldn't quite read. 'Then it's agreed,' he said. 'No deals with Leopold and Inge. And we must be prepared to take the consequences.'

Liesel didn't like the sound of that. But then she thought of Idris still languishing in his prison cell, and the words of Prince Gavan came to her. 'We must steel ourselves,' she said.

At council, Esterel was hard to read. He always gave the impression that he agreed with her, but Peyre's words had made Liesel doubt that a little. Had he really invaded the empire to avenge Walter's death, or because he'd seen a chance for conquest?

Fortunately, Liesel and Peyre faced no opposition in the meeting. Whatever they really thought about it, none of the king's friends were ready to express a view of their own. They looked to Esterel for a lead, agreeing with whatever he said. Farred, meanwhile, beamed with delight at the direction things were heading, though kept his thoughts to himself this time.

'Very well,' Esterel said at last. 'We'll send that witch off with nothing. The plan was always to take Coldeberg. If we can do that by the end of the summer, then consolidate our hold over Barissia, we'll be in a good position to make decisions for next year. From what you say, however, it sounds like the Kellish will respond to our snub.'

'Almost certainly,' Peyre agreed. 'Salvinus has already been unshackled. The Kellish army has plenty of targets to strike. If you refuse to back Leopold for the imperial title, I can't see him holding back any longer.'

'Then let's make sure we are ready for an attack here. Miles, send messengers to Thesse and Rotelegen, let them know the outcome of these negotiations, tell them to beware. I hope that by siding with them against Leopold, it encourages our allies to stand firm. Peyre, you're willing to inform Inge?'

'Aye.'

'I'll go too,' Liesel said.

'That's not necessary.'

'I want to.'

INGE SEEMED to know what their response would be before Peyre and Liesel gave it. Liesel could see her disappointment, but the witch contained her emotions. There was no shrieking or smirking. She looked resigned to what was to come, a thought that didn't make Liesel feel any better.

Inge locked eyes with her. 'Once before, I gave you the chance to avoid bloodshed. You didn't take it then, either. I'm coming to believe you enjoy the drama.'

Liesel looked straight back. 'If my father really did ask you to look after us, think about what you are doing. I want peace in the empire. You have the power to achieve that. Persuade Leopold to accept Jeremias. Let Brasingia heal.'

'Pah. If you think either your brother or your husband will accept

Jeremias as emperor, you're dreaming. The two of you and Esterel have made a bad mistake today. Youthful arrogance. Only the harshest of lessons can cure that.' With that, she turned and left.

When she was gone, Liesel and Peyre shared a look. 'What do you think she will do?' Liesel asked him. She wished her voice didn't sound so childish.

'She does what she wants, whatever we say to her. They're bullies, Liesel. Plain and simple. That's all they know. If we'd caved in today, Inge would have sensed weakness. Now we've stood up to her, she wants revenge. The outcome's just the same. The only thing we can do is beat them.'

'You're right. Thanks for helping me stand up to her. It's so much easier when you're here.'

'That's alright,' Peyre said gruffly, his eyes darting to the side.

There was an awkwardness between them. Liesel didn't know when it had started or where it came from. She was Peyre's queen now, she supposed. Such things put up barriers. She wished it wasn't there, but despite it, she and Peyre wanted the same things. It was a pleasant surprise to have friends and allies when for so long she'd felt alone. She wished she could explain all this to him. But now that Inge was gone, it seemed her brother-in-law wanted to be elsewhere as soon as possible.

SANC

LISTSHOLD, KASSITE LANDS, 676

The night had been full of screams. They didn't stop when daylight came. Sanc and Mildrith evaded the marauding bands of Gadenzian horsemen who chased down the fleeing Kassites.

But these screams were the worst of all.

They hid behind the wooden wall of a house, catching their breath. The area was teeming with Gadenzian warriors, who'd got here well ahead of them. Mildrith had thought List's fortress would be a haven —a place to rally and stop running. But they were far too late for that. They were lucky they'd crept along the edge of the settlement without being spotted. Lucky that everyone's attention was on the man being tortured.

Unable to stop himself, Sanc craned his neck around the side of the house and peeked. List the Castrator was tied against a tree, ropes pulling at each limb. He continued to scream, but his throat was hoarse now, and it came out as a grating, raspy noise that was hard to listen to. List was a man who had prided himself on his nickname— built a reputation and a following on his cruelty to his enemies. One might argue he was getting what he deserved. But Sanc couldn't help feeling sorry for him, as the Gadenzians carried out their retribution —cutting him up, one piece at a time.

Sanc pulled back and faced Mildrith, who was wide-eyed with fear. Exhausted, Sanc had nothing of his magic left to help them escape. Mildrith had used what little she had during the night. *We need to get out of here,* he mouthed at her.

She nodded, a determined look coming to her face. Sanc was relieved to see it. If Mildrith lost her courage now, they were done for. It felt like the sun had betrayed them, exposing them with its light, making them even more vulnerable. Now that this destination was compromised, Sanc had to rely on Mildrith leading him somewhere else.

She gestured for him to follow and moved, fleet-footed despite her fatigue, to the next house. Sanc followed, crouch-running, concentrating as best he could on not making a sound, until the second house hid him from view. Mildrith peered ahead and pulled back. She gestured for him to look and as he drew level with her, she pointed to a Gadenzian warrior who stood alone, looking north towards a patch of trees that thickened into woodland. The shelter of the trees was agonisingly close—there were a few hundred yards of levelled land before they would reach them.

Mildrith was gesturing towards a second warrior. He stood a fair distance to the right of the first warrior. Then she spotted a third, the same distance to the left. The Gadenzians had placed a ring of warriors to the north of List's settlement, on lookout in the unlikely event the Kassites mounted a counterattack. But they were loosely spaced.

Take out the nearest warrior, and Sanc thought they would have a reasonable shot at making it to the treeline before they were noticed. It would have been so easy to do it with magic. But he had expended everything on teleporting the Kassites away from Jackdaw Hill. It felt like a waste now, since so many of those warriors had since been caught and cut down. *But surely some have escaped.*

He met eyes with Mildrith once again, and they nodded at one another. Using her fingers, she counted down from three, and then they left their hiding place, making for the Gadenzian warrior. Exposed, out in the open, there was nothing for it but to roll the dice and hope they got away. The warrior turned and Mildrith stopped. Sanc ran, hoping to reach him before he could raise the alarm. A hand axe flew past him and connected with the Gadenzian. The warrior went down with a cry. At the same time, List let forth a great roar of pain that echoed around the settlement.

Sanc reached the warrior and struck with his dagger. Blood spurted as he stabbed the blade into his enemy's neck, not stopping until he was sure he was dead. Then he was up and running, Mildrith by his side. There was no point in looking to the sides or behind them to see if they'd been spotted. They had to get to the trees as quickly as they could.

Sanc ran at full speed, fear pushing him on. He knew he could trip and fall at any moment. *Either we're lucky or we're not*, he told himself. He reached the first trees, could hear that Mildrith wasn't far behind. He turned around. The moment of truth.

No one had followed them. There was no time to give thanks or celebrate. They kept going. Once the trees grew thick around them, they risked slowing down and speaking.

'List might have saved us back there,' Mildrith said between gulps of air. She was red-faced and tired looking, but Sanc could see the relief on her face.

'Maybe,' Sanc acknowledged, still not quite believing they'd made it out. 'Where to now?'

Mildrith looked grim. 'With Grindan and List gone, I fear the south is lost. We've no choice but to head north. If we keep going, we'll come to the lands of Rinc the Black. I hope he's made it out. If not—' She gave a helpless shrug.

Mildrith didn't need to finish the sentence. They were running out of options. A few days ago, the Kassites had been marching on Mournai. Now they were close to losing everything.

RINC THE BLACK LIVED. He'd escaped with enough warriors, and attracted enough survivors from the other Kassite tribes, to still call his dishevelled band of fighters an army. If one was feeling generous.

Rinc had word from the west. Holt Slender Legged lived and was said to be fighting a guerrilla campaign in his forested homeland. There was no word from Tredan, but Rinc said that didn't matter. 'Whether Late to Battle is alive or dead, it's the same difference. We won't be seeing his face again.'

All of which should have mattered greatly to Sanc, but it felt less important to two other matters. First, he was reunited with Rab, who seemed to have been well cared for by Sweterun. Second, he saw the Irgasil for himself. Until now, he had assumed that all references to the Great Tree of the Kassites had been to a purely metaphysical entity; a spiritual symbol of their people. Yet here it was, dominating the landscape of the northern Kassites, visible for leagues in every direction.

The roots that erupted from the ground reached as high as a house. The thick brown trunk was the width of the Bastion back in Valennes. Above, huge branches lunged in every direction, bedecked in green leaves. Crows cawed down from the branches and there were countless other birds calling and flying about their huge home. The canopy of this single tree was so thick and wide that it cast a vast, permanent shadow over the ground beneath. Some plant life still grew there, barely touched by the sun but fed by bird droppings. Meanwhile, when Sanc stood back from the tree and looked up, he struggled to get a good view of the top of the Irgasil.

Mildrith smirked every time she caught him peering up, convinced that if he were just to stand at the right place and look at the right angle, he would get a glimpse of what was there.

'So, Ymer really lives up there?' he asked her.

'Yes.'

'Has anyone climbed to the top?'

'No. It is forbidden. It is Ymer's realm.'

'Has Ymer ever descended?'

'You've asked me this before. Ymer chooses not to live among us.'

'Alright. But has he ever done so in the past? In history?'

'Of course. The stories tell us Ymer descends from Irgasil for many reasons. To punish the wicked, or to lead the Kassites against their enemies.'

Sanc studied her. She looked back, clearly uncomfortable with his questions, but held her chin in the air with a defiant look.

'Come on, Mildrith,' he said at last, exasperated. 'You've never used your powers to ascend to the top and see for yourself? When you first experimented with them? In the middle of the night, so no one could see you do it?'

'No,' she said angrily.

'Alright. It's just a bit hard to believe, that's all.'

A hurt look came to her face. She marched away and Sanc was left with little choice but to leave the subject alone.

MORE STRAGGLERS CAME to join Rinc's army over the ensuing days. Their news was ominous. Lothar was set on a full conquest of the Kassite lands. Any opposition had been crushed and new forts were being built, forts that would hold down the Kassites for good. It was only a matter of time before the self-styled Emperor of Silb marched on Rinc's position.

And Rinc's position, Sanc judged, wasn't good. His tribe's lands were flatter than the others, with few points of natural defence. Not that Rinc would hear of leaving his capital, built close to the Irgasil. Wooden palisades surrounded a small wooden fort. Easy for the Nerisians to reach and no great hardship to take. Sanc despaired. It would be Scorgia all over again.

As the Scorgians came to Sanc's mind, word came from the coast that an armada had anchored in Rinc's lands. He had not heard from Lenzo since the prince had left him here to support the Kassite uprising. The thought had crossed his mind that he would never hear from him again. Now that Lothar had left Scorgia, Lenzo had what he wanted. Sanc was pleased that the prince hadn't abandoned his allies.

Lenzo came to Rinc's settlement with a score of companions. When Sanc met the prince, he was surprised at the emotion he felt at seeing him again. It seemed Lenzo shared some of the same feelings, giving him a big grin and embracing him.

The prince wore a woody perfume and was dressed immaculately. It was strange that after so short a time Sanc now looked at Lenzo from a Kassite's perspective. He looked too clean, and gaudy, and Sanc supposed that he in turn must smell no better than pig shit to Lenzo. Gaida, the prince's trusty lieutenant, slapped Sanc on the back, as if even he was pleased to see him.

But the cheerful faces of the Scorgians soon disappeared when they observed the dour looks of the Kassites. Lenzo kept quiet as Sanc led him to a meeting with Rinc. Last time, all five chieftains had met with Lenzo. Now that he was meeting Rinc alone, on the northern edge of Kassite territory, he surely didn't need telling how badly things had gone.

The prince sat and listened impassively as Rinc and Mildrith explained what had befallen them, as his Scorgian warriors and many Kassites stood around listening. Only once did Sanc detect a reaction, a slight raising of one eyebrow when Rinc told him of their march on Mournai. It quickly disappeared, but Sanc could tell Lenzo was surprised they had overreached in such a way. Sanc now saw it as foolish. Rinc hadn't been keen at the time, and he told the story with the shame of a man who had known better and should have put his foot down. But there was no point in dwelling on it. They had to decide what to do from the position they were in.

Lenzo was clear what he thought. 'I've enough space on my ships to get you and your people to safety. Perhaps to Ram. You'd all be safe there. One thing Lothar doesn't have is control of the sea.'

Rinc was equally adamant that he and his army were going nowhere. 'We're not leaving. We'd rather die than leave the Irgasil to our enemies.'

Murmurs of approval greeted this pronouncement from the other Kassites.

'But you'll return,' Lenzo pursued. 'I have been speaking with Ordono of the Rasidi. He is ready to ally with us against Lothar. He says he can persuade the Telds to join as well. Think of that. As they strike from the west, you could return and liberate your lands, while the Scorgians attack from the east. It will be too much for the Nerisians to deal with.'

Rinc waved a hand. 'All you Scorgians ever do is make grand promises. We're still waiting for you to stand and fight with us.' He looked around. 'There is a special place in hell for those who betray Ymer. You think, of all the chieftains of our tribe who have protected the Irgasil over the years, I will be the one to leave it to the enemy without a fight? We will give our blood for Ymer, and if we die here, he will reward us in the afterlife.'

The Kassites gave their approval to their chieftain's words. Lenzo looked at them, as if lost as to how he might make them see sense. The meeting broke up with nothing agreed and Rinc told the prince he should return to his ships and leave.

Lenzo took Sanc aside, an intense look in his green eyes. 'The remnants of the Kassites will die here,' he said. 'Is there nothing you can say to persuade them?'

Sanc looked across at the Irgasil. 'I don't think so. No one's said it, as such. But I think they believe Ymer will intervene on their side, should the Nerisians come here.'

Lenzo sighed, ran a hand through his hair, then gave a nod of acquiescence. 'People were just the same in Scorgia before the invasion. They'll only learn when it doesn't happen, and by then it's too late. But what about you and Mildrith? Surely you'll come?'

'I can't leave without her and she's staying.'

'But Temyl and Guntram will come for you. You may not escape a second time.'

'I know.'

'Sanc. The Rasidi have a champion. If you two work with him, you'll have the edge, at last. If you or Mildrith should fall, we'd lose that advantage. If both of you are lost, we're done for.'

'I'm sorry, Lenzo.' Sanc could see the prince's anger and he could understand it, too. But there was no way he was going to forsake Mildrith when she needed him.

'My ships will stay at anchor,' Lenzo said at last, 'for as long as it's safe to. Get to us if you can.'

Sanc nodded. 'Will you take Rab with you?'

Lenzo's serious face broke, and he allowed himself a grin, then shook his head. 'Sure. I recall sharing a boat ride with him once before, and he was no trouble. Also, if you die, he'll be a way to remember you.'

BELWYNN

KALINTHIAN/JALAKH BORDER, 676

Belwynn waited with an elect group of champions and rulers on the Kalinthian border with the Jalakh Empire. Maragin, wielder of Bolivar's Sword, had returned from the Blood Caladri with their king, Lorant. Lorant held Onella's Staff. *That was my brother's*, she thought, experiencing an irrational sense of fury.

The truth was the staff had originally belonged to the Caladri. Lorant was an old ally from the Isharite Wars. He told her how he had spent the last years using the staff to vanquish his people's rivals, the Shadow Caladri. Those bastards had sided with the Isharites, and Belwynn was pleased to hear it had been put to good use.

Theron had been equally successful. King Zared had come for the meeting himself, bringing with him the Shield of Persala. He was also amenable to Gansukh's demands on Haskany. More than amenable, it seemed. Theron told her Zared had already given up on keeping Haskany from the Jalakhs. The Persaleians saw the conquest of Haskany as inevitable and were keen for a solution that didn't drag them into a bloody war.

Finally, Jesper and Stenk had returned from Halvia. With them was Oisin, King of the Orias, and the Giants' Spear. His huge frame towered over everyone else, but Belwynn had always found something reassuring about his presence. There was a gentleness to him, despite his fearsome appearance.

Their reunion had been emotional. It couldn't help remind Belwynn of those desperate moments in Heractus. The city crawling with Isharites; the brutal combat against the Seven, their crystal swords tipped with poison; and the fatal meeting between Diis and Madria. For all that, the conversation with the Giant had been strained—the happy, carefree Oisin of old seemed to have disappeared. It was only when she interrogated Jesper that she learned why. He had left behind a pregnant wife in Halvia.

A dark feeling that this was all wrong came to her. Why was she having to do this again? Why Oisin, who had first taken up the burden of the spear hundreds of years ago? But it seemed events were in motion, and it was too late to stop. They had gathered five of Madria's seven weapons already. And now they had come to negotiate for the sixth.

They saw the Jalakh horsemen first. Then the ground rumbled beneath their feet. The Jalakhs pulled up. A few armed warriors dismounted and walked over to meet Belwynn's group.

Gansukh was first among them. He walked with confidence, though Belwynn thought there must be an element of fear, somewhere within. Their little group could strike him dead in a matter of moments. But the bow wasn't with him. Neither could Belwynn see his mother, Bolormaa, though that didn't mean she wasn't ready to intervene.

The Jalakh khan gave an elaborate bow, and the rulers Belwynn had gathered responded with stiff-backed bows of their own. This was a meeting of kings, and she allowed them to talk with the khan. *Even though I am Belwynn Godslayer,* she reminded herself.

'At last,' Gansukh said, 'you consent to discuss Haskany with me. I have been waiting a long time for this and shown much patience.'

'We have come to you with a proposal,' Theron said. 'You already know the first part. The Jalakh Bow.'

Gansukh inclined his head. 'You shall have the bow when I have Haskany.'

'Agreed,' Theron said. 'Second. Kalinth will take the fort of Masada and its environs. This territory will be added to my kingdom.'

'Third,' said Zared. 'Persala will take a strip of territory, up to and including the watchtower of Simalek, all the way east to the Itainen. These are our conditions for allowing you the rest of Haskany.'

They had left Gansukh the lion's share of the kingdom, but claimed a sizeable buffer for themselves. If the khan was surprised by their demands, he didn't show it. Indeed, a knowing smile had come to his face. Belwynn had spent enough time in his presence to read it. Gansukh believed he would take those lands claimed by Theron and Zared, eventually. He still believed he would take Persala and Kalinth, too. For him, this deal was just another step on his path to glory.

'Very well. I shall grant you those lands as a sign of my good faith. Are we to coordinate our attacks? It would make the invasion that much easier.'

'That makes sense. There is one other piece of news to give you,' Theron said. 'In light of our agreement today, the treaty of mutual defence between Persala, Kalinth, and Haskany, has ended. But I should tell you about a new one. The Krykkers, the Blood Caladri, and the Grand Caladri have joined Kalinth and Persala in a new alliance. It will keep the peace in the north after the annexation of Haskany is complete.'

Maragin and Lorant, both stern-faced, nodded their agreement at Theron's words.

That knocked the smile from Gansukh's face. He didn't like it, of course. But he was getting Haskany, and no doubt he judged he would still get more in time. 'Very well,' he said. 'I wish your new alliance every success, of course. Though maybe you'll need to look to your southern borders more than to my empire.'

That, unfortunately, has a ring of truth to it, Belwynn admitted to herself.

Gansukh turned to go.

'And the bow?' Oisin asked, his voice a deep rumble.

Gansukh pointed a finger at Belwynn. 'She can come to claim it once our new borders are settled.'

With that, the khan and his warriors left them. With a display of agility, he leapt onto his saddle and turned his horse about. The Jalakhs left at a canter and were soon gone.

Theron let out a sigh.

'Something troubles you, King Theron?' Lorant asked him. The Caladri's head dropped to one side, vividly reminding Belwynn of a bird's movement.

'Not the noblest day in the history of Kalinth,' Theron admitted.

'Ah. Perhaps so. But you are now a part of a much stronger alliance. And we are closer to assembling the seven weapons of Onella. Today has made your people a little safer, and that is your job, after all.'

Theron nodded, perhaps a little reassured. But Belwynn knew him well and knew he felt a stain of dishonour on his character after betraying the alliance with the Haskans.

Still, she recalled, it wasn't the first time he'd been willing to commit a wrong to achieve what he thought was right. Which of the heroes and monarchs stood here could claim otherwise? *The end justifies the means, some people believe,* she told herself. *But where does all this end?*

Not well, some part of her warned. But Belwynn was worn down. Burned out. *An end, of any sort, would be a blessed relief.*

PEYRE

COLDEBERG, DUCHY OF BARISSIA, 676

At last, Esterel had given the order to storm the castle. The Kellish army was finally on the move. Reports said Leopold had sent it north, against Jeremias and Auberi. If that were true, it was time to risk an assault.

Peyre understood his brother's reluctance to this point. It could only result in significant loss of life on both sides. But they had the numbers for the task. They had been working on the walls for weeks and had identified a few weak spots to exploit. Most of all, though, they faced an enemy who was half-starved by now, while the Guivergnais had kept their warriors fed and healthy. When it came to the brutality of hand-to-hand combat, how many of them would be prepared to die for their new duke, who had led them into this misery?

Peyre readied his Morbainais troops. They were positioned outside the city, facing the north walls. These walls doubled as the walls of the castle, and they'd had weeks to work on them. On top of the walls, the Barissian defenders waited. They would have archers, rocks, burning oil and sand, and all manner of other unpleasantness ready for them.

Close to Peyre's position, on the northeast side, Miles commanded a similar sized force. The rest of the army was inside the city, led by Esterel himself. They would target the gatehouse of the castle to the south, with its stone walls, portcullis, and murder holes. Attacking at any of these locations was a murderous task. They had to hope that attacking all three would leave the defenders too stretched to withstand them.

Peyre stood with his Barissian Guard. They were his best warriors, led by Elger, containing the most promising of the younger generation. They would have to be risked in the initial assault. The sooner they broke into the castle, the sooner it would be over, and he trusted his Guard not to shrink from the danger.

He missed having Umbert at his side. They had fought together enough times to know what the other would do. His friend had not yet returned from escorting the Cordentine refugees to Valennes.

In his place, Farred stood on Peyre's left. The Magnian stared at the walls with intent. He had waited a long time to retake his home and avenge Walter's death. Peyre decided he would be a more than adequate replacement for Umbert. On his right was Benoit, the Viper, heir of Saliers. In contrast to Farred, this would be his first taste of real battle. Peyre judged he had the stomach for it, but one could never say for sure until someone was face to face with an enemy baying for your blood, desperate to hack you to pieces.

To one side lay the equipment they would need to attack. Ladders tall enough to reach above the height of the walls. Crabs: wheeled wooden structures, with a protective canopy of soaked hides, that allowed a group of warriors to reach the walls safely, whatever might be thrown their way. Some had battering rams attached that could be swung back and forth and were strong enough to punch a hole in the walls.

They were ready. Armour had been strapped tight and helmets covered heads, uncomfortable on a warm summer's evening. But Peyre had to wait for his miners. Their tunnel reached all the way to the walls they faced, where wooden buttresses held the roof up. When they fired those buttresses, the earth above would collapse into the tunnel and hopefully, the walls above would fall, too.

Peyre had been shown the tunnel. It was an impressive feat of engineering, tall and wide. But he wasn't going to get his hopes up. These things were notoriously unpredictable. And while the walls in question had taken a heavy battering in the last couple of months, they still looked close to impregnable.

A rumbling noise was easy to hear, soon followed by the excited whoops of the miners exiting their tunnel with alacrity. All eyes were on the walls now. Peyre stared in wide-eyed wonder. Cracks appeared from the bottom, quickly rising in jagged lines. Lumps of masonry were dislodged. He could see the defenders running from their positions on the wall walk above. Then, a massive shifting, as part of the wall sank into the ground. The wall was ripped clean apart. Stone fell out, towards Peyre's position, covering the ground in front of the city in lumps of debris. Other parts of the wall fell inward into Coldeberg. A cloud of dust. As it settled, the devastation was clear to see. A massive gap had been rent. It was more than Peyre could have hoped for.

Some of his soldiers moved to grab their siege equipment.

'Leave it!' Peyre shouted. It wasn't needed. There were no longer any defenders above to drop things on their heads. Projectiles that came their way could be blocked by shields. They had an opening, and to exploit it efficiently, one thing was needed above all others. Speed. They had to get through before the Barissians gathered their wits and responded.

'Shields ready!' he bellowed. 'Charge!'

He led the Barissian Guard to the opening, and he heard the march of feet and the clank of armour as the rest of the Morbainais followed behind. They reached the first chunks of stonework that now lay on the ground. It wasn't easy to spot through the sight holes in his helmet, even though they had a sloping design to cope with just this kind of problem. Everyone slowed as they picked their way past or over the obstacles.

Arrows came at them. It felt like from all angles. Peyre held his shield out in front of his head and kept his eyes on the ground beneath him. He could hear arrows flitting overhead, scraping off or sticking in the armour of those around him. His shield slammed into his helmet, and he saw an arrowhead had pierced through its wooden boards. He kept moving. A scream to his right told him one missile had found flesh. But it wasn't his role to stop and help. Those behind had to help the injured. Those at the front had to get into the castle.

When they reached the gap in the wall, the Barissians met them. They lunged with spears, shoved with shields, and hacked with axes. Peyre was quick to recognise he was facing Mixo's best warriors, desperate to stop his progress.

He blocked with his shield and held his sword ready. He told himself to stay patient, to wait for an opening. He was desperate to break through this line of defence, for it would allow the Morbainais behind him to pour into the castle. But there was no point in getting himself stabbed to achieve it.

Benoit was more aggressive. He knocked a spear to one side with his shield, then he was forcing the spearman to the ground, pushing down until the sharp side of his sword blade was pressing through the man's coif.

Peyre rushed in to support him, as the Barissians targeted the young warrior. He blocked a spear thrust with his shield. An axe whirled towards him. It was a wild swing, but this one was lucky. He had no choice but to throw himself backwards out of the way. He felt the rush of air as the axe blade passed within inches of his face.

His back landed on a rock, and the air left his body. But he had to move. He scrabbled onto his hands and knees, pain flooding his chest and back, his armour weighing him down. He couldn't stop his neck tensing, expecting the second axe blow that would finish him. He grabbed his sword and used it to lever himself back to his feet.

He focused on the fighting. Farred had saved him, moving into the space he had vacated. The axeman lay on the ground by the Magnian's feet. But he was dangerously isolated.

Peyre moved to help, but he was too late. Spears and swords lashed Farred, and he couldn't block or avoid them all. A spear had impaled him at groin height. Benoit grasped the stave, and Peyre, roaring in outrage, launched himself, the side of his blade cutting round at neck height into the spearman's coif.

The spearman went down, and a frenzied melee followed as the warriors of Morbaine and Barissia clashed at this spot, both refusing to back down. With a force born of fury, Peyre battered with his sword—brutal, crude strokes that Brancat would have disapproved of. Elger appeared at his side, dancing forward with a two-handed spear thrust. Peyre was forced to block a spear that came for his captain, the blow sending a numbing pain along his hand, wrist, and forearm. Benoit now grabbed this spear, yanking on it with all his strength. As the Barissian stumbled towards him, the young man sank a thin-bladed dagger into an eye socket.

Peyre and his comrades shoved, battered, sliced, and stabbed. The Barissians fought with equal ferocity. These were no weakened fighters ready to surrender. They were well armed, knew how to fight, and were ready to give everything. But as they were pushed back, more and more of the Barissian Guard got involved, outnumbering them. Only at the last did some attempt to surrender, but it was too late. They were hacked down in moments and, at last, Peyre's men could take a breath.

A scattering of Barissian soldiers who had declined to join the melee looked at Peyre and his warriors with fear. They dropped weapons to the ground, putting their hands in the air and calling out their submission.

'Accept their surrender,' he called out. These fighters who had served Mixo would switch their allegiance to Esterel in time. Clemency would serve his brother better than a massacre.

He turned around to find Farred. Inhan knelt by the Magnian's side.

'How is he?' Peyre demanded.

The young man shook his head.

'Damn!' Peyre shouted at the sky. He closed his eyes, fighting off the fog of grief that threatened to overwhelm him. *You still have work to do*, he told himself. *Put aside your feelings for later.*

Opening his eyes once more, he scanned the section of the castle they had taken. To his right were the castle stables. Long empty, he presumed, of even the finest beasts. When he looked to the left, he realised the damage to the outer walls of the castle had extended to the inner walls, too. A ground floor room had been exposed—the castle kitchens. He could walk straight in and take his force through the castle. Wherever Mixo was holed up, he would find him in short measure.

'Elger,' he said. 'Take the third and fourth divisions to the gate-house.' He pointed south, where he could hear the royal forces battering the gates of the castle. 'When it's safe to do so, accept the surrender of the defenders.'

'Your Grace,' Elger acknowledged with a nod. He eyed the gap in the kitchen walls. 'You're going in?'

'I know the castle as well as anyone.' *Now that Farred's dead.* 'With any luck, I can end this quickly.'

Peyre and Elger shouted their orders, splitting the Morbainais soldiers into two forces. When he had his soldiers ready, Peyre led them into the castle. He glanced cautiously at the stone ceiling above them. Part of it had fallen in, dust covering the floor of the kitchen. He feared the whole thing would collapse on top of them.

He hastened to the nearest staircase. There was no one around to stop his troop's advance. The winding stone steps went down and up. 'Inhan,' he called. 'Hold this position with the second division.'

Inhan nodded, peering down into the murky depths of the castle.

'The dungeon,' Peyre murmured. 'Not likely to be anyone down there. But be alert.' He glanced upwards. The stone steps to the next floor twisted around at a sharp angle. A perfect place for an ambush. But the duke's private rooms were up there and that was the most likely place to find Mixo.

'Let me go first, Your Grace,' Benoit asked him.

Peyre considered it. The young man was keen to prove himself. 'Very well. I'll leave a gap between us. Retreat if you are attacked.'

They moved one step at a time, anticipating an attack. Peyre's grip on his sword hilt grew sweaty and his neck muscles tensed as he peered upward. Ahead of him, Benoit moved lithely, his dagger held at the ready—the perfect weapon to use in such a confined space. But the farther they went, the more the threat dissipated. At last, Peyre reached the landing of the castle's top floor. Benoit gestured with his dagger at a man dressed in servant's garb, who had silently sunk to his knees, hands held up.

'This way,' Peyre whispered, indicating the direction where the duke's private rooms were located. They moved slowly, stopping at each doorway to peer inside. Behind them, his warriors gathered on the landing, more than enough to deal with any force that might have gathered here.

The first rooms were empty. They came upon the room Peyre had shared with Umbert during their year's exile in Barissia. Benoit gently pushed the door open and Peyre looked in. He met eyes with a young woman. Her chin trembled in terror. She was dressed in the fine clothes of a noblewoman and looked vaguely familiar. But he had met many noble families in his time here and few stuck in his memory. Then, behind her, he saw two small children, a boy and girl. He put a finger to his mouth. She gave a jerky nod, and he carried on.

Memories of his time in Coldeberg castle threatened his concentration. It was strange to be infiltrating the place where he had lived. Strange that Walter and Farred, men who had been steady rocks during the most tumultuous time in his life, were now both gone. Strange and unfair.

'Halt!' Benoit called out sharply.

Ahead of them, a Barissian held out one arm, palm up, while unbuckling his belt with the other. His belt and scabbard fell to the floor. He looked at them, arm still held out, keen to show he was no threat. 'Duke Peyre?' he asked.

'Aye.'

'The castle is yours. Mixo is dead. When he heard you had breached the walls, he took his own life.'

PEYRE

COLDEBERG, DUCHY OF BARISSIA, 676

Mixo's suicide made things easier, ridding Esterel of one problem. He fined the Barissian's family for Mixo's treachery, and in return they were allowed to take his body home.

There was still much to do. They buried Farred beside Walter in the cathedral's crypt. Ancel, the bishop of Coldeberg, proved to be a strong support, smoothing the transition from the old regime to the new. Not long after Farred's funeral, in the same building, their Barissian allies joined the Guivergnais nobility in witnessing the inauguration of Esterel to the duchy of Barissia.

It had taken months of hardship, but now that Esterel was indeed a duke of the empire, the reality of it almost took Peyre by surprise. Such a turn of events would have seemed unthinkable a few years ago. But here they were. Esterel had made Guivergne the dominant power of central Dalriya. An ambition that countless kings of Guivergne had failed to make reality, he had achieved in a year.

Today, the royal council would discuss leaving Coldeberg. The days of holding meetings at The Boot and Saddle were over now. A space was made in the grand hall of the castle. Ancel attended the meeting, demonstrating the bishop's close relationship with his new duke. Otherwise, it was the usual faces who attended.

'Any news from Kelland?' Florent wanted to know.

'Nothing new,' Esterel said. 'The Kellish are still believed to have Burkhard Castle surrounded. But Rotelegen is making their life difficult. I'm hopeful Famiens can hold out.'

'What if we sent a force to Essenberg?' Florent asked. 'Might force them to withdraw and defend the city.'

'I don't think it would,' Esterel said. 'The campaigning season is almost over. There's no way we can take Essenberg in a few weeks and the Kellish know it. All we'd do is sit outside the walls, posturing. Hostilities are over for this year. The queen and I will leave for Valennes tomorrow. I don't mind if others leave sooner. Morbaine, I know, wishes to take his army home at the earliest opportunity.'

'Thank you, Your Majesty,' Peyre said. He had indeed expressed his concerns to his brother that the southern border of Morbaine should be defended as soon as possible. He counted it remarkably fortunate that Ezenachi had not taken advantage of the war to relaunch his attacks. But he knew the uneasy truce that had held since the invasion of Magnia would not last forever.

'Corbenay will act as regent here in my absence,' Esterel said, with a nod to Miles.

Peyre hadn't been informed of this. But it seemed a solid choice. Miles was a safe pair of hands, and he *was* marshall, after all. It was about time he was given the freedom to exercise the role.

'He will be left with a sizeable garrison to defend the city. More expense, of course, but necessary. I would like to give him the Barissian Guard to help with the task,' Esterel said to Peyre. He gave a little smile. 'It makes more sense to have the Barissian Guard in Barissia than in Morbaine, don't you agree?'

Peyre knew his mouth had dropped open. He knew everyone was staring at him. But his brother's request had come out of the blue. He had formed the Barissian Guard three years ago, when leaving this very city. He had recruited the finest warriors into it, trained them up. And now Esterel wanted him to give it to Corbenay? And why ask him in this manner, in the middle of a council meeting, instead of privately?

He studied the faces of the others present. Liesel looked worried; Miles at least had the good grace to look embarrassed. Esterel maintained that fake smile, though one eyebrow was slightly raised now. 'Of course, Your Majesty,' he said. What choice did he have?

The meeting ended soon afterwards, and Peyre wasted no time in ordering the Morbainais to pack up and get ready to leave. He then had the task of addressing his Guard. Elger got them ready. He told them they had been asked to stay at the king's own request. That it was a great honour they had been given. Somehow, he got the words out. When he was done, he prepared his own things, getting ready to leave. A cold rage had come over him and he didn't want to stay in Coldeberg a moment longer than he needed to.

It was as his soldiers were lined up and ready to march that Liesel and Miles came to see him.

'I didn't ask for the Guard, Peyre,' Miles said, looking uncomfortable.

'You didn't decline them, either.'

'True. I didn't really understand what was happening. I thought it might be something the two of you arranged.'

'I didn't know about it either,' Liesel said. 'I'm not sure why he did it. Maybe I can talk to him?'

Peyre shrugged. It was done, and he was too angry to discuss it. 'It's the king's prerogative to assign his soldiers where he wishes. Sorry I can't talk longer. But we're moving out.'

Part of him felt bad for his abruptness, especially to Liesel. It wasn't her fault. But he didn't trust himself to say any more.

PEYRE MARCHED HIS MORBAINAIS HARD, in no mood to cut anyone slack. They made camp outside the town of Schilling. Arnoul of Saliers still controlled the town and invited Peyre and Benoit to his new castle for their evening meal. Saliers had little news to pass on, save a message from Umbert that he and Tegyn had arrived safely in Valennes with the Cordentine refugees. He agreed to ensure Liesel got the message on her way here.

No doubt it was because Peyre had not seen Saliers in so long and had spent more than enough time with his other acquaintances in the last few months. But he had to admit he enjoyed the man's company more than he ever thought possible. Peyre gave him chapter and verse on the siege of Coldeberg and the final assault, and Arnoul was interested and made intelligent comments. He was clearly pleased when Peyre praised Benoit's contributions. Perhaps it was the fact that his wine cup was never left empty, but Peyre continued with the story, telling him about the morning's meeting of the royal council and the loss of his cherished Barissian Guard.

'Ah, well,' Arnoul said in his dry voice. 'Petty, but not entirely surprising, given recent events.'

'It was surprising to me!' Peyre said. He could tell his voice was loud. 'I'm sure I don't know what I have done to deserve a public humiliation like that,' he added, trying to keep his volume at a normal level. But he could feel his anger, bitten down on all day, threatening to spill over.

'I'm sure no one truly doubts your loyalty to your brother. But consider what you have achieved in the last year. Took your army alone to Magnia, where you saved that kingdom from total conquest. Stopped the Middian revolt in its tracks. Even at Coldeberg, it was you who took the castle. Esterel has the glory of his new title. But your reputation now shines just as brightly.'

Peyre considered this, wondering why he had not seen it before. 'But I am not interested in competing with Esterel,' he protested.

'Indeed. But your honour only adds to your deeds. Even if Esterel is not naturally the jealous type, he will have people around him who whisper against you. That is always the way of things.'

Who might the whisperers be, Peyre asked himself. Not Liesel or Miles, he was sure. Both came to see him after the meeting, and he couldn't imagine either of them as backstabbers. *Sacha of Courion?* That was a different situation. They had never got on. And Peyre had bedded his sister. Beaten him in the melee tournament. Did he envy Peyre's position in Guivergne?

He caught Saliers studying his reaction. *The man is a snake*, he reminded himself. *That must never be forgotten.* But that didn't mean he never spoke the truth.

* * *

PEYRE DIDN'T SLEEP WELL, despite being given a good bed in Schilling's castle. His dreams brought him back to the assault on Coldeberg Castle—to the axe blade that came so close to ending it all. Then it was Peyre himself, instead of Farred, impaled by a spear. He awoke, heart beating frantically in his chest, covered in sweat, his mind racing to determine what was dream and what reality.

Saliers had to wait in Schilling for the arrival of Esterel to find out where he would be stationed for the winter. But he offered Peyre the continued services of his son. Peyre wouldn't put it past him to have an ulterior motive. But losing the Barissian Guard had left him bereft of his most trusted followers, and he was grateful to have someone of Benoit's efficiency by his side.

The army of Morbaine continued its progress northwest, each footstep bringing them ever closer to the empire's border with Guivergne. Even if Peyre's own mind still swirled with discontent, he couldn't help noticing the high spirits of his warriors. It had been a dreary summer for them, waiting day after day outside the city, tasked with building work, guard duty, or tunnelling. They were happy to be heading home.

The two riders from Guivergne arrived in the wild no-man's-land between the two realms. As they slowed, Peyre recognised them both. Umbert had come with Ragonde. They were both tired and shared the same sombre expression. He could tell the news they brought was not good.

Peyre and Benoit pushed their horses ahead to speak with them in private.

'News out of Rotelegen,' Umbert told Peyre, as he eyed Benoit. 'The Kellish stormed Burkhard Castle, forced their way to the top. Jeremias says he couldn't break through and relieve them. Famiens had no choice but to surrender.'

Peyre made a face. 'It's not good. But Burkhard was only ever a diversion, not an actual target.' He smiled. 'And there is good news. Coldeberg has fallen.'

Umbert and Ragonde shared a look. 'We heard,' Umbert told him. 'But that's not all. The messenger from Rotelegen says the army of Famiens was punished.'

'Punished?'

'Those who weren't executed were blinded. Duke Auberi included, so the messenger said.'

A dense heaviness hit Peyre in the stomach, expanded to his chest. Blinded? He wouldn't have believed it, but Leopold had been there, and he knew Leopold. Knew him well enough not to question the story. His thoughts jumped from picturing Auberi, eye sockets empty, to Loysse, devastated at the cruelty to her husband. Then to Esterel and Liesel. He recalled their meeting with Inge and the witch's parting words. *'The two of you and Esterel have made a bad mistake today. Youthful arrogance. Only the harshest of lessons can cure that.'*

He shook his head, trying to clear it of the sense of guilt he felt. 'The king and queen need to be informed as soon as possible.' He looked at Umbert and Ragonde, exhausted from their journey from Valennes. 'Benoit, return to Barissia for me and tell their majesties the news. They will want to make all haste to Valennes.'

ESTEREL AND LIESEL did indeed make haste, leaving the Guivergne army behind and reaching the border with a small company of riders. Peyre asked Umbert to take the army of Morbaine south while he joined the royal party on their journey to Valennes.

Evening was already drawing in and Gosse offered them shelter in one of his villages. Peyre could see in his brother's face he felt the same as him. He didn't want to stop for the night—wanted to keep riding all the way to Valennes. But the horses had already been pushed hard, and he consented to Gosse's hospitality.

Gosse organised the billeting, putting Peyre in a house with Jehan and three other royal guards. It was cool inside, despite the heat of summer, no doubt the benefit of the long straw roof. Nonetheless, he was in no mood for sleep. He left the house and perched himself on a log at the edge of the village, watching the sun slowly set.

He turned at footsteps and shifted over so that Liesel could sit with him.

They shared a look, each knowing the other wrestled with a sense of guilt.

'Can't sleep either?' she asked.

'My dreams were already full of Farred's death,' he admitted. 'I don't want what happened to Auberi added to them. Not sure I could take that.'

'I hope you don't blame yourself for either. Farred wouldn't want you to. He knew the risks he was taking in attacking the castle. And he wanted it done more than anyone else.'

'I know. Auberi, on the other hand. It has Leopold written all over it. But Inge allowed it, and she did so as a message to you and me.'

'Yes,' Liesel agreed, her voice quiet, making her sound younger than she was.

Peyre's teeth gritted. He wanted nothing more than to spare her from all of this. Even now, far from Essenberg, Queen of Guivergne, they could still hurt her.

'That was the decision we took,' she said. 'To steel ourselves. I knew something would happen, even if I didn't foresee this.'

'Did you both advise me badly, then?'

Peyre turned to see Esterel. He'd approached them quietly. *Eavesdropping on us?* Peyre wondered. His brother stood, hands on hips, his jaw set. He looked tired. Peyre couldn't recall Esterel ever looking tired before.

'No,' Peyre answered. 'I'd advise you just the same again. There's no dealing with Inge and Leopold. If anything, what they did should confirm that.'

'Yet now I must look my sister in the face and take the responsibility for what's happened. It's very easy for you to give your advice, Peyre. I'm the one who must live with the outcome.'

'Then why did you send Auberi to Burkhard Castle in the first place? You put him there, in Leopold's own duchy, taunting him. What did you think might happen?'

'We needed a diversion. All we lost is Burkhard, which we never wanted in the first place. Better to have lost Guslar, or Lindhafen, in your estimation? And if not Auberi, then who? You? Auberi tried to kill us all and take my throne in case you've forgotten. Why shouldn't he be the sacrifice?' Esterel sighed, running a hand through his hair. 'I had thought they might kill him and free Loysse from the marriage. This... just makes things worse for her.' He clenched one hand into a fist, his fury plain to see.

Peyre and Liesel just looked at him. She had one hand over her mouth. *So, he had sent Auberi to Burkhard expecting him to die?* He knew his brother had a ruthless streak. He hid it well, but it was there. But to admit to such a plan? Peyre's thoughts turned to the Barissian Guard and his conversation with Saliers. He'd thought of confronting Sacha about it, but the steward had been left in charge of the royal army. Now he wondered if it hadn't just been Esterel all along, managing his game pieces to suit his own ends.

The three of them looked at one another for a while, each in their own thoughts. *Are we all afraid of what to say next?* Peyre wondered. Some things said can never be taken back again.

'Whatever blame we apportion ourselves or each other,' Liesel said at last, 'we mustn't lose sight of who actually did this. Leopold and Inge. They're our enemies and this doesn't change that.'

Esterel released a breath. 'They've left me little choice now. This isn't something that can just be forgotten.' He looked at the sunset. Searching for answers, perhaps, or a sign of what the future might bring. 'We do it all over again next year. Take Essenberg if we have to. Keep going until I have Leopold in chains.' He looked at Liesel, then Peyre. 'Until the Brasingians agree to make me their emperor.'

SANC

RINCSHOLD, KASSITE LANDS, 676

Drums and trumpets gave the defenders ample warning of Lothar's army. The noise was brash. Confident. Made by people who believed they had already won a great victory. The Nerisian infantry, the foundation of Lothar's power, had marched all the way from Scorgia to the farthest reaches of Kassite territory. With them came the Gadenzian cavalry, who had given the retreating Kassites no rest in the last few weeks. His magic sense warned Sanc that the two champions, Temyl and Guntram, were also with their king.

Sanc and Mildrith's powers were replenished after the battle at Jackdaw Hill. But Temyl and Guntram would still be a match for them, while Lothar's army—well provisioned and armed, thousands strong, was superior to Rinc's by every measure.

That didn't stop the Kassites from lining up to meet the enemy. Sanc was glad there had been no attempt to hold out in Rinc's fort. Extremely vulnerable to fire, it would have been a death-trap that few could have escaped from. Instead, the chieftain positioned his warriors in front of the Irgasil.

This decision spelt out the true motives of the Kassites. They were not fighting to defeat and drive away the enemy. They were fighting to defend their sacred tree of life. They would give their lives to demonstrate to Ymer, high in Irgasil's crown, that at the very end, they held true to what mattered.

The Nerisians came into view. Just as at Jackdaw Hill, Lothar was in no rush to attack. His infantry was placed in lines facing the Kassites, both longer and deeper than Rinc's forces. To each side of the infantry, hundreds of Gadenzian horsemen moved into position. Rinc had none.

Sanc scanned the enemy, looking for Temyl and Guntram, or even the king himself. He saw no sign of them. The men and women beside him readied themselves to fight their enemy. He couldn't decide if they were brave or mad. Many glanced behind them, necks craning up to look at the Irgasil. Or, he considered, they were simply people of faith and conviction.

The ranks of Nerisian infantry marched towards them—slow. Inexorable. Rinc readied his best warriors in the front rank, their shields interlinked, spears and axes ready to deal death to the invaders. No one could say these Kassite warriors weren't a match for anyone. There simply weren't enough of them.

From his position next to Mildrith a few rows back, Sanc observed those around him continue to cast anxious looks back and forth from the approaching enemy to the top branches of the Irgasil. Their faith would be put to the test now. For Sanc doubted Ymer would come to save them.

The front ranks met one another in a cacophony of shouts and challenges, clashing shields, and the ring of steel weapons. Sanc placed a protective barrier over Rinc and those warriors on either side. If the Kassites were to have any chance of holding off the enemy, he had to keep their chieftain alive. Soon, he felt the tug of another sorcerer trying to disrupt his magic. Fending off the attack, he searched for its source. Amongst one of the two groups of Gadenzian cavalry, either Temyl or Guntram targeted him. No doubt Lothar was there, too. They could afford to sit and watch the Nerisians take apart the Kassite defenders.

Next to him, Mildrith took on the role of defence, waiting to repulse any magical attacks that came. The long lines of the Nerisian warriors began to wrap around each end of the Kassite front rank. Lothar didn't need to deploy his sorcerers while his infantry was able to do his work for him.

'Perhaps you should try to stop them?' he suggested to Mildrith. Already, it felt like they were trying to resist the inevitable.

Mildrith chewed her lip, as if thinking the same thing. She glanced from the Irgasil to Sanc. 'I have an idea,' she said. 'Of using the tree against them. If nothing else, it might strengthen the resolve of my people. It would be better if I could use your power to help.'

'Why not? I don't see what we have to lose.'

Sanc broke off the protective barrier he had constructed over the Kassite front rank and offered his hand to Mildrith. She took it, wasting no time in drawing from Sanc's reserves, while her other hand twisted and pulled in the air, as if she tugged against an invisible weight. Sanc could feel the ground shake. He wasn't the only one, and when a rumbling noise came, the fighting stopped, both sides pulling back a few feet.

Roots erupted from the ground. Sanc had seen Mildrith perform this magic before. But it was different this time. The roots of the Irgasil were wider than a house. When some rose high into the air, the Kassites gasped. It was as if their god had answered their calls.

The roots came for the Nerisians, from below and above. They were skewered; crushed; tossed aside. It was enough for them to break, running back towards the rest of their army. The roots followed them.

'If I can just reach Lothar,' Mildrith said through gritted teeth.

But if they had been surprised in the first few deadly moments, Lothar's champions acted now. Sanc could see Guntram, the tall Gadenzian, had nudged his horse forwards, positioning himself in front of his countrymen. He sent bolts of magic at the giant roots coming his way. His attacks sliced through the wooden worms, dropping them to the ground. But the severed ends kept coming, propelled by Mildrith, faster than he could cut them down.

Then, the sound of an explosion. It was like Jackdaw Hill all over again. And it came from the Irgasil. Moments later, every root fell to the ground, dead. Sanc turned to look at the great tree. He could hear earth moving, deep underground. The ground on which the tree stood shifted, subsiding into the underground chasm. Then, the Irgasil itself moved. It sank, and when it stopped, it was tilting to one side.

All eyes seemed to be on the great tree and for a few moments, no one on either side spoke or moved. But Sanc had no doubts what would happen next. Temyl had changed the course of the battle once more. A great cry rose from the Nerisian side. Both groups of Gadenzian cavalry had been unleashed. They whooped with delight as they gathered speed. Soon they would be on the Kassites and all Sanc could see were dull eyes and stooped postures.

'We have to leave,' he whispered to Mildrith.

'I can't.'

He pulled her hand, and she tore it away.

'You go,' she said, eyes locked on his. There was defiance and grief in them.

'I can't leave you. And if we both stay, Silb is lost, and Dalriya too.'

Mildrith tore her eyes away. Sanc followed her gaze to Rinc the Black. He had turned to her, his face even paler than usual. Behind him, the Gadenzians, long spears held at the ready, would hit his front line in moments. *Go*, he mouthed to her. She shook her head.

Sanc grabbed her hand a second time. This time, she let him drag her away. He forced his way through the last row of the Kassites. Guntram, or Temyl, or both, might be amongst those riders. He couldn't leave anything to chance, cloaking himself and Mildrith in invisibility. Then he ran, pulling Mildrith with him. His magic couldn't conceal them completely as they ran away—the movement might reveal them. But their enemies would be focused on Rinc and his warriors.

They ran north, for the coast. They heard the clash as the Gadenzian charge hit the Kassites. Screams from both sides, human and horse alike, echoed around them.

Mildrith pulled up. 'I can't,' she said, ripping her hand away from his grip a second time.

Sanc understood exactly how she felt. In her situation, he wasn't sure what he would do. But he had his own needs. 'Mildrith. I have to go. But I can't lose you.'

A small frown came to her face at his words. Did she only now understand what she meant to him?

'Please,' he said, almost begging.

A calm seemed to come over her. 'Alright, Sanc.'

They turned and fled.

LENZO HADN'T LIED. Most of his fleet was already at sea, but the prince had waited for them. As soon as Sanc and Mildrith were aboard, his ship cast off. As the distance between the dock and the ship grew, Sanc's fears slowly eased.

Mildrith didn't speak. They huddled together on the port side of the ship, looking across the waves at her homeland. Reunited with Rab, she held the dog tight, absently stroking him. Rab sensed her mood and accepted the prolonged attention without fuss. She gasped. Sanc followed her gaze. He caught the last moments of the fall of the Irgasil; witnessed it toppling to the ground.

It was quiet aboard ship in the aftermath of the fall of the great tree. Even the Scorgians seemed to feel the sense of loss.

Silent tears rolled down Mildrith's cheeks. Sanc put an arm around her, not knowing what else to do to comfort her. She leaned into him, resting her head on his shoulder.

'I lied,' she whispered.

'What?'

'About the Irgasil. Of course, I used my magic to fly to the top. To find Ymer and his realm.' She sighed, and he felt her body shudder. 'There was nothing there. No god, no divine palace, no kingdom in the sky. It was just a tree.'

* * *

THE SCORGIAN FLEET SAILED WEST, then south, keeping the lands of the Kassites on the port side. To starboard, there was simply endless ocean. No one Sanc asked knew for sure what was out there, and if the Scorgian sailors didn't know, then no one did. Some gave him stories, matching the one he had learned in Arvena, of the seven peoples crossing a wide ocean to settle in Silb. This was the legend of the arrival of the Scorgians, Nerisians, Kassites, and the other peoples who made up the seven nations of Silb. But it was vague. No one could tell him about the place they had left, or the reasons why.

As he looked to the horizon, Sanc wondered if his own land of Dalriya was somewhere out there, reachable without magic, if one could just sail far enough. For the first time in a while, he had the time to think about the people he had left behind. His siblings; Jesper and Rimmon. It was harder to picture their faces than it had been a few months ago. The defeat of the Kassites left him further than ever from his goal of returning with an ally capable of defeating Ezenachi. If only there was a way for him to reach out to Dalriya and discover what was happening there.

Mildrith sat on the deck and talked to no one except Sanc. And hardly to him. She had retreated into her own world, unwilling to share her thoughts or emotions. Sanc supposed this was normal enough and that she needed time to process what had happened.

It meant Sanc caught up with Lenzo. The prince shared news from Scorgia, the upshot of which was little had changed. He'd done nothing to challenge the Nerisians on the mainland, focusing instead on negotiations with the Rasidi. In the south of the country, Duke Atto maintained his grip on the mountainous region of Sinto, the Nerisians making minimal effort to take it from him. Ships travelled back and forth from Arvena to the duke's lands, trading supplies and sharing information. But no closer relationship had been formed.

'So, we're going to the isle of Ram?' Sanc asked the prince. 'What's there?'

'Not an awful lot. It's said to have been a holy place of the native people before we came. A few Kassites settled there, but it's lightly populated. It has good beaches for our ships, however. And it's a suitable location to meet with the Rasidi.'

'Their king. I forget his name. He will meet us on Ram?'

'Ordono. He could come to Ram, or I can cross the sea to the Rasidi lands. I was hoping to bring the Kassite chieftains to meet with him.' Lenzo glanced across to Mildrith, still huddled at the port side of the ship, Rab napping at her feet. 'Maybe she can speak for the Kassites.'

'I'm sure she will. She's lost much, you know,' Sanc said, feeling the need to defend her.

'Yes. I do know how that feels, Sanc,' Lenzo said wryly.

'Of course,' Sanc admitted. Lothar had now conquered both the Scorgians and the Kassites. Had a tipping point come already? The point at which the Nerisian emperor could no longer be stopped, and the whole of Silb was his? Much now depended on the prince's new allies, the Rasidi.

* * *

THE ISLE OF RAM rose from the sea at a point roughly equidistant from the coasts of the Kassites, Nerisians and Rasidi. As the fleet approached from the north, all Sanc could see was uninviting rock. It was only when they sailed around and approached from the east that the beaches Lenzo had mentioned were revealed. Here the waters were calmer, and the Scorgian sailors could row their vessels onto the strand.

Most of the Scorgians were left at this spot. The sailors had repairs to make and were content to sleep in their usual spots on deck.

Prince Lenzo led a small group of warriors, commanded by Gaida, who had loaded them up with large packs, towards a nearby settlement. With him went Sanc, Rab, Mildrith, and a small, moustachioed man by the name of Dag. He was an agent of the merchant, Amelia the Widow, whose trading ships regularly came to Ram. With experience of the people here, he would do a lot of the initial talking.

As the sun beat down and the sea wind gusted, he led them to the settlement, no more than a fishing village. Sanc could see a team of locals foraging along the beach, while half a dozen boats were visible out at sea. They passed wood and earth houses as Dag led them to a larger building, built of rough stone, sited in the centre of the village.

Upon entering, they found it empty, save for a dead fire pit in the centre and benches lined around the walls. It was cool inside and, like the warriors who shrugged off their packs, Sanc sat and rested on a bench, his back against the uncut stones of the wall, while Rab flopped on the cold floor. Dag disappeared to find the village elders.

Eight men and women came to speak with them. Most were older, presumably past the days of going out to sea or working all day in the sun. Instead, they had the role of governing their little community. They sat around the fire pit. Lenzo, Mildrith, and Dag joined them, while Sanc and the others stayed on the benches, looking down at proceedings.

Dag performed the introductions. Then Lenzo was soon speaking, explaining his mission here and referring to events in the rest of Silb. The elders raised voices of concern at his news of the invasion of Kassite lands. It seemed their loyalties and bonds were with those people, even if they were isolated from events on the continent. Mildrith took over from Lenzo, giving them the details of what had happened and ending, of course, with the fall of the Irgasil. Each of the elders made a complicated hand gesture, too fast for Sanc to follow, at this news, and many muttered prayers to Ymer.

As this took place, Sanc studied the eight individuals. Amongst the Scorgians, there had been a division between the tall, blond-haired invaders like Lenzo and Gaida, and the smaller, dark-haired natives, like Tassia. The Kassites had all looked like the Scorgians, with no sign of a native people at all, except perhaps in the colouring of some individuals, such as Rinc the Black. Here, he detected a different story. These people of Ram shared the features of both races, in differing proportions from one to the next, but still—it suggested there had been an intermarrying of the two groups that hadn't happened elsewhere on Silb.

The meeting ended with Lenzo presenting the elders with gifts—

precious stones worked into jewellery, cloth, furs, and other luxury items. They agreed to give the prince's small group lodging in the village and gave their consent to his plans for a conference with the king of the Rasidi.

One elder offered her house to Sanc, Mildrith, and Rab. It was a tiny little hut, but she explained her husband had died, and her daughter had married and moved out. There was enough space to sleep comfortably, and she fed them soup while they talked about her life on Ram. It was good to hear about something other than war for a change.

Once the meal was over, and with nothing to do except sit in a tiny hut, Sanc suggested they explore the area. He wasn't keen on allowing Rab into the sea, fearing he would end up stinking out the little house. The woman recommended a walk that would climb to a good view of the local area. Sanc, Mildrith, and Rab were soon following the small trail inland.

Much of Ram was rock, but where water flowed from the central hills to the coast, there was opportunity for agriculture. They walked through an orchard of apples, pears, and mulberries. Sanc and Mildrith took an apple each, and she fed a little to Rab. He was pleased to see her looking more at peace than she had since they escaped Rincshold. Perhaps telling the elders about what happened had been a release.

'What was that gesture they all made?' he asked her, recalling the meeting.

Mildrith shrugged. 'I don't know. Not a Kassite ritual. The people of Ram are said to cling to their old beliefs as well as embracing Ymer. Not a bad way to live, I always thought.'

'I suppose so.' If one was going to worship gods, why not worship them all?

The track wound its way higher. More exposed, they were buffeted by the wind. Suddenly, Rab darted off the trail. Sanc watched as he ran into a crack in the rock wall.

'Rab!' Sanc called, angry that the dog would disappear like that.

'Was he spooked by the wind?' Mildrith asked.

'I doubt it. More likely he's smelt something interesting. I'll have to go fetch him.'

They approached the crack, tall and wide enough for them to get through one at a time. Calling the stupid dog to come back still didn't work, so Sanc and Mildrith passed through into a cave. It was very dark, with no light elsewhere to indicate any other entrances. Mildrith raised a hand, and a warm light flooded the space, allowing them to see the confines of the cavern. It was tall and narrow, with grey walls rising all around them.

'Rab!' Sanc shouted again, increasingly irritated, and worried that he was nowhere to be seen.

'There,' Mildrith said. She pointed to a hole in the opposite wall. It was plenty big enough for a dog to get through, but humans?

'I can't get through there,' Sanc complained.

'You can,' Mildrith reassured him.

She led him to the hole. It was horribly small, not even large enough to crawl through on hands and knees. They'd have to lie down and use their elbows to squeeze through.

'Alright, let me rephrase that, then. I don't *want* to get through there.'

'I'll go first,' she said. He watched as she slithered through.

Despite their predicament, a little grin came to his face. 'Well, I've got a very nice view of something from here.'

He heard a distant muttering from Mildrith, and then her voice was closer. 'If you want to see it again, you'll have to crawl through.'

That was a good secondary motivation to finding Rab, and Sanc made himself lie down and squeeze his way through the hole. The sensation of tonnes of rock pressing down on him was nearly enough to make him stop. But turning around wasn't an option. 'Find Rab,' he muttered, as his shoulders scraped along the rock. 'See Mildrith's butt,' he encouraged himself as his head poked free. Mildrith stood waiting for him, and she folded her arms in mock indignation.

At last, Sanc got to his feet. Mildrith flooded the space with light and he looked around. They were in a second cavern, much larger than the first, as wide as it was long. An underground stream entered from their left and much of the floor space was taken up by a pool of water. The sounds of running water and dripping filled the space.

'There,' said Mildrith, pointing.

At the far end of the cavern was Rab, his neck moving up and down as he ate something.

'Rab!' Sanc admonished.

At least he had the good grace to look guilty as he trotted over. But something else had caught Sanc's eye. 'What's that writing on the wall?'

They approached the pool. Peering down, Sanc got the first look at himself for quite some time. He'd changed. The boy he had been when he came to Silb had transformed. With his bearded face and long hair, he looked no different from the Kassite warriors he had fought with. Except for the eyes. *They'll always be different.* He used to hate his eyes. Countless times, he had wished and prayed that the red would turn brown or blue. Now, he didn't mind them. The people he'd met in Silb seemed to accept them, in a way Dalriyans never had.

They walked across the cavern, their reflections disappearing as they splashed through the pool, the water only reaching their shins. Sanc turned at a slurping sound, to see Rab lapping at the water. He sighed angrily. That guilt hadn't lasted long.

'Looks like fish guts,' Mildrith said, gesturing at the indistinct lump of matter Rab had been eating.

'Serves you right if you get sick,' Sanc told Rab, who turned his head to one side, unsure how he was supposed to respond.

Pictures and words covered the wall in blacks, browns, and blues. Sanc might have thought they had discovered some lost, ancient site, if it wasn't for the fish guts. Clearly, *someone* knew about this place.

Mildrith was reading it, her lips moving silently and a finger tracing a path along the wall.

'You understand it?' Sanc asked.

'Yes. There are prayers offered to Ymer, but to a second deity as well. It's a name that simply means ruler.' She turned to him with a confused frown. 'Ezenachi.'

Ezenachi? One thought after another struck Sanc, too fast for him to process before the next came. Was there any reason to doubt that what Mildrith was telling him was true? None he could think of.

His mind raced, putting together the pieces of the puzzle. 'Then this means Ezenachi was worshipped here on Silb, by the native people of the continent? When the seven peoples and the seven gods came here by sea, they defeated not only the people who lived here, but their god, too. Seven gods against one.'

Mildrith nodded slowly. 'Perhaps so. But this Ezenachi survived? For all this time? And how did he get to your land of Dalriya? Why?'

Sanc shook his head. 'Hard to say for sure.' He thought some more, using the few facts he knew to form a coherent narrative. 'He was defeated, but not destroyed. Waiting for an opportunity, while all but a few of his followers forgot him; worshipped the new gods of Silb.

'Then, in Dalriya, not one god but two are destroyed: Diis and Madria. Suddenly, there is a land where he can become all powerful again. No one to stop him. He can begin again, creating new followers who will worship him after so many years alone. Raising armies, expanding his power, until there is a new world under his control. And this explains something I never understood. How did Rimmon find your world and decide to send me here? It must be that the gateway from Silb to Dalriya had already been opened. Rimmon discovered the pathway here that Ezenachi created.'

There was a lightness in Sanc's chest, a confidence he had not felt before. So many niggly, unanswered questions now made sense. And he felt he had learned something about his enemy. Ezenachi— implacable, mysterious—now he had a history and a motive. What was more, it was a history of defeat and loss. If he had been defeated before, then he could be again. He looked at Mildrith, surprised to see a tension in her face and body. 'What is it?'

Mildrith bit at her lip. 'What if he wants more?' she said in a subdued voice. 'What if Dalriya is just a means to an end? Surely, if what you say is true, he desires revenge for what happened. And now our gods sleep while we fight one another.' She looked at Sanc. 'When he conquers Dalriya, what's to stop him returning here?'

PART III
THE PROMISE OF VICTORY

SANC * PEYRE * LIESEL * IDRIS * BELWYNN

SANC

ISLAND OF RAM, 676

Negotiations between Prince Lenzo and Ordono, the king of the Rasidi, continued at a snail's pace. Lenzo sent Gaida and Dag across the sea to the king's port city of Aguilas in the hope that a face-to-face meeting might pin the monarch down to a decision.

'How hard is it?' Lenzo chafed. 'Either we go there, or he comes here.'

Sanc shared his frustration. Lothar was free to consolidate his control over the Kassite lands while they sat on a rock in the middle of the ocean, doing nothing.

That said, after the trauma of the Nerisian invasion, doing nothing was perhaps what they needed. Mildrith had seemed to be in a state of shock after their escape from Rincshold. Gradually, day by day, she recovered her energy. She talked more, took walks with Sanc and Rab, and began to eat properly.

Sanc set her the task of asking the people of Ram about Ezenachi, the old god they still worshipped. What they said was of little use. Ezenachi was a stern ruler, it seemed, demanding sacrifices from his people in exchange for his help in times of famine or disaster. Mildrith explained they worshipped Ymer alongside him. They looked to the Kassite god to manage the sea for them: keeping their sailors safe and ensuring their catch was plentiful. The Kassite champion had a raised eyebrow when she explained this, making it clear to Sanc that such things were not the traditional role of Ymer at all.

'If their beliefs have diverted from the rest of the Kassites since they settled here,' Sanc said, 'what chance is there that their knowledge of Ezenachi bears any resemblance to the truth?'

'Quite,' Mildrith agreed. 'Though there is one thing they say that is of interest. They believe Ezenachi lived a long way from this island. At Peramo, in the land of the Scorgians.'

'Peramo?'

'The legends say that after they conquered Silb, the seven gods took their rest at Peramo. It's striking that Ezenachi's worshippers believe he also lived there.'

Sanc nodded, full of questions.

'If you want to know more,' Mildrith said, a little smile at the corner of her mouth, 'I suggest you talk to Lenzo. He must know all about it.'

LENZO LOOKED pleased to see Sanc and Rab when they paid him a visit. He petted Rab, who then barked at him.

'He's hoping you'll go play with him.'

'He remembers me?' Lenzo asked.

'Of course.'

'He's a clever beast, considering his size.'

Unsure how to respond to the comment, Sanc simply agreed. He looked about the house Lenzo had been housed in. It was the home of one of the elders, bigger than most. Local stone had been used for the walls, the gaps filled in with mud and straw. But it was crude and cramped compared to the prince's mansion back in Arvena. Sanc said as much.

'I can't wait to get back to Arvena,' Lenzo admitted, letting out a sigh. 'I had thought coming here myself would speed things up. If we didn't need Ordono's support so much, I'd tell him to shove it up his arse and sail home.'

'I've come to ask you about Peramo. Mildrith told me it's the resting place of the seven gods. When she spoke with the locals here, they told her it was where Ezenachi once lived.'

'As I've told you, I'd never heard of Ezenachi before you arrived here. But Mildrith is correct about the seven gods. Each has a tomb dedicated to them at Peramo. I've seen them for myself. It is the holiest place in Silb, that is for certain.'

'If I remember correctly, Lothar had his imperial coronation at Peramo.'

'Correct,' said Lenzo, a sneer coming to his face. 'He made the priests there conduct the ceremony. It's a place that symbolises the unity of the seven peoples. He's a clever bastard. I have to give him that.'

'So it's possible Peramo was a holy site before the seven peoples came?'

'Possibly. I've never heard it said. Unless I was taught it by my tutor. I didn't listen much to him. Why? Is it important?'

'I don't know. Probably not. But I now think Ezenachi came to Dalriya from Silb. I may have come here using the same path. And when I did, I arrived very close to Irpino—'

'—and close to Peramo,' Lenzo added, following his chain of thought. 'So now you know a little more about your enemy. But knowing doesn't bring us any closer to victory. For that, we need an army.'

'I suppose you're right.'

When Gaida and Dag returned from their visit with the Rasidi, they brought the news their prince had been waiting for. Ordono and his royal court were already travelling to his palace at Aguilas. Lenzo, Mildrith, and Sanc were invited to stay with him and agree the terms of an alliance.

Lenzo was in high spirits as he ushered them aboard his ship. Virtually the entire fleet left Ram and set sail for the Rasidi coastline.

Summer had given way to autumn during their stay on the island and the winds that whipped them had a cold bite that they hadn't felt during the passage to the island. The sea moiled around them, waves crashing over the side of the ship with regularity. Sanc's stomach protested at the rocking of the ship and once he and Mildrith found a spot on deck that stayed relatively dry, they huddled under a blanket with Rab and waited for the journey to end.

On the starboard side, the Rasidi coastline came into view. The wind eased and as they approached Aguilas, the sun appeared, as if it were still summer in this part of the world. Sanc left his hideaway and joined a few others in looking out from the bow. He was rewarded by being one of the first to see the city come into view. Aguilas sat either side of a great river mouth that emptied into the sea. The city stretched out over the low ground, covering a wide area.

'It's huge,' he muttered.

'Aye,' Lenzo agreed. 'One of the greatest cities in Silb, for certain.'

'No doubt,' Dag said. 'I'm told the capital, Corbila, is smaller.'

Close to port, Lenzo ordered his captain to wait for the rest of the fleet to catch them up. 'It's wise to make a good first impression,' he confided to Sanc. 'We have the biggest fleet in Silb. Seeing it will encourage the Rasidi to do business with us.'

The biggest fleet but no army to speak of, Sanc told himself. His chest tightened as his mind turned to the failures of the Kassite campaign. *I should have persuaded them not to fight the Nerisians out in the open as we did*, he lectured himself, reliving the war yet again. *Peyre would have known it was foolishness and counselled against it. But I've never had the head for war.*

Lenzo was looking at him. 'The Kassites' defeat wasn't your fault, you know?'

'How did you read my mind like that?'

Lenzo laughed. 'I didn't. I read your face. Anyway, with the Rasidi alliance, we'll have an army to match our fleet. All is far from lost.'

Sanc nodded, turning his gaze back to the city before them. *Perhaps all isn't lost. But this visit really needs to be a success.*

* * *

THE STREETS of Aguilas were an assault on the senses. The wares of spice merchants mingled in the air, creating a heady aroma; while in the background, the fishmongers' stalls added a salty tang. All the vendors shouted their offers, competing with one another in volume to attract the many citizens who strolled the streets. The numbers told Sanc this was a populous place—far larger than any other settlement in Silb he had been to. He estimated it was comparable in size to Valennes. He could tell it was all a little overwhelming to Rab, who stuck close by his side.

The noise and smells were arresting, but the sights drew his attention with equal pull. He had expected the Rasidi to look the same as the other seven peoples he had met—whether Scorgian, Nerisian, Gadenzian, or Kassite, there was little difference in appearance, save for the height of the Gadenzians. But the typical Rasidi was brown-eyed, olive skinned, and smaller in stature. The climate was certainly warmer than it had been on Ram. But the physical differences were so noticeable it made Sanc think there must be more to it than that.

Their buildings were unlike anything he had seen before. The smooth, plastered walls were regularly interrupted by arches of different shapes and sizes. Wood was cut in a lattice design, giving the houses privacy but allowing air inside. The larger buildings were topped by magnificent domes and the exteriors were a blaze of colour, their walls covered in thousands of mosaic tiles.

Finally, being led or ridden in the city, was a strange looking animal. At first sight, Sanc told himself it must be a horse. But these gangly looking things were taller, with a thick-lipped, ugly looking face, and a humped back.

'What is it?' he uttered.

Rab was as interested in it as he was, putting his nose in the air and taking several sniffs, as if the smell might tell him what kind of creature they had come across.

Mildrith followed his gaze, then grinned. 'A camel. You do not have them in Dalriya?'

'No.'

'The Rasidi use them as we use pack horses.'

'Why? They have none of the beauty of a horse.'

'True. But they are hardier and stronger. And the Rasidi have horses as well.'

'I suppose that makes sense.'

'Well, good. I'm sure the Rasidi will be pleased to have your grudging approval.'

Before Sanc could think of a witty retort, he was distracted by a whistle from Lenzo, who was taking in the building ahead of them. They had turned a corner that left them facing a huge archway. It led into what must surely be the largest and most magnificent building in the city—the royal palace. Sanc had seen the rose-coloured dome atop the palace at various points on their journey from the ships. Now that he could get a full look at the walls, he could see the building was octagonal. The walls were adorned with a breath taking mosaic design in cerulean blue, cream, and rose. Wooden latticework was painted to blend in, acting as huge windows.

Outside the archway, which rose half way up the wall they faced, Rasidi guardsmen halted them. While Dag explained their business with the king, Sanc shared looks with Mildrith and Lenzo. He almost felt it an honour to be there; especially since the rest of Lenzo's crew had remained behind on the ships, under Gaida's supervision.

'It is impressive,' Lenzo said. 'I am sure some of these designs would look equally good in Arvena.'

'Or in my kingdom of Guivergne, for that matter,' Sanc said.

'And this isn't even Ordono's main palace,' Lenzo reminded him. 'The finest Rasidi architecture is in the capital, Corbila.'

'Huh,' Mildrith said, lips pressed together as she eyed the decoration with distrust. 'Such ostentation has no place among my people.'

'Which is why the Kassites will always be our most barbarous cousins,' Lenzo said. 'Come,' he added, before she could respond. 'We have been granted entry.'

The interior of the palace was just as beautiful as the exterior, with mosaic floors and decorated columns that reached to the ceiling. Sanc could see how the light came in through the latticed windows, striking the floor and the far walls. It was a maze of corridors and walled off rooms—so unlike the open halls he was used to, where everyone ate, and most people slept. They passed walled gardens, attached to different parts of the palace, each for the private use of the royal family, their officials, or their guests. They were deposited into a guest suite, divided up into different areas accessed through archways, which all faced onto a small garden. There were many rooms and beds to choose from.

'I suppose you two will be sleeping together,' Lenzo said with an arched brow.

It wasn't so long ago that Sanc would have gone red at such words, but now he just grinned as he and Mildrith left the prince and Dag while they toured the suite, Rab padding behind them, before choosing a secluded area with a large bed and colourful bedspread.

Just as Sanc sat on the mattress to test its give, a servant approached them. She looked a few years older than Sanc, and nothing like the Rasidi—tall and fair, with honey coloured hair that was bound in a bun. Her eyes were a distinctive violet colour. Her linen clothes were plain and grey, a contrast to the brilliant colours of the palace.

Nodding her head in a show of deference, she placed a pile of folded clothes on their bed. 'A change of clothes,' she explained, 'for you to wear when you meet with the king.' She had an accent different from any Sanc had heard before.

'Thank you,' said Mildrith, sifting through the clothes. She held up a long dress of forest green, that was patterned with pinks, blues, and yellows. One repeating design was an octagon, the same shape as the palace. Next, she found a headdress. She pursed her lips. 'I don't wear dresses,' she commented.

'I suggest you do here,' Sanc said. 'Besides, I imagine you will look beautiful in it.'

The Kassite gave him a piercing stare and Sanc realised he had said something wrong.

'I didn't realise my purpose in life was to look beautiful for you. Thanks for explaining that.'

Sanc's mouth dropped open a little, though he certainly didn't dare say anything else. He turned to the servant, hoping to find some relief there. There was a tiny smirk at the corner of her mouth.

'If there is nothing else, may I be excused?' she asked.

Sanc disliked the idea that she had to ask his permission to leave. 'What is your name?' he asked her.

For a moment, he saw a look of fear cross her eyes, as if she thought she was in trouble. But it left as soon as it appeared. 'Domeka,' she replied.

'You don't have the same looks as the other Rasidi I have seen,' he said.

Domeka tilted her head at him, as if trying to decipher whether there was some hidden meaning behind the comment. 'I am Teld,' she said simply.

'Thank you,' Mildrith said to her. 'We don't need anything else.'

Domeka left, and Mildrith turned to face him. 'You *are* a little obsessed with everyone's looks, you know.'

'It's not that,' Sanc replied, feeling defensive. 'I just struggle to place people. It's something that comes easy to you.'

'Sorry. You're right,' Mildrith said. 'The Telds have lost much of their ancestral lands. To campaigns by the Nerisians, Egers, and Rasidi. Many now serve the Rasidi as slaves.'

'Slaves?' Sanc repeated, shocked. He knew full well there were different social classes in Guivergne and the other kingdoms of Dalriya. Among the Scorgians, too, and even the Kassites. But slavery he considered an evil. That was one of the things that had made the Isharites a hated enemy; and now Ezenachi did the same—made slaves of those he conquered, controlling everything, even their minds. To learn that the Rasidi owned and sold other humans made him think of them differently.

'That turns my stomach,' he admitted.

'What do you think is happening to my people right now?' Mildrith demanded of him. 'What crimes are being visited on a people we have left defenceless? We need the Rasidi as allies. You'll have to swallow your disdain and smile and bow at the right times. Otherwise, we're finished and Lothar has won. And if that comes to pass, you'll have no one to help you rescue Dalriya.'

Sanc nodded. She was right, he knew. 'True. But if I can do that, you can wear a dress.'

'I can. Why don't you take your clothes and find a bed for yourself and give me some privacy while I change?'

'Sure.' He grabbed his clothes, not looking at her; not wanting to show how her words hurt him. He left, turning back once to see whether Rab was following. The dog sat resolutely next to Mildrith. Sanc wandered around the suite looking for a bed. He found Lenzo. The prince was half-dressed as he changed into his new clothes.

'Trouble in paradise?' Lenzo asked, eyeing the pile of clothes in Sanc's arms.

'We had a fight,' Sanc admitted.

'About what?'

'I'm not even sure.'

'Ah. One of those. That happens in a relationship, so I'm told. Apparently, the making up part is fun.'

'You're not an expert yourself?' Sanc asked him.

'No. I prefer whores, Sanc. You know where you stand with a whore. But I'm in the minority. And you and Mildrith seem well suited. So don't worry about it too much.' He gestured with his thumb. 'There's another bed round the corner there. Get dressed. When Mildrith sees you in your new finery, she might get interested in making up.'

'Not Mildrith. She's not into that whole looking good thing.'

'Sanc, everyone likes to look good. Everyone likes to be told they look good. Even those who claim they don't. That's a universal piece of advice for you, whether it be your wife, lover, or whore.'

'Right. Thanks.'

'Well, off you go then. Unless you want to watch me take my trews off. I don't mind if you do. I like an audience. But you're a bit funny with that stuff, aren't you?'

'Yes. I am,' Sanc said, and hurried away.

* * *

AFTER THEY WERE DRESSED, Domeka and another Teld servant returned to their suite.

'The king has requested your company,' Domeka explained.

'Very good,' Lenzo answered for them.

They led Sanc and the others from the suite and along corridors to a new part of the palace. Everywhere, he saw Teld servants—young and old, male and female. In the palace, they appeared to outnumber the Rasidi. The guards they passed, armed with spears and swords, were all Rasidi.

Sanc was surprised their final destination was a garden. Enclosed by walls with arches on opposite sides, he could smell the fragrances from the flowers and plants, arranged with precision in their beds. A shallow, stone-built pool lay at the far end of the space. The grass was green and neatly trimmed. In the centre of the lawn was a table, shaded by a gazebo made from a light fabric and decorated colour-fully, like everything else in the palace. Domeka gestured towards the table.

Lenzo led them towards the table, where four men rose from their seats. All shared the same Rasidi looks, wore similar robes to the ones Sanc had changed into, and were of a similar age—perhaps all in their fifties. It meant he had no idea which of the four was the king. He could sense the presence of power, though, and assumed one must be the Rasidi champion.

'Your Majesty,' Dag began, facing the man on the middle left. He was of medium build, with a moustache and trimmed beard. He was studying them all, his eyes alive with interest. 'May I present Prince Lenzo of the Scorgians.'

'I am honoured to meet you at last,' said Ordono, extending his hand.

Lenzo took it and the two of them spent a moment looking into each other's eyes. Neither face seemed to give much away. 'Likewise,

Your Majesty. May I present the new champion of the Scorgians, Sanc. And this is Mildrith, champion and representative of the Kassites.'

'Welcome,' said Ordono. 'Mergildo, our champion,' he said, gesturing to his right. Mergildo was taller, and the bags under his eyes aged him. 'I have also asked Guillen, Mayor of the Palace, and Barros, our General Commander, to attend. Please, sit,' he added, directing them to cushioned seats that faced the Rasidi.

Sanc took a seat opposite the champion, next to Mildrith. The titles of Ordono's officials were new to him, but he supposed the mayor to be equivalent to the position of steward that Lord Russell had held under his father, while a general commander sounded like a marshal—a military position.

'Bring the refreshments,' the mayor, Guillen, said to the two servants. 'We are free to speak openly here,' he said once they were gone.

Indeed, Sanc thought, such a meeting place was quite unusual in his experience. Often such conversations were held in a great hall where anyone might overhear. He recalled the tradition of the Kassites, where the chieftains were used to discussing alliances with their people stood around them, listening. The Rasidi did things quite differently. 'Dag and your other man, Gaida, made it quite clear what kind of deal you were proposing when they visited last month.'

'It's quite straightforward,' Lenzo said. 'The Nerisian aggression of the last few years should make every ruler in Silb feel the need for action. Lothar's attacks on the Scorgians and Kassites have been serious, and his ambitions don't end there. He has already crowned himself Emperor of Silb.'

A slight smile came to Ordono's face. 'He's an ambitious one, it's true. From what I've heard, there is little left of the Scorgian and Kassite peoples for us to deal with.'

'Making a deal with a bunch of renegades is beneath the king,' Barros, his other adviser, said. It was far ruder, but more to the point.

'I have already demonstrated the power of the Scorgian fleet by bringing it here so you can see for yourselves,' Lenzo said.

Barros shrugged, but Ordono nodded in apparent agreement. The king's gaze turned to Mildrith.

'The Kassites are ready to fight,' she said. She sounded less sure of her words than Lenzo had.

'My reports say Lothar has conquered it all,' the general commander retorted.

'Not true. Holt resists in the west and Tredan in the east,' the Kassite answered. Sanc kept his expression neutral. The truth was they'd heard nothing from Tredan, but he supposed the Rasidi would know no better. 'And the rest of the Kassites will rise up, given the chance. An attack on Nerisia will force Lothar to withdraw his occupying forces and then my people will be free to take their revenge.'

Ordono looked less than impressed.

'The key point,' Lenzo said, 'is the three champions gathered here.' He gestured towards Sanc and Mildrith, then Mergildo, who nodded his head in acknowledgement but said nothing. 'Working together, they can outmanoeuvre Temyl and Guntram. That will give us the edge in the end, regardless of the size of Lothar's forces. Yes, we need the Rasidi army, too. But we're not asking you to charge headlong into battle. Simply opening a new front will leave the Nerisians stretched too thin to hold down what they've taken.'

Ordono nodded slowly. Servants appeared with food and wine, filling up the table with choice offerings. Sanc's stomach rumbled at the smells as he watched the Telds work.

The king smiled, gesturing at the spread before them. 'You have answered our concerns well, my friends. Come, let us feast together and celebrate an alliance between our peoples.'

Mildrith allowed herself a small smile. Lenzo's was bigger, a mixture of delight and relief.

AFTER THE MEAL, Domeka led the four guests back to their suite.

'I will return with water for bathing,' she informed them before departing.

'Are they trying to tell us we stink?' Lenzo demanded.

'They bathe frequently here,' Dag said. 'The water is warm and scented. You'll enjoy it.'

Lenzo, Sanc and Mildrith looked at one another awkwardly. Things still felt difficult with Mildrith, and without a conversation, Sanc returned to his own part of the suite. He visited the garden that was accessed by a nearby archway. Confined by four walls, it had palm trees, flower beds, a small lawn, and a bench to sit upon. Beyond the garden, he could see the sun was setting, casting an orange haze across the sky.

Footsteps made him turn. They sounded like Mildrith's, but he discovered Domeka instead.

The Teld servant looked hesitant and fearful, as if she was in two minds about approaching him.

'What is it?' he asked her, speaking with care, as if he might frighten her off.

A look of resolve crossed her face. 'A warning,' she whispered. 'Not to trust the Rasidi.'

'Why?'

She pursed her lips together. 'Your bath is ready,' she said, and left the garden.

SANC

AGUILAS, KINGDOM OF THE RASIDI, 676

Sanc held Mildrith close, not wanting to let her go. Beneath the blankets, he trailed a hand down her back, over her hip, then squeezed a buttock. She turned to him, and they kissed. Lenzo had been right. The making up had been worth the fight.

The noise of a partition scraping on the floor pulled them apart. The prince appeared, a glass of wine in one hand and a leer on his face. 'Well, well. This is what you two get up to while I am meeting with Ordono. Looks cosy in there. I'm feeling a little tired myself.'

'Get lost, you Scorgian deviant,' Mildrith growled.

Lenzo broke into a broad smile, enjoying her anger.

'Is there something you've come to tell us?' Sanc asked him. 'Because if this is just a social call, we can send you back the way you came. Very fast. And very hard.'

'Ooh. Fast and hard. Just the way I like it, Sanc.' Lenzo held up his hands as he saw Sanc grimace. 'Come now, no need for threats. There is a very specific piece of news. Mergildo has invited you both to a meeting this evening. He wants to assess your magic and discuss ways for the three of you to work together.'

'Makes sense, I suppose,' Sanc admitted. 'What of the king?'

'His council has agreed to war,' Lenzo said, that familiar look of

relief and pleasure on his face. 'Orders must be sent across the kingdom. It is too late to do anything this year, but Ordono is confident he
will have an army ready to invade Nerisia as soon as spring arrives.'

'What do we do in the meantime?' Sanc asked.

'We need to agree on a strategy. After your meeting with Mergildo,
we may have a better idea about who should go where. As soon as the
Rasidi attack, the Scorgians and Kassites need to be ready. Well,' he
said, as Mildrith's eyes continued to bore into his, 'I'll leave you to it.'

'I can't stand him,' Mildrith hissed as soon as the prince was gone.
Throwing the covers aside, she began to dress.

Sanc watched, taking in her body. Surely, he could never get bored
of such a sight. Mildrith never said anything, but he thought she liked
him looking. He remembered Lenzo's advice. *Everyone likes to be told
they look good. Even those who claim they don't.* Mildrith was different,
though. If he'd said it in words, she'd have told him to shut up. When
only his eyes said it, an almost invisible smile came to her face.
Like now.

'He's not really that bad,' Sanc said. 'He's just looking for a rise
from you.'

'One day he'll get it. A knife to the throat.' She fastened her cloak,
then studied him, concern on her face. 'What is it, Sanc?'

'I was thinking of Domeka.' The Teld slave had warned him about
the Rasidi on his first night in the palace. Since then, she had disappeared. He had asked one of the other servants where she was. But the
woman had looked at him warily and just shaken her head. Had she
been replaced? Worse? Sanc didn't know how he could find out.

Mildrith studied him. 'You obviously feel something is wrong, or
you'd have forgotten about it by now. You need to trust your gut,
Sanc.'

Her words strengthened his resolve. For all her outward surliness,
Mildrith listened to him. She had faith in him. Such things meant a
lot. 'Then I think I need to investigate the Rasidi to put my mind at
rest. Before we meet with Mergildo.'

'Agreed. You need to move around with no one knowing you're
there. If only you could go invisible, or something.'

'Alright, smart-ass. What about you?'

'It would be less suspicious if I were to stay here and be seen. I could tell people you're sleeping. What about the Scorgian? Do we trust him enough to tell him where you've gone?'

Sanc thought about that. 'Maybe not. He has his heart set on this alliance. With any luck I'll find nothing, and he never need know.'

SANC TRAVERSED the corridors of the palace. His magic told people they saw nothing. Heard nothing. His spell had become more powerful than when he had first experimented with it, in the east side of Valennes. Then, he had to keep to the shadows; he had not dared move. Now, he could walk past the Teld slaves and they didn't know he was there. Still, he found he walked on tiptoes, as if a part of his mind didn't comprehend the magic he deployed. When he passed someone, he held his breath and felt his heart beat hard in his chest.

He had yet to learn the full layout of the palace and had to suffer several false turns until he found himself in the restricted area where the king and his advisers operated. He halted. Ahead of him, Mergildo had emerged into the same corridor. The old champion was alone, but that didn't make him any less dangerous. Sanc watched as Mergildo stopped walking and tilted his head.

He senses me, Sanc knew, concentrating hard on his magic. *It's not just sight and sound I need to disguise,* he told himself. *I need to hide my magical presence as well.* Carefully, wary of a sudden burst of power that would reveal himself, Sanc hid his magic. It felt like throwing out plumes of smoke, or mist, that acted as a veil over his magic casting. Mergildo looked his way. *What if he can see through it?* Sanc asked himself. But after a moment, the Rasidi sorcerer turned away with purpose and set off in the opposite direction.

Sanc allowed a breath of relief to escape. If Mergildo had come his way, he felt sure he would have been revealed. As it was, he had found one of the Rasidi leaders. With no better plan, he followed the champion, keeping to a safe distance and suppressing his magic casting.

Enveloped in his magical veil, it was like walking through an early morning brume.

He had assumed, at first, that following Mergildo might take him to the king or other powerful figures of the Rasidi court. Instead, he found he had followed the champion to a palace exit. Remembering there had been two guards stationed outside when they first entered the palace, Sanc sped up.

The guards parted promptly to allow the champion past without slowing his pace. Before they closed ranks, Sanc followed him out. He crept to the side, nervous about getting too close, and leaned against the palace wall.

For a moment, Mergildo looked around, taking in the bustling city. Then he was off, clearly to some specific destination.

Still with no better plan, Sanc waited for the gap between them to lengthen, then dogged his quarry.

The sights, sounds, and smells that had filled his senses on first arriving in Aguilas returned. Now, however, they were pushed to the edges of his consciousness. Sanc's focus was on Mergildo, as the sorcerer's long legs carried him rapidly along the city streets. The champion of the Rasidi must have been as well recognised a figure as anyone in the kingdom, and his compatriots were quick to move out of his way.

Sanc changed his speed to suit his task, never letting his quarry leave his sight. He followed him across a bridge that seemed the only way to cross the river on which the city stood. The bridge was busy with pedestrians, vehicles, horses, and camels. They closed in around Sanc, restricting his movement. It was a tight squeeze to move in and out of the obstacles without brushing an arm as he passed by. It was a relief to descend onto the southern side of the river and resume his pursuit through the streets.

The farther they travelled, the farther they got from the affluent environs of the palace, and the more intrigued Sanc became about their destination. The streets Mergildo led him down weren't cleaned to a polish like those in the palace district. Animal and human waste lay where it fell, creating a new sort of obstacle for Sanc to avoid.

Some citizens he passed didn't even try, squelching through whatever filth lay on their route without care.

The champion's journey ended at a ramshackle tavern, a faded and rotting sign that may have once shown green foliage, or a bunch of grapes. Sanc stopped for a moment, watching Mergildo enter the establishment. The wooden swing door was an obstacle, but Sanc reckoned he could get past it. He'd need to follow behind the next customer and slip through after them.

Sanc's interest was truly piqued now. Everything pointed to a clandestine meeting. But why would someone as powerful as the champion of the Rasidi feel the need to meet here, far from the palace? And there was something else, too. A warning feeling in Sanc's gut that something wasn't right. *You need to trust your gut*, Mildrith had said, and the advice made him pause outside.

Sanc calmed himself, trying to identify the source of his concern. Then it struck him. He could sense Mergildo's power emanating through the walls of the tavern. But it was stronger than before.

'No,' he whispered to himself, moving around the outside of the building until he reached a window. 'It's more than that.' One of the wooden shutters was half open, allowing him to peer inside. He scanned the interior with a rising sense of dread, hoping he was wrong. His eyes settled on a table. Mergildo had taken a seat, his back to Sanc's position. Facing the Rasidi were a Nerisian and a Gadenzian. Temyl and Guntram.

He moved aside, fearful they would sense him, as questions and answers raced through his mind. Any way one looked at it, this wasn't good. Mergildo was in league with Lothar's champions. The chances were that King Ordono was, too. The most logical explanation for their secret meeting was to keep it from Sanc and Mildrith. His gut clenched, remembering that Mergildo had invited them to a meeting this evening. What else could the three champions inside the tavern be discussing, except how to kill them? That would extinguish any remaining hope for Lothar's enemies.

Even such a cursory examination of the facts told him he only had one option.

Run.

'WE NEED to get out of here,' Mildrith said as soon as Sanc had told them what he'd seen.

Lenzo and Dag, on the other hand, were a picture of inaction.

'It can't be,' Dag stammered.

'I know what I saw,' Sanc said sharply, no patience for such denials.

'I believe you,' Lenzo said.

That was something.

'But what if we take what you've seen to the king?' he suggested.

Sanc studied the prince. It was hard to see the hope slowly dying on his face.

'What will that get us?' Mildrith asked Lenzo. 'Either way, he'll deny any involvement. The longer we tarry here, the greater our chances of capture. If Temyl and Guntram are here, Lothar will not be far away. With an army. He'd prefer the Rasidi to offer us up, but he won't think twice about coming for us himself.'

'But the negotiations,' Lenzo said weakly, clinging pathetically to his dream of an alliance. 'Ordono has sent orders out to his noblemen.'

Sanc shook his head. 'Remember how long it took before he granted us an audience? Left us waiting on Ram for weeks. He was probably in negotiations with the Nerisians even then.'

That provoked an angry clenched jaw from Lenzo. It was good to see. 'Alright,' said the Prince of Scorgia. 'Let's get to the ships and get out of here.'

Sanc nodded. 'I could try to get us out of the castle under my spell of invisibility.'

'But?' Lenzo asked, sensing Sanc's reluctance.

'I've already used a good deal of energy following Mergildo. And I need some in reserve. Just in case.' Three champions against two were far from good odds as it was.

'I've got it,' Mildrith said. 'Come into the garden. And bring your blankets.'

. . .

MILDRITH WAS in no mood for questions or debate. She had the three of them lying on the grass of the Rasidi garden, under the palm trees. Then they wrapped themselves up in their blankets. She studied them, nodding. 'Now close your eyes.'

'I—' Dag began.

'Just do it,' Lenzo growled at him.

Sanc held Rab tight and closed his eyes, waiting for Mildrith's magic to begin. It didn't take long. He felt his leg grasped by the sinewy strength of a tree root. Soon, his other limbs were gripped in the same way, holding him tight.

'I suggest you hold your breaths,' Mildrith said.

As Sanc sucked in a last gasp of air, he began moving, dragged along the ground. He gripped the ends of the blanket tightly. Then downward. He knew he was being pulled underground, and a terror struck him—the thought that if, for whatever reason, Mildrith's magic was stopped, he would be left buried alive. But he didn't stop, the roots kept dragging him, in what direction he no longer knew. Then, at last, he and Rab were flying, no longer surrounded by earth. He opened his eyes as he landed, gently enough, on the ground.

Sanc was quick to wriggle out of the dirty blanket and get to his feet. Lenzo and Dag were with him, staring about wild-eyed. As he looked around, he saw Mildrith burst from underground in a spray of mud and rock. The roots that had carried her retreated into the soil, their work done.

He took in their location. It was another garden, but larger than any he had seen inside the palace, with paths made of crushed stone that wound their way around flowerbeds and manicured trees. As he turned, he saw the walls of the palace at the far end of the garden.

'I saw it from the minaret,' Mildrith said, as she stood and brushed clumps of mud from her clothes. 'Reckoned this would be a safe spot to come out.'

Sanc smiled. 'Well done. Come on,' he said, pointing to a low part of the wall. 'We can get over there and into the city.'

The four of them helped one another climb the garden wall, low enough to clamber over without the need for magic. Rab stayed still as Sanc passed him over the wall to a waiting Dag, who was balanced on Lenzo's shoulders.

'Which way?' Mildrith asked.

'This way to the docks,' Dag said.

'Good,' said Lenzo. 'Lead on. With any luck we reach the fleet and leave before anyone realises we've gone.' He sighed. 'Salacus help me. You know things have turned to shit when you're hoping to leave with nothing.'

They walked into the city, the streets bustling with activity just the same as when they arrived.

'If we need to,' Sanc said, eyeing two soldiers patrolling on the other side of the road, 'I can hide us. But it's harder than you think. When people don't know you're there, they try to walk through you.'

Lenzo looked at him with distaste. 'We'll save that for an emergency.'

'Sanc,' Mildrith said sharply.

Sanc followed her gaze, his stomach dropping. He scanned the crowd for the three sorcerers, but couldn't find them. Then he spotted someone else he recognised. It was Domeka, the Teld slave, who had disappeared from the palace. Her gaze locked on his, her eyes widening with shock. But instead of running away, she lifted her skirts and dashed towards them.

'You are out already!' she said breathlessly when she joined them. 'I was coming to fetch you.'

Mildrith put a hand to Sanc's arm, stilling him. 'Why?' the Kassite asked, an edge to her voice.

'The Rasidi will betray you to the Nerisians. You need to leave the city.'

Mildrith nodded, relaxing a touch at the Teld's words. 'We know. We're heading to the docks now.'

'No! They are heavily guarded by the Rasidi army. It looks like they are planning to seize the ships. You must follow me.'

'Not my ships!' Lenzo hissed. 'We have to get to them. Sanc, teleport us there. We need to escape with them. If the fleet is taken, we truly are lost.'

Sanc looked from the prince to the slave, unsure what was for the best. He tried to calm himself—tried to think carefully. Then he sensed them.

'They're near,' he said to Mildrith, fear gripping his chest. 'They may be after us already.'

'Or come for the fleet,' Mildrith said.

Domeka was scanning their faces, a worried look on her own. 'Listen to me. I come from the Teld king. I spy for him in the palace. He has sent his champion here to get you out. We don't have time to waste.'

Lenzo shook his head. 'I'm not putting my trust in anyone again.' He put a hand on Sanc's shoulder. 'We need to get out of here. Now. We can talk with the Telds later. Our priority is not letting Lothar get his hands on us.'

'There is another who has come here to get you out. Someone from your world,' Domeka said, looking at Sanc, her violet eyes full of desperation.

Sanc turned to her with a frown, the prince's hand dropping from his shoulder. 'What did you say? Someone from my world?'

Domeka nodded. 'He says you are a friend of his and must be rescued. He has been looking for you ever since he came to Silb.'

'What?' Sanc said, trying to make sense of the woman's words.

'His name is Herin.'

SANC HAD to find out if Domeka's words were true. To Lenzo's credit, he didn't argue.

'I can't abandon the fleet,' the prince said simply.

'Even if it means capture?' Mildrith asked him, a little harsher than Sanc would have said it.

Lenzo shrugged. 'I'm nothing without those ships. Lothar might as well have me.'

Sanc nodded. 'Their champions are after me and Mildrith. They can sense where we are. With any luck, that might allow you to slip through.'

'Alright. I'm due some luck,' Lenzo said wryly. He offered his hand, and Sanc took it. The prince gave a nod to Mildrith, no attempt at humour for a change. 'Come, Dag.' They strode off before Lenzo turned one last time. 'If I make it out, I'll find a way to contact you.'

Sanc and Mildrith followed Domeka through the streets to the south side of the city. All the while, Sanc felt for the location of the three enemy champions. They got no closer, nor further away, which at least reassured him that Domeka wasn't leading them into a trap.

Then, standing innocuously in an open square, he saw Herin. Jesper's friend looked healthy enough. He had his sword at his belt, but his clothes were different—a loose, flowing cloak over woollen trousers. A brown leather satchel hung from one shoulder.

He was standing with a woman—another Teld. As they closed, Sanc could see the woman was older than Domeka, about Herin's age. She had the same violet-coloured eyes as Domeka and held a walking stick. Sanc desperately wanted to call over, but he controlled himself. Even when Herin turned his way and his eyes widened, Sanc somehow kept a straight face.

'Sanc,' Herin said simply. 'I've been looking for you.' He gestured at Rab. 'That damned dog of yours really messed things up.'

Sanc nodded. 'I'm sorry. But I'm pleased to see you. This is Mildrith.'

'That was quick,' the woman next to Herin said to Domeka.

'They'd already left the palace, suspecting something was up.'

The older Teld nodded at them appreciatively. 'That may have saved your lives.'

'This is Kepa,' Herin said. 'Champion of the Telds. We came here once Domeka sent word of your arrival.'

'How much trouble are we in?' Kepa asked them.

'There are three champions in the city,' Mildrith said. 'Temyl, Guntram, and Mergildo. They may be looking for us already.'

'Three on three then?' Kepa asked, eyeing Sanc and Mildrith. 'Maybe we should take them on?'

Sanc smiled. There was something mirthful in the way Kepa said it that made him warm to her.

'Sanc and I have already used magic,' Mildrith said seriously. 'And we have the Rasidi soldiers to deal with, too.'

'Then discretion is the better part of valour today,' Kepa agreed. 'We should retreat to the Teld lands.'

'Then there are the ships,' Sanc said.

Herin and Kepa both raised an eyebrow.

'The Scorgian fleet is docked in the city,' Sanc explained. 'We don't want the Rasidi to grab it. Prince Lenzo left us to put to sea before it's too late.'

'That would give our enemies control of the seas as well as the land,' Mildrith emphasised.

'Hmm,' Kepa said. 'Perhaps I can provide something that might help both our escapes. The king is still in his palace?'

'As far as we know,' Sanc said.

'Then maybe if I send something over there, it will draw the attention of the champions and the soldiers.' Kepa raised her arms into the sky. Looking above, Sanc saw grey clouds arrive above them, blocking the sun. With a hand gesture, Kepa sent the clouds north, towards the palace district. As they moved, a spiral of wind formed, growing in size. When the weather arrived where the champion wanted it, Sanc could hear the squall and wondered at what damage it might be doing.

'With any luck,' Kepa said, 'that should occupy people's attention. At least give the Scorgian a chance to get to his craft.'

'You control the weather?' Sanc asked her.

'Sort of. I can move the air and that amounts to the same thing, near enough. I know the Kassite can manipulate plant life. What is your specialty outlander?'

'I'm not sure I have one. Not like the champions of Silb.'

'He can go invisible,' Mildrith said. 'For one.'

Kepa pursed her lips. 'Interesting. Anyway, I suppose we should go. Before our enemies locate us. Herin, would you do the honours?'

Herin reached inside his satchel and pulled a brown coloured rug from it, laying it neatly on the ground.

'Everyone on,' Kepa instructed, sitting at one end of the rug and facing outward. Sanc may have refused if Herin hadn't sat down in the space next to her. The fact that he seemed prepared to go along with it somehow made it more acceptable. Sanc and Mildrith took their places, and Rab curled up beside Mildrith. She put an arm around him.

'What about me, mistress?' Domeka asked.

'You are compromised, dear. Get on.'

Mildrith pushed at Sanc to shuffle over and guided the Teld to sit down between them.

Sanc felt the air gust in, seemingly from all directions, flapping his hair. With a lurch in his stomach, the rug rose from the ground. Somehow, the air pressure kept their seat rigid. Then, changes in the force of the surrounding air caused the rug to move. They rose and moved; rose and moved; reaching the height of the houses and still going.

Shouts of alarm and surprise rang out around the square. Sanc looked down on the Rasidi gesturing up at them and felt the terror of heights for the first time in his life. He reached out a hand toward Mildrith, forgetting Domeka was between them. The Teld grasped it instead. 'Don't worry,' the girl said. 'It'll be alright.' Sanc was sure he could hear Mildrith sniggering at him.

Once Kepa had the height she wanted, she turned around to face them. 'Here we go, then. I'll get you to the safety of my homeland. It's not too far away.'

The Teld champion turned back. The rug sped forward. In the distance, Sanc could see a chain of mountains.

'Don't worry,' Domeka repeated. 'But if you don't mind, please don't squeeze my hand quite so hard.'

BELWYNN

MASADA, KINGDOM OF KALINTH, 677

The winged horse of Kalinth flew from the fortress of Masada.

It had been a bloodless conquest. Many ex-Knights of Kalinth had set up in Masada in recent years, and they had infiltrated the fort with apparent ease. Belwynn allowed herself a grim smile. It was almost as if Theron had been planning such a move. His talk of honour didn't prevent his plotting.

In the end, most of the Haskan garrison had chosen to stay and give their oaths to the king of Kalinth. They had few options. To the east, Zared of Persala had taken a swathe of territory that reached all the way to the Itainen. The rest of Haskany had fallen to the Jalakhs, and few Haskans would choose to live under the khan's regime. His horsemen had swept across Haskany, putting out resistance as soon as it was formed. The Haskan king, Koren, had tried to hold out in his capital. But even stone walls had only kept the Jalakhs out for days. Koren was dead, and Gansukh hadn't bothered to take his crown. Haskany no longer existed, its people under the rule of one foreigner or another.

The Jalakhs patrolled the borders of their newly won territory, and it was impossible to say whether the fighting was over or just beginning. The fact that Theron himself had come to Masada and was overseeing its defences said much about his fears.

It was, therefore, with no pleasure that Belwynn left the relative safety of the fortress and rode out into Jalakh occupied Haskany. She rode alone, having decided that was the best way to get what she wanted. For Khan Gansukh owed her his bow, and she had come to collect.

Winter had not yet decided to leave the northern lands completely. It froze the ground at night. Not that it bothered Belwynn. But she had to take extra care of her mount, ensuring he was well fed and rested. During the days, the sun rose high in a clear sky and then it was a matter of keeping him cool and well-watered. She knew better than to push him too hard and her progress was slow. *But so be it. I'll still return to Kalinth at the beginning of Spring. That is when our company will set out.*

At night, while her horse slept, she wondered about the new group she was a part of. Maragin and Oisin, keepers of the sword and spear, she knew of old and trusted no one more. Lorant, King of the Blood Caladri, she had to admit was an able replacement for her twin, Soren. He now carried Onella's Staff and, from what Belwynn had learned of him over the years, probably wielded as much magic as her brother had. Belwynn herself carried Toric's Dagger at her belt. That left three spaces to fill. Who was picked might make all the difference. Or it may not matter at all.

Her thoughts would then turn to Theron, and her once-daughter, Lyssa. To her stepdaughters and their children, dangerously close to Ezenachi's realm. To Clarin. To Soren, of course. To lose someone you love is a cruel wound to carry, but that ache at the loss of her twin seemed to only grow as the years drifted past, while all other pain had faded.

When dawn came, it was a relief to move again and escape her thoughts.

It was four days in when the unit of Jalakhs intercepted her. There were six of them, all men with hard eyes.

'I am travelling to a meeting with your khan,' she explained to their leader when he pulled up alongside her.

'I was told we might come across you,' he said.

Indeed, he had shown no surprise at finding her travelling alone, or at her words. Belwynn supposed what he said was true.

'My orders are to escort you to Samir Durg.'

Her escort travelled north, at a faster pace than the one she had set. Her horse kept up with them, and she supposed that if he pulled up lame, there were now spares for her.

On the evening, the Jalakhs made a fire, cooked supper, and spoke together. Belwynn sat apart, declining the offer of food. Whenever one of them looked her way, she stared right back and they were the ones to give in first, letting sleep take them, while she looked out across the land that was the latest addition to their empire.

When they attacked, it took her completely by surprise. A blow to her head knocked her from the horse onto the ground. One did not recover quickly from such a fall, and by the time she had Toric's Dagger in her hand, they had her surrounded. Maybe someone like Clarin, or Moneva, could still have recovered from such a position, but Belwynn had never been a warrior.

They clubbed her arms and she felt bones break. She dropped the dagger. Tempered steel swords pierced her body, and hacked parts off. They placed a hemp bag over her and tied her up. They bundled her onto a horse—her own horse, she guessed—for some reason that caused her more anger than anything else. They led her, slumped over the back of the beast, for some time. Occasionally she would get another beating, or one of them would rip a new injury into her body.

At last, they stopped. From inside the bag, she heard their muffled voices. She was dragged off the back of the horse, landing on the ground once more. They picked her up—perhaps two of them holding her legs, one her head, one her back. Then they threw her.

She hit the water with some force. It stank—some stagnant pond, the water brown and fetid. Tied up as she was, she quickly sank to the bottom. The floor of the pond had some give in it. Probably some godforsaken bog, which would pull her down into the muck.

Belwynn closed her eyes. It wasn't the way she had thought she would go. Nibbled at by whatever disgusting creatures inhabited such a place. But under the water, pulled into the bog's embrace, she was surprised to learn it was an ending she could settle for. There was an undeniable appeal. Every story must end, and even with the very best, there is always a yearning for closure. For peace.

* * *

SHE DRAGGED herself from the pond and stood on what was left of her two legs. It had been as much a test of her emotional and mental resources, as her physical ones, to make herself return from her rancid grave.

In the light of morning, she studied her reflection in the water.

'I'm sorry, Elana,' she said, as she studied the ravaged body she inhabited. The face was unrecognisable. Her voice sounded different, as if her attackers had even damaged that. 'What have I allowed to happen to you, old friend?'

Belwynn was surprised to feel a tear coursing down her cheek. She had thought she was long past crying. She turned away, looked to the sky, and found north. A bitter smile came to her face at the lopsided gait she now walked with. But still she walked, for Samir Durg.

BELWYNN LOST count of the days. She walked day and night now, no horse to care for. Riders intercepted her as she approached the huge walls of the Jalakh fortress. She didn't speak to them or even turn to look their way. But she sensed the fear in the hard men of the steppe. They left her, returning to Samir Durg. When, at last, she shambled her way to the gates, they had been opened for her. She was led through the fortress to the palace.

The sun had set, and no light came in through the golden dome of Gansukh's throne room. Instead, flames flickered and smoked on each side, casting shadows in the great space that gave it an eerie feel. Gansukh eyed her as she hobbled towards his throne, making no effort to increase her pace. As before, he was flanked on one side by his advisers, on the other by armed warriors. All of them observed her with the same dread look. To the side, the khan's mother, Bolormaa, had put her knitting down. She also studied Belwynn, her lips pressed tight.

'I have come for the Jalakh Bow,' Belwynn said.

Gansukh turned to one of his warriors with a sneer. Belwynn realised it was the leader of the group who had tried to kill her. Confirmation, not that it was needed, that they had been following the khan's orders. The man met Belwynn's eyes and gave her a gloat of a smile.

The khan glanced at his mother before returning his gaze to Belwynn. 'Of course. That's what we agreed, after all.' He reached to one side and took the Jalakh Bow in his hands. Reluctant, it seemed, to part with it.

'King Theron is pleased with his new conquest?' he asked her.

'The bow,' Belwynn repeated. 'I'll not ask again.'

'Don't threaten me in my own palace,' Gansukh warned her. He looked her up and down. 'What kind of fiend are you, that you can survive such injuries?'

'I am Belwynn Godslayer. I have nothing to fear from mortals.'

'Hmm.' He fingered the stave of the weapon that had given him such power. Belwynn understood that parting with it went against his every instinct. 'What guarantees do I get that you will return it once your purpose is done?'

'Give her the bow,' Bolormaa spat, her patience gone.

'Very well,' Gansukh said. He rose from his throne and approached Belwynn. With a mocking bow, he presented her with the weapon.

Belwynn took it. There was a sense of relief that at last she had it in her hands, but also a fury at the cost. 'I will need two more things.'

'What now?' Gansukh asked her.

'First, return my horse.'

The khan gave an easy shrug. 'It's yours. What else.'

Belwynn pointed to the warrior. 'Does he have a wife?'

The warrior's face creased in a frown.

Gansukh turned to him. 'You should have cut her head off.'

'Great Lord, please. I did as you asked.'

'That wouldn't have stopped me,' Belwynn said.

Gansukh gave her a look of scrutiny, trying to assess if her words were true. He glanced at Bolormaa, who gave an almost imperceptible nod. 'Very well. I shall give you this man's wife. Then I don't expect to see you again unless it is to return my people's bow to me.'

'Of course,' Belwynn said, giving in to sarcasm. 'We made a deal, did we not?'

LIESEL

VALENNES, KINGDOM OF GUIVERGNE, 677

The wind harried her, a wintry bite to it that required her warmest clothes, as she observed the activity on the archery field. The crossbow bolts made a whipping sound as they flew, then a thud when they hit the hard wooden targets.

Liesel had to admit it had become a terrifying noise. There had only been a few weapons at first, the Cordentine refugees she had taken to Valennes training a small band of citizens how to use them. But the training was simple—little more than point and click to fire. Anyone could do that.

Liesel and the other trainees had found drawing back the string was the difficult part. But once the Cordentines taught the correct method—sitting on one's bottom with your feet on the stave and pulling it back—most had the strength for it. Certainly Liesel, with her big shoulders, wide chest, and thick limbs, found she was one of the quickest. 'At last, a benefit to being built like a cow,' she would say, to which Tegyn always rolled her eyes.

Liesel had no problem in recruiting archers. They could be women; young or old; from any background or profession. Not everyone liked it. There were many who were appalled at the idea of arming townsfolk and peasantry. More than one lord had complained to Esterel. But the king had little time for their reservations. His goal of becoming emperor of Brasingia now consumed him, and Liesel was churning out units of arbalests in weeks, when otherwise it would have taken years.

Others, like Tegyn, had different criticisms. She would complain the machines broke down too often. She pointed out that the Cordentines themselves warned about getting the weapons wet—more of a problem in this climate than in the south of Dalriya. She mocked the idea of sitting down in the middle of a battle to reload one's weapon. She demonstrated how many more arrows she could fire in comparison.

Liesel would nod in agreement. But privately, she always believed the benefits outweighed such problems, and looked for solutions instead. She knew, too, that a part of Tegyn's objection was personal. The bow held a special place amongst Atrabians, and Liesel was, in a way, cheapening her friend's skills. She understood, and she refrained from arguing about it.

With a huge supply of arbalests, Liesel's principal task became making the weapons. Esterel gave her the money she needed. It might have been different had Miles, the king's marshall, been in Valennes instead of spending the winter in Coldeberg. But he was absent, and Liesel was allowed to spend his budget on her project.

She had to persuade the Cordentines to do things her way. They were used to spending days and weeks on one piece, producing every part themselves and making a unique, expertly finished weapon. But such an approach didn't suit Liesel's goals. She wanted quantity over quality. So she had the stocks, strings, and bolts made separately by Guivergnais crafters, asking the Cordentines to focus on assembling the pieces. They would complain when rushed, but Liesel explained that if any broke, they would simply be replaced by a spare. In the end, they did what she asked. She had brought them from Thesse to Valennes, where their families were housed, and they had the income and pride that comes from steady work once more. Liesel was their saviour and protector, and the refugees were fiercely loyal to her.

Esterel arrived on the field. He walked alone, the days of Gosse lurking by his side gone now they were safely in Valennes. He gave a nod to Tegyn, but otherwise said nothing, watching Liesel's arbalests at work.

'Well?' she asked after a while. 'Can you see how they will be of use?'

'I can. The range is impressive. And you say they are more accurate than a standard bow?'

Tegyn snorted in derision but kept her views to herself.

'The great benefit,' Liesel said, ignoring her friend, 'is that you can hold your aim for as long as you need to, while waiting for the perfect shot.'

'So I could have them aim at the walls of a city or castle?'

'You could. They would hit defenders at a safe distance from the walls, as well.'

Esterel nodded. She could see he was considering this new addition to his army, working out how best to incorporate the units she had created. Abruptly, he turned to her. 'Liesel, I wish to talk. Will you walk with me?'

'Of course.'

'Lady Tegyn,' he said with a farewell nod.

'Your Majesty,' she replied.

Esterel led her back in the direction of the Bastion. The conditions during the siege of Coldeberg had persuaded Liesel that the fortress where the royal court lived was not as bad as she had first thought. But it still stank, and she spent most of the day outside.

'Was there something you wished to talk about?' she asked.

'Yes. I am wondering, now you have everything in order, whether you need to spend so much time on this crossbow business. It doesn't require your personal supervision all day.'

'What else would you have me do?' Liesel asked, surprised. It wasn't like her husband to fuss over what she did with her time.

'I would like you to rest more. The doctors say it would help you conceive.'

Oh. This, Liesel said to herself. Esterel had got it in his head that she should be pregnant by now. 'I don't see how sitting around all day will help me get with child.'

Esterel ignored her. 'They have also advised me we should try at different times of the day. Not just at night, when you are tired after your exertions.'

'I'm not tired at night,' she said irritably. She hated the idea of Esterel talking about such matters behind her back. They had been married less than a year—it was hardly such a length of time for concern. And why, she asked herself, was it assumed the problem lay with her and what she did?

'I thought we could try now?' he asked, a mischievous grin on his face.

'Oh.' Liesel sincerely hoped she wasn't turning red. 'That's why you're leading me to the Bastion.'

LIESEL TRACED a finger down the king's chest and belly. 'I could get used to doing it in the middle of the day,' she admitted.

'Me too,' said Esterel. He sat up and swung himself from the bed, searching for his clothes. 'Though unfortunately, I have meetings to attend, and I'm already late. I want you to stay in bed, though. Lie flat. The doctors say—'

'Oh, please. Enough with the bloody doctors!'

'Sorry,' he said, looking hurt. 'I'm just trying to help. We both want this, don't we?'

'Of course,' Liesel said. What else *could* she say? It wasn't as if she had a choice.

Esterel got dressed, throwing her clothes back on the bed for her when he found them. 'I'll see you at dinner,' he said and quickly departed.

Liesel lay on the bed. She felt strange. Used, somehow. Yes, she wanted to give Esterel children. But he had become obsessed with the need for an heir recently. It was clearly something to do with the upcoming war that made him worry about it. But it felt like the affection between them had gone. As if he wanted sex for that reason alone. And what if she didn't fall pregnant? What if she couldn't? Would he get rid of her?

Esterel told her he loved her. But in the last few months, he had revealed the depths of his ambition. 'He wants an heir,' Liesel warned herself in a whisper. 'If he doesn't get one from you, he'll go elsewhere.'

* * *

THE DAYS PASSED, and it seemed winter had done its worst. Preparations for war had to be advanced, including ensuring the realm was ready to cope with the pressure. The biggest problem for Esterel was the duchy of Famiens. Its loyalty had always been suspect, but since the blinding of its duke and many of his warriors, its relationship with the throne had never been more strained. After several requests, Loysse had written to Esterel, agreeing that she would visit him at the Bastion.

As the day of her sister-in-law's arrival approached, Liesel became ever more nervous of it. In sending Auberi to take Burkhard Castle, Esterel had turned the warriors of Famiens into bait—a diversion to occupy the Kellish while he conducted the siege of Coldeberg. He'd admitted as much to Liesel and Peyre. If he hadn't anticipated the brutality of the Kellish punishment, he'd still knowingly put them in harm's way.

Liesel had got on well with Loysse when they had met last year. The duchess of Famiens had been friendly and honest, even taking her side against Esterel. Now, Liesel's guilt over Auberi's injuries weighed her down. She imagined looking at the world from Loysse's perspective. Surely, she would hate Esterel's Brasingian wife, who had encouraged this war; at least as much as Esterel, who had sacrificed her husband for his ambitions.

IT WAS Sacha who came to find her, as she waited in her room with Tegyn.

'Her Grace, Lady Loysse, has arrived in Valennes,' Esterel's steward informed her.

Liesel stood from her chair. 'Thank you. Where do you want me?' Now it had come, she was keen for the meeting to happen. Even if for no other reason than it would then be over.

'You and the king will formally greet her in the Great Hall. After-wards, Esterel expects to talk with her in his private rooms. He antici-pates you will accompany them, but—' Sacha spread his hands, suggesting that much would depend on Loysse's mood.

Liesel met Esterel in the Great Hall. The fires had been stoked high, though any warmth soon seemed to escape the vast chamber. Together, they waited for his sister. When Loysse came, it was only with a small entourage. Four attendants trailed her, carrying travel-ling bags. Next to her was Syele, dressed for battle, wearing stiff leather armour and a longsword scabbarded at her belt. Loysse herself was wrapped up warmly in her travelling clothes, her blonde hair, so like Esterel's, coiled into a bun. Her face was not so different to how Liesel had imagined it—set hard and unsmiling, while emotion was plainly visible in her blue eyes.

'Welcome back to Valennes, sister,' Esterel said, his voice airy, as if oblivious to the tension in the room.

Liesel turned to look at him, worrying that it was the wrong tone entirely—it would do no good, she believed, to behave as if nothing was amiss. She therefore caught the rapid change in his features—his face lost colour and his mouth opened in shock. Returning her gaze to the duchess, she saw for herself. Loysse had removed her thick outer cloak, handing it to Syele. Revealed was an unmistakable bump.

Liesel's mind raced. To be showing already meant Loysse must have fallen pregnant months ago—before Auberi left for Rotelegen. The most likely scenario was that he had returned to Guivergne, blinded, to be told by Loysse they would have a child. She tried to imagine Auberi hearing the news; or Loysse doing the telling. She found she couldn't.

'You asked me to attend you?' Loysse said, her eyes boring into Esterel's.

Liesel had rarely seen her husband lost for words, but now was such a time. 'I thought we might speak in my apartments?' he got out, as if his sister were ruler and he was asking permission.

'Wherever you wish,' Loysse answered.

LOYSSE HAD A LOT TO SAY. It came out in a flood as soon as Esterel asked after Auberi. 'How would you feel, knowing your wife was with child and you would never get to see it?'

Liesel got the feeling many of the lines were things she had already said to Esterel in her mind many times, and she didn't hold back in saying them now. She castigated him for pursuing the war—Liesel herself got a glare at this point, though Loysse spoke as if it were all Esterel's fault. Liesel felt both relieved and guilty that she was let off so easily. Most of all, of course, she castigated him for his decision to send Auberi and the army of Famiens to take Burkhard Castle. Exposed, Loysse told him, they hadn't stood a chance against the Kellish.

'If I could take the decision back, I would,' Esterel said.

Loysse sneered. 'Then at least end the war now. Find a peace before more of your people end up mutilated and broken.'

'It's impossible now,' Esterel said. 'I can't let this atrocity stand. Everyone knows it, here and in Brasingia. A line has been crossed. War is coming.'

'Gods,' Loysse said, furious. 'I used to hero worship you, you know that, Esterel? And what kind of king have you become? A thoughtless, self-centred tyrant.'

'Enough!' Esterel said, his voice rising at last. 'You've had your say, Loysse, and I've listened to it. But I am still your king. And I tell you now, this war is not over. Not by a long stretch. I require your obedience and loyalty in what is to come. If you can't give it, say so now, and I will find someone else to govern Famiens for me.'

'Good luck with that,' Loysse spat out.

Esterel stared at her, saying nothing, his face implacable;

dangerous looking. Loysse stared back. In the end, it was Loysse who backed down.

'What is it you wish of me?'

'I will take a great army into the empire once more, led by the magnates of Guivergne. I will require you and Auberi to come to Valennes and rule in my absence.'

'Why us?' Loysse asked. She glanced at Liesel, and Esterel followed her look.

'Liesel needs to be with me. She is my claim to Kelland; to the empire.'

'So that's it? You intend to make yourself emperor?'

'Aye.'

'And there is no one else who can rule from the Bastion instead of us?'

'Everyone else will be coming. And if we fail...' Again, Esterel glanced briefly at Liesel. 'If we fail and Peyre and I don't return, you are my heir.' He gestured to her belly. 'And your child will be next in line.'

Liesel stared at him. What was Esterel planning in the empire? Was this the source of his obsession with getting an heir of his own? Had she failed him, causing him to turn to his sister and her child instead?

Loysse shared Liesel's look. 'Gods, I hope you know what you're doing, Esterel. This could be the end for all of us.'

He nodded, pensive looking. 'I won't lie. It could be. But we've started something now, and it can't be stopped. You think Leopold will stop now? That he can be reasoned with, after what he did? That a peace treaty with him and that witch would actually mean anything?'

Loysse shook her head. It seemed her rage was spent at last. All that was left was sadness. 'If that's true... and I suppose it is. You had better win, Esterel.'

He grinned, a small glimmer of that easy confidence returning. 'I intend to.'

IDRIS

ESSENBERG, DUCHY OF KELLAND, 677

T he key turning in the lock woke him. Idris sat upright. *I must have dozed off. Again.* He found he was doing so more frequently. Imprisoned in his small room, there was little else to do, save for the exercise routines that got him through each day.

The door opened and the man who had killed his father walked in, two guards hovering behind him. Their eyes met. Idris wanted to kill Salvinus, and Salvinus knew it. The small quiver in his mouth said that Salvinus enjoyed the knowledge.

The bastard dropped a pile of clothes onto the bed. 'Get dressed. The emperor wishes to speak with you.'

Idris fingered the items. A gambeson and quilted breeches. Military clothing. Idris fought down the hope that the items elicited, keeping his expression neutral. It could mean many things. 'You wanted to watch?' he asked Salvinus.

Salvinus made a face. 'No. Unlike his imperial majesty, I have no wish to look upon your scarred torso. It knocks me sick.'

SALVINUS LED him along the corridor and down the stone steps of the castle to the ground floor. It was the first time Idris had been this far from his room in months. The ceilings were high and the rooms wide. The size of the space triggered an anxious reaction in him. *By the gods. What will happen if I ever stand in the outside world again? Will I run to hide under some rock?*

It was evening and fireplaces, candles, and lanterns were all deployed to shed some light in the great hall. Leopold was seated on a carved wooden throne. Cresting one stile was the eagle of Kelland. Opposite was the seven antlered stag of Brasingia. It was new, no doubt commissioned to satisfy Leopold's ego. Standing next to him was the witch, Inge. *All my favourite people in one place.*

Leopold smiled as they approached. 'Idris. I have a proposition for you.'

Whatever it is, play it right, Idris warned himself. He got to one knee, bowing his head. 'Your Majesty. I am all ears.'

He stole a glance at Inge. She liked to see such displays of obeisance as much as Leopold. She eyed him with a predator's gaze.

'It's your uncle,' Leopold continued. 'Treacherous bastard. After all we've done for him, getting rid of his brother, giving him control of Atrabia, he proved false.' As Leopold spoke, his voice got louder and his face grew more twisted, ending in an animal expression of anger. 'Salvinus here called on him to aid in the conquest of Gotbeck. He made his promises, but they were weasel words. He never came. You tell it, Salvinus.'

'You've said it, Your Majesty. Attacking from two directions, we could have rolled over the Gotbeckers in a matter of weeks. As it was, the bishop was able to bring all his forces against my Luderians and defend, slowing us down. All I got from Emlyn were pathetic excuses about a threat from the Confederacy. Who knows what the truth is? He's been bought off by the Guivergnais, most likely.'

Idris had learned something of the conflict with Guivergne. Liesel was their queen now, and she had brought that kingdom into a war against Leopold. How he had prayed that the enemy would come to Essenberg and burn it to the ground. That hadn't happened. But clearly, things weren't going well. Not if the mighty Kellish were relying on the Atrabians to help them. Come Spring, the war would resume, and Inge was moving her pieces into position. He knew for sure now that this wasn't some prank to dangle freedom before him, only to take it away. This was his chance.

'I'm not surprised,' Idris said. 'He may have been in talks with the Guivergnais, but the truth is, my uncle is a coward. He will always find an excuse not to fight, however pathetic.'

'Yes,' Leopold agreed. 'That's the truth of it. And you're no coward, eh, Idris? You may be cracked in the head, but you can fight.'

'Indeed, Your Majesty. It is precisely because I am cracked in the head that I can be relied upon to fight, whatever the odds.'

Leopold laughed and slapped his thigh. 'See. That's what we need.'

'All of which may be true,' Salvinus said. 'But he can't be trusted. After what happened to his father.'

'I can be trusted. I've learned my place.'

Salvinus sneered, unconvinced.

'Salvinus is going to Atrabia,' Inge said.

Finally, the real ruler is speaking. Idris turned to her. *Careful now,* he warned himself. *If she doesn't trust you, this is over.*

'He will remove your uncle. He could place you in his stead.'

Idris nodded. 'I will serve you,' he said simply. 'You think I want to stay in my little room forever? I understand the position I am in. I will be Prince of Atrabia by your gift. It is a gift you can easily take back. I am neither stupid, heroic, nor craven enough to cause you to do so.'

She studied him. Close to making her decision. He understood her predicament. She wanted the Atrabians to fight with them. Kill Emlyn, and they'd likely face an Atrabian revolt. That was the last thing the Kellish needed. They didn't have the time to chase Idris's people over hill and through forest. They needed a new prince who did as he was told. They needed *him*.

'Understand this,' the witch said. 'If you prove false, it won't just be the end of you. You will be the last Prince of Atrabia. Atrabia will be annexed, garrisoned with imperial forts, and ruled directly from Essenberg.'

'I understand,' Idris said, looking from Inge to Leopold. 'And you have my word.'

* * *

IT TURNED out being out in the fresh, crisp air, with a clear blue sky above, didn't make Idris want to hide under a rock. He loved it. Even though he was riding amongst Salvinus's band of cutthroats, it was a little taste of freedom. Something, in his darkest moments, he had doubted he would ever experience again.

Not that everything was perfect. Idris had done his best to keep his strength, exercising in his room—even in his dank cell before that. But he found that his body had lost its stamina. Travelling all day— something he had taken for granted before his imprisonment—was now exhausting. Unused muscles ached, his lungs gasped, and he wanted to lie down and rest. When they stopped, he was ravenous. He hadn't noticed how much his appetite had dwindled during captivity until he could now compare it with other men. He ate quickly, but was soon full.

He also compared his stick like frame and limbs with the warriors Salvinus commanded. He had always been thin, but now he was self-conscious about his fragile looking body, even when wearing the quilted trews and top he had been provided with. At least they hid his scarred body, though he was sure that everyone already knew about that.

Salvinus's personal band were mercenaries, many of whom had been under his command for years. But the rank and file of his force were Luderians. Leopold was the duke of Luderia, but it seemed he had allowed it to become Salvinus's personal fiefdom. Idris studied the warriors of Luderia. They were quick to do as they were told, but stony faced. He could tell few of them loved their commander or were happy with their new mission. They might have been told that the Gotbeckers, or the Atrabians, were their enemies; but most men know a barefaced lie when they hear it.

Each day they got closer to Idris's homeland until one evening, he could make out the hills and mountaintops of Atrabia. Another thing he thought he might never see. He was surprised when, sat around the fire during supper, Salvinus sought his advice.

'I've taken a force into Atrabia once before, you'll recall,' he said, a comment that got a few grins from the surrounding warriors. He was referring, of course, to the moment he had captured Idris, his father, and Liesel. 'But any thoughts you have on strategy are welcome.'

'You may find it harder this time round,' Idris suggested. 'The Atrabian army had been in Thesse, and no doubt you caught our remaining defenders by surprise. Unless you had a deal with Emlyn beforehand?'

Salvinus smirked. 'He knew nothing about it. We had him and his family in our hands before he knew what was happening.'

Interesting, Idris said to himself. 'Impressive,' he said out loud. Of course, Inge had been there that time, and the credit probably fell to her. But he wasn't about to say that.

'So, if the Atrabians are on the lookout for us this time, what do you suggest?'

'I would get your warriors fully armoured well before we reach the border. Atrabian archers are plentiful and skilled. Their arrows can get through this, no trouble,' he said, picking at the quilted gambeson he wore.

Many of his lieutenants wore the same grudging look of acknowledgement as Salvinus did. They thought his advice sound. Because it was.

* * *

THEY WERE NOT TROUBLED on the first day. Salvinus's scouts ranged ahead but found nothing. The army spent the night in the open. Salvinus doubled the numbers on watch. It was wise, and Idris had to admit the man knew his business.

The second day was different. Idris saw the Atrabian scouts watching them long before the Luderians did. He knew where to look. But eventually, word got to Salvinus that they were being tracked.

'Emlyn knows we're here?' he asked Idris, as they rode near the van of the army. He'd sent his scouts ranging ahead and to each side, but in the broken countryside of Atrabia, it was easy to hide.

'If he doesn't yet, he soon will. But no matter. All we need do is get to Treglan and have me declared prince. He can't stop an army this size.'

'You have so little faith in your own countrymen?'

'Oh, they're capable of making our lives very difficult if they put their minds to it. But they don't have the numbers to defeat us. Plain and simple.' Idris noted the look of relief on Salvinus's face.

'And you think they will? Make our lives difficult?'

'That depends on how loyal they are to my uncle. Locked away the past two years, it's hard for me to say how things stand in Atrabia.'

'Has it been two years? Don't time fly.' Salvinus gave him his mocking smile, and Idris had to stop himself from drawing his sword. They'd armed him, a sign Salvinus was gradually coming to trust him. Having a weapon at his side made using it far too tempting. But after so long, he knew he couldn't throw his life away now. *Steel yourself,* his father had told him. *And by the gods, I have done my best to do what you asked, father. I have encased myself in so much steel that I fear I am cold metal all the way to my centre.*

IDRIS

ATRABIA, 677

A rrows flitted down at them. A score of cloaked archers stood on the brow of the hill. The long column of the Luderian army was an easy target. Those men nearest the enemy held up shields to protect themselves. Following Idris's advice, Salvinus had ordered his men to wear whatever armour they had. Idris himself had been given a chain mail hauberk and a boiled leather helmet. *It's as if they actually want me to survive. I should feel honoured.*

Other warriors, the poorest of the Luderian infantry who had walked all this way, had no such protection. Some arrows found their targets and, as Idris had warned, the arrows came fast enough to pierce mere linen or wool.

Salvinus turned around on his mount at the cries of pain amongst his army. 'Maybe we should send a cavalry force at them to clear them away.'

Idris made a face. 'They'll only retreat and lead your men a merry chase, or into a trap. Then reappear and begin again. Better to ignore them. All we need do is get to Treglan.'

'Why listen to this Atrabian?' one of Salvinus's lieutenants spat. 'Better to make a defensive camp than wander so far into enemy territory.'

Salvinus considered the words. 'Well?' he said, looking at Idris.

'We could build wooden walls and become sitting ducks if you wish. All the while the men are working, they'll be getting stuck with Atrabian arrows. They'll shoot at us all night as well, only pausing to bring fire and burn us out. Far better to keep moving and reach Treglan. We'll suffer far less attrition. That is my view, at least.'

Salvinus sighed. 'The Atrabian is right. Staying put gets us nowhere.' He looked at the hill. 'It's not like they have the numbers to do more than irritate.'

THEY CONTINUED THEIR MARCH, but the Atrabian landscape gave them no respite. More archers came, tracking them on each flank. A seemingly endless supply of arrows rained on them. Idris kept his head down. It would only take one bit of bad luck to be looking the wrong way and catch one in the face.

The van of the army had stopped at a thicket of trees. Salvinus rode ahead with his lieutenants, Idris with them. It was a grisly scene. Captured scouts had been hacked to pieces, body parts nailed to the trees.

Salvinus ground his teeth. 'Damn it. Without scouts, we could be walking into anything.'

His lieutenants said nothing, peering uneasily ahead, where the trees grew thicker.

'What say you, Atrabian? Treglan is due east.' He peered at the sky. 'Can we make it before nightfall?'

'I would have said yes.' Idris peered in the same direction as Salvinus's followers. 'But I have my concerns now.'

'What concerns?' Salvinus demanded.

'They know the route we take. If we follow this trail into the trees, they may have a trap for us. Blocked the path with felled trees, for example. Keep us busy until night falls. Then fall on us in the dark. It could be a massacre.'

'You wait until now to express this concern?'

'It's now that your scouts have been taken out. You want to carry on blind?'

'What then? Make a camp here?' Salvinus and his men looked about them with unease. It wasn't a great location. 'Well?'

'I'm thinking,' Idris said irritably. He took a deep breath. 'Alright, I have a suggestion. We leave this path and go cross country.' He pointed approximately southeast, where the rugged terrain was covered with thick woodland. 'It'll be difficult going for a while, I won't lie. But it then breaks out into open land, all the way to Treglan. We'll have sight lines in every direction. They won't dare attack—we'll have superior numbers and cavalry.'

'Sounds good,' Salvinus said. 'I can't wait to leave this scabrous land behind.'

'Ha! You should see the mountains in the north. This is nothing.'

'No thanks. This is your shithole of a country, not mine. I have no interest in it, save that you bring it into a state of obedience. How long will this difficult going last?'

'An hour at the most.'

Salvinus puffed his cheeks out. 'That's long enough.'

Idris said nothing. Salvinus's lieutenants had uneasy looks, but not one had come up with an alternative plan.

'Alright,' said the mercenary leader.

IDRIS LED them through the trees, the land dipping to a hollow. Navigating past the branches of the first dozen trees was fine; the next dozen bearable; after that it was a chore that drew complaints from the riders in their party. It was underfoot that was the most problematic. The ground was uneven and often hidden with bracken and other vegetation. The horses disliked the confined space. Some riders had to fight them to keep them going. Idris's beast chewed on its bit. He gave it a gentle pat, doing his best to exude confidence.

'What kind of treacherous hole are you leading us into?' one rider complained.

'At least we're safe from the archers in here,' Idris said.

It was true. The Atrabians had enjoyed a free shot at their column for most of the day, but here the woodland was so dense that they were safely hidden. The comment seemed to stay further complaint, and they kept going.

'We'll need to walk the horses up this bit,' Idris warned.

He'd reached the end of the hollow and now looked on a steep bank that rose so high he couldn't see the top. Still crowded with trees and other vegetation, the ground was a mix of mud and rock and looked like it might easily give way underfoot.

'By Gerhold's hairy balls!' Salvinus cried when he saw what they faced. 'You didn't tell me we had a scarp to climb! We'll have broken necks and everything.'

'Just take it nice and slow,' Idris advised, dismounting. 'Once we reach the top, we're in open farmland. We'll have a clear route to Treglan.'

'Go on then, Atrabian. Show us how it's done.'

'Very well.' Idris held his mount's lead rope and set off. He didn't pull on it, and his gentle persuasions encouraged the beast to walk with him. Taking it one step at a time, he began to climb. His foot slipped once, but he quickly righted himself.

He stopped about a quarter of the way up. 'See, there's nothing to it,' he shouted, ensuring his voice carried. He turned around to look at the column of the army, the Luderian infantry marching towards their position. He heard booted feet shuffling on the top of the bank above him. They were descending the bank in his direction, moving with care, yet he could still tell there were scores of them.

Taking care to give nothing away, he manoeuvred himself so that he was positioned behind his horse. The last thing he wanted was a stray arrow striking him. He heard the creak of staves being pulled back. As soon as the first sound of a string being released came, he got to the ground.

The arrows cut through the air above Idris, slamming into the horses and riders gathered below. His horse bolted, charging down the slope into the riders. Those riders had nowhere to go. The sheer slope was ahead of them, and their infantry were behind. Horses panicked, some men forced from their mounts or choosing to dismount. A second hail of arrows struck them.

Some of Salvinus's mercenaries, those still in control of their horses, began moving to the flanks, perhaps seeking a way around the bank. But they soon stopped. Only now did they realise how much trouble they were in.

More archers moved in from the sides, flitting between the trees. The invaders were trapped. The order was given, and the archers released. Salvinus's mercenaries were overwhelmed as arrows hit riders and horses alike. Some warriors fell; others were luckier, saved by armour and shield. One of them, somehow staying mounted, charged at the new arrivals. He fell in a second volley.

There was no means of escape, except perhaps back the way they had come. Orders were shouted, but others didn't wait, pushing themselves through the mass of milling soldiers to get back to the path Idris had taken them off. He heard the archers above him on the bank moving and twisted to look. They came into view, dressed in light armour with small bladed weapons at their belts, relying on their bows to make an impact. They shot once more, and the panic amongst the enemy increased.

Amid the scrambling, Idris spotted Salvinus. He knew he should leave him or risk being struck by an arrow. But Salvinus was the kind of man who would escape while his men died around him. *I'm not having that,* Idris decided. He got to his feet, drew his sword, and went for his target.

He passed dead warriors; warriors clutching at wounds, shafts sticking out of their bodies, while their blood leaked onto the ground. But Idris only had eyes for Salvinus, boring into the back of the man's head as he tried to leave. Perhaps Salvinus felt the stare because he looked behind him. His eyes widened when he saw Idris.

'I thought you dead!' he shouted.

Idris couldn't help the sly smile coming to his face. He desperately wanted Salvinus to know that he'd played him. His enemy's face fixed into a cold mask and Idris saw the mercenary's knuckles tighten on the hilt of his blade. Only now did Salvinus realise what Idris had done. Perhaps he was so used to betraying others he hadn't conceived someone might do the same to him.

'There's no escaping,' Idris shouted over. 'Atrabians will be waiting for you back there,' he added, nodding in the direction the Luderians were retreating.

'Then I might as well gut you while I have the chance.'

Salvinus walked straight for him, giving Idris no time for second thoughts. The man oozed confidence, his sword gripped loosely now, wrist twirling. No doubt he believed he could take out Idris with ease. But Idris had spent almost two years fantasising about a moment like this. There was no way he was going to walk away from it.

Salvinus went on the offensive, his strokes hard but controlled, using his aggression to elicit a weakness in Idris's defences.

Their blades struck one another. Idris hadn't traded blows in nearly two years. The impact ran up his arms into his hands. Salvinus was a touch faster, and Idris was nervous of his blade. The steel gleamed in the fading light and the edge looked razor sharp; no doubt it was better quality than the one he held. But Idris knew his defensive moves, and he'd always been good with a sword—deceptively so, some said, given his gangly limbs.

At the end of his flurry of blows, Salvinus sidestepped and swung his blade at Idris's side. But Idris had a long reach, and he moved aside at the last moment. The tip of the blade caught him on the hip. His hauberk protected him there, and he doubted he'd be left with more than a bruise.

He was tempted to strike back—a wild swing that would catch Salvinus on the side of his head, or neck. But if he should miss, he would leave himself open and Salvinus would pounce. His father's last words to him rang out in his head once more. *Idris, Liesel. You must steel yourselves now. If you do, you will survive this and be stronger for it.* He would listen to his father—retain the iron control that had kept him alive.

In all the time that had passed since Liesel told him of Prince Gavan's death, he felt his father's presence now more than ever. Watching over this encounter. He wasn't desperate for revenge on the man who had killed him. That wasn't his father's way. He was looking out for Idris—reminding him of how he could win.

Salvinus and Idris clashed once more. This time Idris gave as good as he got, giving Salvinus something to think about. Nevertheless, when they tore apart, he'd come off worse. A slash to his thigh had gone through his armour and he could feel a wetness there, even if the battle fire that pulsed through his body masked the pain of it.

'You're better than I thought you'd be,' Salvinus conceded.

The mercenary was short of breath, and that gave Idris renewed belief. 'You too. I guess you were a formidable fighter. Before you got old.'

Salvinus didn't like that. He came for Idris, putting all his efforts into an attack. Idris backed away, feinted, moved to the side. His reach kept Salvinus from landing the strike he was so desperate for. The mercenary growled with a final effort, trying to get inside Idris's defences. Idris concentrated, unwilling to make a mistake, refusing to listen to his body that pleaded with him to stop.

Salvinus took a step back, his chest heaving. He allowed himself a grin and opened his mouth to speak.

Who knew what he intended to say? Because Idris wasn't about to let him rest. Now he attacked, forcing Salvinus to defend. He'd started the slower, but they were evenly matched now. It was a battle of wills. One of them would tire, slow down a little. Idris knew it wouldn't be him.

He gave his strikes more back-swing, hitting Salvinus harder than he had yet. It worked. A swing knocked Salvinus' arms away to one side. Still, Idris waited for the right moment. When Salvinus, desperate to recover, brought his arms back to centre, Idris struck them again to the other side. The momentum produced an even greater gap. Idris took one long-legged lunge and struck. His blade caught Salvinus on the side of his head and the hilt slammed into his chest.

Salvinus fell backwards onto the ground, unable to roll or catch himself. Idris's blade came down on his wrist. With a cry of pain, Salvinus lost his grip on his weapon. Idris stood over the mercenary, various locations available to strike a killing blow.

'Finish him, Idris,' came a voice.

In a rush, the rest of the world returned to Idris's perception. The Atrabian archers stood around in a rough semi-circle. They'd watched the fight, but not intervened. He wondered what they would have done if it had been Idris laid out on the ground.

Twenty yards away, Salvinus's army also looked on. Between the two groups, more bodies lay prone, stuck with arrows. In the trees to either side, Atrabians, armed with bows, waited for the order to draw and release again. Even so, the Luderians hadn't surrendered. Those closest to where he stood held up shields, as if that was going to stop the Atrabians should they fire once more.

Idris looked at the speaker and got a surprise. It was Ilar. Even broader than he'd been when Idris had left, he looked different in other ways, too. He held himself with a confidence that suggested he was a leader of these warriors.

'No, cousin,' Idris answered him. 'Not yet.'

He leant down and pulled Salvinus up by the collar until he was back on his feet. Ilar approached them, putting his own meaty hand on Salvinus's shoulder. The mercenary captain stared at the ground, defeated, tucking his injured arm under his armpit.

Idris looked across at the army that had come into his people's lands. He shouted, his voice so loud it surprised himself. 'If you haven't realised yet, you are surrounded. These woods are full of Atrabian archers in every direction. This invasion is over. But that doesn't mean anyone else has to die. The only one who has to die is him,' he said, putting the tip of his blade to Salvinus's chest. 'Lay your weapons down now and you have my word that there will be no further reprisals, and your injured countrymen will be treated.'

Idris wasn't surprised at the haste with which the Luderians threw their weapons down. This wasn't a war they cared about. Salvinus's mercenaries were more reluctant—more suspicious, perhaps, that they would be allowed to live. But without the Luderians, they were hopelessly outnumbered. They had no choice but to do the same.

. . .

IT TOOK a while to ensure the enemy were fully disarmed and to identify and treat the injured. But eventually, Idris climbed the bank out of the hollow and reached the higher ground. His legs shook with the effort. He had little energy left now that the battle fire had deserted his body. But there was still work to do.

A group of Atrabians accompanied him, including Ilar, who pushed Salvinus up the bank ahead of him. Salvinus had opened his mouth to speak once, and Ilar had punched him square in the face, probably breaking his nose. They heard nothing from him after that, save for a rattling sound as he breathed.

A few hundred unmounted Atrabian warriors met them on the edge of the treeline. His uncle, Emlyn, was there, a contented grin on his face at the sight of Idris and Salvinus. Next to him was his second son, Macsen, who also seemed to have grown substantially. He, too, looked pleased. As well they might, after such a victory. Idris looked around for other faces he knew.

'Your mother stayed in Treglan,' Emlyn informed him quietly. 'Your sister is still in Guivergne, as far as I know.'

Idris nodded. It was better like that. He needed to hold himself together, and he would have struggled at the sight of his mother.

Others came forward to congratulate him, but he held up an arm to stop them. 'Help me, please,' he said to Emlyn and Macsen, as he tugged on his hauberk. They helped him to pull the thing over his head. Then he beckoned Ilar to bring Salvinus with him. He nodded to the ground, and Ilar threw him down.

Idris stripped free of his gambeson so all could see the silver marks on his skin in the dwindling sunlight. He saw the looks of anger, sympathy, and horror on the faces of his countrymen. Nodding at them, he raised his arms. 'I am free,' he proclaimed, his voice sounding strange even to his ears, like the cry of an animal. 'Free from the murderers who took away your prince and killed him.' Reference to the crime brought bloodthirsty looks from the Atrabians to Salvinus.

Idris stared at the man for a moment, hesitating. He was slumped over, defeated looking. But that was a show. He deserved a slow, painful death. Idris wanted it to last; he wanted to look him in the eyes and be the one to give it to him. But that wasn't the way of his people. It wasn't what his father would have done. And there was another thought in the back of his mind. *Kill him while you have the chance.*

'Now we shall have our revenge!' he cried.

With his free hand, he pulled at Salvinus's hair; with his other, he slit his throat. He let the body slump to the ground. Then he hacked at the neck until the head came free. He held it high as gore spattered his chest.

The warriors around cried out their affirmations. Idris, feeling as much beast as man, welcomed their roars as the warriors raised their weapons, howling into the sky.

'Long live the prince!' one cried. Others joined in, getting to their knees. Emlyn didn't hesitate to do the same, and his sons followed his lead.

'This is just the beginning,' Idris told them, a euphoric smile splitting his face. 'I promise you. We shall have our revenge on the empire!'

PEYRE

ARBEOST, DUCHY OF MORBAINE, 677

P eyre rode out from Arbeost with Coleta. He had promised to
take her on a picnic before he left, and the weather was mild
enough for it to be pleasurable. Winter seemed to have lasted forever
and his childhood home felt rather dull compared to Valennes or the
Brasingian Empire. He was grateful Coleta had stayed with him. She'd
been interested in learning about Morbaine. It was nice to have a bed
companion, too.

'This is a good spot,' he said, pulling up. 'See.' He pointed down the
hill to the plain below that extended east and became the Midder
Steppe. 'We have quite a view.'

He dismounted and helped Coleta from her horse, then set up
their blankets.

'You came here often?' she asked, taking a seat.

'Umbert and I did, yes. In our last year or so, before our exile, we
were free to come and go as we pleased.'

'I bet you got up to all sorts. I saw the way that shepherdess we
passed looked at you.' Her brown eyes sparkled wickedly.

Peyre coughed and busied himself with laying out the food. Coleta
was very observant of such things, the kind of things he wouldn't
notice in a thousand years.

She nestled into him, and he wrapped a blanket round them both. 'I don't mind,' she whispered.

Peyre wasn't sure why she should mind, since it had happened long before they had met. Still, he liked her company. He liked her smell; liked to put his arm around someone. She helped take his mind off those things that tortured his mind when he was alone. How Liesel was still with Esterel. Esterel's treatment of him, especially taking away his beloved Barissian Guard. The blinding of Auberi, and how Leopold and Inge still held power in the empire. Ezenachi, still out there—plotting, no doubt. So many things he was powerless to do anything about, they put him in a vile mood if he let them.

'I appreciate the chance to be alone, away from Arbeost,' Coleta told him.

'Aye. We won't be here much longer, you know. I expect a summons from Esterel soon. We have unfinished business in the empire.'

'I don't wish to talk about war, Peyre.'

'Oh. What do you wish to talk about?'

'Us. Our future together.'

'What of it?' he asked. 'I am very fond of you.'

'Oh, gods,' she said, putting a hand to her forehead, then over her mouth. 'I knew it. Sacha warned me, but I never listen.'

'What? What did Sacha warn you of?'

'Esterel made me his harlot. Discarded me as soon as he was done with me. And, shameful slut that I am, I've let you do just the same. You'll get rid of me, too, and I'll be the laughing stock of the kingdom.'

'Come now, don't talk like that. You're not a slut, or a laughing stock. Don't say such things.'

She pulled away from him, looking him in the eye. 'Do you intend to marry me?'

Caught off guard, Peyre heard himself stammering. 'I—I don't think of such things.'

'Then I'm your slut. Let's talk with honesty. I deserve at least that from you, surely.'

Peyre felt a sense of shame, though he wasn't sure why. He'd never promised Coleta marriage, and she'd never talked of it until now. She'd never asked for anything, not really. But did he owe her something more? After all, their relationship had begun almost a year ago. Did that create certain expectations on her part, that he hadn't thought about? *It's quite possible*, he said to himself, *that I have been a little self-absorbed recently.*

'I admit,' he said, 'I haven't given these matters much thought. I've been content to live in the moment.'

Coleta nodded. 'I know. I'm angry with myself, really, not you. There is something wrong with me. No one's said as much to me, but I'm sure you all think it.'

Peyre frowned, taken aback by her words, oblivious of where it had all come from. He'd thought they were going to have a pleasant ride and a bite to eat. He wasn't ready for this. 'No one thinks that, Coleta. I certainly don't.'

She stood. 'Can you take me home?'

'But—'

'Please. Take me back, Peyre.'

* * *

UMBERT AND LORD Russell accompanied Peyre on his mission to the Midder Steppe. He'd originally planned to bring a score of warriors with him, but what was the point? He was entering Middian territory. They could kill him if they wished. It made no difference if he had two or twenty-two with him.

He couldn't help sharing his conversation with Coleta with the two men. It had taken over his thoughts, and he needed to push it away.

When he was done, Lord Russell and Umbert gave him the same, slightly blank, look. It was easy to tell they were father and son.

'In my day,' Russell said, 'one approached a girl's father and asked for her hand in marriage. I know things are very different in Valennes, and I hesitate to pass judgement. I suppose the question to ask yourself is whether Coleta is the woman you wish to spend the rest of your life with.'

Umbert gave Peyre a secret look. It was a look of sympathy, with no humour at his father's comment, and Peyre appreciated it. 'I suppose that's my problem, Lord Russell. I just don't know.'

'Well,' Russell said, with a bemused look, 'one thing I do know is that it is time for you to pick someone, settle down, and produce an heir. And I'm saying this to both of you,' he added, with a glare at Umbert. 'You are men, well past the age of casual dalliances.'

'Yes, father,' Umbert agreed.

Four Middian chieftains came to talk with Peyre. They met where the lands conquered by his father bordered Middian territory. Three of the chieftains he remembered from the last meeting, when he had been only a few misplaced words away from a battle he had feared he would lose.

Cuenin, on whose lands he had built a fortress, was noticeably calmer this time around. It was Jorath who was the more anxious since they would now negotiate on the fate of the disputed lands in the north. Frayne, the chieftain of the far south east, was the man whom Peyre had done business with. The fourth was named Brock. He seemed close to Frayne and was of a similar age—older and hopefully wiser. His tribe's lands lay in the south-west corner of the Steppe, and he was forthcoming with news from that part of the world.

'Ezenachi has control of the Wilderness,' he announced.

'Control?' Peyre asked.

'Meaning, he's turned everyone there. Not just humans. The vossi serve him now. I tell you, the vossi were bad enough to start with. Belligerent little sons of bitches. Turned vossi are going to be a whole new level of nasty.'

The vossi were little more than a name to Peyre. Denizens of the Wilderness, said to be human like but smaller and more primitive.

'So the question,' Lord Russell said, 'is who is next?'

'Well, it's either return to Magnia or come for us,' Brock said. 'And since he came to his little deal with the Magnians, I expect it'll be us. Could be any day now. So I hope this meeting gets us to a place where we start worrying about the real danger.'

'As do I,' said Peyre.

Esterel had written to him over winter, giving him full authority to deal with the Middian question. Esterel's interest was in Brasingia, not the Steppe. His only concern was preventing war. He even hoped to avoid the need to waste troops garrisoning the forts that had been built to hold the conquered lands. All of which was music to Peyre's ears. It gave him the freedom to sort the mess once and for all.

'My proposal is simple,' he said. 'A full withdrawal from the Steppe, by all Guivergnais forces. All lands returned to the Middians. I can't do this overnight. People have made homes here and will need to be found alternatives elsewhere.'

Jorath looked at him nonplussed, as if suspecting it was a jest. 'This is real? You speak for the king?'

'I do.' It had been Peyre's uncle, Nicolas, who had decided to annex the lands in question. Even at the time, no one seemed to know why.

'The price you ask?' Frayne said, looking for the hidden cost.

Peyre smiled at him. 'The right to march our forces through steppe lands. And a formal alliance between Guivergne and all the Middian tribes.'

'We're not fighting your war in Brasingia for you,' Cuenin warned.

'Not against the empire. We can win that war ourselves. Against Ezenachi. And I don't just mean fighting the same enemy. Sharing intelligence and plans.'

'Well, this is exactly what we need!' Brock said. It was said as if the man he'd been told was a devil actually spoke common sense.

Peyre nodded his head in acknowledgement. 'I've said before that Ezenachi is the real enemy. The king understands that.' Whether or not Esterel did, Peyre wasn't so sure. His brother had proven to be ambitious and ruthless. He wasn't sure how those traits would translate into action against Ezenachi.

'We're not becoming your vassals, to order about as your king wishes,' Frayne warned him.

'Of course. I am proposing an alliance of equals.'

The four chieftains looked at one another.

'I'll be honest,' Frayne said. 'I don't think we even need to go away and talk about it. You have given us exactly what we want.' He eyed Peyre. 'I told you I thought you were a man worth trusting. Seems I was right. I usually am.' He squinted, as if studying Peyre's features. 'Are you sure there is no Middian blood in those veins?'

* * *

PEYRE LEFT Lord Russell with the unenviable task of implementing his agreement with the Middians. It would not be easy to undo years of settlement in the steppe lands. But the concessions were worth the difficulties involved. There would be no repeat of last year's Middian attack. The army of Morbaine was free to join with the rest of the Guivergnais army.

He marched his army north, earlier than he'd expected, since the negotiations with the Middians had gone so quickly. He had Umbert lead their vanguard through the steppe. The right to access to these lands had been an important demand of his, one the Middians had been quick to accede to.

He brought Coleta with him, having decided that Valennes would be the safest place for her. Her questions about their relationship remained unanswered. Peyre had no answers for her. His mind was on Brasingia. They would be at war soon, and who knew what might happen? He thought of Farred; of his father. There was a good chance he'd not survive it, then any promises he made would have been worthless. Maybe, when the war was done and the kingdom at peace, he could think clearly about his future.

The temperature dropped during the nights, making the journey a hardship for Coleta and any others not used to such conditions. But Peyre could read the signs of Spring in the grasslands they passed through. As soon as Esterel had his logistics in place, they would set off. They'd have months in Brasingia. Anticipation built in him as he thought of it. Could they really conquer Brasingia and make his brother an emperor?

They crossed into Guivergne and took the roads that led to the capital. Sacha met them on the last day. Coleta gave a little cry of joy upon seeing her brother. As they embraced, Peyre and Sacha's eyes met. Their relationship had become too complex for Peyre to identify any single emotion in that look.

But whatever else he thought of Sacha, he couldn't deny the man made a good steward to the king. He had organised a camp outside the city for Peyre's soldiers, making it easy for Peyre to leave his army to it while their small group rode the last mile to the city. When they reached the Bastion, Peyre's old rooms were waiting for him. The servants had even got a fire going for his arrival. Peyre and Umbert settled in as if they had never been away. Coleta was roomed with her friend in a different part of the fortress. Peyre felt little else than a sense of relief at the separation.

Sacha confirmed Peyre was the last of the king's magnates to arrive in Valennes, and so that evening there was a grand feast to welcome the commanders of the Guivergnais army to the capital. Arriving in the Great Hall, Peyre made his way to the top table. He nearly stopped mid-stride, startled at who he saw.

Resting a hand on Loysse's arm, Duke Auberi stood talking with Liesel. Peyre felt a sense of relief, that immediately dissolved into shame, that the duke had a green cloth tied around his eyes. Despite Sacha's words, Peyre had assumed Auberi would have remained in Famiens. With little other option, Peyre moved over to the group.

Loysse and Liesel turned to him.

'Auberi,' Loysse said. 'Duke Peyre is here.'

'Hello, Your Grace,' Peyre said.

Auberi turned his head in Peyre's direction. 'Ah. Morbaine. I heard you had arrived. We are one step closer to the invasion.'

'I am sorry for what they did,' Peyre said simply, not knowing what else to say.

'Thank you, Peyre. My heart aches for the men who followed me into the empire, not for myself. The gods have still blessed me with a loving wife and, we hope, a child.'

Peyre turned in surprise to Loysse, only now noticing her bump. 'Congratulations to you both.'

'Thank you, brother,' Loysse said. She smiled at him, but it was tempered—of course it was—with sadness. Peyre glanced at Liesel, who gave him a little smile of her own. No one seemed to know what to say.

'I cannot take vengeance for what Leopold did that day,' Auberi spoke into the silence. 'But vengeance is what my people demand. I will have to rely on you and your brother to deliver it.'

'Of course,' Peyre said firmly. 'I will do whatever I can.'

Peyre's words did little to lift the mood. Loysse didn't look pleased, and it was only when he looked at Liesel a second time and took in her expression that he remembered they were talking about her brother.

* * *

NEXT DAY, Esterel held court in the hall with his magnates as they put together the kingdom's final preparations. As well as immediate family, the other great lords of Guivergne were in attendance: Sacha of Courion; Lord Chancellor Caisin; Arnoul of Saliers; Florent of Auriac; and Domard, Duke of Martras. The presence of Auberi and Loysse became clear: they were to rule in the king's absence. All others would accompany him to Brasingia.

Martras, who had stayed behind in Guivergne last year, seemed keen to make up for missing out. He had something to say about every point of discussion. Currently, it was about Liesel's crossbow units. It seemed she had been exceptionally busy: recruiting, training, and arming hundreds of arbalests. Peyre was nothing but impressed, but Martras had a different view.

'It seems to fall on me to say it,' Martras said, 'but I am one of a number who have severe reservations over these units. This is in no way meant to denigrate your work, Your Majesty,' he said, with a nod to Liesel. She returned a frosty look, but it did nothing to put the man off. 'I understand the thinking behind it. But there are dangerous consequences. It is the special responsibility of our estate to defend the realm. Now, imagine the minds of the lowest in our society, who find they have in their power, with these weapons, the means to kill with ease. Yes, we are sending them against the Brasingians today. But these men will—and women, I should add—they will return home. And the thought that they could continue to use them will, inevitably, come to some of their minds. And who might they decide to use them against, you understand?'

He looked around the room for support. But whatever the personal views of these men, they were all loyal to the king. And it wasn't just that. The miseries and realities of war were fresh in Peyre's mind and no doubt in everyone else's. Especially since Auberi was with them, a testament to the enemy's brutality.

He remembered all too well that sinking feeling in his stomach when the Middians had arrived against his army, and how he wished he had the archers to hold them off. No warrior here was about to refuse the aid of these crossbowmen, who might well tip the outcome of the invasion in their favour. Martras, meanwhile, talked as if they were heading to one of his jousting contests.

'I have heard this argument before,' Esterel admitted. 'And while I understand it, my immediate concern is not the stability of this realm. My concern is winning victory against an enemy that, yes, is divided and weakened right now. But is still larger than us, in terms of resources, manpower, and virtually any other measure worth mentioning. So, no, Your Grace. With all due respect. I shan't be leaving the arbalests behind.'

They would never know if Martras planned to dispute the issue further. Because at that point, the doors of the hall opened and two men staggered in. Peyre knew both and all his attention was suddenly fixed on them. One, Jehan, a guardsman of the Bastion, supported the other. It was Inhan, a young man of Peyre's Barissian Guard. Or, at least, what had been his until last year. Esterel had given his Guard to Corbenay, who had wintered in Coldeberg.

Inhan's face was deathly pale and Peyre's eyes were drawn to a makeshift cloth bandage wrapped about his lower arm and hand. It was sodden with blood. The fact that the injury had not been properly treated said everything about the urgency of his mission.

Jehan helped him down to a kneeling position before the king. There was a silent expectancy, save for Loysse whispering in her husband's ear, informing him what transpired.

'Please, speak,' Esterel said to Inhan.

Peyre braced himself for the news that would come.

'They got into Coldeberg, Your Majesty,' Inhan informed him. 'The city is fallen. We didn't know how, but the witch was with them.'

'Then that was how,' Esterel said. 'With magic. What of Miles? Of Corbenay,' he corrected himself, clearly desperate to hear about his friend.

Inhan bowed his head in grief. 'Dead, Your Majesty, like many others. I'm sorry. They—' he swallowed, then looked up again. 'They have put his head on the walls of the city as a warning. Leopold wanted me to tell you that.'

'Leopold was there?' Esterel asked.

'Aye. He supervised the killings.'

'Elger?' Peyre asked, unable to wait any longer to hear the fate of the leader of his Guard.

'Elger is dead, too, Your Grace. They spared me so I would take you this news and tell you to desist from returning to the empire. But —' he choked, and tears streamed down his face. 'But they took my sword hand,' he said at last, holding up what Peyre now realised was a bloody stump. 'So that I could not raise a blade against the empire again.'

Peyre could feel a terrible anger rise in him. He looked around the room and saw many faces as wrathful as his own. Miles was a close friend of Esterel, Sacha, and Florent. They had always seemed inseparable. Each now seemed to have the same look. A hunger for vengeance that needed to be sated.

'Then Leopold has sealed his fate,' Esterel said.

SANC

KINGDOM OF THE TELDS, 677

S tress and strain had become so much a part of Sanc's life that he only noticed it when it stopped. Winter had come to the lands of the Telds—a high, mountainous kingdom. When the snows fell here, they fell thick, and there was nothing to do but sit it out. Long nights and short days spent by the fire were what Sanc needed. There had been some attempt by the Rasidi to track their escape from Aguilas, despite the imposing territory the Telds controlled. It had been the weather that had forced Ordono's forces to withdraw. A welcome relief, but a warning that they might return.

Sanc talked with Herin. He told him everything that had happened since his arrival in Silb. It felt good to share his story with someone else who understood what he was going through.

Herin, meanwhile, had been teleported to the land of the Telds. With no magic, and no ability to understand the language, he had faced hardship of a different sort to Sanc. 'It wasn't until I was taken to see Kepa that things started moving. Until then, most people assumed I was a madman. She realised there was something else going on. She took the trouble to teach me the Teld language. Gods, it was frustrating. But that moment when I could tell her who I was and where I was from.' He sighed, relieving the relief. 'It was like when you freed me from Ezenachi's control all over again. After that, she agreed the Telds would look out for any signs of a sorcerous outlander. It was when we heard news of the fighting between the Nerisians and Kassites that you were described. Of course, I knew it was you immediately. The Telds sent spies out to locate you. It was Domeka who found you.'

'She is a spy?'

'It's easy enough to infiltrate Ordono's palaces, apparently. He uses Teld slaves as his servants, almost exclusively. Once Domeka was in, she could report back to us here. Now they'll have to find someone else to replace her.' He looked at Sanc. 'It's something I'd like to help put right if I get the chance. That Telds live as slaves sticks in my craw.'

'You like these people?' Sanc asked him. Herin had never given the impression of liking much at all before.

'I do. They cared for me, even when they thought I was mad. Especially then, in fact. I feel more at peace here than I ever have. My mistakes hung around my neck in Dalriya. Here, those seem like distant memories. Almost as if they happened to someone else.' He grimaced. 'You're too young to understand.'

'I do understand. I, too, feel different here. In Dalriya, everyone else had decided what I was. There is more freedom here, even if we have only come here for a very specific reason.'

Herin grunted. 'And how close are we to achieving that goal? Rimmon wanted us to bring someone back to defeat Ezenachi. I suppose these champions are the key to it. But we only have two on our side and three against us.'

That was the crux of the matter, and Sanc had no answer to it.

SANC HAD the time to practise his magic with Mildrith and Kepa. It was the first time since his lessons with Rimmon that he felt like he had a mentor to guide him. If not necessarily more powerful than

Sanc or Mildrith, Kepa had wisdom to impart. She would lead them up into the mountains, where they could be alone. She leaned heavily on her walking stick, and it took Sanc a while to realise that her left leg was badly damaged, unable to bend at the knee. When Mildrith asked her, Kepa spoke of having to defend against other champions. With Temyl and Guntram on one side and Mergildo on the other, Sanc respected her ability to hold her own for so long.

She tested their magic and encouraged them to learn from each other. 'Your strength is in mind control,' she informed Sanc. 'You can shape what others see and what they do not. Part of your task is to learn to maximise this power and be open to all the possibilities it provides. But you also need to be open to other kinds of magic, Sanc. Learn to use the world around you. It is easier than drawing all your magic from within.'

'Sanc's is a power from *his* world, do you think, Kepa?' Mildrith asked. 'The champions of Silb all wield magic that controls an aspect of the natural world, do we not? In my case, flora. In yours, the air. Temyl seems able to control the earth—and the metals and rocks that lie under the soil.'

'That is hard to say,' Kepa answered. 'It seems to me that it is similar to the powers wielded by Ezenachi. Herin has told me how his own mind was imprisoned for years, while Ezenachi forced him to do his bidding instead. If what you two discovered on Ram is true—that Ezenachi was a god here in Silb, before he reached Dalriya—then you could easily say Sanc's is a power of *this* world. For the seven peoples arrived in Silb from elsewhere, after all.'

Mildrith nodded, and a thoughtful expression came to her face. She seemed to consider Kepa's point of view carefully, as if it contradicted her previous understanding of the world. As he observed this, Sanc had a renewed appreciation for Mildrith's abilities. She had never, until now, had a teacher of any kind. How she had developed such strength by herself was incredible.

'What do you know of the history of the seven peoples?' Sanc asked Kepa.

'All I really know are the legends of my people. All seven peoples crossed to Silb by sea.'

'The Scorgians took them all by boat, so their legends say. They consider themselves to be the leaders of the seven peoples, for this reason.'

'That is not how the Telds see it. In our stories, all seven peoples were equal. Upon landing in Silb, they divided up the continent fairly, according to the resources available and to how each part of the continent suited their skills. The Telds had come from a land of mountains and valleys, and so claimed a similar realm to the one they had left.

'But the other peoples became corrupted by greed and ambition. They stole what was not theirs and lay claim to even more. They forgot the unity that had allowed the seven peoples to conquer Silb. Instead of harmony, they brought war. The Telds were forced to defend their realm from their neighbours. But they had so many: Egers, Gaden-zians, Nerisians, and Rasidi. When one war ended, another began. And so, our lands were taken from us, one piece at a time. Even our children were taken, to be treated like slaves by the Rasidi; or turned into Egers. The champions of the Telds have always had to defend their homeland from aggressors. But I, like all my people, still believe that one day we will regain everything we have lost.'

* * *

KING HARITZ of the Telds was a bag of skin and bones, always wrapped in furs. His home was a wooden hall, situated on the short Teld coast. It was one of the few areas in his realm that sat at sea level. His hall was not unlike those owned by the Kassite chieftains—far from the magnificence and luxury of Ordono of the Rasidi. His authority over his people was more limited than other kings of Silb. Kepa explained each tribe had its own chief. These men owed loyalty to Haritz but had to be convinced, individually, to lend their support to war or other endeavours.

Still, when they met with Haritz, Sanc soon learned this was a man with a grasp on the politics of Silb. 'Prince Lenzo misjudged Ordono and the Rasidi,' he commented, when Sanc and Mildrith had shared their experience in the city of Aguilas. 'He is more scared of a direct confrontation with Lothar. Scared of losing everything. Even though an alliance makes him a junior partner, he'll believe that is a situation that can change.'

'He risks losing his throne without a fight,' Mildrith said, her anger at the Rasidi unabated. 'It's the action of a coward.'

'True enough. But conquering the lands of the Rasidi would be no easy task, even for the army Lothar has. So long as the Rasidi stay in line, I can't see Lothar trying it.'

'All of which is a problem for us,' Sanc said. He could feel the urgency of his situation pressing down on him like a great weight. His reunion with Herin only put his responsibility for Dalriya in sharper focus. It was well over a year since he had arrived in Silb. Who knew what gains Ezenachi had made since he had left? And the situation in Silb was getting worse, not better; the chances of returning home with aid as far off as ever.

'These are dark days,' Haritz agreed. 'The Scorgians and Kassites subdued; the Rasidi willing to do Lothar's bidding. We are now the only ones standing against him and that will bring his retribution onto us.' The man's hair had long ago turned white, but he had the violet eyes of the rest of his people. They still sparkled with vigour. 'But sometimes, when you are at your lowest, your choices become that much clearer. Or, as Telds say, "in the darkness, it is easier to see the light".'

Mildrith harrumphed. 'What can you see, Your Majesty? I see no way out.'

'I can see the only option left. The Egers.'

'Those barbarians? Murderers and despoilers? Even the Kassites have heard of their crimes.'

'The crimes of the Egers are numerous,' Haritz agreed. 'We Telds have been the victims many times, so believe me, I know about the Egers. But they are the last opponent of Lothar. The last of the seven peoples to be brought into this war. It is, perhaps, time to unleash them. See what comes of it.'

'And what if we unleash hell?'

'The alternative is submission and slavery. A slow fading away of who we are. The loss of identity. The loss of self.' The king studied Mildrith. 'The time has come for us to decide, which would we prefer?'

* * *

A FEW DAYS after their conversation with King Haritz, a lone vessel sailed into the royal port. It was a small craft with a small crew of Scorgians, who Haritz hosted as honoured guests. The captain, Dag, had been sent by Prince Lenzo.

'Not an easy voyage,' he declared to those assembled. The Teld champion, Kepa, was with the king, as Dag patted Rab and rubbed his hands by the fire. Sanc, Mildrith, and Herin were also in attendance. 'Set out west from Ram, staying well clear of the Rasidi coast. Severe storms coming around the western point of their kingdom.'

'I can imagine,' Harith said. 'We get few visitors by sea. I presume your prince wants to share information, if not strategy?'

'Indeed. Wanted to check you lot are alive, first of all.'

'Did you rescue the fleet from Aguilas?' Sanc asked him. The last he had seen of Lenzo and Dag, they were heading for the docks, where the Rasidi army was said to have a presence.

'Aye. Most of it. Gaida was ready to go, having caught which way the wind was blowing. He was just waiting for his prince, didn't want to pull anchor and leave him stranded. Lenzo gave him a right rollicking, telling him he should have left at first sign of trouble. But his heart wasn't in it. Gaida's as staunch as they come. Anyway, we set sail, all but a few ships making it back to Ram. We wintered there. You can imagine what the prince thought of that. A near empty island is not his idea of a good time. He did manage to—'

'What news from the Kassites?' Mildrith interrupted, clearly not interested in what Lenzo's idea of a good time was.

'Holt holds out in the forested parts. We are supplying him with food and resources. Everywhere else in your lands is held down by the Nerisians, in new forts. Lenzo and the bulk of the fleet returned to Arvena a couple weeks ago. But he sent me to warn you.'

'Warn us?' Kepa asked.

'Lothar's plans for this season look set. His forces will attack Teld lands from the east, while Ordono and the Rasidi strike from the west. Seems they intend a full conquest. They're preparing for a lengthy campaign.'

Haritz nodded. 'Such news is no surprise. But I thank you for risking such a voyage to tell us.'

'The prince wishes he could do more to help. He said to tell you he can send the fleet here and attempt a rescue. If you agree with me the place, I can return with enough deck space to rescue a few thousand.' Dag eyed Sanc and Mildrith. 'I can take some away now if need be.'

So Lenzo wanted Sanc and Mildrith out of Teld lands. But where should they go? Sit in Arvena? Leave the continent to Lothar? If that was all that was left to do, he and Herin might as well leave Silb and return to Dalriya.

Haritz was eyeing him. Sanc had a decision to make.

'We have a plan, of sorts,' he said. 'Travelling from here to the land of the Egers with the goal of recruiting them to our side.'

'The Egers?' Dag said warily. 'Has it come to that? Then I shall tell my prince of your quest and we shall wait to hear from you. Perhaps we can work with the Egers, somehow,' he added, though he sounded less than convinced. 'Who is accompanying you, Lord Sanc?'

'I am going with him,' Mildrith said.

'And me, I suppose,' said Herin.

Sanc looked at Kepa.

'The three of you,' she agreed.

Ah. Sanc had thought the Teld champion might accompany them.

She gave him a smile. 'I will be of little use. The Egers kill Telds on sight. Besides, with the armies of three of the seven peoples descending on my homeland, I am needed here.'

'Hmm,' Dag said. 'I was under the impression the Egers kill *everyone* on sight.'

Sanc exchanged glances with Mildrith and Herin. He had no idea what they were letting themselves in for, but it didn't sound good.

'We cannot say that for sure,' King Haritz replied to Dag with the thinnest of smiles. 'The Egers have yet to meet outlanders.'

BELWYNN

MASADA, KINGDOM OF KALINTH, 677

Belwynn's companions studied her with unease. She had the Jalakh Bow, and in her opinion, that was what mattered. Instead, they focused on her new body. The Jalakh woman had been strong and healthy. Belwynn's new vessel would get her to her destination—the lands of the Lippers, where they would find Ezenachi.

'What happened to Elana?' Lorant asked. The Caladri's head twitched to one side.

'Elana died twenty years ago,' Belwynn said.

'Alright,' he said, persisting. 'What happened to her body?'

'It was mutilated, bones shattered, and thrown in a bog.'

They all looked at her, appalled.

'What did you think?' she demanded, anger seeping into her voice. 'That I just fancied a new look?'

'I'm sorry,' Oisin rumbled, a mournful look on his face.

'It's alright. Here,' Belwynn said, offering the bow to Jesper.

The Halvian took the weapon, examining it reverentially. 'Me?' he asked, sounding almost incredulous.

'Who else was going to have the bow? Lorant has the staff already.'

'Seven weapons and seven champions,' Oisin intoned in agreement.

'Let's get going, then,' Belwynn said. 'We need two more champions to complete our group.'

THEY SET off south from Masada, travelling along the border between Kalinth and Persala. Belwynn had found herself in strange company before and it was easy to forget it until they passed wide-eyed farming folk on their route. The mothers made warding signs with their hands, while their children gaped open-mouthed, on the edge of wonder and terror.

Leading their small party was Jesper. He took on the role of ranger naturally, reminding Belwynn of Gyrmund. There was nothing unusual about his appearance, except for the recurve bow stowed in an open quiver. People knew it to be a weapon of the Jalakhs, a people who were feared in these parts.

King Lorant of the Blood Caladri rode his horse well and often ranged ahead like Jesper. His people rarely left their homeland, and he drew quite a few stares, Madria's Staff hung on one side of his mount.

Maragin, chieftain of the Grendal clan and unofficial leader of the Krykkers, rode her horse badly. Krykkers were not quite such a rare sight in these parts, but one on horseback certainly was. She rode next to Belwynn, a look of discomfort etched on her face. Belwynn wondered if it was outright pain, but knew the Krykker would never admit if it was. She carried Bolivar's Sword in her scabbard, the greatest treasure of her people. On her back, she carried the shield of Persala. They would need to find a suitable champion for that weapon.

Belwynn now looked like a Jalakh, which made her far more conspicuous than she used to be. But better that than the maimed body she had left behind. She needed no possessions, save for the dagger at her belt, and she could ride all day without the need to stop.

Finally, there was Oisin, King of the Orias, and the truth was he made the rest of them look perfectly normal. His green skin was marked with blue tattoos. Over twelve feet tall, there was no horse that could carry him, but he could keep pace with them, running with

435

a loping stride that he could maintain for hours at a time. He held the Giants' Spear as he ran. It was a fearsome weapon and, if there had been any doubt about who he was to passersby, his spear removed it.

Some cheered and called his name. For with that spear, Oisin had killed the Isharite dragon that had terrorised half of Dalriya. To most of the common folk, that was the moment that had saved them and won the Isharite wars. Of course, there were stories of Belwynn and the killing of Diis, as well. But no one had witnessed that, and it wasn't so spectacular as a giant fighting a dragon.

* * *

Maragin and Lorant had both made representations to the Grand Caladri to allow them passage through their lands. That once great power, with so many wizards, had been conquered by the Isharites. Belwynn had been there when Edeleny fell; had escaped with Madria's staff just in time. Over half of the population had died in those years, including most of its magic users. Under the protection of the Krykkers, the Grand Caladri had regained their independence. But their days of glory, it seemed, were over.

There were enough Caladri wizards left to help them cross the Caladri lands from north to south. Wooden poles acted as way-markers—with enough magic, they could move from any one pole to another. With Lorant contributing his own magic, enhanced by Madria's staff, they were teleported to the border with Guivergne. Belwynn remembered the feeling of nausea such magic had caused in the past. But while Jesper and Maragin looked pale and sick after the journey, she was unaffected this time.

Belwynn had only ever travelled through Guivergne to get some-where else. But this was territory Jesper was especially familiar with. He led them south through a duchy named Famiens. Its duke, they were told, was in Valennes, and the group agreed to head for the capi-tal. The rulers of Guivergne had shown support for their task, and Jesper had personal reasons for going.

Once they reached the city, their party was offered proper

bedrooms and an invitation to eat at the top table in the great hall of the city's fortress, named the Bastion.

Their hosts were the duke and duchess of Famiens, named Auberi and Loysse. The duke wore a green band of cloth around his eyes and, once the conversation began, they learned he had been blinded as a punishment in the fighting last year. The more Belwynn heard, the more it sounded like a madness had descended upon this part of Dalriya. Guivergne and Brasingia were locked in a bitter struggle—the king, Esterel, had recently taken all his great nobles and a great army into the empire to wreak his revenge on his enemies. With Ezenachi at their border, threatening to overwhelm this whole region, Belwynn couldn't understand why the resources of the two greatest realms were being wasted on such a pointless conflict.

'Any news of Sanc?' Jesper asked Loysse.

Belwynn recalled Jesper telling her about this young man. A red-eyed sorcerer, like Pentas, he was the duchess's youngest brother. He and Herin had left on a mission to distant lands.

'Nothing,' Loysse said. She looked emotional, as well she might, Belwynn supposed. The woman was pregnant, on top of everything else that was going on. 'No one even talks of him any longer,' the duchess admitted.

Eyes turned to Belwynn, as if she could offer some comfort. 'Perhaps,' she said, feeling obliged to say something, 'once we kill Ezenachi, Sanc and Herin will be able to return.'

This brought a few nods, as if anyone knew where the pair were, or how they might return to Dalriya.

THE ROAD SOUTH from Valennes was well kept, and they made good progress to the Midder Steppe. According to Loysse, relations between the Guivergnais and the Middians had been complicated in recent years. But Belwynn had never heard of the Middians interfering with foreigners crossing the Steppe, and they were not challenged. They passed one burned out and abandoned Guivergnais settlement, evidence of the conflict the duchess had alluded to. But the others they passed through on their journey did not seem nervous and held only tiny garrisons. Most warriors, it seemed, were in the empire.

They continued south along the border between the Steppe and the duchy of Morbaine. There were no forts or defences of any kind here, just a flat terrain with few permanent settlements.

Belwynn's thoughts turned to Magnia. In her homeland lived the two girls she had raised as her daughters, now with families of their own. Her cousin, Edgar, had been killed by Ezenachi, leaving his wife and son to rule a severed kingdom. Cut in half by the god's peace offer, it was a country that now teetered on the brink of destruction. Their quest to kill Ezenachi would save Magnia, and that was what had persuaded her to act in the end. The rest of Dalriya seemed determined to destroy itself. Maybe, in Magnia, there would still be a land of reason and hope.

They had to travel west to get to the royal court, to the estate of Wincandon. Their presence excited the Magnians, no doubt hoping for saviours to arrive. The king's hall was packed with people getting a look at the visitors, as they presented themselves to King Ida. All five of them knelt, even though Lorant and Oisin were kings themselves, and Maragin was more or less the equivalent. Oisin took it upon himself to make the introductions. When he introduced Belwynn Godslayer, there were gasps and frowns aplenty.

It was the first time she had lain eyes on Ida. He looked a lot like his father, with some of the colouring from his mother's Middian heritage. He seemed so young—too young for the burdens thrust on him. At mention of her name, a look of shock and fear passed over his face. She wore a different skin than the one he had expected. For a moment, the idea of trying to explain herself came into her head, but she rejected it. She was a monster. Attempting to justify herself had no purpose.

'It is an honour to finally meet my kin,' he said. His voice was rich and commanding. There was something else there, too. A note of hostility. 'And I am grateful for the arrival of such great champions in

Magnia. We hope you are here to help us against the foe who killed my father and laid Magnia low.'

'The honour is mine, Your Majesty. And yes, that's the idea.' Belwynn looked about. 'Is your mother not here?' It was Elfled, after all, who had put her up to all this. For her not to be here to meet them was strange.

'She is missing,' Ida said, that strained note in his voice there again.

'Missing?'

'Perhaps you recall the last conversation you had with her?'

Belwynn racked her brain. 'I—'

'You gave her the burden of finding the cloak of the Asrai. Since that day, we lost our mother. She became obsessed with finding a way to reach the island of the Asrai. She charted boats that sailed westward, but nothing worked. She would stand for hours, staring out to sea. Then, one day, she walked into the waves. She never came back.'

A hush descended in the hall. All eyes were on Belwynn. She thought, perhaps, some emotion was expected of her. Sorrow, maybe. Guilt, almost certainly. But it had been twenty years since she had been human and such feelings were distant, tenuous things. Recently, she had become especially detached from the passions that had once governed her. To pretend in front of these people would be more of an insult than saying nothing.

'Where did she enter the sea?'

She saw a muscle in Ida's jaw move as he ground his teeth together. 'I can have someone take you there.'

BRICTWIN, Ida's bodyguard, led them to the stretch of stony beach where Elfled had last been seen. There they could see a solitary figure and his horse, waiting a lonely vigil.

'It is Morlin, Elfled's bodyguard,' the Magnian said sombrely. 'He waits for her.' With that, he left them to it, keen to return to his own master.

Belwynn and her companions dismounted, leading their horses to the position where Morlin waited. He looked tired, his face weather beaten and streaked with lines. His eyes met Belwynn's and there was the barest nod of acknowledgement. He returned them to the grey sea and Belwynn followed his gaze. There was nothing out there.

'How long ago did she enter?' Belwynn asked.

'Many days. I should have restrained her. But she ordered me not to.'

'Is someone checking up and down the coastline?' Jesper asked. 'A body is unlikely to wash up in the same spot.'

'People have been checking all along the coast,' Morlin confirmed. 'But I am not waiting for a body.'

'What are you waiting for?' Belwynn asked him.

'I am waiting for Queen Elfled to return.'

They all looked out to sea. Belwynn cast her mind back to Tana, Queen of the Asrai. She had worn the cloak of the Asrai and joined Belwynn's group as one of Madria's champions. She had lost her life in the final battle and Belwynn had never had the time to get to know her. It had been Soren who found the isles where the Asrai lived. He had used magic to get there. Maybe Lorant could do the same?

Just as she thought of him, the Caladri spoke up. He pointed at the waves. 'There.'

Belwynn looked, but saw nothing. Neither did the others, even though Morlin stared with intensity. The Jalakh woman must have had good eyes, because Belwynn was the second to see something. Shapes on the water. They disappeared and returned, as if coming up for breath and returning to the sea. As if swimming.

'They come,' she said, and walked closer to where the waves lapped in and out. Everyone came with her, and now Jesper confirmed her sighting. There were four of them, human-like figures, heading in their direction. When they got close to shore, they stood. They were as Belwynn remembered: naked, with pale skin, dark eyes, and green hair that trailed down across their bodies. Three stood still while the fourth approached them.

She had two features about her that were different. First, from her shoulders, down to her thighs, something shimmered. Belwynn recognised the Cloak of the Asrai. Second, her skin was not pale like the other Asrai. It was a warm brown colour, like the skin of the Middians.

Belwynn was not the only one who started at what she was seeing. *Who* she was seeing. Her mind struggled to comprehend it. Her eyes looked from the webbed fingers and toes to the delicate facial features.

Elfled had returned. But she was an Asrai.

'Welcome back, Elfled,' Oisin rumbled. The Giant was the only one who seemed able to process what they were seeing.

She stopped before them, the sea only up to her ankles now. Her gaze was direct; provocative, even, as if she knew the cloak did little to hide her body. Her lips parted, and she gave them a sharp-toothed smile.

'Your Majesty,' Morlin got out, his voice confused. 'What happened?'

'At last, I discovered the secrets of the Asrai.'

'The secrets?' Belwynn repeated. 'What are they?'

'They are secrets, Belwynn Godslayer.'

'I am sorry,' Belwynn said to her. 'When I asked you to get the Cloak, I didn't envisage what sacrifices you would have to make. That you would have to abandon your children.'

'You were right,' Elfled replied. 'I was the one who had to do it. I came to understand that. And, of course, I did this *for* my children. But I know Ida will make a great king. I was promised that a long time ago.'

'But,' Jesper said, 'your children. When they see you... they will not understand.'

'Perhaps the youngest shouldn't see me then. That is up to others to decide now. That Elfled—the queen, wife, and mother—that Elfled died. She drowned in the Lantinen. I am someone else now.'

'Then we two are alike,' Belwynn muttered, to which Elfled nodded in agreement.

'But, Your Majesty, you still live,' Morlin protested. 'I am still honour bound to protect you.'

'Very well, Morlin. You waited for me. Our bond remains.'

Maragin grunted as she shifted the Shield of Persala from off her back. 'Here you go, then,' she said, shoving the weapon into Morlin's grasp. 'The seven weapons are together once more. Each has its champion. It has taken long enough. Now it is time to rid Dalriya of our enemy.'

IDRIS

KINGDOM OF CORIELTES, THE
CONFEDERACY, 677

I dris slithered along the rocky ground on knees and elbows. He stopped at the edge of the cliff and peered down.

It was his first proper look at the enemy. A horde, one might call it, sent to destroy the Confederacy. A creation of Ezenachi, it contained peoples one would never naturally see together. Lippers, Caladri, Cordentines, and Magnians. And now, men and women of the Confederacy.

For Ezenachi had worked his dark sorcery on this land. Doica, the southernmost kingdom, was completely overrun, its people turned to do the god's bidding. Corieltes was all but lost. Little wonder that Gethin, King of Ritherys, had begged him for aid. For his kingdom was next. And even though Idris would have preferred to turn his troops on the empire, he could hardly say no. Because after Ritherys, came Atrabia.

Rhain, King of Corieltes, joined him. Behind them, hidden in the craggy landscape, was a small force. Small, but hand-picked. It was unclear how the Turned decided where to go or what to do. But for now, they marched through the lowlands, towards the last defenders of this tiny kingdom.

'You think this will work?' Rhain whispered to him.

'Is it not working so far?'

'It is their sorcerer that concerns me.'

'Aye. But sorcerers can be killed.'

Rhain turned to him, fixing him with his brown eyes. The man was slim, dark hair half grey now. He was a cautious type, Idris felt, but then that caution had probably kept him alive this long. But his time had almost run out. The armies of Atrabia and Ritherys had given him a lifeline. 'You have had experience of this, I know. Inge, the Brasingian. But she still lives, Prince Idris.'

'She does. But not for long. Look, however they do it, the Turned know what opposition to expect. And they are expecting the last of your forces. Maybe they anticipated the army of Ritherys coming here.' He looked down at the lines of the enemy. Little discipline to it, the different peoples marching together, no discernible units. But enough numbers to finish the Confederacy forces. 'But they haven't planned for my Atrabians. And certainly not for an army of Luderians, as well.'

'You think the Luderians will fight for us?' Rhain asked doubtfully.

'I am sure they care little about saving your kingdom. But I think they will fight if it seems like we will win, and if the consequence for desertion is death.'

The sound of fighting came from the front lines of the Turned army. They had engaged with the warriors of Ritherys and Corieltes. Idris trained his gaze down below, as the remaining Turned marched towards the engagement. 'You'll tell me when you see him?' he asked the king, a nervous energy rising in his body now. He welcomed the feeling. Welcomed the imminent bloodshed and danger. Imprisoned for so long, it reminded him he was free. Reminded him he was alive.

'I know him when I see him,' Rhain confirmed.

'I thought all Caladri looked the same.'

'Not this one. He's always mounted, surrounded by others. And there's something—an arrogance to the way he holds himself—that marks him out.'

The Turned moved quicker now, and the sound of fighting grew fainter. Gethin was retreating his unit. It was all according to the plan

Idris had framed. The Atrabians and Luderians were waiting to ambush them. And the belief in victory might reveal the sorcerer.

'There,' Rhain said.

It was as the king had described. A cavalry force of about a hundred Caladri came into view, at the rear of the Turned army. Idris could see some of them looking up the steep slope on which he perched, wary of the terrain they rode through. But their infantry had walked past unmolested and had engaged with Gethin at the far end of the valley. There was little reason for them to suspect Idris's tiny force was lying in wait.

He saw the sorcerer, about a third of the way in from the front rank of the cavalry. There was indeed something about him that said he was in charge. Idris had been around powerful people enough to read such body language.

He and Rhain shuffled backwards, careful not to let their movement alert the enemy. Twenty yards behind, waiting patiently, were the best archers the Atrabians had. And that made them the best in all of Dalriya.

'It's time,' Idris told them. He described the precise location of the Caladri sorcerer. His archers understood that was the target. But Idris knew there were enough of them to make mincemeat out of the entire cavalry force. He readied his own bow. A childish part of him wanted to be the one to hit the sorcerer first. He grinned as the anticipation of the day drew to its climax. His archers copied him, sharing the same grin. It seemed people liked a leader who enjoyed his work.

Wordlessly, in almost total silence, he led them to the edge of the cliff. A long line of them, all nocking arrows and pulling back bowstrings. He knew exactly where to look, but it would only take a moment longer for the rest to sight their target. Idris released his arrow, and two score followed it.

Fear struck Idris in the gut. For the sorcerer nearly saved himself. Somehow, he sensed the arrows coming for him. With a wave of his hand, he sent most of them flying away. But a dozen got through, and half of those struck their target. Six arrows are enough to fell most anyone.

The Turned sorcerer fell from his horse and the Caladri around him turned to face the source of the attack. As they looked up, they saw forty archers nocking their second arrows and pulling back the strings of their bows. Most had no time to move out of the way. Some put up arms to protect themselves, a few even managed to grab shields. The arrows tore into them. No magical protection this time.

Now, the Caladri moved, some towards Idris's position, some away from it. The oddest part about it was the lack of shouts or any voices at all. He pushed that thought from his mind.

As his archers readied their third arrows, Idris descended the cliff towards the enemy. There was no path here, and it was steep. He slid a few yards before righting himself. A dozen Caladri horsemen narrowed the gap towards him at a frightening pace, but they were the ones cut down when his archers released their third volley. Idris had the time to draw and release an arrow of his own, hitting a Caladri in the back. His victim fell from his horse, and Idris let out a cry of glee. They were winning. Any moment now, Emlyn would execute the ambush and they would have them trapped.

He continued his descent, with no concerted effort by the Turned to stop him. He heard the slips and slides, the falling stones, of his archers following behind. As they came, they would stop to release more arrows, flattening the nearest of the enemy. Idris reached the valley floor. He cared little about those few Turned who had escaped south. They could run all the way to Doica or further for all he cared. He faced north, toward the main Turned army. He heard the cries of the Atrabian army as they sprang from their hiding places. More arrows would be fired, and spear, sword, and axe would drink enemy blood. He knew the Turned would be forced back this way.

As his small force gathered with him, Idris placed his bow behind a rock. A thin smile came to his face as he drew his sword. He yearned for that unique, terrible violence of hand-to-hand combat. He still had revenge to mete out. The Turned weren't the objects of his vengeance. But today, they would do.

* * *

IT WAS A MASSACRE. Merely a setback for Ezenachi, Idris was sure. He had entire countries at his disposal. But they had killed one of his sorcerers, and hundreds, if not thousands, of his better warriors.

For the kingdom of Corieltes, it had made the difference between destruction and survival. Rhain had less than half of his country intact, the rest occupied by a Turned population. He would have to do his best to hold on to what he had for the time being. Idris had waited long enough to follow his real ambition.

'Now we head for the empire,' he told the leaders of his army. Emlyn and the Atrabians were behind him.

Gethin was not keen. Idris was not surprised. The fate of the empire meant little to his kingdom.

'The Confederacy is in a precarious position,' the king of Ritherys said.

The Confederacy was screwed. That was the truth of it. But that was a problem for another day. 'We had a deal,' Idris reminded him. 'I have fulfilled my side, have I not? Where would you be without us?'

Gethin couldn't wriggle out of his obligations. 'I'll keep my word,' he said.

But Idris knew his composite army had weaknesses. The fighters of Ritherys had no interest in the empire. The Luderians, meanwhile, wanted nothing more than to return home. But how much could Idris rely on these soldiers he had spared, to support him out of choice? He knew they'd had no love for Salvinus. That didn't mean they had any more for him.

A speech to the assembled seemed his best option. He gathered the army about him, telling the officers to keep men quiet. He stood atop a rock, alone, making them look up. Bare-chested, he made sure everyone could see the marks that were now a part of his legend.

'Wherever we have come from,' he began. 'Wherever we thought we were going in life, we have all had a rude awakening these last few days. We have seen the dark reality of what Ezenachi has done. And we all know it is coming for us. There is nowhere to hide.' He looked about him. Maybe some of those gathered didn't want to hear it, but not one of them could deny he spoke the truth. 'A crucible of fire and steel is coming to Dalriya. Stand still, and we will be swept aside. But act with courage and purpose, and we can fashion the world as we wish it to be. So, to Brasingia we must go. Corrupt and decaying from the inside, the empire is there for the taking. We can be the ones to grab it, in both hands. Lend me your swords, and I can make it a beacon of purity. Together, we can face any force that threatens us.'

Idris surveyed the warriors of three nations. Not everyone was persuaded.

But enough are.

* * *

IDRIS LED HIS ARMY NORTH, through Ritherys and Atrabia. He knew no one in the empire would suspect he might launch an invasion. No doubt they had heard of Salvinus's fate by now. But their sense of superiority over Atrabia prevented them from imagining a situation where he was the conqueror and they the conquered. Despite all that, he only crossed the border into Luderia at the closest point to Witmar. The capital would get little or no warning of their coming.

Now he marched his men hard, every hour counting. Witmar would get little support, he knew. Leopold and the Kellish were surrounded by enemies, most notably the army of Guivergne. They'd not be sending any help. Much of the regular Luderian army was in his hands already. And with Salvinus dead, the leadership in the capital would be weak. The only figure of authority left in Witmar was the dowager empress Hannelore. And whatever authority she had, he doubted it extended to military leadership.

They had to spend the first night in Luderia camped outside. Idris posted only his most loyal Atrabians on guard duty. Not so much to watch out for an attack, he explained to them. To watch out for Luderian deserters.

Most Luderians were still there the next morning. Some had drifted away in the night. Some had been caught, and the only answer to that was execution. But that was it, now. Their last chance. For they would reach Witmar today.

As they approached the city, doubts inevitably crept in. Was his confidence misplaced? There was Inge, of course, and it would be a mistake to underestimate her. But as the walls of Witmar came into view, there was no army waiting for them. The walls were wooden. Tall and thick, but wooden, and therefore susceptible to fire. Idris hoped it wouldn't come to that, but he didn't rule it out.

By evening, his army had made camp outside the city. He did not try to encircle Witmar. Let those inside come to terms with what kind of force lay outside their walls. It might help them see sense.

After a while, he left his uncle in charge of the camp and approached the city with a small entourage—King Gethin, and those men amongst the Luderians who were of influence. A gate opened and a similar sized party came to meet them. It was an encouraging start.

Each side introduced themselves. Idris found he was talking with four of the highest-ranking noblemen of Luderia. 'We are here to speak for Lady Hannelore,' one of them said. Lord Teuchenberg, an older man, was white haired and officious in manner.

'Ah,' Idris replied. 'And I suppose the dowager empress is against opening the gates to me.'

'She is.'

'Have you explained to her what she can expect if you do not open the gates?'

'We have. But you can hardly be surprised that she stands with her son against you.'

'And where do you stand, my lords? With Leopold and Gervase Salvinus?'

'I thought you killed Salvinus?' another lord asked. He wore a goatee, was squat and well built, and seemed the most forthright of the group.

'I did. You regret that action?'

'Certainly not. You did everyone in the empire a favour.'

'Wechlitz!' warned Teuchenberg.

'What? I speak for everyone, do I not? The man was a boor who showed us nothing but disdain.'

'And did Lady Hannelore defend her people against him?' Idris asked mildly.

'She did nothing of the kind,' Wechlitz said, still with the bit between his teeth. 'Ignored our remonstrations and gave herself to the filthy savage.'

'Wechlitz, enough!' the older man said. 'I see your line, Your Highness,' he said to Idris. 'We have had poor government here since Duke Arne passed away. But you have said nothing about your intentions.'

'I intend to become Duke of Luderia with your support,' Idris replied. 'I put myself forward as a better ruler than you have had recently. I hope my colleagues here, who have fought with me in recent days, can vouch for that.'

It was the turn of the Luderians to speak and they did their job, summarising what had happened since Salvinus had led his army against Atrabia. Most significant, Idris was sure, was when they described the threat from the Turned of Ezenachi. It seemed enough to make the four noblemen take consideration of the wider picture.

'All well and good,' Wechlitz bristled. 'But you have brought foreigners with you.' He gestured at Gethin. 'You think we will let foreign soldiers into our capital?'

'Gethin?' Idris prompted.

'I have sworn an oath to fight with Prince Idris,' the king explained. 'But I have no interest in Witmar. As soon as these gates are opened, I will take my soldiers with all haste back to Ritherys, and never return.' It was said with such fervour that the Luderians could hardly doubt he told the truth.

'Then I have learned all I need to,' Wechlitz declared, with a pointed look at Teuchenberg.

The older man was more reluctant. 'What promises can I get from you, Your Highness?'

'I will rule Luderia in full consultation with the noble council. The rights and responsibilities as they existed under Duke Arne will be restored. You must know, my lords, that Atrabia is my home. My quarrel is not with Luderia. I will submit to your greater knowledge on all matters concerning the governance of the duchy. The only exception is my war with Leopold. That will be prosecuted as I see fit.'

Teuchenberg studied Idris for a while, before nodding. 'Leopold has lost his right to the loyalty of Luderians. With our support, a peaceful transition can be made to your rule, Your Highness. But I have one demand. Regarding Lady Hannelore. She has her faults, but she is still the daughter of Duke Arne and the former wife of Emperor Baldwin.'

'I will treat her with the utmost respect.'

'Then we are agreed. The gates will be opened, the soldiers from the Confederacy will return home. And you, Your Highness, will become Duke Idris of Luderia.'

LIESEL

DUCHY OF BARISSIA, 677

It was a miserable march from Valennes, along the Cousel, then across the border and into Barissia. No one knew what to say to Liesel. Or Esterel. Or Peyre. Even Tegyn avoided Liesel, knowing her friend was not in the mood. Among the three of them, all they were capable of was the most minimal, bitten off word. Instead, they rode each day, their warriors marched, and they remained impatient for the resolution of a conflict that had made them bitter and jaded.

Messages had been sent to their allies in the empire. Liesel's brother-in-law, Jeremias, was beset by enemies to his north. The rulers of Grienna and Trevenza, now styling themselves as dukes of the empire, remained loyal to Leopold. Liesel thought of her sister in Guslar, no doubt worrying for her children. Liesel desperately wanted to see them again. But that was a relationship full of uncertainty. If Esterel took the imperial title for himself, as he had made plain was his ambition, where did that leave Jeremias? He was the man lawfully elected emperor two years ago. Liesel had been there to witness it. But was he in any position to enforce that result? In her more optimistic moments, Liesel thought Katrina might be pleased. Her sister had never wanted to be empress.

The south was slightly more promising. Archbishop Emmett of

452

Gotbeck offered no support, his duchy recovering from the savaging it took from Salvinus last year. But Friedrich of Thesse had a fresh army, and he was bringing it to Coldeberg. The thought of having to retake that city filled Liesel with dread. It had taken them all last year's campaigning season to do it. What, exactly, Esterel's plans were, she didn't know. She didn't even want to ask him. But she was in no doubt that, amid his genuine grief, her husband knew exactly what he intended to do.

THE TWO ARMIES met outside Schilling, west of Coldeberg, the Thessians arriving only a couple of hours after the Guivergnais. Loyal forces still held the town.

Esterel and Friedrich met alone to discuss strategy. When they were done, Esterel announced a feast would be held in the keep to celebrate their continued alliance.

As Liesel was preparing for the event, Tegyn entered her room.

'Liesel? Duke Friedrich found me. He's asking for a private word with you if you're willing?'

Liesel smoothed down her dress. 'Did he say what about?'

'No.'

'Alright. Help me put these boots on, will you?'

Friedrich waited alone. Thanking Tegyn, he invited Liesel to stroll about the streets of Schilling with him.

'I spoke with Esterel.'

'He has told me nothing.'

'Ah. He asked me to besiege Coldeberg with my forces. The army of Guivergne will march straight for Essenberg.'

'I see. If you do not want to do so, Friedrich, you must say.'

'No, it's not that. It's a reasonable use of my army and we both agreed there is likely to be little fighting. The garrison inside is probably small and will surrender when Essenberg falls.'

He looked at her with a smile. She found it hard not to think of the Friedrich she knew as a child. He seemed to have the same innocence about him even now, when discussing the most serious matters.

'Esterel clearly intends to take Essenberg and make himself emperor. With the size of his army, I think he'll do the first part. But I admit, I am a little nervous about what happens next. You know Jeremias was elected emperor. If your husband turns that aside, will he stand by the result of a new vote? What else might he turn aside?'

'What are you asking me, Friedrich?'

He sighed. 'I suppose I am asking what kind of man he is? What kind of emperor will he be?'

'Compared to Leopold?'

'No, not compared to Leopold. Compared to my father, or yours.'

Liesel nodded. It was a fair question. 'Our fathers faced great evil. Neither survived. Esterel is not a perfect man. He is ambitious certainly, but then how many emperors of Brasingia have not had ambition? But he would be the kind of emperor who might face Ezenachi and somehow win. And that is who we need right now. Don't you think?'

Friedrich nodded. 'Yes. I see a winner, too. And there is indeed a great evil, stretched out along my duchy's southern border. So, I'm prepared to support Esterel, for that reason. And because you are his queen, Liesel. I just wanted to hear it from you. That there are no nasty surprises coming down the road. Because it feels things are moving very fast now.'

Liesel smiled, though she didn't feel like smiling. 'I'm glad I could reassure you,' she said.

She wondered who there was to reassure *her*.

* * *

THE ARMY MARCHED NORTHEAST, leaving Schilling in the hands of Friedrich. Esterel seemed uninterested in Barissia, despite the fact it was now his duchy, and its capital was occupied. He was fixed on Essenberg.

'You are agitated,' Tegyn said, as they rode together near the front of the armed column, just behind Esterel. Next to her husband was Gosse, taking up the role of bodyguard she had given him last year.

Ahead, Florent had scouts ranging out across the Barissian countryside.

'We are close to the border with Kelland,' Liesel replied. 'I am queen of Guivergne, but Kelland was my home. My family's province, going back to before the founding of the empire. And here am I, with an army come to invade it. I don't know what to think. Sometimes I think it's wrong, sometimes right, sometimes neither, just necessary. But it's certainly sad that it's come to this.'

Florent reported to Esterel when his scouts crossed the border. The Kellish were waiting for them, he explained, riders of their own tracking the Guivergnais advance. But so far, they were falling back, allowing Esterel to enter the duchy.

Esterel nodded, pensive looking. 'I am a little surprised,' he admitted.

'What?' Liesel asked him, trying to keep her voice calm.

'If I was Leopold, I would fight here. With the Kellish and Luderians, his army must match ours in size. And his warriors would be motivated to keep out an enemy. I'm not sure what retreating from us gets him.'

'Perhaps he simply intends to hold out in Essenberg?'

He shrugged. 'We won't have long to find out.'

Soon afterwards, they crossed into Kelland. The reality of the situation pressed down on Liesel with even greater weight. They passed a small wooden watchtower, abandoned by the Kellish. Otherwise, there was nothing to see except the rich farmland they passed through. The Guivergnais ignored it, their carts still full of food. That was a testament to Sacha, who managed their provisions with a miser's attention to detail. Everyone was given the bare minimum in rations, and even Esterel had to cajole his friend if he wanted anything extra.

Florent returned, giving Esterel more information. Liesel saw her husband's eyebrows rise, and he looked in her direction.

'Come, wife,' he said. 'We have a meeting. You too, Lady Tegyn.'

'Me?'

'Yes,' Esterel replied, straight faced. 'You.'

. . .

ESTEREL REQUESTED the attendance of Peyre and Duke Martras as well. Once they were gathered, Florent and half a dozen of his scouts led them to a small village. There was only one inn, and that was where their meeting would be held. Florent waited outside with his scouts while the five of them dismounted and entered the building.

A familiar face stood to greet them. Lord Kass. He looked at them nervously, a sheen of sweat on his forehead. He was tired and haggard —even his moustache had more droop than flourish. He was at a table by himself. A few tables over were what Liesel guessed were his personal entourage. It looked like his wife and children, with personal servants, only a couple of whom were armed.

'Your Majesty, I am much obliged,' he said, offering them seats at his table.

Esterel drew a chair for Liesel, then sat himself; Peyre, Martras, and Tegyn took up chairs beside them. Esterel, it seemed, didn't even consider ordering from the bar. This must be serious.

'I know I do not deserve your trust,' Kass began, eyes flicking toward Liesel and Peyre.

'Why not?' Esterel demanded.

Peyre reminded his brother about Kass's history—how he had done Inge's work, visiting Arbeost all those years ago with talk of a marriage between Liesel and Esterel, while secretly bringing with him killers, who had come close to murdering Esterel's brother, Sanc. It was a story that seemed as strange now as ever, not least because that alliance in marriage, seemingly a ploy, had come to pass.

'I regret my part in that and more,' Kass said earnestly. 'When Duke Walter found out about it, he had every right to have me executed on the spot. He showed mercy, gods bless his soul. Whether or not you choose to believe it, after that, my allegiance changed. Not outwardly, it has not been safe to do that. But I have hoped that this day might come—that the witch is finally driven out of the empire. Anyway, I am eager to give you the latest news. I am recently come from Essenberg. I took my leave of the city with my family in the dead of night. We travelled in this direction, hoping to be of service.'

Esterel made an impatient hand gesture. 'Speak, Lord Kass.'

'Of course. First, from the north, Leopold's allies in Trevenza and Grienna have invaded Rotelegen. The king received news that, outnumbered, Duke Jeremias has withdrawn his forces into Guslar and hopes to hold out there. But it is the news to the east that will be of most use to you. Salvinus is dead. Killed by Prince Idris in Atrabia.'

Nine words. Only nine words, but they came as such a shock to Liesel that she found she could not make sense of them. Had she misheard? Had Kass lost his mind?

'Hold up,' Tegyn said. 'You talk of my brother in Atrabia. Back-track, so that this makes sense to me.'

'Apologies, my lady,' Kass said. 'This story began a few weeks ago. Patience worn out with the lack of support from Emlyn, Leopold and his advisers sent Salvinus with an army into Atrabia. Salvinus took Idris with him. The plan was to replace the uncle with the nephew, so that they would have a loyal man on the throne, who would supply them with Atrabian soldiers. They were worried, of course, about this very moment. When the army of Guivergne would come. The Atrabi-ans, they decided, might make the difference.'

So far, Liesel was following. Emlyn, it seemed, had grown a pair of balls, and stopped cooperating with Inge. That had prompted the release of Idris. If Emlyn still lived, Liesel resolved to find and thank him personally. She had badly misjudged the man.

'It seems Idris led them into a trap. The Luderians were forced to surrender. Excuse the bloody details, ladies—'

'Spit it out,' Tegyn encouraged.

'The story is that Idris took Salvinus's head himself.'

Liesel couldn't stop herself from releasing a gasp of satisfaction. She hadn't even dared to dream of such good news.

'There is more,' Kass warned. 'Idris took an army to Witmar. The city surrendered and agreed to make Idris duke.'

'What?' Tegyn demanded. 'Idris is now Duke of Luderia?'

'Yes, so they say. And the rumours coming out of that duchy before

I left were that Idris does not intend to stop there. With an army at his disposal, there was much fearful talk in the streets of Essenberg. That he intends to come to the city and finish the job he has started.'

'That explains the Kellish retreat,' Esterel said. 'They have lost a good part of their army. Not only lost the Luderians, but now find them an enemy force at their back.'

Peyre and Martras nodded, both men sharing the same look—astonished that fortune was shining so brightly.

'Beware, though,' Lord Kass added. 'Leopold is weakened, but you have a new opponent to contend with. Idris has turned the tables in a matter of weeks. He is an adversary not to underestimate.'

'Adversary?' Esterel repeated. He pointed with a finger at Liesel and Tegyn. 'We benefit from the presence of his sister and my wife, who knows him well. Idris is an ally, not an enemy. I have no quarrel with him.'

'Aye, maybe,' Kass said, looking at each face slowly. 'But I have never heard of such a complicated state of affairs. Leopold, Idris, and yourself. Each with an army within a matter of miles of one another. And only one of you can be emperor.'

* * *

Esterel sent Lord Kass to Coldeberg, so that he could tell his story to Friedrich. They resumed their march on Essenberg. Florent continued to send his scouts ahead, but now there was less expectation of finding an army waiting for them. If the Kellish truly were threatened from the northeast as well as southwest, they had little option but to retreat to their capital. *Little option but to surrender*, Liesel thought, though she knew Leopold would never do that.

The misery of the first days of the campaign had disappeared since hearing Kass's news. The odds were suddenly in their favour. They had to be careful to avoid overconfidence, of course. But Liesel couldn't help hoping that this war might soon be over, without the need for brutal battles, drawn out sieges, and the misery and loss that came with those things.

She recognised every place they marched through. Even so, she felt a sense of disbelief when the familiar view of her childhood home appeared before her eyes. The Great Road, the river Cousel, and the stone walls of Essenberg.

In some ways, those walls seemed impregnable. But she knew they weren't. As a child, she had witnessed the Drobax overwhelming the defences, forcing her mother to flee the city. Salvinus had got them out. Of course, for his own ends. But he'd got them out, nonetheless.

Is this what happens when people you hate die? she asked herself. *You grow fond of them? For the gods' sake, Liesel, get a grip.*

Esterel ordered the army positioned a safe distance from the walls, spread from river to road. Each sector would be managed by one of his generals: Peyre, Martras, Florent of Auriac, and Arnoul of Saliers. They would report to Esterel, positioned in the royal tent, to the rear of the camp, while Sacha would continue to manage the logistics.

Each general had been given a unit of Liesel's arbalests. They were positioned to the front, ready to break up any attempt by the defenders to sally from the city. She couldn't help a feeling of pride at the role they played, despite hoping they would not be used against her own people.

While all this is happening, Liesel told herself, *the soldiers on the walls are watching. Reporting back to Leopold and Inge.* She tried to imagine what the atmosphere would be like in the royal castle. Scared? Angry? Desperate? The Kellish army was intact, and no doubt could hold out for weeks, if not months. Inge had magic, and that still frightened Liesel. But still, Leopold and Inge were a wall's width away from defeat.

Then, one final twist. Peyre arrived at the royal tent. 'I sent Sul to scout around to the far side of the walls.'

'Hmm, that's brave, trusting that idiot with an important job,' Gosse ribbed with a grin.

Peyre smiled. 'I must be losing my mind. Still, he did alright.' He looked at Esterel. 'Found Idris's army, camped about as far from the walls as we are. Has the Luderians and Atrabians with him, at least three thousand warriors.'

There was a silence for a while as the news sank in.

'It's about time I meet this prince,' Esterel said.

IDRIS CAME to the Guivergnais camp. Esterel ensured he was taken the long route, so the Atrabian could see just how many soldiers Esterel commanded.

Even so, Idris still walked in as if he owned the place. He was flanked on one side by Emlyn, Ilar and Macsen, the two boys smiling goofily at Liesel: on the other, by Luderian lords.

Idris had changed. Liesel shouldn't be surprised. He'd always been thin; now he was gaunt. It was his eyes that were most different. They surveyed the scene like a predator, an animal intensity there that spoke of tempers bubbling just below the surface. He grinned when he saw Liesel and Tegyn. She hoped it wasn't maliciously. She got the impression that her old friend's real thoughts and emotions were well hidden.

Esterel, affable as usual, invited him into the royal tent. A rich spread of food and drink was on display. Even that was a statement on her husband's part. *Look at my army. Look at the supplies I have spare. I'm the one in charge here.*

Esterel's generals and Idris's lieutenants ate, drank, and talked of meaningless things. They guessed at how many men Leopold had inside the city; compared thoughts about how long his food would last. Eventually—at last—Idris and Esterel began to talk.

'I congratulate you on your military successes,' Esterel said. 'The queen has told me about your treatment, and we are both pleased to see you free. We are also pleased to hear about the demise of Gervase Salvinus. To be the man who finally ended that bastard's life—well, you've made a name for yourself already.'

'There are two more who I mean to see buried before I pause to pat myself on the back.'

'Quite. I hope we can work together on that. I have my own reasons to see Leopold and his witch dead.'

'Good to hear. Then we need to work out the arrangements for afterwards, do we not?'

'Yes,' said Esterel. 'And if I can rely on your support, I am more than happy to confirm you as the duke of Luderia.'

Idris raised an eyebrow at that. 'Confirm me? But I am already the duke of Luderia, am I not?' Idris asked, looking to his Luderians for confirmation.

'That you are,' one of them said, a squat man who didn't seem the slightest bit awed by the company. 'No one makes a man duke except for the people of Luderia.'

'You see,' Idris said, turning to Esterel with a smile. 'I am already the duke, so you are offering me nothing, King Esterel. I am Duke of Luderia and Prince of Atrabia. You, sir—with all due respect—are a foreign monarch with no legitimate claim to authority in Brasingia. So let me propose a counter offer. If I can rely on your support, I am ready to confirm you as the Duke of Barissia.'

Ilar and Macsen grinned stupidly at their half-brother, and Liesel had to stop herself from smiling with them.

Esterel returned an equally pleasant smile. 'From my wife, I inherit my claims on Barissia and Kelland. And, with all due respect and without wishing to appear a brute—I have an army in Brasingia a good three times the size of yours. I have lands that bring an income many times those of yours. As much as I admire you, Prince Idris, I haven't marched all the way here to put *you* on the throne.'

'I see. I hope your good lady wife has not been remiss to educate you on how things work in the empire. Our emperors are elected. I have two votes. The dukes of Rotelegen, of Thesse, and Emmett of Gotbeck have one each. When it comes to it, do you expect them to elect a king of Guivergne as emperor of Brasingia?'

For the first time, Esterel's forced pleasantry slipped. His lips were pushed together, and a dead eyed look had come to his face. 'Are you suggesting that you intend to campaign against me? I advise you not to.'

Liesel looked from one man to the next, growing nervous for the first time. Surely, with Leopold not yet defeated, they would not fall out over what might or might not happen afterwards?

'Your Majesty,' Idris said, his smile also gone now. 'I mean no offence. I wish to come to an accord. I am merely trying to demonstrate what an alliance with me is worth to you. My two votes, and your two votes, well... we can make you emperor here and now. But your initial offer of confirming my rights over Luderia values such an alliance too little.'

Esterel frowned. 'I see. And I take your point. Then what else can I offer you?'

'I wish I could take your beautiful wife,' Idris said.

Liesel reddened, fighting off shock, as all eyes turned to her. She made herself give a little smile. 'I am sure my husband sets too high a price on me to give me away.' She turned to Esterel. 'At least, he better.'

Several men laughed, and Esterel smiled. With a forced sigh, he held up both hands. 'Alas, it's true.'

'Ah. Then make me your heir,' Idris said.

'My—what? My heir? My children shall be my heirs.'

'Of course,' Idris agreed. 'When you have a child, they shall become your heir. Until then, it will be me.'

'What? You're hoping I die soon and that you replace me? Is that it?'

'Not at all. I wish you a long and healthy life. But emperors *are* popping off quite quickly these days. Call it a nicety. In return for me withdrawing my claim, and supporting yours, you make me your heir. No doubt, only temporary.'

'You just lectured me about the constitutional rules in the empire,' Esterel complained. 'How can I make you my heir?'

'Not to the imperial title, you can't, no. I meant to Kelland and Barissia. And Guivergne.'

There was a shocked intake of breath from the Guivergnais at that.

'What?' Idris said, turning at the sound. 'If your king can rule in Brasingia, I can rule in Guivergne. Fair's fair.'

Liesel could see Esterel think about it. He looked to those he trusted—Sacha and Peyre. He looked at her. She gave him a tiny shrug. It didn't seem like much of a price to pay.

'Very well,' Esterel said, holding out a hand. 'We have a deal.'

SANC

KINGDOM OF THE TELDS, 677

They sped through the air. The only thing separating them from a great fall onto the rocky terrain below was Kepa's magic, and a rug only a few inches thick. Sanc considered himself brave enough after all the dangerous experiences he had endured. But there was something about this mode of travel that set off a phobia. He had a physical reaction to it: short of breath, trembling, and wishing it was over from beginning to end.

Kepa brought them down at a point where three realms met: the southern edge of Teld and Gadenzian territory bordered the Khanate of the Egers. Here, the land flattened. It was the beginnings of the great southern plain that the Egers controlled.

'They'll spot you not long after you cross into their lands,' Kepa told them, as they stared south. 'It's up to you how you want to proceed. But you might find they are more interested in you than if it was a Teld incursion.'

'You mean they might wait a moment before deciding to hack us to pieces?' Herin asked dryly.

The others looked genuinely fearful about what they might find. Sanc didn't feel scared. Not yet. He was still glad to have both feet on the ground.

Herin and Kepa held each other's arms as they said farewell. There was an affection there, and Sanc supposed he shouldn't be surprised to see it. Maybe not the same relationship he had with Mildrith. But Herin had been alone for so long, for one reason and another. Sanc was pleased to see the friendship, or whatever it was. And then he felt sorry for the Magnian when Kepa left them, flying away into the distance.

Herin arranged his array of weapons. He had a longsword at his belt and a shorter bladed weapon that he called a seax. Strapped to his back was a bow with a quiver full of arrows. He had clearly come ready to fight. But for all his prowess, Sanc knew it was his magic, and Mildrith's, that mattered.

THE FLAT GRASSLAND of the Eger Khanate reminded Sanc of the Midder Steppe, the land where he had first learned about war from his father. Rab seemed to like it. He roamed ahead, a useful scout to have, even though he struggled to see over the top of the grass.

As they walked, Herin shared what he had learned about the Egers. 'They are a race apart from the other peoples of Silb. This is of the Egers' own doing. Kepa told me they bind the heads of their babes, making their skulls look unusually long and fearsome. They steal young children as the spoils of war, binding their heads and forcing them into their own way of life. Anyone older, they kill. It is a ruthless way to fight. They have taken much Teld land over the years.'

'They also won many victories over the Gadenzians,' Mildrith added. 'It is said that kingdom was all but finished, its royal line destroyed, and its army broken. That was when Lothar's father was made king of the Gadenzians. He, and then Lothar, pushed the Egers back. The Eger Khan was killed in a great battle by Temyl and Guntram. The southern lands of the Gadenzians were divided into three margravates, responsible for holding the border against the Egers. Ever since, the Egers have been kept at bay. That was the beginning of Lothar's rise. He found himself with the resources of two kingdoms, and the freedom to turn his army elsewhere.'

'The Egers have a new ruler now?' Sanc asked.

'I am sure we will find out,' Herin said. 'There is one other thing to warn you about, Sanc. The Egers don't ride horses to war. They have giant lizards, large enough to be saddled.'

'Dragons?' Sanc asked, reminded of the beast that the god Diis had brought to Dalriya.

'No. Wingless creatures, so Kepa said.'

'But still to be wary of,' Mildrith said. 'Some can rip open a horse with their sharp claws. The stories say it was those lizards that helped the Egers get the better of the Gadenzian cavalry.'

Long-headed killers and giant lizards. Maybe that flying rug wasn't so bad, Sanc conceded.

RAB WARNED them of the ambush. His growl was easy to interpret. The dog's precise location wasn't so easy to pinpoint, nor that of whoever he could smell.

Herin was quick to get his bow in his hands, his quiver swung around to rest against his waist.

'Careful,' Mildrith warned Sanc as he marched towards the sound. He nodded back, taking the time to cast his invisibility spell. Then he crept through the grass, worried as usual about Rab's safety. A hissing sound, ahead and to his right, caused a shiver to run down his spine. He'd been warned of lizards, but to hear one close by was something else. He peered through the grass but couldn't see anything, while he had the distinct impression his own movement had been noticed. Being invisible wasn't so useful if the enemy was also well hidden.

Mildrith shifted the encounter in their favour. He heard shouts about thirty yards ahead of him, and then saw missiles fly into the sky above. Following their flight, he saw her. She was floating in the sky, drawing the attention of the Egers. With one hand gesture, then another, she deflected the missiles that came her way.

Sanc knew it was time to move. He stood straight and moved through the grass. Half a dozen Egers had revealed themselves. They wore leather armour and carried spears and axes. One went down from an arrow, whistling in from the side. A second cried out as first one leg, then another, was caught in the grip of thin roots that spiralled up his limbs.

Too distracted to have noticed Sanc's approach, it gave him a free strike. He sent one sprawling with a blast of magic, then another.

Rab's warning bark made him turn, just in time.

The lizard was thick and muscular, with a broad snout. It was an earthy colour, except for its top part, where its scales were pale green. Two great leather bands were wrapped around its torso, holding a saddle. It moved at a frightening pace.

The animal took up so much of his attention that Sanc saw its rider's spear strike late. There was a glint of metal and he dived out of the way on instinct. He landed hard on the dry ground, and then rolled to the side, concerned that the lizard would stamp down with its claws. He stopped, stretched both hands out to where he thought the beast was, and released his magic. He was rewarded with a shout and the thudding sound of what could only be the huge beast landing after being sent flying.

Sanc got to his feet, still worried about Rab. He found the trampled grass left by the lizard, then a great gash in the ground where it had landed after his strike. After sliding a few more yards, it lay on its side. It was still, but Sanc couldn't tell whether it was dead. For all he knew, it could even be pretending.

Rab was making a strange noise, somewhere between a growl and a whine, as he padded around the lizard, nipping at its scales.

'Back off, Rab,' Sanc said as he got close. Thrown to one side, he found the rider flat out on the ground.

'Rab!' he repeated when the dog didn't listen the first time.

Rab moved away a little but wouldn't stop making his noises.

Sanc approached the Eger rider. They had the long head described by Herin. The face had feminine features, and Sanc wasn't sure if he was looking at a man or woman. Their ribs looked crushed, almost certainly caused when the beast landed on them. He took his dagger in one hand and carefully lowered himself to his knees, keeping a wary eye on both rider and mount. Neither moved, and he placed his free hand on the rider's neck, feeling for a pulse. There was nothing, and he returned to his feet.

Studying the lizard more closely now, he could see its chest rising and falling. But it seemed out cold and, content to leave it that way, he retraced his steps, calling Rab to come with him. He headed for the position where the other Egers had been. He found Mildrith and Herin there. The Egers lay dead, except for one warrior. With the same elongated head as the rest of his people, he sat on the ground, the tip of Herin's sword hovering near his neck.

Mildrith was speaking to him. 'Who else is out there?'

'I will tell you nothing, foreigner. Don't waste your time asking.'

The Kassite turned at Sanc's approach. 'Well?'

'A giant lizard,' Sanc said. 'Its rider is dead, but the mount is unconscious. I couldn't see an injury.'

Herin shrugged. 'Then let's just kill this one and get out of here.'

Mildrith made a long-suffering face at Sanc, probably to empha-sise that Herin was *his* friend, not hers. Not, Sanc thought to himself, that List the Castrator would have said anything different.

'Kill a prisoner?' Sanc asked, unhappy with the idea.

'You had better kill me,' the Eger warrior said, 'or I will follow you and kill you.'

'See?' Herin said.

Sanc made a face. Whatever this warrior said, killing someone they had captured was a low thing to do, and unnecessary. And after all, weren't they here to form an alliance with these people? 'Where is the Eger Khan?' he asked the man.

The warrior looked at Sanc with derision. 'He will come soon enough. He will pull your spine from your body and make a display of your body parts for daring to enter our lands.'

It was clear they would get nothing from this man. Sanc sighed. Their task was going to be more difficult than he imagined if the Egers simply attacked on sight and refused to talk.

Mildrith gestured at the Eger's fallen comrades. 'They have leather belts. We can tie him up.'

'You had better kill me than let me live.'

Herin shook his head but relented, tying the man's limbs together with the belts and placing a jacket over his head. 'With any luck, that lizard will wake and eat him.'

* * *

THEY CONTINUED THEIR JOURNEY EASTWARD. Rab had as much idea as any of them about where they were headed. Mildrith spoke of a place called the Eger Ring. It was said the Egers took all their looted treasure there and that it had grown into the greatest hoard in Silb. But its location was, by design, remote and secret. Otherwise, they saw no permanent settlements. The Egers, like the Middians in Dalriya, were nomadic. That made it rather difficult to find their khan.

Meanwhile, small bands of Egers trailed behind them. Some rode parallel, perched atop their lizards that came in a variety of shapes, sizes, and colours.

None approached. Perhaps they had heard what happened to the last group who tried to ambush them. After a while, the Egers seemed to get bored, and left. Perhaps, when Sanc and his companions had walked through their territory, their responsibilities were done. Herin suggested capturing one or two and interrogating them, but Sanc had the feeling they would get as much out of them as their last captive.

The nights were chilly, and they would stop when they reached a place of relative shelter, since such places were hard to find. Stands of trees were preferred, so they could build a fire. It wasn't as if they were trying to hide, so they allowed the flames to burn high. If they struggled for firewood, Mildrith would encourage the local plant life to provide more. They would go hunting with Rab, and Mildrith would find edibles among the trees. Most evenings, they succeeded in supplementing their rations.

It went on in this way for several days. Then, the bands of Egers grew larger and didn't leave. Before long, they were being escorted by hundreds of warriors. Still, none of them attempted to interfere with their progress. Ahead, they heard a fast-flowing river. It was the first time the monotonous landscape threatened to give way to something else.

Before they reached the river, they sighted a camp. Hundreds of tents had been pitched this side of the river. There were enough to accommodate thousands of people. At last, they had got somewhere.

As they made their way towards the camp's outskirts, a group of around two hundred left the camp and approached them. Most were on foot—men, women, and children. All had the Eger shaped heads, and all wore similar items—baggy trousers and colourful jackets with warm linings. Those with armour wore leather, often with lizard scales sewn on.

Those not on foot rode lizards. Sanc studied them. Those riding the smaller, leaner lizards were themselves smaller in stature—often younger in years, or female—suggesting that there was a limit to the size of rider these beasts could carry. If a full-grown man had a lizard, it was broad and heavy, capable of taking the extra weight.

Sanc and his companions stopped, waiting for the Egers to approach. He put a leash on Rab, unsure how the dog would react as those great beasts got closer.

One rider, a tall youth who looked a few years younger than Sanc, raised a hand. The Egers stopped, looking from him to Sanc's group and back again. There seemed to be an air of uncertainty, as if the Egers themselves were unsure what would happen next.

'Why have you come into our lands and killed our people with magic?' the youth asked.

'We apologise for the deaths of your people,' Mildrith said quickly, as if fearful that Herin would speak first. 'I am Mildrith, champion of the Kassites. This is Sanc, a sorcerer from the outlands, and his servant.'

Herin opened his mouth to protest at this, but Sanc stared at him to stay quiet.

'We are come to meet with the Eger Khan,' the Kassite continued, 'and offer our powers to him.'

That was a good way of putting it, Sanc had to admit.

The young Eger studied each of them, apparently deciding what to do. Sanc readied himself. If necessary, he would blast his way through the Egers, sending their great lizards flying in all directions.

'Very well,' the Eger said at last. 'I am Hamzat. I will take you to see the khan.'

THE TENT BELONGING to the Eger Khan was bigger than those around it, but otherwise no different in design. Such details gave an insight into how a people were ruled. The Egers were the last of the seven peoples of Silb Sanc had encountered, and were as unique in their ways as any other.

Hamzat led them inside, the members of the entourage he had led either waiting outside or returning to their chores. Inside, the tent was airy and spacious, divided into several rooms. It was full of colourful rugs and decorative hangings and objects.

Hamzat clapped his hands. 'Come, out,' he snapped. 'I have guests to introduce to my family.'

A few servants moved quickly at this, vacating the space. Hamzat led them on through a dividing curtain. Only three people waited for them in here. Two were older and looked to Sanc like Hamzat's parents. The fourth was a young boy, who looked like he was about to enter his teenage years, with the same looks as his family.

The khan waved them in. He was bearded, average height and build, and wore a colourful robe, open at the chest. His wife dressed more plainly and looked at them nervously.

'This is my father, Tagir,' Hamzat introduced him.

'Please, sit,' Tagir said, gesturing to the floor. Everyone except Tagir's wife took a place, forming a circle. She fetched a large bowl and cups, handing them to Tagir, who poured out drinks.

'Thank you for seeing us, Your Majesty,' Sanc said, as the cups were passed around.

Tagir frowned and looked at Hamzat. 'Why does he call me that?'

Hamzat gave a small smile that had an edge of contempt to it. 'The foreigners do not understand. This is the Eger Khan,' he said, gesturing to the boy.

'Your brother?' Herin asked.

'Yes.'

Sanc was confused. The father was not the khan; not even the older brother. It didn't seem to make any sense, and he wondered if it was a joke at their expense. He and Herin looked at Mildrith. She shrugged. 'I know no more than you. This is the first time I have met the Egers myself.'

'It is simple enough to explain,' Hamzat said. He gestured at Mildrith. 'You are the champion of the Kassites?'

'Yes.'

'Among the Egers, our champion *is* the khan. When my brother was discovered, he was made khan.'

'Discovered?' Mildrith asked.

'When he was found to have magic. The last Eger Khan died in battle twelve years ago. My brother was born with Anada's grace. But it is only recently that his powers revealed themselves.'

Sanc nodded, finally understanding. It wasn't so long ago that his own powers had revealed themselves. At that point, this boy, who was probably from an ordinary family, had been made khan. And the lack of activity from the Egers in recent years was because they were waiting for their new khan to emerge. It seemed a strange way to organise themselves—to suffer years of weakness while they waited for a new ruler. On the other hand, combining the roles of king and champion must make the khan incredibly powerful.

He took his cup. Steam rose from it, and it smelled strongly of alcohol. He took a sip. 'What is his name?' he asked Hamzat.

'The Eger Khan is his title. He needs no other name.'

'I see.' Sanc turned to the boy. 'Your Majesty—'

'You do not speak to the khan, foreigner!' Hamzat exclaimed.

Tagir looked offended, and the khan's mother had put a hand over her mouth.

'Apologies,' Sanc said quickly.

'You can speak to me,' Tagir said. 'The khan will listen to your words.'

'Of course.' Sanc struggled now with what to say; where to begin.

All the time, a single thought taunted him. They had come all this way, desperate to bring the Egers into their war with Lothar. Only to find their ruler—and champion—was still a child.

'It's like this,' Herin said, rescuing him. 'We want to kill Lothar the Nerisian. And we wondered if you want in?'

PEYRE

ESSENBERG, DUCHY OF KELLAND, 677

The trebuchets and catapults had all been given the same target. The pounding sound they made was so regular now that it had become background noise. Not a single engine had been taken out by the enemy. The army of Guivergne dominated the siege, and that was down to Liesel and her arbalests.

They had cleared the city's walls of defenders within moments. So many bolts had been fired, with such accuracy, that it wasn't a matter of *if* a defender would be struck, but *when*.

Now, the unit under his command was divided into smaller groups. Each group took a turn to train their weapons along the length of the wall while the others rested. Peyre had responsibility from the river to the other side of the Valennes Gate, where his forces met those commanded by Auriac. The arbalests could hold their weapon for hours, bolt loaded, looking for any sign of movement. Should a Kellish archer poke his head above the walls, or the engineers attempt to access the catapults positioned on the bridge, a flurry of bolts would be released immediately. And there were three other units to his right, doing the same thing.

It made Peyre think. He'd been anticipating a bloody campaign—

assumed they'd be fighting their way to Essenberg, struggling to get inside. But it had not turned out like that, and their superiority could now be made to count. He'd already ordered his craftsmen to construct a wooden tower. He hoped they could build it at least as high as the city walls, allowing him to station arbalests at the top and give them a better angle to shoot from. But the more he thought about it, the more he asked himself why they waited for the siege engines to break through. The dominance of their crossbows would give them almost total cover to get ladders up against the walls. Do it at the right time, and they could get soldiers inside those walls.

On the evening, he left Umbert in charge of his position and walked to the back of the camp where the king had his headquarters. On the way, he met up with the other three commanders: Florent of Auriac, Arnoul of Saliers, and Domard of Martras. They shared something between a bond and a healthy rivalry. Each had been as taken aback as the other by the effectiveness of Liesel's units.

Martras had originally argued against their use. To be fair, that hadn't been because of any doubts about how deadly they were. But whatever reservations the duke still held, he could hardly ignore such a weapon now it was here.

'Before we speak with the king,' Peyre said, 'am I the only one who thinks that a hundred ladders would get us over these walls?'

'With these crossbows, we could do it,' Saliers said, always quick to discuss tactics. 'But the loss of life would be significant, on both sides.'

'We stand to lose people one way or another. Waiting around for a bout of plague to spread would be worse.'

'I think the king would rather avoid a bloodbath, if possible,' Martras said. 'After all, he intends to rule this city when all is done. Those soldiers who are now our enemies will become liege men. Better to keep them alive. Would you say those are his thoughts, Auriac?'

'I am sure. But as Morbaine says, we have other options, and must ensure his majesty can weigh all alternatives.'

'True enough,' Martras conceded. 'You still favour a direct approach, Your Grace?'

'I prefer to take the initiative than wait and hope for things to turn our way,' Peyre said. 'Let's see what the king says.'

IDRIS, the new duke of Atrabia and Luderia, was of course present for the war council, as well as several of his followers. *And now he is heir of Guivergne*, Peyre thought bitterly. No one gave a fig that making Idris Esterel's heir had stripped Peyre of his own inheritance. Esterel had not said a word to him about it afterwards. Idris acted as if he and Peyre were great friends. Even Liesel seemed pleased with the deal.

Peyre struggled to figure the Atrabian out. He seemed a very different man to the prisoner he had visited in Essenberg Castle. Inordinately confident and sure of his own worth. But Peyre simply couldn't see what Prince Idris brought to the table that had persuaded Esterel to give in to his demands. Yes, he had brought an army to Essenberg. But he had no siege equipment to speak of. He'd never have got inside the city walls, not in a thousand years. Indeed, Peyre reckoned the Kellish army could have broken his force comfortably if the Guivergnais had not arrived at the same time. Meanwhile, he was so short of supplies that Esterel had already ordered Sacha to send rations to keep his soldiers fed.

The only thing going for him was his enthusiastic support for Peyre's aggressive approach.

'A night time attack,' the prince urged. 'Ladders up wherever they least expect it. All we need do is get one of their damned gates opened, and they're finished. No chance for the witch to escape. I guarantee few Kellish warriors will lay down their lives for Leopold. We could end this in a day or two.'

Esterel was more cautious. 'Something to think about. But there are risks inherent in all of that. We have the upper hand and time is on our side.'

Peyre watched his brother study the reaction of his generals to his words. He still had enough support to get his way. But Peyre had identified a potential ally. He swallowed his pride and lingered about after the meeting to share some words with the Atrabian.

Peyre made casual chat with Martras as the generals left the royal tent. Idris made no hurry to return to his own camp with his officers. Peyre noticed him catch Liesel's eye, and they wandered a little way off to the side. Peyre knew full well how happy Liesel was to see her childhood friend free. No doubt they had much catching up to do. But that could wait.

'Excuse me, Your Grace,' he muttered to Martras, and made his way over to the pair.

'—don't know what you are thinking,' he caught Liesel saying, before she turned at his approach.

'I'm not interrupting?' Peyre said, knowing full well that he was.

'Of course not, Your Grace,' Liesel said.

Idris looked at him with his dark eyes, saying nothing. Was there a challenge there, Peyre wondered. The Atrabian certainly didn't appreciate Peyre's appearance.

'I wondered if we three could talk,' Peyre pushed on. *Who cares what the Prince of Atrabia does or does not appreciate?* 'About persuading the king to launch an attack.'

'I don't know that *I'm* persuaded,' Liesel said.

'Come on, Your Majesty. It's your crossbows that have put us in this position. They can win us this siege. What say you, Your Highness?'

'I say you are a most pugnacious fellow, Your Grace,' Idris said. His voice had a levity to it that Peyre didn't appreciate. 'Why, did you know, Your Majesty? One of these many scars I bear is courtesy of this man?'

Peyre went cold as he returned to that room in Essenberg Castle, a knife in his hand, and Idris sat with his back to him, already scored red three times. A white-hot anger followed soon after. Had Idris not asked him to do it? Had he not been trying to free Liesel at the time? What other choice could he have made, with Leopold watching?

Idris watched Peyre closely, a small smile of pleasure on his face.

Meanwhile, Liesel was frowning in consternation. 'Is this true?'

Peyre looked at her, unsure how to admit to it.

'Of course not, Liesel!' Idris said, his face suddenly jovial. 'I jest, silly cow! Sorry, Your Grace,' he said, turning to Peyre. 'That is an old term of endearment I used to have for the queen. She knows no offence is intended by it.'

A cry rang out from the royal tent.

'That sounds like Gosse!' Peyre said, the difficult conversation with Idris suddenly forgotten.

He trotted over, his hand on the hilt of his sword. As he peered into the depths of the tent, his blood ran cold. Gosse had his great sword drawn. He had positioned himself in front of Esterel. Before them stood Inge.

Peyre drew his blade from its scabbard. He wasn't the only one. Martras and Auriac did the same.

Esterel looked their way and put out one arm. 'Hold! I'm fine.'

Peyre heard Liesel gasp behind him.

'The witch!' Idris said, drawing level with Peyre, a dagger in his hand. 'At last, the moment has come.'

'Wait,' Peyre said, grabbing his arm. 'Esterel told us to hold.'

'I'm not waiting for her to escape,' Idris said, pulling free and striding to the tent.

This idiot will get my brother killed, Peyre told himself. He dropped his sword and launched himself at the prince. Grabbing him from behind, he put his arms around him and threw him to the side. He positioned himself between the prince and the royal tent.

Idris was quick to recover, his dagger pointed at Peyre. 'Out of my way,' he demanded.

'Stop it!' Liesel shouted. 'You're going to get someone hurt! Esterel!' she called. 'Are you alright?'

'I am going to speak with Inge,' he replied.

'She'll kill him,' Idris hissed.

Peyre couldn't say for sure that the Atrabian was wrong. 'Let me come in with you, Esterel,' he called over. 'The others will wait. *Won't you?*' he said, directing the last words to Idris.

Esterel gave Inge a look.

'Very well,' she said. 'But tell that Atrabian to keep his distance, or so help me, I will burn him to the ground.'

'Good,' Idris whispered. 'Here.' He offered the hilt of his dagger to Peyre. 'You know what to do.'

Peyre ignored him and walked over.

'Close the door, will you Peyre?' Esterel asked him as he entered. 'We need some privacy.'

Peyre pulled the cloth across. He took a last look at Liesel, fear written across her face. *There is Esterel, Gosse, and me*, he reassured himself. *Surely, she can't kill all three of us?*

The four of them looked at one another for a few moments. It felt like this was the moment the fate of the empire would be decided, the siege of Essenberg suddenly of secondary importance.

'You've either come to talk, or kill me,' Esterel said at last. 'Which is it?'

Peyre observed Gosse adjust his grip on his sword. The wrong move or word and the big man wouldn't hesitate to swing.

'It is time to talk,' Inge said. 'I have done my best for Leopold. But the strain has seen him grow more erratic. The atrocities at Burkhard Castle and Coldeberg... I can no longer control him.'

'Those were Leopold's actions?' Peyre asked her, unable to keep the scepticism from his voice. 'Not yours?'

'They were.' Her voice was even, no trace of the mockery he associated with her. 'There were witnesses to both. You can ask them.'

'And this willingness to talk has nothing to do with the fact that we have you pinned in Essenberg?'

Esterel gave him a warning look. He wanted Peyre quiet now and he would have to oblige his king. Esterel, as ever, was in the saddle.

'Of course it does,' Inge said. 'Our gamble in Atrabia backfired. Those crossbows of yours have made defending the walls all but impossible. Leopold isn't so stupid that he doesn't know, deep down, that he's lost. He's desperate, and desperate people do terrible things. You should hear him talk. I don't pretend to have any compunction about killing his enemies for him. But we're talking about the blood of innocents now.' A look of distaste crossed her face. It was the most human Peyre had ever seen her. 'It's over.'

'Then you will bring him to us, to give him justice?' Esterel asked.

'I will.'

'And you will now serve me faithfully?'

Peyre looked at Esterel, doing his best not to speak out and keep a lid on his shock. *Esterel was not only going to spare this witch, but take her as a minister? She had as much blood on her hands as anyone. She was a treacherous snake!* But after his emotions came spilling out, Peyre's logic followed. *She was a sorcerer. Could Esterel kill her even if he wanted? And of course, he didn't want that. A sorcerer serving him made him more powerful.*

Then there was Ezenachi. Always Ezenachi, a shadow that hung over everything they did. Esterel needed her to keep the god at bay. By magic, by diplomacy, by whatever means necessary—she was their best hope of keeping him from crossing the border. At least until Sanc returns, he thought, sparing a thought to wonder where his younger brother was.

'I will,' Inge replied to Esterel. 'You will become Emperor of Brasingia as well as King of Guivergne. With such power, and with my support, you will be strong enough to be a barrier to Ezenachi's expansion.'

Esterel sighed. It looked like relief was his brother's primary emotion. He rarely shared his most intimate hopes and fears, Peyre knew. But he'd glimpsed the weight his brother carried. He resolved to put aside the personal slights he had suffered and support him. He glanced at Inge. After all, his brother would need someone to watch his back.

* * *

THE GREAT CITY of Essenberg surrendered to Esterel. He and his immediate entourage took over the castle in the northwest quarter of the city. Some of his soldiers had been given lodging in the Imps, the imperial barracks in the city. Many more remained outside the city in their temporary camps. A degree of normality had returned. The merchants and farmers were returning to sell their wares at market, which was just as well, because there were many mouths to feed.

There was still much organising to be done to transfer to Esterel the titles he wanted. But first, they had to strip those titles from Leopold.

Peyre had been appointed as a judge in Leopold's trial. He was just one of the magnates seated in the Great Hall, listening to the prosecution give their evidence. There were dukes of the empire: Idris, Friedrich, and Archbishop Emmet. Coldeberg had surrendered soon after Essenberg, and there was no longer a single city anywhere still loyal to Leopold. The only absentee was Jeremias, who still faced trouble in Rotelegen from his enemies to the north. Just as importantly, there were Kellish nobility and churchmen. Leopold had inherited his title of duke, legally, from his father. Only the Kellish could reject him, just as the Luderians had done weeks before.

Inge was absent. She knew when not to draw attention to herself. Peyre knew that rumours already swirled around the capital about her new relationship with Esterel. But it was Leopold who would be blamed for their collective crimes, not her.

Of course, everyone knew Leopold would be found guilty of all charges against him. There was no defence offered, and it didn't look like the man cared. He sat under guard, muttering to himself. His wavy brown hair was long and unkempt, his moustache now joined by a new beard. Sometimes, his eyes would explore the ceiling of the hall. If he was listening to the trial, he hid it well. He looked a broken man, if not mad. It was almost as if they would be doing him a favour. Something about that bothered Peyre. After all his crimes—Auberi, Miles, Elger, and countless others—he wanted him to suffer.

The archbishops of Gotbeck and Kelland were the ones who declared his guilt, and the sentence—death by beheading. Why the Brasingians believed it sounded better coming from two churchmen, Peyre didn't know. Leopold didn't react at all. It was a strange experience to be part of.

'May I have leave to speak?' came a familiar voice.

Queen Liesel approached her husband, going down on her knees. All eyes were on her.

Esterel had remained strictly neutral in the trial. Now he leant forward, a mixture of confusion and affection on his face. Whatever this was, it wasn't something he had been warned of. 'Of course, wife.'

'I would plead for my brother's life. Not that I wish to defend or mitigate his crimes, for which he has rightly been found guilty. But a simple plea of a wife to her husband, to spare the life of her younger brother.' She looked earnestly up at Esterel. The hall had gone deathly silent. 'And if I could say more, it would be that Leopold was led astray as a young boy, and surely the person who corrupted him should be held at least as accountable.'

There were murmurs at this. Everyone knew of whom she spoke.

'He can be exiled, kept a prisoner,' Liesel continued, emotion plain in her voice. 'Any such method to ensure he is no longer a threat.'

'Thank you, sister.' Leopold. Like a nightmare from which one couldn't avert one's eyes, everyone's head swivelled to the condemned duke, who at last had decided to participate. 'That you are the one to defend me at the last humbles me. I know I have done wrong. A life of exile, on a farm maybe. And a promise from me never to return.'

It was a surreal end to the trial. Peyre was surprised at Liesel, a woman he still adored and had always used sound judgement in the past. But such a plea to Esterel only made things more difficult. He tried to imagine himself in her position, and it was Loysse or Sanc who had been condemned. It was a difficult thing to imagine. Maybe he would have wanted them to live.

'Of course, when a wife makes her husband such a plea, I must grant it.'

Gasps followed Esterel's statement. If it wasn't for his complete control of those in the room, there would have been shouts of protest. He stood. 'Now, I am done here.' He wasted no time in heading for the exit at the back of the hall.

No, Peyre thought to himself, and got to his feet. *This can't stand.* There were a hundred reasons Leopold's sentence had to be carried out, from the personal to the political. And as much as he and Esterel loved Liesel, they were too important to be ignored.

He followed Esterel, and he wasn't the only one. Idris, Sacha, Emmett of Gotbeck, a few others. They joined Peyre in swiftly exiting the hall, pushing aside the drapes that protected the king's private space. 'Your Majesty,' some called. 'Esterel,' demanded Peyre and Sacha.

Esterel turned to his chasing pack. 'I know, I know,' he told them. 'He must die. But I couldn't deny her. For the gods' sakes, someone tell me I have no authority to revoke the sentence and get it done.'

* * *

IT WAS A WARM MORNING, the sun spilling into the castle yard. It seemed somehow wrong, to Peyre, to have an execution on such a day.

He was pleased he'd had no role in such details. He didn't even know whether Liesel was aware it was happening. It wouldn't surprise him to learn it had been kept from her. They just had to get it done, was his opinion. Then she could come to terms with it.

There was some mercy to the proceedings. It was carried out in a private space in the castle, without a mob of commoners baying for blood and making a holiday of it. There were still plenty of people squeezed into the space to watch. Such things had to be witnessed, and all estates were represented, from the highest to the lowest. The lowborn citizens would tell what they had seen, and Leopold's death would be accepted as fact.

Peyre had no idea why Idris was the one wielding the sword. Maybe there was some law that a duke could only be killed by someone of his own station. Maybe Esterel had surrendered to the man's demands yet again. Peyre didn't want to know. He just wished it over.

Leopold placed his neck on the block. Idris stood over him, not attempting to wipe the smile from his face. It was strange how Peyre no longer knew what he thought about it. A part of him had wished Leopold dead for a long time and took the same pleasure as the Atrabian in his demise. Another part was sickened by it. How preferable it would have been if Esterel and Leopold had met on the battlefield, and Esterel had struck him down. That was how things should be done—a clean end to it all. This felt grimy and unsatisfying.

The sword fell.

'Oops,' Idris said, a lopsided grin appearing as he studied the mess he had made.

Three more chops and it was over.

BELWYNN

KINGDOM OF MAGNIA, 677

They said their farewells at the new Magnian border. Elfled shared a few private words with her son. King Ida looked pale and shaken. Belwynn supposed Elfled had been his rock since his father died. Her disappearance, and strange reappearance, would be enough to wound a man of mature years. He was still a boy, really.

There was no doubt Magnia was weak, on the brink of destruction. The king didn't have an experienced adviser to lean on. Belwynn's people needed her expedition to be a success. But those gathered believed in the seven champions. They smiled and cheered, the bravest of the youngsters approaching them and asking to touch the sacred weapons. After all, Belwynn, Maragin, and Oisin had been there in the final confrontation between Madria and Diis. Why shouldn't they win the day again?

'I have kept to Ezenachi's demands,' Ida told them, 'and respected the border. The Caladri fleet patrols the Lantinen, preventing us from observing their coastline. So my knowledge of our lost lands is limited. But the evidence we have suggests they are lightly populated. There are rumours the Turned have been sent elsewhere. I am hopeful the resistance you come across will be limited.'

'Whatever we find, we shall face with determination and bravery,' Oisin said, holding his huge spear aloft. He still stood ready to travel by foot, while the others were mounted. The Magnians cheered his words. Some champions looked a good deal less confident than the Giant. But the time had come to find out.

Seven crossed the border. The deal with Ezenachi, that had kept the kingdom of Magnia extant, was broken. They had to find and kill this god. The price of failure would be high.

* * *

THE KING of Magnia was proved correct. Morlin led them through territory with which he was familiar, and they encountered no one.

'The Turned don't operate like a normal enemy,' Jesper said. 'Anyone else would have built fortifications to defend their new conquests. That doesn't seem to have been Ezenachi's thinking at all.'

'It is as King Ida suggested,' Lorant said. 'The Turned have been sent after their next targets. That is the key to their success, it seems. They overran the realm of my cousins, the Sea Caladri, by stealth. Before they knew it, thousands of their people had become their enemies, and were prepared to kill their own folk. It is a strategy built on constant expansion, adding to their manpower each time they conquer a new realm.'

Everyone seemed to agree with the king of the Blood Caladri in the discussion that followed.

'What say you, Lady Belwynn?' Oisin asked her. 'You have not said a word.'

Belwynn thought about it. 'My family's estate of Beckford is only a few miles from where we are now. The farmers would keep beehives for the honey. Each hive had a queen who laid eggs and made new bees.'

'So Ezenachi is like a queen bee?' Jesper asked her with amusement.

'In a way. But the queen bee could be replaced, and the colony still survive. There is no one to replace Ezenachi. I don't know how the Turned work exactly. But I don't think it matters too much. Kill Ezenachi, and it's over.'

It was not until they travelled farther south that they came across any Turned Magnians. They were living in their old settlements—primarily the young and the old, no adult males at all. They were farming: tending their fields, gardens, and livestock.

They would turn and stare, not saying a single word, before silently returning to their chores. It was eerie. It made Belwynn wonder what was going on in their minds. Were they even thinking in the way she understood that word? It was impossible to know.

'Those of fighting age are elsewhere,' Morlin noted. The Shield of Persala was strapped to his back. He still had the habit of staying close to Elfled, even though the Asrai didn't look like she needed a body-guard any longer. 'It is said they have turned the vossi of the Wilderness to their side. The Middians are nervous they will be next.'

'It makes one wonder,' Lorant said, 'whether these people can be freed. Once Ezenachi dies, is his bewitchment of these poor people over?'

'Sanc did it,' Jesper said. 'He released my friend, Herin.'

Herin, Belwynn thought. *That rogue.* There was something reassuring in the thought that he was still around, involved in all of this. *I hope you are looking after this boy, old friend.*

'How did he do it?' Lorant asked.

Jesper shrugged. 'He placed him inside a box. I don't know what else. I know nothing of sorcery.'

'Then perhaps a way can be found to free these people, even if Ezenachi's death doesn't do it,' mused the Caladri.

* * *

Six champions travelled together, south along the road that ran through the centre of the isthmus, connecting Magnian lands with those of the Lippers. Morlin led a spare horse. The seventh champion, Elfled, had gone ahead.

'The Red Fort,' Jesper murmured, the first to see their destination.

Red sandstone caught the eye, even if the construction itself showed little artistry. 'You think if we assault this fort,' Belwynn asked him, 'it will draw Ezenachi here?'

'I can't say for sure. But he came once before.'

They waited for Elfled. Belwynn saw Lorant turn to the empty road with a frown. There was a shimmering, and then the Asrai was there, walking towards them.

Elfled gave them her sharp-toothed smile. 'It is well garrisoned with Lipper warriors. Somewhere around three hundred, I would guess.'

Belwynn looked around at her companions. 'Does everyone agree with this? Tell me now if you have any doubts.'

Jesper reached behind and took the Jalakh Bow from his back, studying it with a smile. 'I must admit, I've been itching to use it. And it's a good idea to get some practise, right?'

'Young Jesper,' Oisin said, hefting his spear. 'I am afraid you will have little time to use it. I will smite our enemies with great speed.'

'Give me some time to get into position first,' Elfled said. She turned to Morlin. 'Stay here. Protect the archer.'

'Very well,' he agreed, fitting the straps of his new weapon to his shield arm.

Elfled departed. Belwynn tracked her for a while. Then, with another shimmer, she was invisible once more.

Lorant and Oisin left next, skirting around to the side of the fortress. When enough time had passed, Jesper approached the Red Fort. Morlin accompanied him. Maragin and Belwynn were comfortable to wait—they had no hanker to use their weapons as if they were toys.

A crack echoed across the landscape. It was a noise Belwynn had not heard in a long time. Jesper had released his first arrow. It soared up to the battlements, taking their first kill. He shot once more before the Lipper defenders answered, a hail of arrows coming for Jesper. Morlin placed himself before Jesper and his shield sent the arrows skittering away. Jesper fired again, taking out an archer.

This time, the defenders answered with their ballista. The machine was set on the wall and could be swung in any direction. When the huge bolt was fired, it made a noise as loud as the Jalakh Bow. As it came for him, Morlin punched out with the Shield of Persala. The bolt was returned the way it came, crashing into the ballista and splintering wood.

'Over there,' Maragin murmured.

To the side of the fortress, there was a blast of air as Lorant used Madria's Staff. Oisin went hurtling high into the sky, over the fort's battlements. He landed with a crash on a wall walk and Belwynn could see the Giants' Spear swinging about him. The Caladri used his magic again, pointing his staff at the wooden gates of the fort. With a rending noise, they were torn from their hinges, crashing to the ground. With such ease, the Red Fort was breached.

'Time to go,' Maragin said.

They joined Jesper and Morlin, the four of them trotting to the gates. Only a few sporadic arrows came for them now, the attention of the defenders on the walls taken by the Giant wreaking havoc amongst them. Maragin held Bolivar's Sword in front of Belwynn, defending her as she always had done. Never mind that Morlin had the shield. Never mind that if Belwynn had been struck, it wouldn't have stopped her. But she appreciated it all the same.

She had expected resistance at the gates, but there were no Lippers there. None alive, at any rate. A few corpses lay about, their throats ripped open.

'Elfled is inside then,' Maragin said dryly.

Morlin looked at the men in horror. Perhaps only now he realised what his queen had become.

'Let's get going,' Maragin said, striding into the fortress. 'Where are most of the defenders likely to be?'

'The main hall is this way,' said Jesper. He fitted an arrow to his string and walked beside Maragin.

'Come,' Belwynn encouraged Morlin.

He nodded, pulling himself together. He drew his sword and walked beside her, his shield out in front.

Much of the hall was in shadow, with flickering candlelight, making it difficult to see. But after Maragin and Jesper burst in, the Lippers inside rushed to meet them. Jesper only got off a few arrows before the press of enemies forced him to draw his sword instead.

Maragin swung Bolivar's Sword with ease, and the weapon sliced through armour, even shattering a Lipper sword when the blades met.

Morlin put himself before Belwynn, his instincts as a bodyguard kicking in. His shield saved him more than once, as the numbers in the hall overwhelmed them.

Belwynn had to help. She struck out at the Lippers with Toric's Dagger. Its blade was short, and she had to get in close to use it. She took a shield to the face; a sword blade to the stomach; a blunt weapon struck her shoulder, nearly making her drop her weapon. But none of the injuries stopped her, and she thrust her dagger into necks and faces.

The fighting was fierce at first, but then eased as the numbers of Lippers diminished. The last few ran for an exit at the far side of the hall.

'Let them go,' Maragin said breathlessly. 'There is an Asrai stalking these corridors. They'll not get far.'

Piles of bodies lay about the Krykker, and she stood in a pool of blood. The hall had the stench of an abattoir, and Belwynn wanted to leave. 'Let's get to the walls.'

They climbed the twisting stone steps, Morlin leading with his shield in case anyone was waiting to pounce in the confined space. On the battlements, it was no better than in the hall. Bodies lay broken, carved in two, even spitted by the huge spear Oisin wielded.

'Ah, dear friends!' the Giant called across from the opposite side. 'It is good to see you safe and unharmed. The parapets have been neutralised.'

'The rest of the place is emptied as well,' Maragin said. 'What do we do now?'

'Wait, I suppose,' said Jesper.

* * *

BELWYNN FELT the coming of the god in her gut. It was a reverberation in her body; in the building on which they stood; in the ground and in the air.

He approached from the south. A lone figure, walking to the Red Fort. His power emanated and drew her in. As she looked at him from the battlements, her mouth fizzed with the taste of iron. Ezenachi inhabited the body of a Lipper man. Her eyes and her mind warred with each other, disagreeing on what they saw. He was a man—vulnerable looking, dwarfed in size by Oisin. But Belwynn knew, better than anyone, that wasn't true. The body was merely a vessel for a god, and what she couldn't see with her eyes, she could still sense.

He stopped when he saw them atop the fort. 'At last,' he said, his voice as dry as desert, as deep as a bottomless pit. 'I have been waiting a long time for the seven weapons of Madria to find their way to me. I see only five champions, though.'

From the side of the fort came a blast of magic. It was Lorant, Madria's staff held aloft in both hands, the force of the magic he unleashed blowing his hair back. His claws dug into the ground to stop him from toppling over.

Reacting quickly, Jesper had his string pulled back and released an arrow, the sound adding to the Caladri's blast.

Doubt assailed Belwynn at the ease with which the god dealt with the attack. One hand pointed at Lorant to block his magic, while with his second Ezenachi turned the arrow to dust. Then, a flick of his wrist and Lorant let out a cry, his arm snapped. Ezenachi made a pulling motion, and the staff flew from Lorant's grip and sailed through the air. The god caught it, studying the weapon.

Oisin leapt from the battlements, landing with a thud on the ground below. He reached his arm back, ready to throw his spear.

There was a humming in the air and nausea forced Belwynn to her knees, her hands gripping the stone of the embrasure in front of her. On either side of her, Maragin, Jesper, and Morlin were equally unable to resist. She watched with dread as Oisin struggled, willing him to stay on his feet, to throw that huge weapon. But even he succumbed, buckling up into a ball, the hand that still grasped his spear shaking. To Oisin's right, Lorant was on all fours. To the giant's left, Elfled was revealed, her fingers scrabbling in the dirt. No doubt she had thought to come at Ezenachi by surprise. That stratagem now looked as pathetic as everything else they had done.

It was a terrible thing to realise they had failed so pitifully. Even worse, to realise she had known they would all along. She had hidden this moment from herself. In the grip of Ezenachi's magic, she couldn't explain why.

Seven champions wielding seven weapons, Ezenachi intoned.

Belwynn knew immediately he was speaking inside her mind. Madria had lived there once. Now another god had intruded into her most private space.

You are exactly what I need to complete my conquests. At last, I have subordinates worthy of the role. You will serve me now.

Belwynn could feel Ezenachi's clench on her mind, closing off her own thoughts.

'Yes, master,' she heard Jesper and Morlin chorus.

'Yes, master,' Maragin said soon afterwards, and as the Krykker said the words, she could hear the rumbling of Oisin on the ground below.

So, instead of killing Ezenachi, they would help him win. Belwynn fought him. Her mind was being encircled, and when that process was complete, she would be his. Lost.

Fight, Belwynn, she told herself.

But she had no powers to stop a god. It had been Madria, working through her, who had killed Diis. And she had only killed Madria with trickery. Belwynn Godslayer was a fraud of a sobriquet. She couldn't stop Ezenachi. And she was so tired of it all. Tired of the expectation.

The circle closed.

Yes, master, Belwynn said.

* * *

THIS IS *the end of Book Two of Heirs of War. Sanc, Peyre, and Liesel return one last time in Book Three,* A Reckoning of Storm and Shadow. *Grab your copy now!*

ABOUT

Thank you for taking the time to read *A Crucible of Fire and Steel*. If you enjoyed it, please consider telling your friends or posting a short review. Word of mouth is an author's best friend and much appreciated. Thank you, again. Jamie

Sign up to Jamie's newsletter and get a free digital copy of his short story collection, *Mercs & Magi*
subscribe.jamieedmundson.com

f facebook.com/JamieEdmundsonWriter
X x.com/jamie_edmundson
BB bookbub.com/authors/jamie-edmundson
g goodreads.com/Jamie_Edmundson
a amazon.com/Jamie-Edmundson/e/B06ZY1WDPH

Printed in Great Britain
by Amazon

37231024R00290